"We found these," he went on, opening his big fist under my nose, "in your pocket. They belonged to my father, you thieving little shit."

He was scaring me. They do bad things to thieves. Odd that it should have slipped my mind before I embarked on this idiotic escapade.

"I'm sorry," I mumbled. Not perhaps the smartest thing I ever said.

"But," Nicephorus said, "in a funny sort of a way it's all to the good. You see, we need you to do something for us, and there's a remote chance you might not want to do it. And we're not savages. If you'd turned us down, we couldn't have forced you. But now, we can quite legally and legitimately make you an offer. You do what we want, or we'll hang you."

My mouth had gone horribly dry. "I'll do it," I said.

"You don't know what it is yet."

HOW TO RULE AN EMPIRE AND GET AWAY WITH IT

HOW TO RULE AN EMPIRE AND GET AWAY WITH IT

K. J. PARKER

www.orbitbooks.net

Copyright © 2020 by One Reluctant Lemming Company Ltd.
Excerpt from *The Last Smile in Sunder City* copyright © 2020 by Luke Arnold
Excerpt from *The Mask of Mirrors* copyright © 2020 by Bryn Neuenschwander and Alyc Helms

Cover design by Lauren Panepinto
Cover images by Shutterstock
Cover copyright © 2020 by Hachette Book Group, Inc.

Orbit
Hachette Book Group
1290 Avenue of the Americas
New York, NY 10104
www.orbitbooks.net

First Edition: August 2020
Simultaneously published in Great Britain by Orbit

Orbit is an imprint of Hachette Book Group.
The Orbit name and logo are trademarks of Little, Brown Book Group Limited.

The publisher is not responsible for websites (or their content) that are not owned by the publisher.

The Hachette Speakers Bureau provides a wide range of authors for speaking events. To find out more, go to www.hachettespeakersbureau.com or call (866) 376-6591.

Library of Congress Control Number: 2020933510

ISBNs: 978-0-316-49867-8 (trade paperback), 978-0-316-49865-4 (ebook)

Printed in the United States of America

LSC-C

10 9 8 7 6 5 4 3 2 1

Oh, the man who can rule a theatrical crew,
Each member a genius (and some of them two) [...]
Can govern and rule, with a wave of his fin,
All Europe – with Ireland thrown in!

W. S. Gilbert, *The Grand Duke*

The history of how the City was
saved, by Notker the professional
liar, written down because eventually
the truth always seeps through.

Act 1

1

It wasn't going well. He was polite enough – he was always polite – but I was losing him.

"It's a fantastic story," I said. "There's this man – Einhard would be amazing in it. It's the part he was born for."

A little ground regained. Einhard was hard to find parts for, and under contract. "Go on," he said.

"There's this man," I went on. "He's a nobleman by birth but fallen on hard times. He's begging in the street."

"That's good," he said cautiously. "People like that."

"And one day he's sitting outside the temple with his hat on the ground and his dog on a bit of string—"

"No dogs. We never work with dogs."

"With his hat on the ground, when who should walk up but the lord high chamberlain and the grand vizier. In disguise, of course."

"But we know it's them."

"Of course. And they point out that the man bears an uncanny resemblance to the king. Yes, the man says, he's my umpteenth cousin umpteen times removed, that's why I grew the beard, because it's embarrassing sometimes, but what can you do? And then the grand vizier says, we need you to do a job for us, and you'll be well paid. And it turns out that the king's been abducted by traitors in the pay of the enemy, who want to start a war, so we need you to pretend to be him, just long enough so that—"

He raised his hand. "Let me stop you there," he said.

Oh well, I thought.

"It's a great story," I said.

"I agree. It's a fantastic story. Always has been. It was a great story a century ago in *The Prisoner of Beloisa*. It was even better in *Carausio*, and *The Man in the Bronze Mask*—"

"A hundred and sixteen consecutive performances," I pointed out.

"Still a record," he conceded. "It's one of those stories – well, a bit like you," he said with a smile. "Starts off really well a long time ago and just keeps on getting better and better, no matter how many times you see it, up to a point, but after a while—" He shrugged. "Best of luck with it," he said, "but I don't honestly think it's for us, thanks all the same."

"There's a siege in it," I told him. "And a love story."

He hesitated. "Sieges are good," he said. "Tell you what. Why don't you go away and rewrite it with just the siege, and forget about the other stuff? Sieges are going down really well right now."

Which is bizarre. Seven years into the great siege of the City; that's real life, for crying out loud, surely the last thing you go to the theatre for is real life. But (he explained to me, when I objected) what the people want is something that looks at first sight like real life, but which actually turns out to be a fairy tale with virtue triumphant, evil utterly vanquished, a positive, uplifting message, a gutsy, kick-ass female lead and, if at all possible, unicorns. Also, I told him, what they want is something that looks new and completely original but is actually the same old story we've all known and loved since we were kids. Exactly, he said. But, knowing you, what you'd give them would be something genuinely new and original *disguised* as the same old same old; and if I were to put that on in my theatre, after a night or two the actors would start to feel terribly lonely.

So I went away. As it happens, I wrote him a positive, uplifting piece of shit about a siege where virtue triumphed, evil was vanquished and Andronica looked stunning in slinky black leather as she kicked enemy ass from one side of the proscenium to the other. It ran twenty-six nights and more or less broke even, so that was all right.

Virtue triumphant, evil utterly vanquished, a positive, uplifting message, a gutsy, kick-ass female lead and, if at all possible, unicorns. I have to confess I'm no scholar, so for all I know there may be unicorns, in Permia or somewhere like that, so maybe one component of that list does actually exist in real life. Wouldn't like to bet the rent on it, though.

2

I left the theatre and walked down Fishtrap Hill into Paradise. Curious thing about this man's city. All the really horrible bits of it have absolutely charming names. Like the Old Flower Market, which at one time must have been a place where you could buy flowers, but not in my lifetime. It burned down in that big fire about five years ago and nobody's missed it; the inhabitants moved out and separated strictly on Theme lines – all the Blues went to Old Stairs, all the Greens to Paradise – with the result that there's no longer anywhere in town where Blues and Greens can be found living side by side. No great loss. Theme-related murders are down about ten per cent since the Flower Market went up in smoke. It's so much easier to tolerate your deadly enemies if you never see them from one year's end to the next.

A respectable professional man like me has to have a reason for setting foot in Paradise; not something you'd do frivolously, or unless you absolutely had to. I walked down a couple of alleys, with that dreadful twitchy feeling you simply can't help, like painfully sore eyes in the back of your head, then stopped at one of twenty or so identical anonymous soot-black doors, wrapped a bit of cloth round my knuckles and knocked three times. The door opened, and this woman stood there staring at me.

You wouldn't put her on the stage. You wouldn't dare to. Stereotypes and caricatures are all very well – our life's blood, if the truth be told – but there's such a thing as overdoing it. So, if you want an obnoxious old hag, you go for two or three out of the recognised iconography: wrinkles, hooked nose, wispy thin white hair like sheep's wool caught in brambles, shrivelled hands like claws, all that. You don't use them all, because it's too much. Which is why you don't get much real life on the stage. Nobody would believe it.

"Hello, Mother," I said.

She gave me a sour look. "Oh," she said, "it's you."

"Keeping well?"

"Like you give a damn."

You don't stand talking in doorways in Paradise. "Can I come in?" I asked.

"Why? What do you want?"

She loves me really, but I'm a great disappointment to her. "I haven't been to see you for a while," I said.

"Six months and four days. Not that I mind."

"Can I come in, please?"

My mother owns her own spinning wheel, which in Paradise makes you aristocracy. She's also the widow of a Green boss, so nobody's stolen it yet. And that's not all. She spins high-grade coloured yarns for the daughters of the gentry, who sit doing embroidery all day; the difference being, my mother gets paid. She's practically blind, but she's still very good at what she does, very quick and never any problems with the quality

of the product. I once figured out that she'd spun enough silk
thread to stretch from here to Atagene and back. I told her
that. She has no idea where Atagene is, and couldn't care less.

"Is it money?" she asked.

Hurtful. True, very occasionally I've been obliged to borrow
trifling sums, but not recently. Not for at least six months.
"Certainly not," I said. "I just wanted to see you, that's all.
You're my mother, for crying out loud."

She sat down on that ridiculous looking low chair, put her
foot on the treadle and picked up her clawful of yellow frizz,
all hairy, like a fruit with mould. The wheel started to hum,
as it's done all my life. I told her what I'd been doing, or an
artistic version thereof, in which virtue was triumphant and
evil utterly vanquished. She pretended she couldn't hear me
over the noise of the wheel. Like I said, I'm a disappointment
to her. She wanted me to be a murderer and an extortionist,
like my father.

A man can take only so much of the bosom of his family, so
I steered my narrative to an aesthetically pleasing conclusion,
told her to take care and left.

Back up the hill, and fortunately the wind was from the sea,
so by the time I emerged into Buttergate I'd left the smell of
home behind me. There was a line in a play I was in once: *home
clings close*. Which is true, but only if you let it.

From Buttergate I headed uptown. I had a paying job;
private after-dinner entertainment in a fashionable house in
the Crescent. Impersonations of leading figures of the day,
needless to say, and as I turned the corner into that magnificent example of early Mannerist architecture I was desperately
trying to remember which side my hosts were on. I hoped they
were Optimates, because I can do Nicephorus and Artavasdus

standing on my head (literally, for two thalers extra; goes down very well, but makes me dizzy), whereas the Populars are a bit too nondescript for easy mimicry. The house I was looking for was the third from the south (more fashionable) end, with a blue door.

I heard this whirring noise. It was just like the whir of my mother's wheel, but it couldn't be, could it, in context. I listened to it for maybe three heartbeats, and a shadow passed over my head and put me in the shade for just a split second, and then there was that impossibly loud thump and a big cloud of dust where the house with the blue door used to be.

There's almost always a moment of dead silence, before all hell breaks loose. When you've been around as long as I have, you know what that moment is for. It's the Invincible Sun giving you just enough time to choose: do I charge in and help and get involved, or do I discreetly turn round and walk away?

When the bombardment first started, about eighteen months ago, nobody thought about choosing. Didn't matter who you were, when one of those colossal slabs of rock fell out of the sky and flattened something, you didn't walk, you ran to help, do whatever you could; even me, once or twice. I remember the dust blinding me and coating the inside of my mouth with cement, and ripping off two fingernails scrabbling at a chunk of stone with a man half under it – his eyes had been squeezed out of his head by the pressure, but he was still alive. I remember my fellow citizens jostling me out of the way in the rush to get there first.

But that was eighteen months ago. Since then, we've settled down into a sort of a pattern. The enemy secretly builds a new super-trebuchet, capable of reaching over the walls; they haul it up to within range at first light, spend the day setting it up and loose their first ranging shot around dusk. It takes them six hours to wind it up again; only by then, our intrepid commandos have darted out through a sally port, punched through the lines, smashed up the trebuchet beyond repair and rushed back to the safety of the walls, sometimes with fewer than sixty per cent losses. So the enemy go away and build a new one, and so it goes on, pointlessly and catastrophically, like the siege; and once or twice a month, a house near the wall gets smashed (because you can't lob a stone over the eastern end of the wall and not hit something) and that's just life. Occasionally, there are dire personal consequences to ordinary people like me, who would have been paid good money for performing to a select audience in what's now a mess of smashed bones and rubble. That's real life, in this man's town. You can see why nobody wants any more of it than they can possibly help.

I used my moment of absolute quiet sensibly. I turned round and walked back the way I came, quickly but without breaking into a run.

I'm not a writer (as you'll agree, if you read this book). I only reach for the pen when times are hard, business is slow and nobody wants me. Then I write a part for myself – a flashy cameo, usually – and a play to go with it, and tout it round the managers until one of them is gullible enough to accept it. Because I'm better at writing for other people than for myself, my fellow actors generally like my stuff; and what the big names in the profession like, the managers like, and what the managers like, the bit players and the small fry like. In fact, everybody likes my stuff, except for me (and the public, but they don't like anything) and as often as not we break even. Since three out of five plays in this man's city close inside of a week and make a loss, that makes me a bankable proposition. But I'm not a writer, and I don't want to be one.

Nor do I want to do what I mostly do for a living, which is impersonations. However, Destiny or the Invincible Sun or someone like that doesn't really give a damn about what I want, which is why I was born and grew up looking totally, absolutely nondescript, and why I have this uncanny knack of imitating other people. Protective mimicry, possibly; or the basic actor's urge, taken to extremes.

Not that I'll ever be a proper actor, let alone a great one – for which I'm profoundly grateful. There's an immutable rule that only jerks and bastards can be really fine actors. Take Psammetichus, or Deuseric, or Andronica – loathsome, arrogant, self-centred as a drill bit, and the rest. It's easy to explain. If you spend most of your life being Psammetichus or Andronica, think how wonderful it must be to be someone else, for three hours every evening. I can imagine no greater incentive for mastering and perfecting your craft. And doing matinees.

It's not quite like that for me. Mostly the people I impersonate are serious public figures: politicians, generals, the occasional actor, athlete or gladiator. Most of them are profoundly unpleasant people, and on balance I'd rather be me than them. Actually, there's a remarkable paradox here. Nobody in his right mind would pay good money to see me, when I'm out of character. And nearly everybody in the City would pay very good money for a guarantee that the First Minister or the Leader of the Opposition would never been seen or heard of again. But when it's me pretending to be the First Minister or the Leader of the Opposition – well, there aren't exactly queues stretching down the street, but a steady trickle each night, enough to pay the rent and a very modest profit. Make of that what you can. I regard it as rather more curious than interesting.

Brick dust all down my sleeve and in my hair, and an unexpected, unwanted, free evening. I put my hand in my pocket and dredged up what at first sight looked like a promising catch of shiny silver coins; but half of them turned out to be that week's rent, a quarter were what I owed to various friends with an unhappy knack of being able to find me, and the residue was food and a new pair of second-hand boots – not a luxury, in my line. You go and see a manager, first thing he looks at is your feet. If you've been walking around a lot lately, you're probably unemployable.

I tried the other pocket, because you never know, and to my great surprise and joy I found a silk handkerchief, which I remembered picking up off the floor at a rehearsal about three weeks earlier. At the time I was in the money and had every intention of finding out whose it was and giving it back – very virtuous of me, and now my virtue was about to be rewarded. I took it to the place I usually go to, in Rose Walk, and they gave me about a quarter of what it was worth, which if you ask me was downright dishonest.

Since I was in Rose Walk, I figured I might as well go the extra fifty yards and show my face in the Sun in Splendour. I hadn't been in there for a while, on account of not wanting to meet certain people who'd been kind and understanding when I was down on my luck, but for all its faults it's a useful place; and I reckoned I'd be safe, since my golden-hearted creditors were both appearing in a revival of the *Two Witches* at the Golden Star, and therefore would be on stage at that time of day. I deliberately trod in a muddy rut in the road before I went in. Caked mud can happen to anyone, no matter how well shod, and hides cracks and splits. Attention to detail is everything.

The Sun never changes. They'll tell you that's because those are the exact same rushes on the floor that Huibert would have stood on when he was rehearsing the King in *Dolcemara*, and it would be sacrilege to replace them; likewise, that's the very same soot on the back wall that Saloninus scraped a bit of to mix the ink with which he wrote *Dream of Fair Ladies*, sitting in that very corner, on the chair that wobbles a bit, next to the table that it doesn't do to lean on too hard if you don't want your drink all over the floor. Steeped in tradition, like the Empire itself.

The usual crowd, too; mildly surprised to see me, after so long. They knew I'd been pitching to a manager – everybody knows everything – so I didn't have to buy my own drink. Various good friends brushed the dust off me and I made a bit of a stir explaining where it had come from, though their interest in current affairs waned considerably once they were reassured that none of the theatres had been hit. They were more interested in what I'd be writing for the Rose, with particular reference to any small but lively roles for which they might just possibly be available. I promised something nice to everyone who asked me, the way everyone always does. It's remarkable how hope breeds in this city, like rats.

"Someone was in here looking for you," someone told me.

Note the grammar. If the subject of the sentence had been a proper noun, nothing out of the ordinary; A, a manager with a part for me, good; B, a creditor, bad; the two sides of life's endlessly spinning coin. But somebody meant somebody we don't know (and in the Sun we know everybody). My wings tensed, ready to launch me into flight, like a pigeon in a tree.

"And?"

My friend grinned. "Not in the business," she said. "Wouldn't last five minutes if they were."

"Ah." I picked up the bottle and held it over her glass without actually tilting it.

"Not very good at acting," she explained. "We're old friends of his, haven't seen him in ages, got the impression he hangs out here. Like hell they were."

She'd earned an inch, which I duly poured. "In what sense?"

She frowned. "Enter the Duke and his courtiers, disguised as vagabonds. Shoes and jewellery all wrong. Not a clue."

Unsettling. I wasn't always an actor, believe it or not, and not everyone I've ever known was in the trade. "What did you tell them?"

"Haven't seen you for ever such a long time, no idea where you might be, thought you were dead, never heard of you." She smiled at me. "Of course, I wasn't the only one they asked."

"When was this?"

"About an hour ago."

So they'd left very shortly after I arrived. Without being too obvious about it, I glanced round. Everyone who'd been in when I arrived was still there; no, I tell a lie. One face was missing. I slid the bottle – still a third full – across to her, picked up my hat and slipped out through the side door.

I walked back up Crowngate, where I was nearly trampled to death by a half-company of heavy infantry. I stepped back into a doorway and let them pass. No prizes for guessing where they were off to in such a hurry. If I was a soldier on a mission from which I wasn't likely to come back, I don't think I'd stomp along quite so briskly. There you go. Presumably they all reckoned they'd be the lucky ones, or one. See above, under hope.

It's awkward keeping your head down and staying clear of people who are looking for you if you're an actor, so I decided it was a stroke of luck that I didn't have anything on at present. Correction: I had a play to write for the Rose, something I could do anywhere. It irked me that I wouldn't be able to go back home but I'd still have to pay the rent, which would eat horribly into my capital. I resolved to channel my righteous indignation at the unfairness of it all into my writing, which I'm sure is what Saloninus or Aimo would have done in my shoes.

If you want to lie low in this man's town, the closer you can get to the docks the better. Ever since the siege began, and we won back control of the sea even though the whole of the land empire had gone down the drain, there's been an awful lot of foreigners living in and around the docks, where rents are cheap. Nobody knows them, they don't belong to a Theme, and their money is as good as anybody else's. They're traders, factors, agents, sailors discharged from foreign ships, and a lot of them can't even speak Robur; and you know what we're like with anyone we can't understand. I figured that if I pretended I was foreign and replied in gibberish, if anyone spoke to me I'd be left blissfully alone. I could write my play, get paid for it and stay out of sight until whoever was looking for me decided I must be dead or overseas, and all that at a price I could afford. Magic.

So I wandered around for a bit – it was dark as a bag by then – until I reckoned I'd found somewhere suitably anonymous, but where I could bear to live for a week or so, and knocked on the door. Long wait; then a panel in the door shot back and a little round bloodshot eye glared at me.

"Room," I said, with my very best Aelian accent. I'd wrapped my scarf round my head to hide the colour of my skin.

The panel snapped shut and the door opened. The man with the eye saw what he expected to see. "Forty trachy a night," he said. "Meals not included."

I held out my gloved hand palm upward, with a silver quarter-thaler gleaming in the middle of it. "Room," I said.

"Sure." He stood aside to let me pass. "Heard you the first time."

The skin-colour thing would be a problem, of course. As it happens, I have a genius for makeup, but all my stuff, goes without saying, was back home, and I couldn't afford to go out and buy any more. Just as well I know how to improvise. I learned how to do a really effective whiteface with chalk, brick dust and goose fat back when I was in the chorus of *The Girl with the Red Umbrella*. For chalk, substitute flour, and I was able to find the whole caboodle later that night in somebody's kitchen.

The room wasn't bad. It had four walls, a tiny, tiny window and a door that shut if you slammed it.

3

My business requires me to keep fully abreast of current events. Talking of which, I'd like to protest in the strongest possible terms about the public's – that means you – deplorable lack of loyalty and patience. Just because the minister for this or the secretary of state for that is no bloody good and couldn't find his own arse with both hands, that's no valid reason for turning him out of office and replacing him with someone else, almost certainly with an entirely forgettable face, a squeaky little voice that won't carry to the back of the hall and no known mannerisms. It's bad enough when a general gets killed leading from the front; desperate waste of my time and trouble learning him like a book, but I do understand, these things happen in war. But getting shot of a perfectly good politician just because he's useless strikes me as downright perverse.

It wasn't like that in the old days, of course, before the siege. High officials were appointed, not elected, and you knew you could spend the necessary time and trouble on them

with a reasonable prospect of seeing a return on your invest-
ment. But when the emergency government deposed the last
emperor, sidelined the House and set up direct elections – I
don't suppose they deliberately set out to make my life hell.
The unfortunate consequences to me personally probably
never crossed their minds; which makes it worse somehow, in
my opinion.

Following the news when you're effectively confined to a
fifth-storey saltbox isn't the easiest thing in the world, particularly if you're playing the part of an ignorant foreigner who
knows nothing about City politics and cares less. Some news,
however, gets everywhere, the way sand gets under your collar
on the beach.

I'd ventured out, well wrapped up and in full whiteface, to
buy a loaf and a bit of cheese – which I didn't actually need
straight away, but when you've been banged up for three days
with nobody but characters of your own creation for company,
any excuse will do. The stallholders in the little market in the
square opposite the dock gates are used to foreigners, though
they tend not to look at them when they're taking their money;
all to the good, as far as I was concerned. Anyway, there was
this fat woman, and she was talking to the woman on the next
stall down, who I couldn't see. I wasn't really listening, but
then I caught: "All lies, of course."

"That's not what I heard," offstage, behind me.

"Lies," the fat woman repeated, inadvertently spraying my
cheese with spit. "They'll say anything, the damned Opties."

"It's true," asserted the voice off. "They were talking about
it in the King of Beasts last night, my brother heard them.
They were saying, he's dead."

"Bullshit," said the fat woman.

"It's *true*. Lysimachus is dead. He was at a party and a stone fell on him. Squashed flat, like a beetle."

That got my attention. It's a cliché, but icy fingers touched my heart. It's only when it happens to you that you realise just what a top-flight metaphor it actually is.

Let me make one thing clear up front. I don't care. I couldn't give a damn. I don't regard myself as involved.

Accordingly, the death of Lysimachus – if true – was a devastating blow to me personally, purely because imitating him accounted for something like forty per cent of my income. Sure, you can still imitate people after they're dead, but there just isn't the same demand. Also, in bread-and-butter burlesque work, once someone's dead he's only ever going to be a supporting character, not the lead, a cameo at best: and even if you stop the show every night you don't generally get paid extra.

On the other hand – so my train of thought ran as I wandered back to my room, devastated, hardly aware of where I was or what I was doing – on the other hand, Lysimachus isn't, sorry, *wasn't* just anybody. He was the *man*. At the darkest hour in the City's history – five hundred thousand bloodthirsty milkfaces camped outside the walls, the regular army all dead or scattered and the Fleet still trapped on the far side of the Ocean; with a garrison of a few hundred untrained men, he held the line against the darkness; his determination, his dauntless courage, et cetera. If he hadn't been there, we'd all be dead. Not opinion, fact. Therefore – I consoled myself – there's *always* going to be a demand for a really first-class Lysimachus impersonator, and more so now he's dead (if he's dead), because he'll become the ultimate symbol of hope, and what's the theatre about if not peddling hope to people who ought to know better? In fact – all false modesty aside, by the time I got back to my room I already had a plot and rough outlines of acts one and three, in which the Invincible Sun sends the spirit of Lysimachus back from the Elysian Fields to save the City in its darkest hour. And there'd be a siege in it, you bet, and surely someone with my incredibly fertile imagination ought to be able to figure out a way to shoehorn in a strong female lead –

Turning it over in my mind as I ground my way through the last scene of Act 2 of the Rose piece, I tried to think about it logically. What had actually happened? I'd overheard two market women sharing a rumour; and one of them swore blind that it wasn't true, just a pack of lies put about by the Optimates. Hardly proof beyond reasonable doubt. I felt an urge to go out and listen some more, maybe in places where they might be even better informed than my two current witnesses. But then I thought, what the hell. If Lysimachus was dead, he'd still be dead tomorrow, possibly even the next day. Death is like real estate; it's different from everything else in its category because of its permanence. Meanwhile, I had work to finish, and people I didn't know were looking for me. Perspective is everything.

Act 2 is always a grind. With the exception of Acts 1 and 3, it's the hardest part of your standard three-act play. So I tend to write fat – scribble down any old thing, just so long as it moves the action forward and gets you to the bits you know and give a damn about; edit and rewrite later if you absolutely have to. That way you don't have to think too hard, which was just as well in this case, because my mind kept wandering. He was at a party and a stone fell on him. Indeed. Common knowledge by now that a trebuchet shot flattened a house in the Crescent the other day; and rumour is the ultimate oyster, building layer upon layer of glittering shiny stuff round a tiny speck of fact. Cue the venerable rumour-monger's syllogism; somebody got killed that night; Lysimachus is somebody; therefore Lysimachus got killed.

All right, now let's try using a tiny bit of intelligence. I was hired to perform at that party. Lysimachus is one of my best characters. Would the host have hired a Lysimachus specialist to perform at a party where Lysimachus was going to be a guest? At the very least, I'd have been told – don't do Lysimachus, for crying out loud, unless you want to get us all hanged. Exactly. Therefore, Lysimachus wasn't a guest at the party, therefore he wasn't flattened by a rock, therefore he must still be alive.

I reckoned I was on fairly solid ground there. Yes, the host might have come up to me just before I went on and murmured: by the way, don't do Lysimachus, there's a good fellow, he's in the front row. People do that to me more often than I care to think, and suddenly your entire plan for the evening is lying in more pieces than a broken pot. But think about it. It's hardly a secret that Lysimachus is my best thing. I'm very good at him, though I do say so myself. Presumably Lysimachus knows this; from what I've heard about him and the nature and quality of his sense of humour, he's not likely to be amused. So, if you've managed to lure the most famous and important man in the City to your dinner party, are you really going to risk mortally offending him by bringing on the world's most celebrated Lysimachus-baiter as an after-dinner turn? No, of course not. Therefore, see above, the rumour isn't true. Worrying yourself to death over nothing at all. Pull yourself together, for crying out loud and get on with some work.

Getting Act 3 out and down on paper was like having a tooth pulled, but I managed it somehow. By that point I was sick to death of that horrible little room and the smell of cardamoms and lavender from the warehouse three doors down subtly blended with the open drain under my window, so I slapped on my whiteface, rolled up what I'd written and crept out into the street. I felt as bad as I must have looked. For ten days, all I'd had to wash in was the piss-pot, and the nearest water was the pump, five flights of narrow, winding steps down, and loneliness had been the least of my problems, if you count tiny things that bite as company. I'm not the most fastidious of men, but I don't like it when I turn into the sort of creature I'd cross the street to avoid.

I'd written the bloody thing, but how was I supposed to deliver it and get paid? If the men I didn't know were serious about finding me, they'd have found out by now that I was writing something for the Rose, so I couldn't go there myself; therefore I had to get someone to go for me. One of those utterly depressing times when you find out who your true friends are.

To get from the docks to the Gallery of Illustration you have to walk right across the City, not something I really wanted to do in broad daylight, in homemade whiteface. For a start, the stuff melts, which isn't a problem you get with proper greasepaint. I muffled myself up as best I could, which only made me more conspicuous on a hot day, and everybody knows milkfaces don't like the heat, so which was more likely to attract attention, a walking cocoon in a heatwave or a normally dressed milkface with brown streaks? I decided to go with the muffled look, and it must have worked, because people looked away rather than stared.

The Gallery of Illustration started off as a theatre for people who don't like to be seen going to a theatre, of whom there are quite a few in this incurably stage-struck town. Instead of plays, therefore, the Gallery put on illustrated lectures on uplifting themes, and even though the writers and the cast were basically the same people as you'd find in the dens of iniquity ten minutes away down the hill, the high-minded types reckoned it was all right and the Gallery did a roaring trade for many years. I played there myself quite a few times on and off. Then a new manager took it over and changed it into just another second-rate playhouse, and for various reasons my face didn't fit any more. That was the manager I was going to see.

Her real name's Hodda and she's been specialising in pure unsullied girlhood for about fifteen years. She gets abducted by slavers in Act 1 and rescued just in time by her childhood sweetheart in Act 3, which is exactly what they want to see north of the river; and when she isn't doing that, she runs a painfully tight ship and drives the hardest bargain in the City. She's also an exceptional dancer, in spite of a stiff left leg where someone kicked her over a business disagreement ten years ago; when she's not on stage, she walks with a stick. She is, come to think of it, the nearest thing you're likely to find in real life to a strong kick-ass female lead, a dignity to which she's been able to aspire by virtue of her doll face and simpering skills. She can't sing worth spit, though.

"What the hell do you look like?" she said.

I looked over my shoulder. "Keep your voice down, for God's sake."

She rolled her eyes. "You're in trouble again."

"Yes."

"How much?"

"Actually," I said, without thinking, "it's not money."

I had her attention. "What have you done?"

"Can we go inside, please?"

"You look absolutely ridiculous, do you know that?"

The Gallery of Illustration used to be a warehouse, with a high roof and a loft for storing bales of cloth or whatever. The loft was perfect for a gallery, with an outside staircase going up to it. Backstage is one poky little room, with hampers of old costumes, two or three tables where you can make up, a big old trunk with three padlocks where she keeps her money and a couple of rickety old chairs. "Well?" she said.

"Has anyone we don't know been here asking after me?"

She knows I don't drink during the day so she didn't offer me one, but her hand shook slightly as she poured her own. "No. Why?"

"People I don't know are asking after me," I said.

She raised her eyebrows. "Why would anybody want to do that?" she said.

"Don't ask me."

"You're not in the habit of pissing off strangers," she said. "Only your friends and colleagues."

"Exactly."

She drank her wine, looking at me over the rim of the glass. It's a mannerism that has made her very popular with men over the years, and I guess it's like the violin: you have to keep practising even when you're not performing to an audience. "What's any of that got to do with me?"

"I need a favour."

"Of course you do, why else are you here? Not to see me, bet your life."

Well, yes, we were sort of good friends once, and then we weren't friends at all. "I've got a play for the Rose."

"So I heard. Any good?"

"Garbage," I said. "Good part for Einhard, and Andronica fighting a sword duel in skin-tight chainmail. Anyway, it's finished, and I need someone to deliver it for me."

"And collect the money."

"Quite."

She nodded. "Ten per cent."

I gazed at her. "Are you out of your mind?"

"It's you I'm thinking of," she said, butter wouldn't melt. "I go into a manager's office, hand him a manuscript, fine, I'm just the messenger. But he's not going to hand over cash money to me unless I'm your duly accredited agent. And the going rate—"

"Hodda, I need that money. I may have to be invisible for quite some time."

"Take it or leave it."

"Fine." I stood up and grabbed my hat. That's all I did.

"Well?"

I sat down again. "Hodda," I said, "In the past I may not have been strictly honest with you."

"You can say that again."

"About – well, things that happened long ago and far away."

She has this nasty sceptical streak. "Don't tell me," she said. "Really you're the crown prince of Olbia in disguise."

I scowled at her. "Something like that. The point being, for all I know these people might be very unpleasant indeed, and obviously while they're on the scene I can't work, so I really do need that money. All of it."

She pursed her lips. "I could do with a two-handed curtain raiser," she said.

"I could do with a hundred per cent of what I'm owed."

She smiled. "Deal," she said. "You write me fifteen minutes of cheerful froth, I'll go and get your money for you."

Like I said, I'm not a writer. "Usual terms?"

"We can discuss that later," she said. "And I tell you what. I'll throw in a stick of whiteface absolutely free. Just to show there's no hard feelings."

I hung around just long enough to patch up the worst of the damage to my codbelly complexion, then stomped off in a huff back to the docks. I really didn't fancy another three days or so cooped up in that loathsome smelly room, writing light comedy for free, but that's what happens when your oldest and dearest friends help you out.

4

While I was gouging myself inside out trying to be amusing in my dockside hutch, things were happening in the outside world, although nobody saw fit to tell me about them. There was another trebuchet bombardment, which hit a dancing academy for daughters of the nobility; no survivors. There was a riot – not Blues against Greens but Blues and Greens against the government, and some clown sent in the cavalry and there was a horrible mess. I very much doubted that the two were related, since the Themes don't tend to send their kids to learn the *pas de deux*, but it all went to add to my general sense of gloom and unease. I like a quiet life, with money and things to spend it on, and clean clothes, and soap.

No point trying to find out what the riot was supposed to be about, since a foreigner wouldn't be interested; couldn't really eavesdrop effectively because people have that tendency to clam up if they think a milkface is listening. All I gathered was that there were now soldiers on the streets as well as on the wall – oh, and all the theatres were closed until further notice. That made me grin, until it occurred to me that Hodda might not have been round to the Rose yet; in which case I was screwed. So, I reflected a moment later, was she, not to mention the whole profession, but probably not nearly as screwed as I was.

Trouble was, I had no idea where to find her. Presumably she lived somewhere, in the sense of an enclosed space containing a bed, as and when she needed one of her own, but under normal circumstances that would be none of my business. Nobody knows where anyone lives when they're not at, in or fluttering moth-like around the theatre; it's not relevant. The Gallery would be locked up, and I daren't show my face in any of the usual places, not even covered in pink grease. I couldn't even stay where I was for more than a day or so, unless I wanted to exhaust my tiny treasury. I counted my blessings and found that I had a hundred and six trachy, nowhere to sleep, a two-handed curtain raiser with original songs to popular melodies that I couldn't sell, boots with holes in them and strange men looking for me, and all because a bunch of idiots felt like tearing up the pavement and throwing things. I do wish people would have more consideration.

I can imagine what you're thinking – not telepathy, just a process of logical deduction. For a start, you're reading this, so you can read, so obviously you're educated, therefore you belong to the better sort – and I know you people like the back of my hand. You're thinking: if he's starving it's his own stupid fault, because there's always work in this man's town; not the sort he's used to, maybe, drooping around theatres and rich men's drawing rooms for a few hours in the evening parroting someone else's words (he doesn't even have to make up what he says, for pity's sake: a writer does that for him). No, proper hard work, toting barges, shifting bales, fetching, carrying, digging holes in the ground and filling them up again. But that wouldn't occur to him; he's too proud. Nobody to blame, therefore, except himself.

Couldn't agree with you more, except for one thing. Not pride, because someone who spends day after day trudging from one audition to another, to be politely told he's no good nohow, doesn't have much of that commodity left. Not mortal terror of breaking into a sweat – try rehearsing a dance number, full costume in midsummer heat for five hours straight, because we open tomorrow and it's still not right; and show me the bricklayer who could do that without passing out and being carted off in a wheelbarrow; and bear in mind, you've got to smile nicely the whole time, and be *graceful* – no, it's not that. It's simply that if you want to do casual work in this city, you need to be paid up with a Theme; and I'm not, and never have been, and won't ever be if I can possibly help it. And before you ask, it's none of your business. Family stuff. Private. So, you see, my options were somewhat circumscribed; jump off a bridge or starve. Or—

5

Actually, it sort of follows on from my earlier rant, because if I hadn't spent my entire adult life in the profession, I doubt very much whether I'd have had the necessary skillset and physique for burgling houses. Years of song and dance have made me fit and agile; I can run from Cornmarket to Eastgate non-stop, and arm-wrestle stonemasons. And what's the very essence of the burglar's craft? Not being seen or heard. That's something I know all about. There are times on the stage when you want everyone to look at you – your big speech; and other times (her big speech) when you're actively deflecting the audience's attention, unless you want her down on you like a ton of bricks the moment the curtain falls. Or when you're waiting in the wings to come on, or when you're lying dead; you don't last five minutes in the trade unless you can keep perfectly still and quiet for a very long time, and be practically invisible.

Translate all that into mundane accomplishments, such as shinning up drainpipes and walking quietly across dark rooms. You'll realise, if you think about it for a moment, that I left something out.

Something I happen to have, in fairly good measure, because of my theatrical training; but maybe not quite enough. It definitely takes nerve to walk out onto a stage in front of a hundred or so strangers; chills your blood, catches your breath, crimps your guts, see above under hearts and icy fingers. But there's fear and there's fear. Climbing up the side of a house, you can so easily get into trouble. Your foot can slip, or the drainpipe can come away in your hand. Then you reach the window, only to find the shutters are locked, so you try and go back down; only going down is a hell of a lot harder than going up, you're scrabbling for your footholds in the dark and you wrenched the retaining nails half out of the wall on your way up, you felt them go. Or maybe the shutter's not locked, in which case you have to hang by one hand while you fool about with it with the other (and by now your fingers are mortally weary, and maybe you sprained one or two of them, so they really can't be relied on) and then arch your back to wriggle over the parapet before sliding on your gut with nothing to hang on to – and then suppose you actually make it inside, whereupon someone smashes your head with a hammer or a huge great dog tears your throat out. But the worst an audience can do is not like you.

Which is why I chose the theatre, I guess. But there you go. I chose – well, remembered, a house; I'd entertained a select gathering of the best people there with impressions of leading personalities from politics and the arts, only a few weeks earlier. They'd shunted me off into a sort of scullery on the ground floor to get changed and made up, and I distinctly remembered noticing that the shutter didn't close properly, and from the scullery to the drawing room you only had to walk down one corridor and open one unlocked door. No climbing up walls like a crane fly, no floundering about in the dark in unfamiliar surroundings, and I knew there was something worth having, and where to lay my hand on it.

I didn't bother with the whiteface. It makes your hands slippery. I went to bed, hoping to get an hour or two's sleep, but that wasn't going to happen, so I stared at the ceiling until I reckoned it was about time; then I muffled myself up, crept quietly down the stairs (good practice for the main event) and slipped out into the street. I hadn't heard any footsteps while I'd been lying awake, and the street was empty. I made myself inconspicuous all the way down Fish Lane to the wall, then turned right and took the back alleys, eventually coming out at the foot of Hill Street. My house was one of the big villas clustered at the bottom, where the new money lives.

The house was easy to recognise, because some clown with an unfortunate money-to-taste ratio had thought twin gate-posts in the form of winged horses was a good idea. I traced round the western edge of the garden wall until I reached the house proper, then started counting windows. There wasn't a glimmer of light to be seen.

The shutter practically flung itself open as soon as I got the point of my knife into the crack. I stopped, kneeling under the sill, and counted to fifty, just in case I'd woken anyone up with my tiny mouse-like scratching, but no sound and no movement; everything was perfect. I hopped up over the sill, felt the flagstones under my feet, crouched down and waited some more, almost as if I was hoping something would go wrong. But it didn't, so I stood up, walked delicately on the sides of my feet (the quietest way and you keep your balance;

tiptoe is asking for trouble in the dark) until my fingertips connected with the door latch. Now latches sometimes rattle like hell, but this one didn't, bless it, and I was out in the corridor, lined with rush matting (because nobody likes to hear servants clattering about when they're trying to have a civilised conversation). By rights I should have stopped and listened some more, but it was obvious there wasn't any point; you can feel when a house is alive, and this one wasn't. Fifteen paces took me to the drawing-room door, which didn't creak, so I needn't have bothered with the pat of lard in my coat pocket. Directly opposite that door, unless some thoughtless idiot had moved it, was a cabinet, and in that cabinet was a collection of antique rings, cameos and brooches – I knew that, because they'd been stupid enough to have it open when I was there entertaining.

I found the cabinet by walking into it, very slowly and softly; I felt one of the brass handles against my kneecap. The top drawer squeaked ever so softly, but I took my time and I knew the sound wouldn't carry outside the room. I filled my left pocket with small, cold things. Job done. There were at least five more drawers, but greed isn't one of my many faults. The pocketful would tide me over for a good long time. Taking more than I needed would be the act of a criminal. Then back the way I came; careful not to rush, which is the classic beginner's mistake.

Nobody in the pantry. I opened the shutter, poked my head out, nobody in the alley; climbed through, taking care to close the shutter behind me. Deep breath, then I walked briskly down the alley, each step severing the connection between me and any crime that may have been committed. At the end of the alley I turned left into Hill Mews, where someone stepped out of the shadows in front of me and hit me with a shovel.

6

I think I may have mentioned in passing that my father was a Theme boss, and you may have got the impression that I'm not proud of that fact. I'm not.

He came to the City (God knows how often I've heard this) with fifty trachy in his pocket, from a mining camp in the Paralia. He was fourteen years old and he'd already killed three grown men; one in self-defence (he asserted) and two for money. Not a great deal of money, because life was cheap in the mining camps though everything else was extortionately expensive. The idea was, nobody would suspect a child of being a paid assassin, but a kid can slip something nasty in a grown man's soup or cut his throat while he's asleep, just as well as anyone else. Which was true for a while, but then the authorities (such as they were) got wise, and another good idea bit the dust; rough on my father, because he nearly got caught – standing over the foreman's bed with a knife in his hand, hard to explain your way out of that. He didn't try. He ran, and he was as slippery as an eel, and he stowed away on an ore barge and arrived in the City, one more scrap of human trash to add to an already formidable accumulation.

His idea was to pick up where he'd left off back home, and one thing he wasn't short of was nerve. He sneaked into the bedroom of one of the Green bosses with a razor in his pocket, then woke him up. If I can get in here, he pointed out, after the Green boss had let go of his throat, I can get in most places, and out again, and nothing to connect me to you.

The Green boss explained to him that they didn't do things that way, or at least not often enough to support a profession; that said, he could always use young men with guts and imagination, and if he cared to call back in the morning, using the door this time, they could have a useful discussion. Then, when my father was nodding and smiling and thanking him for giving him a break, the boss punched him across the room. Taught you something you haven't learned yet, he explained; never assume you've got away with anything, and don't you ever tell anyone you had me at a disadvantage.

Which is how my father joined the Greens, starting very much the way he was to carry on. Bear in mind that this was before the Themes were made legal (which only happened at the start of the siege, because the provisional government desperately needed manpower). Back then, just belonging to a Theme was a crime that could land you in the stone quarries or the galleys – which was awkward, since the Themes made sure that nobody in Poor Town who wasn't a Blue or a Green could earn a living, on either side of the law. Anyone who tried got his legs broken, and the leg-breaker-in-chief for the whole of the west side of the City was my dad.

It was a good line of work to be in, he never tired of telling me. It was safe as houses, because anyone who gave you any trouble would be floating face down in the harbour within twenty-four hours; you've got to have respect, or what have you got? The pay was good, and everybody went out of their way to be nice to the man who could have their shops burned to the ground on his say-so alone. From time to time there was friction with the authorities, but that was true for all Theme members; and if my father ever needed an alibi, or someone to make a confession on his behalf, there were plenty of men with families who could be counted on to oblige.

It's a great life, he used to tell me. And he watched me grow up big and strong; he used to grab hold of me and pinch my biceps; plenty of meat there, he'd say. And for a while, that was fine. I relished the way the other kids went out of their way to like me, and if anyone was mean to me he'd be sure to apologise first thing the next day, with a sort of terrified look in his eyes, which I thought was just grand. The only thing I found a bit frustrating was that my dad had taught me to fight, really well, but I never got the chance, because none of the other kids would ever stand up to me.

It all went wrong when my dad decided it was time for me to start my apprenticeship, so to speak. The idea was that I would go with him on his rounds, collecting money, showing his face where it needed to be seen, giving the usual one friendly warning, that sort of thing. I didn't mind that at all. I liked the way people went all quiet when we walked in somewhere, and I felt proud of the way they were scared of him – of us, because he made no secret of his plans for my future. Take a good look at my boy, he'd say, so you'll be sure to recognise him. I liked that a lot.

Because my dad was so good at his job he didn't have to do it very often. But from time to time there'd be some poor devil who simply couldn't help breaking the rules, out-of-towners, usually. In this case, it was an Aelian. He'd been bosun's mate on a grain freighter, but he got too sick to work, so they left him behind; get well, they told him, and next time we come we'll take you home. But some scoundrel stole the money they'd left for him, and there weren't many Aelians in town back then, so nobody to look out for him. By the time he was back on his feet, he owed three thalers' rent, and no way of knowing when his shipmates would be back. So he found himself sleeping under an archway in the Old Flower Market; and he made the mistake of putting his hat down on the ground next to him, the way beggars do, only you weren't allowed to beg in the Flower Market unless you were paid up in a Theme. The Blue and Green bosses met up and tossed a coin, and the Greens lost; their job to take out the trash. My dad's job.

When we came looking for him, the poor fool was just sitting there. The hat, I remember, was empty. I could've told him he was wasting his time, because no Themesman would dare to be seen giving money to a scab beggar. But that was beside the point.

Thinking back, I guess my dad was feeling the effect of a long spell of idleness. He hadn't had to hurt anyone for a long time. He explained it to me once. It's like making love, he said (that wasn't quite the term he used); when you've been without for a while, it sort of builds up inside you. That would explain it, I guess; also, the man was a foreigner, so there was no family to get upset if my dad went a little bit further than usual.

He walked up to him with his hands in his pockets, stopped and looked down at him, dead quiet. The man looked up at him, hopefully. My dad nodded politely, then kicked him in the face. I remember the way his chin flew up; I couldn't believe Dad hadn't broken his neck, but I didn't give him credit for his skill, acquired through so much practice. The man was lying on his back, belly up; my dad stamped on him, four times, each time a different place, and I heard things snap, a very distinctive sound, like nothing else. Then he rolled him over onto his side with his foot and kicked him three times more. Then he rolled him over onto his back, looked him over appraisingly, nodded, turned away, turned back, and ground the heel of his boot in the man's right eye. "That'll do," he said cheerfully. "Let's go and eat."

On the way home, I was unusually quiet. But eventually I asked him why he'd turned away and then turned back. He'd done the job, so why the last bit?

He stopped and looked at me, and for a moment I thought he was going to answer. Then he walked on, and I had to jog to catch up with him.

"Dad?" I asked him.

"Come on," he said. "You know your mom hates it when we're late for dinner."

Next morning, when I was supposed to be going with Dad on his rounds, I pretended I had a cough and a sore throat. I spun it out for a week. Then I told him; I wanted to be apprenticed, to a goldsmith or a lawyer, something like that.

Dad took it well, I'll say that for him. I'd chosen well; I made it sound like I was ambitious, wanted to better myself, get out of the Flower Market. He liked that idea; my son the government official (there were a lot of Greens in the civil service). That would show just how far he'd come from the mining camp, that was for sure. In fact, it was my mother who raised hell over it. She was Green to the core, the way some people are. Dad laughed at her, which didn't improve matters. So the boy wants to be a big clerk and sit on his arse all day, he said; bloody good luck to him, he'll go far. She didn't say anything, but she gave me a look that nearly took all the skin off my face.

So I put in for a vacancy in the Treasury. So did a lot of other kids, but, guess what, I got the job, without even an interview. The work was much harder than I thought it would be, but my superiors were amazingly tolerant and helpful, even when I made a series of godawful mistakes. Don't worry about it, they said, and laughed nervously. I promised I'd do better in future. It's all right, they assured me, it's fine, don't give it another moment's thought.

And then something happened. To this day I don't know what it was, though I suspect my dad had taken money to let someone clear out of town before getting what was coming to him. He should have had more sense, but I think he'd been himself for so long, he reckoned he was invincible and immortal. He wasn't, though, not one bit.

There wasn't a funeral, because there was nothing to bury. My mother was allowed to stay in the Theme, as a special favour, but the only work she was allowed to do was spinning, which is badly paid and about as low as you can get. Nobody would employ her or buy from her so she was left doing piecework for foreigners. But she stayed Green, and she blamed me – if I'd only gone to work with my dad, I'd have been able to stop him from doing whatever it was he did, or I'd have been able to protect him, or protect her; whatever, it was all my fault. I couldn't actually find it in my heart to disagree with her, come to that.

And I lost my job at the Treasury, of course; and that's when I became an actor. I don't know why the Themes never bothered to take over the theatres, but they never did. While I was in the Treasury I'd spent a lot of time learning how the people there spoke and moved; educated, refined, sophisticated people, or so I thought, and compared with what I'd grown up with, so they were. In my department there'd been a dozen or so young sprigs of the gentry, younger sons of younger sons, forced to work but with family connections that meant they didn't have to work too hard, and I'd chosen to model myself on them; and, of course, they were all hopelessly stage-struck and theatre-mad, so I was too. Some young idiot I was sort of friends with was spending a lot of money he hadn't got on an actress by the name of Andronica, who'd saved up enough to branch out into management; he introduced me to her, and she took me on as a stagehand, spear-carrier and understudy second romantic lead and third clown. I'd like to say the rest is history, but that would be ridiculous.

All of which may strike you as irrelevant, but I thought I'd mention it anyway, because I know a bit about getting knocked out; not much, but probably more than you do. At least I hope so, for your sake.

My dad could put a man's lights out with one punch. Nobody doubted him on this, but he liked to prove it now and again. He told me, don't do the big swing, like you're drawing a bow. Make it come from your back and shoulders. Move your arm a short way, and his head a big one. And then he demonstrated, on an old drunk who happened to be standing a yard or so away. He was right, of course. His fist probably travelled no more than eighteen inches, but the old man's head snapped back, and he dropped, the way you drop your socks on the floor when you're undressing.

What the hell, it was that kind of neighbourhood, and my

dad wasn't the only one who liked to see men drop. Now, some people get back up after a while and they're more or less fine; no worse than a bad hangover, they say, not such a fun way of getting it but cheaper, and the effect's about the same. Other people are different. Their brains get all rattled up – I felt it once myself, when I was a boy, that absolutely unique sensation of your brain bouncing off your skull. They find they forget things, they lose their rag over stupid stuff, sometimes they mumble, sometimes they say there's always a fog, even when there isn't. Now I've knocked men out on the stage and been knocked out more times than I can say; I fall down rather well, though I do say so myself, I've been complimented on it by managers, who aren't prone to saying nice things about people. On stage it's a great big sweeping swing so they can see it at the back of the gallery, and if you're getting hit you clap your hands together unobtrusively down at waist level, to supply the noise.

7

I came round, and all I could see was a misty blur, and my head hurt so much I wanted to cry. I felt sick and my head was swimming; I closed my eyes, but that made it worse. I couldn't remember anything after walking up the alley. I could hear a voice, very far away, but I couldn't make out what it was saying. Then my stomach heaved and I threw up, but I couldn't move, not even my head, and the puke came gushing out over my chin, and my throat was so raw I couldn't bear to breathe.

Something swooped down on me. At first I thought it was a bird, a hawk or something like that, but it turned out to be a hand, mopping up the sick with a bit of cloth.

Part of my mind – not the bit that had slammed against my skull, presumably – was making a feeble effort. I must have got knocked down, it told me, by a cart or something. No, that made no sense, because I could remember looking carefully, both ways, before sneaking out of the alley. Then I saw this weird image, a man looming up at me like he'd just sprouted out of the earth, and lifting his arms, and the silhouette of a shovel blade, heart-shaped. Somebody bashed me, I realised.

Then I thought; if I've been bashed on the head, does that mean I'll lose my memory? That really scared me; who's going to want an actor who can't remember lines? So I started remembering things, quick sharp, at random: my dad's name, the opening speech from *Hippolytus and Clarenza*, the number of spokes in the wheels of the milk cart I used to hitch a ride on when I was nine, the managers of all the theatres in the City—

"He doesn't look anything like him," someone said.

"Not right now, maybe," someone else said. "I don't think we're catching him at his best."

I remembered that the pockets of my coat were stuffed with stolen property. You clown, I shouted at myself, how could you have been so *stupid*? But this wasn't a sensible time to fall out with myself; save all that for later.

"He's awake."

Immediately I closed my eyes, but not quickly enough. Someone prodded my cheek with a forefinger like a stone-mason's chisel. I could feel the fingernail almost but not quite cut my skin. I opened my eyes and there was this enormous face glowering down at me.

I recognised it.

I remember the first time I saw him. It was at the funeral of that general; you know, the milkface who got killed in the big assault at the beginning of the siege, just before the Fleet showed up and saved the day, his name's on the tip of my tongue. Never mind. Anyway, him; and all the big men in the provisional government took turns to stand up on the rostrum and make speeches about how smart and brave whatsisname had been, and how he'd saved the City, which wasn't true, of course, it was Lysimachus who did that. But never mind. First they had Faustinus, the City prefect, and then the Theme bosses, which I thought was a bit sick even though they were all legal and respectable now, then the Admiral, who was obviously reading from notes someone else had written for him, and finally General Nicephorus, the new commander-in-chief, land forces; and I looked up at him, his broad, noble face, his piercing eyes, his striking profile, and I remember thinking: I could do you standing on my head.

And now here he was, the second most important man in the City, looking down at me, as though he'd just noticed me stuck to the sole of his boot.

"I saw him," he said, in that quiet, measured voice that I do so well, "in the theatre. He can do it."

I had no idea what he was talking about.

"You must be joking," said someone else, and he stepped forward, and I saw him. Artavasdus, his second-in command, who I'd actually met once. A higher voice but well within my register, and useful for comedy scenes, because people think he's an idiot. I don't do him very often, but he's not difficult. "His nose is too short, for a start."

"From a distance," Nicephorus said.

"I saw him in a burlesque at the Crown," someone else said. "He was very good. Actually, he was being me." I knew the voice: Faustinus. And the reason I couldn't move was nothing to do with being bashed on the head. My hands and legs were tied to something, with rope.

"Fine," said Artavasdus, "but we don't need him to be you, we've got you for that. And I say he's nothing like him. Shape of the head's all wrong. And he's a foot too short."

"Actually," Nicephorus put in, "he's six inches too tall."

"You're kidding."

"I had him measured." Nicephorus turned away to shine some personality on Artavasdus. "Which proves my point. You see what you think you're seeing. He's just some low comic, so you think he's shorter. Actually, he's taller. So, if you think you're seeing the real thing, it doesn't matter."

"Nico's right," Faustinus said. "Well, he's obviously taller than me. But when I saw him, I didn't notice that. And when they want to be taller, they wear built-up heels."

Which isn't true, incidentally. You can't walk worth a damn in those things.

"You all appear to be under the illusion that we've got a choice," Nicephorus said. "Look, he'll be with us, so who's going to suspect anything? And he'll be wearing the right clothes, and we'll make sure he's got hats and hoods and God knows what, stand him in the shade, get some short guards to make him look taller—"

"You said he's too tall already."

Nicephorus laughed. "See? You've got me at it now. The point is, nobody suspects. They see what they want to see."

"All right," said Artavasdus. "What about hearing?"

"He does the voice really well," Faustinus put in. "One of my clerks told me. Close your eyes and you'd think it was the real thing."

"Fine." Artavasdus was getting cross. "Let's hear him, shall we?"

"All right," Nicephorus said. "You'll have to make allowances for him being a bit banged up."

I opened my mouth. My palate had been stripped raw by the acid from the vomit. "Excuse me," I said.

"And anyway," Faustinus said, over me, "it's not just the voice. It's the voice *and* the speech rhythms *and* the phrasing, and all the little gestures and mannerisms. And of course we'll tell him what to say, so the words will be right. You know, all the little turns of phrase and pet expressions—"

"He's trying to say something," Artavasdus interrupted.

"Are we going to let the Themes in on this?" Faustinus said.

"The hell we are."

"I agree," Nicephorus said. "This is between the three of us."

Which struck me as odd, because if this was some sort of political thing, then surely Lysimachus would have to know. But, none of my business. "Excuse me," I repeated.

They looked at me.

"Excuse me, but what am I doing here?"

Nicephorus gave me a look that should have squashed me flat. "You know what," he said, "you're a bloody pest."

"Am I? I mean, I'm sorry. I didn't mean—"

"We've been looking for you," Artavasdus said, leaning forward so I could smell almonds on his breath. "The length and breadth of the City, in all the nasty places. And then, just fancy. Where do you eventually turn up? Burgling *my house*."

I was about to object, and then I remembered. He was quite right.

"We found these," he went on, opening his big fist under my nose, "in your pocket. They belonged to my father, you thieving little shit."

He was scaring me. They do bad things to thieves. Odd that it should have slipped my mind before I embarked on this idiotic escapade.

"I'm sorry," I mumbled. Not perhaps the smartest thing I ever said.

"But," Nicephorus said, "in a funny sort of a way it's all to the good. You see, we need you to do something for us, and there's a remote chance you might not want to do it. And we're not savages. If you'd turned us down, we couldn't have forced you. But now, we can quite legally and legitimately make you an offer. You do what we want, or we'll hang you."

My mouth had gone horribly dry. "I'll do it," I said.

"You don't know what it is yet."

"Doesn't matter."

"Some of us," Artavasdus put in, "aren't entirely convinced you can do it."

"Try me. Please."

They looked at each other, and I knew I hadn't made a good impression. They had the look of someone who's just bought something and got it home, and realised it doesn't go with the curtains. "Listen to him," Artavasdus said, "he's pathetic."

"That's his own voice," Nicephorus replied, trying hard to be fair. "Let's try and keep this constructive, for crying out loud." He turned his head and looked at me. "I want you to sound like Lysimachus," he said.

"Imitate him, you mean."

"Yes. Go on."

You know when your mind goes completely blank. "What would you like me to say?"

"I don't know, do I? Say anything."

I could feel myself starting to panic, but then I thought; hang on, I know lots of stuff to say, even if my brain has stopped working. And then I thought: I'm a manager, and Lysimachus has signed up with me for a half-season; what would really suit him down to the ground?

"Oh, pardon me," I said, "thou bleeding piece of earth, that I am meek and gentle with these butchers. Thou art the ruins of the noblest man—" and so on. You can't beat Saloninus, on these occasions. Any bloody fool sounds good saying that stuff.

The speech ran out on me, and I stopped. My throat was sore as hell and my head hurt so much I couldn't bear it. Oh, and I was scared as well. They were looking at me, as if I was a bill they were splitting three ways, and they couldn't decide who'd had the turbot.

"I still don't know," Artavasdus said. "I can see what you mean, but I'm still not sure."

"He's trying too hard," Faustinus said. "Probably nervous." He leaned over me, smiled horribly. "Relax," he said.

"Don't be an idiot, Faustinus," Nicephorus said, "you'll only make him worse."

Faustinus looked at him. "Well?"

Nicephorus sighed. "I think he'll do," he said. "Arta?"

Artavasdus shrugged. "Like you said," he replied wearily. "If we think we've got a choice, we're kidding ourselves. I just have this terrible feeling it's all going to end very badly."

"You're not helping," Nicephorus said. "All right, I'll take that as carried unanimously. You two had better get back out there. I'll brief our reluctant hero."

Artavasdus stood up, shaking his head ruefully, and walked out of my field of vision. Faustinus started to follow him, stopped, turned back as if he was going to say something, thought better of it, went. Which left me alone with the second most powerful man in the City. What joy.

He untied the ropes that were holding me down to the sort of cot thing I'd been lying on. He was clumsy or his hands were shaking; he had trouble with the knots. Personally I'd have cut the ropes and have done with it. "All right," he said, "let's see how smart you are. Tell me what's going on."

"I don't know."

"Extrapolate." He paused. "It means, use what you know to make a guess about what you don't."

I decided I didn't like him very much. "You want me to impersonate Lysimachus."

"Genius. All right, why do we want that?"

I think I mentioned that my head was hurting. Wasn't getting any better, either. "I don't know," I said. "Maybe he's sick, and there's a big occasion coming up." I waited for a reaction. None. "Maybe he's lost his voice, and there's a speech he needs to make."

Nicephorus shook his head. "We'd just postpone it."

"Why don't you just tell me?"

"Why don't you do as you're damn well told?"

Funny, the little things that bug you into doing something stupid. That had been a favourite phrase of my dad's. "Fine," I said. "Maybe you're planning a coup. Maybe you've already done it, and Lysimachus is locked up in a cellar. And you want me—"

He laughed. "Obviously," he said, "we found out all about you. No, Lysimachus isn't downstairs in a cell. Your mother is. And if you don't do as we tell you, we'll make her wish she'd never been born."

You know what? I rather like melodrama, as a genre. It's easy to write and good fun to act, and it fills theatres even in the hot weather. But I don't like it much in real life. And the way he'd said that, about my mother, could have been my father talking, when he was bullying someone. "You know your trouble," I said. "You have problems taking yes for an answer."

That shocked him, and he laughed. "Fair enough," he said. "Yes, we need you to pretend to be Lysimachus."

"Why?"

"He's dead."

My head felt as though there was a wedge in it, and someone had struck the last blow that cleaves down the grain. "A rock fell on him."

"You heard the rumour."

"I was supposed to be there that night. I was the entertainment."

Nicephorus looked at me, shocked and steady. "Just as well for us you weren't," he said. "All right, then. Can you do it?"

"I don't know," I said.

He was starting to lose patience with me. "No," he said, "I don't suppose you do. There's a difference, taking people off for laughs in a burlesque and actually pretending you're them. For one thing, on the stage you exaggerate. You daren't do that if it's for real. You can do the voice when you're declaiming, but conversation's another matter, and I don't suppose you ever heard him just chatting with people."

"No," I said. He looked at me. "But I can extrapolate."

His face cracked into a grin. "Go on, then."

All right. Here's how I do it.

It's not exactly difficult. If it was, I wouldn't be able to. All I do is, I imagine I'm standing in front of a mirror, but the reflection I'm looking at isn't me, it's him – the target, the victim, the subject. I watch his face as I talk to him, observe how his lips move, his eyes, the intonations and where he puts the stresses on words; I hear his voice in my head, though I'm doing the talking. And then, for all intents and purposes, I'm him. I open my eyes and face the audience, and that's all there is to it.

I'm kidding, right? No, actually, I'm not. I'm definitely not thinking out every word and every gesture, because that's suicide. I'm being him, which I can do as easily as I am me – which isn't exactly easy in any realistic sense of the word. Because being me has never been easy. And on balance I'd far rather be anybody else but me.

True. If we were talking to each other right now, face to face, the voice you'd be hearing wouldn't be my voice – not the one I was born and brought up with, in the alleys round the Old Flower Market. I had to work like mad to get rid of that voice, with its sharp, whining vowels, its devil-may-care slovenly aspirates and its smothered, bitten-off consonants. And the words would be all different, if it was really me talking: different vocabulary, different syntax. I had to learn to shape my sentences in a completely alien way when I got out of that horrible place, and that made me change the way I think. And now it sort of comes naturally, but it's also constantly there, a nagging worry in the back of my mind, just in case I let slip a glottal stop or a dislocated conditional clause or an atavistic verb ending. No, being me is hard work, all the time. Being politicians is a walk in the park in comparison.

Which, incidentally, is why I get so few low comedy parts. Your accent's just not convincing, they say, you're laying it on with a trowel. Have you ever actually been east of the Black Cross in your life? And I shrug, and think: small price to pay.

"I'll do my best," I said, sounding just like Lysimachus. "But don't expect miracles."

His eyebrows shot up. "That's not bad," he said.

"Fuck you," I said. He laughed.

"Actually, screw you would be better," he said. "Lysimachus didn't actually swear very much, not after he turned into a big hero. Of course, he wouldn't have thought of *screw you* as swearing."

"Screw you, then."

"Much better. Only then he'd laugh, after he'd been horribly rude to you, to show it was all right."

"Noted," I said, as myself.

"Try it again."

"Cue."

"What? Oh, sorry." He cleared his throat. "Actually, that's not bad."

"Screw you," I said, then grinned; not a laugh, because he wouldn't just then, not out loud. I knew that, even though I'd never met him. I just knew, a laugh wouldn't be right.

"That's much better. You're sure you never met him?"

"Me and a big man like that? Talk sense."

He pursed his lips. "Not big man," he said. "Actually, I'm not quite sure what he'd have said, but I never heard him use big man in that context."

"Boss," I said.

"Yes, you're right." He looked at me. "How'd you—?"

"He came from the Themes, right? Boss, or boss-man, or big boss man. Sort of a technical meaning in Poor Town."

"Yes, well, you'd know about that, wouldn't you? You know, you're really very good."

I didn't say anything, but I gave him the look. In Paradise it means you're asking for trouble. It made him laugh. "Sorry," he said. "Listen to me. I'm apologising to you; you really have got the hang of this. All right, you can stop it now. Truth is, I never could stand the fellow."

For a moment I forgot my headache. "Is that right?"

"Stop it, I told you. No, I never did like him much."

He stopped and looked at me. "What do you know about him, exactly?"

Strange question. "What everybody knows. He was the man. He saved the City."

"Like hell he did." It was sudden, and very bitter. "Let me tell you about Lysimachus. He was a bodyguard. He started as a fighter in the arena; he was a champion; he was very good at killing people. Then the siege happened, and a very great man needed a bodyguard, so we chose the best for him. And, yes, he was a very good bodyguard, and he loved the great man: he was devoted to him, like a dog. But then the great man died, after he'd saved the City, and the people of this town weren't ready to hear that their saviour was dead, so we changed the truth. We told them, Lysimachus was the great man, Lysimachus saved the City; because he looked like a hero, and he was big and strong and he could tear a man to bits with his bare hands in fifteen seconds flat, and people like that. We told them: the man you thought was a great man was really just a geek, an engineer, he tinkered with stuff, but he wasn't a leader. It was Lysimachus who did it all; he really saved your lives when we were this close to getting slaughtered." He stopped for a while; he was feeling uncomfortable. "It was my idea," he said. "We had to do something, quickly. So I said, this is what we'll do, because people have to have someone to believe in or they give up." He closed his eyes, then opened them again. "And here I am, doing the same thing all over again, serves me right, I guess. But it worked the last time, and it's going to work again. This city is not going to fall just because its people are—"

He didn't tell me what its people are. He assumed I already knew.

"I didn't know about Lysimachus," I said.

"Of course you didn't, nobody did, that was the *point.*" He took a moment to collect himself. "But it worked," he said. "And it worked in spite of the fact that they'd been there at the time, they knew who the real hero was, they cheered him in the streets, when they weren't blaming him for every damn thing. But then we told them, it was Lysimachus really. And they believed us, because he looks like a hero, and he's one of them, scum of the earth made good, and because his skin's the right colour."

Ah, I thought, I was right. And the name was still on the tip of my tongue.

"So," he went on, "if we could sell them that muscle-bound thug in place of a real hero, we can sell them you in place of the thug. Just long enough till we can find someone else for them to worship and adore, and then you'll be free to go. Rest of the day's your own, and all that."

I decided he'd forgotten something. I waited for a moment, then said, "Excuse me."

"What?"

"Sorry to bother you, but what's in it for me?"

He turned his head and gave me a look I won't ever forget. "Staying alive," he said. "You want to do that, don't you?"

8

He gave me a book to read: a history of the siege, it said on the spine, which wasn't strictly accurate, since it only went down to where the colonel of engineers (Nicephorus' old boss) got killed. It was quite hard going but I struggled through it.

From it I gathered that at one point things had been very bad indeed. Apparently, the enemy lured the entire City garrison out into the woods and slaughtered them like sheep, at the same time fixing things so that the Fleet was marooned a thousand miles away and couldn't come back to save us. The only thing standing between us and annihilation was a few companies of engineers, who happened to come back to town after they'd finished a job somewhere. Their commander pulled off a series of tricks and scams that made the enemy think we were better prepared than we were, and that bought some time. And then there was a whole load of stuff about the engineer commander having known the enemy leader when they were kids, which I must admit I took with a pinch of salt, because how plausible is that? I guess Nicephorus had it put in the book because he needed something to explain how we managed to survive apart from plain old-fashioned amazingly good luck, which happens more often than you'd think but which no audience ever believes in.

I read the book in a small room – call it a cell, because that's what it really was – in a tower in the Imperial palace, while I was waiting for someone to come and tell me what I was supposed to do. You'd have thought from all that intensity – we have no choice, disaster looms – that they'd be in a hurry to get on with it, whatever it might turn out to be, but apparently not. Still, it gave me time to reflect, get the horrors, overcome them, relapse into a quivering mass and gradually pull myself together again until I resembled something vaguely human. Also, my headache slowly subsided, though I was too busy scaring myself to death to feel the benefit.

You know on the opening night whether it's going to work or not, and sometimes you can hear the death rattle at the first rehearsal. I had a really bad feeling about the whole idea. It was the result of desperation, and that's never good. When you get bounced into something by force of circumstance, you don't have options, and it's in choosing between alternatives that we get a chance to exercise wisdom, whatever the hell that is. It's the difference between riding a horse with a bit and bridle and being tied on a galloping horse backwards. So, if it turned out that I had any say in the matter, I wasn't planning on sticking around. If I saw a chance, I'd take it, simple as that.

Assuming I didn't get a chance, was there anything I could do to improve my chances of survival? Nothing immediately sprang to mind, other than giving this ridiculous job I'd been landed with my very, very best shot. Actually, the book made me feel a bit better on that score, since it purported to record examples of rational human beings believing the most atrocious garbage, on both sides of the City wall. By the same token, there's only so much dumb luck in the world this side of the Great Meathook, and, by the look of it, the provisional government had used up all of it, leaving none for later.

Fine. There's an old saying; the worse the play, the harder you have to try. Which meant, among other things, that I was going to have to take this ridiculous business *seriously*; not just sleepwalk through it looking for an opportunity to sneak away, but actually think about it, focus, concentrate, get every last detail exactly right; not simply do enough to satisfy the management, but put everything into it, as though it mattered, *because* it mattered. Hard to do, given the ludicrous situation, but like the man said, it's not like we have a choice.

For the next five days, the conspirators – let's call them that – worked on me to bring me up to snuff. In practice, that meant that for twenty hours out of twenty-four one of them sat with me, while the other two were off somewhere, presumably running the City, and talked to me; all I had to do was be Lysimachus back at them. If I got something wrong, I was corrected. No, he wouldn't say that, he wouldn't sit like that, he wouldn't laugh at that, that doesn't sound right, try it again. They were patient, I'll say that for them, with the deadly calm of men wound up tight like fiddle-strings; shouting and losing your rag would be counterproductive and we can't afford to waste a second. By the end of the third day I was shattered; that was intentional, they said, no use me only being Lysimachus when I was fresh as a daisy, I had to be him all the bloody time. That night, Artavasdus woke me up after I'd had one hour's sleep. I remembered what was going on just in time and woke up perfectly in character; violent start, a backwards wriggle that put an arm's length between me and him, and my hand on where the hilt of a knife should have been on the bedside table, only there wasn't one. Not bad, though I say it myself, and from then on Artavasdus started treating me with a bit of respect.

"We'll practise that some more," he said.

"No we fucking won't."

He grinned. "Swearing," he pointed out.

"Swearing's called for," I replied. "And if you do that to me again I'll break your arm."

For a split second, he thought I meant it. For a split second, come to that, so did I.

On the sixth day, they showed me in public. It had been a very long time, they said, since anyone but them had laid eyes on the great man, and the City had noticed; there were ugly rumours flying around – true ones, but never mind that – and something had to be done straight away. There had already been riots, which had been put down with considerable brutality, which the conspirators regretted. In consequence, they'd had to issue a statement that Lysimachus was ill, dangerously so, though the doctors were hopeful. It would therefore be in order for me to make just a fleeting appearance on a balcony, well wrapped up against the cold, even if there wasn't any. I'd wave, then stagger back exhausted by the effort, and my faithful comrades would escort me into the palace, and everything would be just fine.

And it was. Playing weak and feeble is harder than it sounds, but fortuitously I had the mountain fever once, and I could remember how my joints ached and how much effort it took to do anything at all. Don't worry, they told me, you'll be twenty feet over their heads and all muffled up. I told them, you do your job, I'll do mine. Idiots. Didn't they realise that it's got to be perfect? Don't suppose they did. You need to have served your time in the profession before you find that out, but it's true. The people at the back of the gallery can't actually see your face, but they know if you're smiling or not, just as they can tell if a girl's pretty. I have no idea how, but they do.

So I did it my way, and it worked. I think that was when I realised exactly what Lysimachus meant to the people of the City. When they steered me out onto the balcony, I discovered I couldn't see anything except people: no pavement, no walls, just bodies squeezed up tight against each other, a solid mass of faces, eyes all fixed on me, as though the stalls had overflowed and flooded the whole of town. And the noise. I don't get cheers like that when I go on but some of us do. I stood there suffocating in the noise, and, God, I was jealous.

"I think we got away with it," Faustinus said, as I tottered away from the window, still in sick and feeble character. "You look awful," he noticed.

"I'm fine," I said, but it took me a moment to pull myself together. "Just acting. Now what?"

"Let's not get carried away," Nicephorus said. "Thirty seconds at an open window is one thing. Besides, we don't actually need you for anything just now."

Nor he did. One thing I'd found out about the First Citizen and Father of his Country: he didn't do much. Hardly anything. It was more a case of keeping him on a leash, to stop him interfering in things he didn't understand and screwing them up.

"He was a clown," Artavasdus confided in me the next

day, over Lysimachus' favourite breakfast of barley rolls, fermented cabbage and green tea. I despise fermented cabbage. "He worshipped the old man, but once he was gone, the fool started believing what we said about him. He forgot he was nothing but the old man's minder, started thinking he'd actually done it all. To tell you the truth, he was starting to get out of control."

They made me do exercises. Lysimachus had been an arena champion, so at that time naturally he was amazingly lean and fit. Once he quit the sand and found himself with access to unlimited food, he started eating with a sort of savage passion. His arena metabolism burned most of it off, but they told me he was starting to get blurred round the edges at the end. But that wouldn't do for me. Everyone expected Lysimachus to have the physique of a heroic statue, and that was non-negotiable.

"Actually," Faustinus told me, as I lay on my back lifting some ridiculous weight on a bar, "you were about right when we caught you. About the same build as him, I mean. But people wouldn't believe that, you see."

I could accept that. A friend of mine who used to make a living cutting dies for counterfeit coins told me once: a forgery's got to be better than the original.

And then there were the scars. Everybody knew Lysimachus had scars, because he'd been an arena champion, and then he'd been speared in the back saving the General's life one time. Actually, they told me, while Nicephorus was stropping the razor, he had remarkably few scars for a sand fighter, because he was good, therefore he didn't get himself all cut up, but that's not what people expect to see, is it?

We'd negotiated a bit on this issue. I'd started off from the position that I was a wizard with sealing wax and greasepaint. They weren't having that. It shows how much I'd managed to please them that they were prepared to modify their ideas at all; they'd figured on leaving me deckle-edged, like a worn-out saw. Instead we compromised on a relatively small number of well-documented scars, which Nicephorus executed himself with a surprisingly light touch for such a big man. They had to be packed with saltpetre to get them to age quickly. It hurt like hell and I had to dig deep into character to stop myself yelling the house down.

Time out, while I make a point that's probably occurred to you already.

Lysimachus was an arena fighter and, until he heard the call to a higher destiny, Blue to the core, the way my dad was Green. The sand boys say: you only get really good at fighting if you enjoy it. A bit like my theory of acting, I guess. You have to take it seriously. Well, yes, obviously you take a fight seriously if you want to stay alive. But that, according to the sand boys, isn't the point. If you fight just to stay alive, sooner or later you'll lose. You need to fight to *win*. You need to enjoy winning, more than anything else in the whole world. To get that enjoyment, you need to relish your opponent's defeat, and his pain, and his death.

Which maybe explains why my dad was so good at what he did. He wasn't the biggest man ever, he didn't have muscles like – well, Lysimachus, or (come to that) me. He was pretty nimble on his feet but he couldn't do back somersaults or jump his own height. But every time he went into a fight – I don't think I can do better than his own favourite simile. It's like going to meet your best girl, he said. Paraphrase that for clarity. It's not just a case of liking to hurt people. You need to be in love with it.

Am I in love with what I do? Maybe I wouldn't go that far. Married to it would be closer to the mark. But, yes, a chip off the old block, to that limited extent. I go about my craft with the same – I'm reaching for a word here – the same *wholeheartedness* that he went about his.

And now the chip stands back and considers the block, by means of a mirror, called Lysimachus. One way of looking at it, it makes the job easier, because I know what makes this man tick. Easy-peasy. Take my dad, and then imagine that, through some inconceivable intervention of the Invincible Sun, he comes across a cause he genuinely believes in, which comes to inform and motivate his every thought and action. That would be Lysimachus.

On the other hand, I told you my trick with the imaginary mirror. I look into it and I see Lysimachus. I look into it and I see my father. I look into it and I see me.

Not a pleasant thought.

9

Once the scars had healed up, I met an ambassador.

No big deal, they told me, because this clown never met the real Lysimachus, but he insists on talking to the top man, and they're prepared to give us credit, and we need the grain shipments. It'll be good practice for you, and we can show the two of you on a balcony, and everyone will know where their next meal's coming from.

I didn't like the idea. The one aspect of Lysimachus I was still having trouble with was his arrogance. That came from me growing up in Poor Town, where everybody knows his place, like in every pack of predators. In the Themes, your place is your most valued possession, because it guarantees that you'll always eat *something* and sleep *somewhere*, and it takes much of the stress and anxiety out of life. You know who you're allowed to beat up, and who's allowed to beat up on you. It's only the highest echelons, the big boss men in each Theme, who have absolute freedom of thought and action, and even they're nominally subject to the law and the emperor and stuff like that – very nominally, but I guess it's the difference between having a sky and no sky at all. And to achieve the status that teaches you how to be arrogant, you need to pass through a lifetime of very vivid and powerful experiences, mostly getting beaten up and beating up other people. I have a fine imagination, but I wasn't sure I was going to be able to extrapolate all that.

Don't be such a prima donna, they told me. Get on with it.

They dressed me up in a senator's gown and trotted me down about a million miles of corridor to the Shell Chamber, so-called because its walls are tiled with mother of pearl, one of the wonders of the City and unbelievably vulgar. I did my entrance, quickening my step as I walked through the door to make sure I was a clean stride ahead of the other three.

The ambassador was a big man, broad-shouldered, fat in that almost elegant way – he bulged all over but nothing wobbled – with a shiny bald head; very dark for a milkface, with a snub of a nose like a thumb and eyes the colour of a clear sky in winter. He wore plain unbleached linen, beautifully tailored, over a yellow silk vest and stockings, and dainty sequinned slippers on his tiny feet. They'd briefed me on his people. They lived a long way away – six weeks across the open sea, which they were able to cross because of their amazing long, low, clinker-built ships, which zipped along at an amazing speed and rode out storms that would send anything we've got to the bottom. Their country was a very big island, by all accounts the earthly paradise. It had a ridiculously long growing season, and the north was flat and temperate, the south was hot with monsoons. Grain was stupidly cheap, grown on slave-worked plantations. What they wanted from us was the better things in life; decorated furniture, quality ceramics, tableware, and most of all books, which they'd recently heard about and thought sounded like a really nice idea.

"Sure," I said to him. "And everything we send you, you'll copy, and then you won't need to buy from us any more. That's not good business."

His translator toned it down a bit, presumably, but I saw his face stiffen. Still, it was what Lysimachus would have said. At the edge of my peripheral vision, Faustinus had that taut look, but I ignored him.

The translator turned back to me. "And why not?" he said. "When we buy something, surely we buy the right to use it as we see fit."

"No, you don't," I said. "You buy *one copy*, that's all. Look, you've come a long way and I'm sorry to disappoint you, but there it is. Our stuff's the best in the world, that's why you want it so badly. We can find buyers for it any day of the week, and they won't rip us off like you're planning to do. Nice to have met you, enjoy the rest of your stay in our fair city."

The translator had trouble with that, I could tell. I made a point of keeping my peripheral vision tight, because Artavasdus was pulling faces at me, I don't know what the other two were doing but presumably something similar. The ambassador stopped to think about it. I waited, looking bored.

"Surely," the translator said, "we can find a compromise."

"Ah," I said, "now you're talking. Fine, here's the deal. You buy what you like, but on the understanding that what you're paying for is the right to copy. That'll be expensive."

I paused. No point going on too long, or the translator would've forgotten half of what I'd said.

"You're thinking: screw him, we'll buy Robur goods elsewhere on the open market. And, yes, you could do that, so I'm prepared to be reasonable. I'll charge you double what the stuff is worth at home, which still works out cheaper for you than getting it from the Aelians. Wheat and oats cost you practically nothing, so it's no skin off your nose. Or we can forget the whole thing, I really don't mind. Up to you."

The ambassador frowned, then stuck out his hand. I grinned and shook it. "How much does he want?" I asked the translator.

"How much can you supply?" the translator replied, without needing to confer.

I was in trouble after that. What the hell were you thinking of, are you out of your tiny mind, you realise you nearly jeopardised, et cetera. I didn't need all that; I was shaking and drained after half an hour of running on sheer nerve – it's a bit like crossing a wide expanse of ice that you know won't bear your weight: you can only do it if you go really fast and keep going.

"It worked, didn't it?"

Yes, they told me, but that's beside the point. No, I told them, it's not; and I realised I was still in character, and they'd stopped yelling and were listening to me.

That was scary. "Look," I said, back to being little contemptible Notker from Poor Town. "It's what he would've done. I know it was, I could feel it in my marrow. If I'd been nice and polite and accommodating it wouldn't have been right. And we'd have got half of what we're going to get."

"It was supposed to be a dry run," Nicephorus said. He was the least upset of the three of them. "That was the whole idea. That man didn't know you, you didn't have to be convincing."

"It's not like that," I said. "It's all or nothing. Either I'm him or I'm me. Otherwise it'll just fall to bits."

"We never used to let Lysimachus see ambassadors until the deal was actually signed," Faustinus pointed out. "But this one insisted."

"Proves my point," I said.

"Be that as it may." Nicephorus was being the boss dog of the pack, but it wasn't the role he was cut out for. "All right," he went on, "you were right, as it happens. But you didn't do as you were told."

"Fine," I said. "So, if you could just clarify. Which is more important, doing it right or doing what you tell me to?"

"He thinks he knows better than we do," Artavasdus said.

"As far as my job goes," I said, "I probably do."

"Smart, though," Faustinus put in. "I hadn't thought of it like that. Them copying our stuff, I mean. You were right about that," he said, actually talking to me, not the others.

"It's the difference between buying a ticket to the play and buying the play," I said.

They looked at each other.

"All right," Artavasdus said, "so he's smart. In the tiny, specialised segment of life in which he has knowledge and experience, he's no fool. But we can't have him making policy decisions."

"That's up to you," I said. "You decide what I do. But I have to do it my way. His way. And would you please talk to me occasionally, not each other."

"Our fault," Nicephorus said, "for running before we can walk. And it hasn't turned out so bad, and we got away with it, so no harm done. But Arta's right," he said, turning to me. "You do not run this city. Got that?"

"He didn't," I said, "so there shouldn't be a problem."

"I'm beginning to wish we'd never embarked on this,"

Artavasdus said. "Still, I'll hand it to you," he went on, addressing me. "You're just like him. I hated the man, just so's you know."

"I can't say I like him much," I replied.

To what extent am I justified in making myself the hero of the piece?

I told you earlier that I'm much better at writing parts for other people, and I imagine by now you'll agree. Also, there's a sort of unspoken law that the principal character has to be the hero; so much so that we use the two terms interchangeably. So, fine. I'm the protagonist of this story, because I'm the protagonist of my life. Hero, though, implies actions of heroic stature – great deeds, brave, clever, both. I'm telling you about bits of my story in which I did well, or I think I did well, and subsequent events don't absolutely disprove my opinion; so, that makes me the hero. For now, anyway.

But – I've glanced back, most uncharacteristically, at what I wrote at the beginning (I rarely read what I've written; usually there isn't time) and I did use that word: history. That implies a commitment to the truth, whatever that may be. So. So what? I'm writing down what actually happened, not making anything up, not leaving things out.

But there's more to it than that, or I'd be able to play Sechimer every bit as well as Otho does, and obviously I couldn't do that. It's the bit extra that you put into the part. We both say the same words, but Otho is a genius and I'm not, so Otho's Sechimer is a real live human being and mine isn't. Also, Otho's Sechimer is completely different from everyone else's.

Words, facts; it's what I put into the facts that makes the subtle difference – between me being the hero, the villain, the comic relief, the guy who comes on to move the chairs at the end of Act 1 so nobody trips over them during the fight scene. And that's all about how you see yourself.

In my case, I see myself exclusively in a series of distorting mirrors, as someone else, see above. To which you naturally and reasonably reply, so what? I'm profoundly interested in myself, nobody else gives a damn, that's how it should be. But not when it impacts on my capacities as a historian. I don't know. Maybe I should've written this in the third person and confined myself to dates and battles.

Three more public appearances: two were just balcony scenes, the third was laying a wreath on the tomb of the first Blue to die in the siege. They didn't want me to, but I said a few words, which went down really well with the Themesmen; they cheered and stamped their feet and threw their hats in the air, which is quite a tribute when you think what hats cost these days.

"You shouldn't have done that," Nicephorus said. "There was no need. He never usually makes a speech."

"He's been sick," I told him. "They've been worried about him, we've had riots because they were worried. So he'd have made a speech."

He had no answer to that, so he let the matter drop.

Next day I was in my room lifting those horrible weights when all three of them came in, and Faustinus shut the door and wedged it with the back of a chair. I wasn't sure I liked that.

"Obviously," Nicephorus said, "he wasn't married."

I shrugged. "Just as well," I said.

"Absolutely," said Artavasdus. "Actually, he was more inclined the other way, if you know what I mean."

"I might have a problem with that," I said.

"Lucky for you, he kept it quiet," Nicephorus said. "But he was definitely both sides of the fence, so we need to take care of that."

"Explain what you mean about *taking care*."

"There was a certain amount of gossip," Faustinus joined in. "He was seeing an actress."

He made it sound so dreadful I couldn't help laughing. "First I've heard of it," I said.

"I thought it was fairly common knowledge among you people."

"We have a first-rate internal intelligence network," I said. "It's vital to know who's screwing who, to avoid unpleasant conflicts when you're casting a piece. So, if one of us had been—"

"But he was." Artavasdus was about to enjoy himself, I could tell. "Pretty well everybody knows about it, except you." He treated me to the nastiest sympathetic smile I've ever had the misfortune to share a room with. "Always the last to know, as the saying goes. Her name's Hodda."

He could have kicked me in the balls instead, but, no, he had to be cruel. "I find that hard to believe."

I'd made his day. "You think you know people," he said. "I imagine your friends kept it from you. Nobody likes to be the messenger."

I took a deep breath. Didn't matter. Hardly anything does. "So," I said. "What's it got to do with anything?"

Nicephorus gave me his steady look. "He's been ill," he

said, "but he's better now. If the affair's suddenly broken off, it'll look funny. So—"

"I think he's dumped her," I said firmly. "Probably found out she's been cheating on him. It happens a lot in theatrical circles."

Nicephorus shook his head. "He needs a girlfriend," he said. "Because of those other rumours. And you know this Hodda."

"I know lots of actresses. What about Andronica? She'll do anything."

"Hodda knows the truth," Faustinus said. "So she's already in on this. The fewer people who get involved, the better, obviously."

Sometimes I hate logic. "So what do you have in mind?" I said.

"There was no settled pattern," Nicephorus said, every inch the trained strategist. "Sometimes she came to the palace, sometimes they met at one of a number of private houses. Never at the theatre."

"If you'd ever been out back of the Gallery of Illustration, you'd know why. What's the plan?"

"It's easier and safer to have her come here, to start with," Faustinus said. "Her carriage is quite distinctive, people will see. Word will get about."

"So I don't actually have to see her."

Nicephorus pursed his lips. "We think the two of you should be seen together," he said. "For one thing, if anybody is harbouring doubts about your identity, that ought to set their minds at rest. I mean, she'd know it was him—" He stopped. Upper-class reticence, rather cute. "And it's just the sort of thing you wouldn't allow to happen if you were running an impostor," he said. "So it makes sense."

"You really think so? I don't."

"We've decided," Artavasdus said.

"We think it's for the best," Faustinus said, with just a faint smear of an apology.

I thought: what the hell. You leave your personal feelings backstage. Besides which, I had a vague recollection that it had been me who left her. Or maybe it was the other way round. Six of one, half a dozen of the other.

10

So they set about arranging a well-publicised clandestine meeting. Screw them. I decided it was high time I took an intelligent interest in the art of war.

There are books on the subject. Can you believe that? Think about it. Either the book is no bloody good, in which case you follow its precepts and you and fifty thousand of your countrymen are slaughtered like geese at midwinter; or the book is true and authoritative and contains everything you need to know about the subject, in which case you follow its precepts and you and fifty thousand of your countrymen, see above, because the other side have read the same book and can predict your every move. Or both sides would wipe each other out to the last man, which really wouldn't solve anything, would it?

Still; there are books on the subject, including the *Mirror of Battles*, by Carnufex the Irrigator, who was a very great general a very long time ago, and which I'd happened to dip into when I was researching a play about, guess what, a siege. I wanted a whole bunch of military technical terms for the low comedian to reel off – ravelins and mamelons, I remember, and enfilades in side and rear, and pavises, and mangonels, and other stuff I never managed to find rhymes for. So I asked Nicephorus if he knew where there might be a copy, and of course the clown owned one. Slept with it under his pillow, probably.

(In case you're wondering; ravelin/javelin; mamelon/camel on; side and rear/hide in here; pavises/sneezes. I managed to find one for mangonel, but it's slipped my mind.)

Anyhow, I read the book, paying rather more attention this time, and I confess I found it illuminating. I also badgered Faustinus into letting me loose in the archive room, where they keep the reports filed by the section commanders for the duration of the siege so far; and other stuff as well, some of which I dipped into while I was at it.

("What do you want all that stuff for?" Faustinus asked me suspiciously. "Hardly in your line, I'd have thought."

"It's all the sort of thing he'd know," I told him. "And I don't know it, so maybe I should."

He peered at me, convinced I was up to something. "We tell you everything you need to know."

"No," I said politely, "you don't. You couldn't possibly. For instance, suppose I'm handing out medals, and some old soldier says to me, remember that time when the Fifteenth held the Southgate bastion, and Marcianus would've got chopped to bits, only you charged in and saved us? I could make a real fool of myself if I said the wrong thing."

He shrugged. "Suit yourself," he said, "I'll lend you the keys. But most of it's incredibly boring.")

So I spent a week in there on and off, when I wasn't needed for balcony scenes, and by the time I gave Faustinus his keys back I wished I hadn't. I'm all for a quiet life, and, generally speaking, if there's bad news I'd far rather not know about it. Worrying just makes things worse, I always say, specially if there's nothing constructive you can do to improve matters.

You remember my scene with the ambassador: let's start there. When the enemy started the siege, we quickly reached the position where they couldn't get inside the walls and we couldn't drive them away; not that it mattered all that much, because once the Fleet came back, we still had complete command of the sea, even though our land empire had been taken away from us. Big deal. Over the last seven years, the City's turned itself into one enormous factory. We import raw materials and turn them into the most beautifully made and finished goods money can buy, which we then sell for a great deal of money, with which we buy everything we could possibly want. Brilliant. Between the factories, the dockyards and the Fleet, there's work for everybody (in theory) and most of the City people are far better off than they were before the siege began.

Except that, quite by chance and on the spur of the moment, I'd hit on the flaw in the scheme. The whole world wanted the things we made, because we made them so well; but we were asking too much money for them. So the foreigners had started making them at home, or trying to. We were losing skilled craftsmen, lured abroad by promises of better money and not living next door to a half-million murderous savages wanting to kill them; we'd made it illegal for a skilled man to leave the City, but that was a bit like punishing a man for committing suicide: once he's done it, what can you do to him?

Fine, I thought. Now let's glance through the minutes of the cabinet meetings and see what they're proposing to do about it. So I did. Nothing. Which left me with the ghastly conclusion that nobody except me had spotted that there was a problem, or else they'd figured it out but weren't proposing to deal with it. I couldn't believe that. It was so obvious, so painfully staring-you-in-the-face obvious that even I could see it. So I read the minutes again, and all I could find was Faustinus bleating at the Theme bosses to stop their skilled people slipping away abroad, and the bosses asking, reasonably enough, exactly what they were supposed to do about it: see above?

Once you find the half-worm of doubt in the apple of confidence, you start to worry. I read the section commanders' reports. A pattern started to emerge.

Basically, the section commanders said, we were fine. Over the last seven years, the enemy had made a dozen all-out attempts at cracking the wall and getting inside, all of which had been beaten off with horrific losses to the enemy. They'd tried every trick in the book to sap and undermine the walls, but we'd read the same book (see above) and were ready for them every time. Therefore, they'd settled down for the long term and basically given up.

Settled down for the long term; I could vouch for that. Go up any of the high towers and steeples in this man's town and you can look out over the wall and see what the enemy have accomplished over the last seven years. What started off as a load of rickety tents has turned into a thriving town – make that city – with wattle-and-daub houses with neatly thatched roofs, which from time to time we set fire to – think pigeons; we put out grain on the battlements to lure in the pigeons that nest in their eaves; catch a pigeon, tie some smouldering straw to its legs, let it go, sit back and watch the fun. Well, they started it. But they rebuild, and improve, and extend, and behind the narrow streets of thatched huts there are ploughed fields as far as the eye can see.

But that's all right, surely; because they can't get inside, we've proved that, so there's no reason why this happy state of affairs shouldn't go on indefinitely. Fair comment, and while we're at it, could I interest you in buying the Blue Star temple? The point being, we can, and do, hurt them regularly, to the fullest extent of our ability; and they're still here. We only have to get it wrong once and we're all dead. It's like the contest of skill, instinct and nerve between the duck hunter and the duck. Nine times out of ten, the duck wins. The tenth time, he gets killed and eaten.

So, obviously, it stands to reason there has to be a long-term plan for evacuating the hundred and fifty thousand people who live in the City, taking them over the vast ocean out of harm's way and starting from scratch in a place where the Robur nation aren't quite so obsessively hated by absolutely everybody. I looked for just such a plan. Maybe I didn't look hard enough, or maybe it's top secret. Or maybe—

It slowly dawned on me that it's possible for the wise men who run your life for you to see disaster coming and not have a plan for dealing with it; because they know what needs to be done but there are vested interests in the way, or they can't figure out the politics, or they think it'll be horrendously unpopular, or it'll cost too much money, a commodity you can't take with you if you get your throat cut by the enemy but never mind about that – it's possible to build a beautiful house on the lip of an active volcano, with all the hot water you could ever want, and restructure your mind so you don't actually think about what you're doing, or what will inevitably happen.

If you value a good night's sleep, don't ever have a similar revelation. True, I worry a lot, always having had plenty to worry about, but was it just me being silly? Don't think so.

So there I was, transformed against my will into the spit and image of the most powerful man in the City, staring at a medium to long term that could only end badly, knowing that if I really was who I was pretending to be, if I made a monumental effort I might just be able to change all that. It was one of those moments of perfect pellucid clarity. I knew exactly what I ought to do, if only I could find a way of doing it. What I had to do was find an opportunity, stuff my pockets with small items of great value, stow away on the next grain freighter out of the docks and leave the idiots to get on with it. Practically a moral duty, when you thought about it.

11

It was all arranged. We were to meet at Faustinus' house at the foot of Hill Street. He and his family would be at the theatre – go and see the new play at the Rose, I told him, I gather it's really quite good – so we'd have the place to ourselves; we being me, her, Nicephorus and Artavasdus, only she and I would arrive at the front door, while the others sneaked in at the back.

("Why?" I demanded.

"She insisted."

"It's an awful lot of trouble to put you to."

"It's no trouble.")

I arrived in broad daylight, because that's what he'd have done. I rode there in an open carriage, with four Green bodyguards; we talked and I told them a dirty joke, which amused them no end. The door was unlocked. I went inside.

It was a nice house, very tasteful, very expensive; lots of small items of great value, and I was wearing a military greatcoat with deep, deep pockets. I was thinking seriously about my future when those two idiots came up from the kitchen.

"She specifically said she didn't want to be alone with you," Artavasdus said. "And she's a well-known actress, a public figure, so we can't just disappear her, not without a lot of trouble and fuss."

It took me a moment to work out what he was getting at. "For God's sake," I said, "it's nothing like that."

"She was very insistent," he replied, looking at me.

People like to believe the worst about me, I have no idea why. "Fine," I said. "We can all sit here in embarrassed silence for an hour, and then go home."

"Let's do that," Nicephorus said, and made himself comfortable in the best chair in the room.

I was beginning to wish I'd brought something to read when I heard carriage wheels outside in the street. They both stood up; so did I. While they were on their feet, I quickly set the scene the way I wanted to play it.

There was a full-length mirror in the corner of the room. I dragged it out centre left, adjusted the position of a chair, sat down in it to make sure I had the line of sight. In the mirror I could see the door she'd come in through, but all she'd be able to see would be the back of my head and shoulders. I took a deep breath and a long look into another mirror, and waited.

Enter Hodda left, advances upstage, sees man in chair. Just for a moment she freezes, like she's seen a ghost. While she's still frozen, I spin round in my chair and scowl at her.

"You cow," I said. "Where's my money?"

She recovered well, I'll give her that. "Hello, Notker," she said, and took off her hat.

Artavasdus was on his feet, in case I made a lunge for her with some weapon I'd managed to conceal from him. I gave him my fish eye, and he sat down.

"I haven't got your money," she said. "There was a close-down, remember?"

"Which lasted three days. That was weeks ago."

"I've been busy."

I'd made my point. Time to let her off the hook. "How's it doing, by the way?"

"The play? Oh, not bad. First night was a bit touch and go, but it's settled down now. Mitto got your part. They say he's the best thing in it."

"He couldn't act his way out of a rotten sack."

"He's always good in cheap melodrama."

She was looking at the wall, not me. But for a split second there, she thought she'd seen him, Lysimachus. I decided to point this out.

"Yes," she said, "that was really quite impressive. Pity, really. If I'd known you could act, I'd have given you a job."

That made Artavasdus laugh out loud, and Nicephorus smiled behind his hand. Not that I minded. Someone has to be the straight man. A bit like fight scenes; you don't mind one bit when he stabs you and you die, so long as he minds what he's doing and doesn't accidentally jab you in the leg first.

"Do you people always carry on like this?" Artavasdus said. We both looked at him. He shrugged. "I was only asking," he said. She looked at him some more. "You wanted us to be here," he said.

"And it was very kind of you," Hodda said sweetly. "But I'm sure two important gentlemen like you have better things to do."

That's the disadvantage you're under if you've been born and bred a gentleman. If you get a direct order from a lady, or someone dressed up as one, you're obliged to obey it. No matter that the carriage wouldn't be there to collect them for another hour or so, and they'd have to walk home through the streets. My heart bled for them, and then they left.

And then we looked at each other for a bit. I've always liked Hodda. She's not as pretty as she looks. Consider her face in repose and you'll see she's quite plain really, nose too long, face a bit thin, forehead unfashionably broad, the first signs of crow's feet under her eyes. But her face never is in repose. She's smiling or frowning or pouting or doing her thoughtful face; she can do a whole three-act tragicomedy without saying a word, all by expressions. She says or does something horrible and you forgive her instantly, because of that little didn't-really-mean-it twist at the corner of her mouth. Her own hair is coarse and wiry and just sort of droops, so she coils it up tight in a bun. Six years ago she was slim but now she's skinny, and the backs of her hands are starting to show. She's got a tongue like a razor, but she's smart. Thousands of men in this city are madly in love with her, and I don't blame them.

"You've really got yourself in a mess this time, Notker," she said.

I nodded. "Not through choice," I said.

"It's not a bad take, though," she went on. "When I saw you there just now—"

"Just so I know," I said. "Were you fucking him while you were with me?"

Her turn to nod. "And there the similarity ends," she

added. "Not that it signifies. Did I ever tell you, I've never really liked sex?"

I took a beat, then my cue. "If I'd known you could act, I'd have written a play for you."

She gave me her genuine smile. It's not genuine, of course. It's better than the real thing. "I don't get what people see in it," she went on. "I've always thought it's a bit like paunching a rabbit. If you stopped and thought about it, you'd never do it. So I don't stop and think."

"When did you ever paunch a rabbit?"

"Didn't you know? I grew up on a farm, in the Paralia. God, was I glad to get out of there. I was betrothed at birth to the local tanner, would you believe. He had three teeth and smelled of brains."

Great line, good character, but not actually true. I met her father once. He was the stage doorman at the old Lion. Still, you can't expect people to remember everything.

"What are you going to do?" she said.

"God knows. See it through, probably."

"You'll never get away with it."

"Probably not."

She gave me the acid look. "That's stupid," she said. "You can't embark on something knowing it'll end in disaster. You've got to do something." She paused. "What are you grinning about?"

"Nothing. No, you're right. I can't keep this up for very long, and I've never tried so hard in all my life. It's crazy."

"And now I've been dragged into it," she said, "and you're playing the lead. Thank you so much."

"Don't start on me," I pleaded. "That's not fair, and you know it."

She sighed. "It's just," she said, "every time my life starts to smell, there you are. Not your fault, maybe, but it's a fact. Can't argue with facts."

She was starting to get on my nerves. "It'd be better if we were on the same side, just this once," I said. "For both of us."

"True." She smiled. "I forgive you. Right, let's start again. What are you going to do?"

A thought had just crossed my mind. "Did you tell those clowns how to find me?"

"Don't be ridiculous. I didn't know where you were."

"No, but you knew where they could start looking."

She closed her eyes, then opened them; she was being patient with an unreasonable man. "They'd closed my theatre," she said. "I had wages to pay. And there wasn't much I could tell them. And if I'd known who they were or what they wanted you for—"

"Fine," I said. "Just clearing the air. Anything else you'd like to tell me?"

"No."

"That's all right, then."

There are times when it's good to claim the moral high ground; remarkably few of them, in my experience. "How's business at the Gallery?"

"Packing them in like dried figs. The script's lousy, but they don't seem to mind. And you never did deliver that curtain raiser you owe me."

"All right," I said. "So what do you think I ought to do?"

Her face changed. "Now just promise you'll hear me out, all right? Only I know you. You can be so quick to fly off the handle sometimes."

"I promise."

She paused, and I knew a Big Speech was coming. "Just ask yourself this," she said. "Precisely what has this city ever done for you?"

I wasn't sure if I was expected to reply. "In what sense?"

"In any bloody sense. Think about it, Notker. Everybody keeps banging on about our Robur heritage and our place in the sun and our manifest destiny, but what does this city mean to you? Because to me it's just a place where I happen to live, that's all. And the people here, they've done nothing for me. I've done it all myself. I've fought like a tiger to get what little I've got; nobody's ever given me anything."

"I wasn't aware anyone was supposed to."

"Maybe not. Proves my point. They don't owe us anything, fine. We don't owe them anything. Oh, and one small detail. At some point, in the course of some enterprise we didn't know about and had no say in, the glorious Empire pissed off the savages so badly, they swore to wipe every last Robur off the face of the earth. Don't know if you keep abreast of the news, but on the other side of the wall there's a lot of people wanting to kill us. Now that makes me uncomfortable."

I grinned at her. "You don't say."

"Not a joke, Notker. And one of these days, they'll come for us. And I don't want to be here when it happens."

"Fine," I said. "I agree with every word you've said, as it happens. So what are you still here for? Get on a ship. Go somewhere else."

She shook her head, and there was something about the gesture. "Last time I saw you I gave you a stick of whiteface," she said. "Trouble is, I don't think greasepaint's going to be enough, when the time comes. Use your brain, Notker. If the City falls and everybody dies, any Robur that're left are going to stick out like a sore thumb. And it's all very well saying, go a long way away, but I don't know how far is far enough."

"You may be right. Not sure where this is leading, though."

"Oh, don't be stupid. If the savages are bound to win anyway, why not be on their side? Why not help them?" She paused, but only for a moment. "Do a deal. Personal immunity, in return for valuable assistance. You can do it. You're him, for crying out loud."

You think you've heard everything. "You're crazy," I said.

"I'm serious. It's the only way out of this."

I remember one time I was cornered by this dog. Bloody thing was obviously mad, it was foaming at the mouth and its eyes were fixed on me; if I'd made the smallest movement it'd have had me. So I kept very still and deadly calm, until its owner came and called it off me. Sorry you were bothered, chum, he said, leaving me sprawling against a wall with pee running down my leg. But nothing is ever wasted. Thanks to that dog, I knew how to handle this situation.

"I think you've got the wrong idea about how things are fixed," I told her. "I may look like him, but I'm me, and those three know it. I can't wipe my arse without their permission, let alone borrow the keys of the City gates and take them for a midnight stroll."

"You're him," she said. "Everybody thinks so."

"Your point?"

She stretched out her arms and fingers downwards, as far as they would go. Very nice gesture, which I hadn't seen before. "You appear in the market square," she said, "all over blood. There's a conspiracy, you tell everybody: Nicephorus and Artavasdus and Faustinus just tried to kill me. Ten minutes later, there won't be enough of them left to fill a pie. Then you'll be in charge. Then you can do what you damn well like."

Didn't I tell you she's smart? Smarter than me, anyhow, by a long mile. "I couldn't do it," I said. "I haven't got that sort of nerve."

"We could do it," she said. "We could've done it tonight: it would've been easy."

I nodded slowly. "Yes," I said, "we could."

"So next time, we do it."

"Let me think about it."

She was that close to hitting me. "What in God's name is there to think about? Let's just do it. Say you'll do it."

First time I met her, I was a shepherd and she was a shepherdess, and we had these appalling fake lambs, on wheels, which we had to drag along on bits of string. It wasn't supposed to be funny. We had a little dance; I could do the steps now, if you asked me to. Now, though, all I could think of was the old proverb about holding a wolf by the ears. You can't hold her; you daren't let her go.

"Fine," she said.

It was as though I'd woken up; and there was Hodda, my oldest friend in the business, kneeling in front of me with her hands in her lap and that you-clown-Notker look on her face. "Think about it," she said. "I wouldn't want you to rush into anything, God knows."

Which must have had the desired effect; because immediately I thought: hang on, though. We *could* do it. Between us we could pull it off, because actually it would be pretty

88 K. J. Parker

straightforward, certainly not much harder than what I was already doing. And the difference would be, I'd have her to help me, and say what you like about Hodda, she's smart, really smart, and cool as an icicle when the heat is on. And, if she hadn't beaten me to it, it'd only have been a matter of time before I'd thought of it myself.

"We'd have to be careful," I said.

I was a shepherd and she was a shepherdess; I was sixteen, she was a whisker under a year older. She'd been on the stage for ten years at that point; it was my first job. They didn't actually throw things at us, but probably only because they were saving their ammunition for the low comedians.

It was an old-fashioned extravaganza; it had a technical meaning back then, sort of a cross between a fairy play and a burlesque. You were supposed to take an incident from myth or folktale, or you could just about get away with a scene from Saloninus; add a crowd of pretty but irrelevant young people singing and dancing, the comics doing their bits, with lots of colourful costumes and clever stage effects and always ending with a dance ensemble. As a genre it went the way of all flesh years ago, and no great loss. Everybody started off in extravaganza, and everybody got out of it and into something better just as soon as they possibly could.

Anyway, at some point during the run (I think we lasted fifteen performances) Hodda and I promised we'd be true to each other until the stars went out and the sky came crashing down. That was some time ago, but the stars still shine and the sky's still up there somewhere, and a promise is a promise, at least as far as I'm concerned. I remember that when I made that promise, my back was aching and my feet were killing me, stuffed in worn-out pumps two sizes too small, and the sweat was running down my face, and we both stank to high heaven. You never forget your first kiss, they say. Mine tasted of pig-fat and rouge.

Of course, a lot depends on your definition of the word *true*.

12

The conspirators were vexed and unhappy. Admiral Sisinna was insisting on seeing all four of us, and wouldn't take no for an answer.

"He's a great man," Nicephorus said grudgingly. "He's rebuilt the Fleet so it's practically back to where it was before the siege, and he sorted out the Eldat pirates, and he's practically never here, which is a blessing in itself."

"But you don't want me to meet him."

"Hardly," Artavasdus said. "He's sharp as a needle."

"Does he know me?"

"I think he's met you maybe half a dozen times, at council meetings. Makes no secret of the fact he doesn't like you."

"We have something in common," I said. "That's nice."

"He needs your support," Faustinus said. "He needs five thousand men for the Fleet, which means reintroducing the press gang, and you can imagine what the Themes think about that."

And quite right too. When I was a kid there was this young

lad in the Greens, a quiet, pleasant boy most of the time, apprenticed to a violin maker and doing very well. But he had a secret vice: he liked to hang out in the dockside bars. He used to go there and sit in a corner, quiet as a little mouse, and wallow in all the raw life and energy (and I've been in those places, and you can have it), and one day the press-gang burst in. Their time-honoured method is to bash everybody's heads with axe handles, tie them up and throw them in the back of a cart, and the next thing they know they're on a ship, proud and fearless sons of the sea. The violin maker's boy didn't really take to the maritime life, and he died of scurvy somewhere off the Five Fingers. They threw his body over the side and sent home his coat and his socks to his mother.

I don't have much time for the Themes, but I'll say this for them: they put a stop to the press, even before they got an official say in the running of the City. It took some doing, and it was all good honest reconnaissance work, no heavy stuff. They had kids watching the Fleet barracks, and when the press-gang set out they were followed every step of the way, with relays of runners to pass on the glad tidings; by the time they fetched up in the docks, there'd be nobody about except old men and a few cats. So the gangs started hitting the bars further inland, but what they mostly caught was drunks, thieves and no-goods, who caused the Fleet far more trouble than they were worth, so the raids gradually died out, and some genius suggested increasing rates of pay as a way of solving the manpower crisis, and, guess what, it worked. So if Admiral Sisinna wanted to start up that old game, no wonder he needed all the backing he could get.

"Just a moment," I said. "Is that actually necessary?"

Artavasdus stared at me. "You what?"

"Bringing back the press," I said. "It's barbaric."

Artavasdus rolled his eyes and Faustinus looked embarrassed. Nicephorus did his look-at-me-being-patient face. "I agree," he said. "But it's necessary."

"Is it?"

"Absolutely. Sisinna's building sixty more ships. He needs crews for them. But the Themes won't let merchant seamen sign up, because Fleet men don't pay guild dues. Therefore we need the press."

"Now look," Artavasdus said. "This is policy. During the meeting, you keep your face shut. Got that?"

I pretended I hadn't heard him. "There must be a better way," I said.

"I wouldn't be at all surprised," Nicephorus said. "Trouble is, nobody's thought of it yet. So we'll do it this way. And you will not rock the boat, understood?"

At this point I was still thinking it over – that stuff I'd talked about with Hodda, you know. And, by coincidence, the stage I'd reached was Admiral Sisinna.

If you took a step back and thought about it clear-mindedly, it was Sisinna and his ships that kept the City safe and functional; not the soldiers on the wall, certainly not the council, the senate or the Themes. As noted above, he spent very little of his time in the City, which was good in one sense and bad in another: good in that he didn't interfere in politics if he could avoid it, bad because he couldn't be used by one faction against another – actually, that was probably good, but you get what I mean. Now, if Hodda and I were going to pull off our little conjuring trick, a great deal would depend on the view Sisinna took of the matter. If Lysimachus seized control, Sisinna was the only man who could bring him down. But if

Sisinna decided he liked Lysimachus after all, he could make Lysimachus' position effectively unassailable.

The third option would be to include Sisinna in the plot against Lysimachus' life, get rid of him and replace him with someone we could control, but I didn't like that one bit. Point one: he was never there, and therefore couldn't be torn to bits by a furious city mob. Point two: everyone knew that Sisinna didn't get involved in that sort of thing, so it'd be downright suspicious if we tried to implicate him. Point three: for what it was worth he was the best admiral we'd had for a generation, and we needed him desperately if we wanted to survive. Not that I'd have tried arguing that one with Hodda; also, come to think of it, with myself. The City and the Robur were past saving, I thought we'd agreed on that. But still two valid points nonetheless.

All right, then.

Believe it or not, I'd never been able to imitate Sisinna successfully, and I gave up trying a long time ago. He's a tiny little man, with small hands and feet and a head rather too big for his body, little narrow, sloping shoulders, small eyes, a lion's mane of wavy white hair and a thin line of beard and moustache that looks like he drew it on with chalk. I'd give a fortune to have his voice; it'd be perfect for Saloninus, Theudric, all the classics. They say he was a fencing champion in his youth, though these days he walks with a stick; also, that he writes theological commentaries in his spare time, and possibly even poetry. He's married into one of the great patrician houses, so naturally he keeps a mistress: a new one every five years, the current one being an actress I was in a revival of *Charity* with, about two years ago, and who'd worked for Hodda until she threw her out.

The meeting went well. Sisinna stated his case briefly and lucidly, the three conspirators agreed with him, and then it was my turn. The Themes aren't going to like this, I said. No, he said, probably not. Never mind, I said, you can count on my support.

He looked at me oddly, sort of shrugged, thanked us for our time and went away. "Well done," Artavasdus said to me, after he'd gone. "Glad to see you can do as you're told at least some of the time."

The actress's name was Auxentia. I managed to get a message to Hodda, who passed it on. The problem, naturally, was getting away from the three conspirators, and finding a place for a meeting.

"There's no need," Nicephorus said. "You don't have to see her again for at least a week."

"But I want to."

He looked at me. "What's that got to do with anything?"

I tried to look embarrassed. "Look," I said. "You probably know, Hodda and I had a sort of a thing once."

"Yes. So?"

"Well, it's come back."

He did his oh-for-God's-sake sigh. "Have you any idea how inconvenient that would be? Arrangements. Making sure you're seen and not seen. Guards' duty rosters. You can't just go flitting about the place—"

"Please?"

I learned how to say *please* from Hodda. She's better at it, but I'm still very good. "Just make absolutely sure Arta doesn't find out," he said. "He reckons I'm far too soft on you as it is. He says, if you want a pet with substandard intelligence and revolting habits, buy a dog."

So it was all arranged. I would be at the house where Hodda and I met, and Auxentia would bring Sisinna. From Auxentia we gathered that he liked black tea, honey-cakes and a straight, hard chair, because of his bad back.

He looked at me when he walked in and for a moment I was scared stiff. But it wasn't that kind of look. He sat down; the girls poured tea and left. I sat down opposite him.

"Thanks for coming," I said.

"This is all a bit cloak-and-dagger, isn't it?" he said. "I thought we settled everything at the meeting."

I nodded. "I've been thinking," I said.

"Is that right?"

Everybody's a comedian. Mind you, he had good timing. "I said I'd try and sell the idea to the Themes," I told him, "and I'll do that, if you want me to. But I don't think they'll accept it, even from me."

He frowned. "Maybe not. I know it's an emotive issue."

"You bet," I said. "And every time I support something and it turns out that people hate the idea, the respect they have for me goes down a notch, and I don't like that."

He dipped his head very slightly to acknowledge a fair point. "So?"

"So," I said, "we need a better idea."

He treated me to a superior smile. "Speaking for myself," he said, "I hate the press. It's a crude and inefficient way of raising men and it causes a lot of ill feeling. Unfortunately, until someone comes up with a better idea we're stuck with it."

"If the Themes let you recruit from the merchant marine," I said, "it wouldn't be necessary."

"Yes," he said. "But they won't. Every merchant seaman has to belong to the Sailors' Guild, and gives a tenth of his pay to guild funds. In the Fleet, belonging to the guild is a court-martial offence, so they don't make any contribution to Theme funds." He sighed. "I know for a fact there's a lot of men who'd jump at the chance of signing on with the Fleet just to get out of the clutches of the guild, but they daren't: they've got wives and families at home." He gave me another of those you-halfwit smiles. "I'd far rather have volunteers than pressed men, believe me. But if there's one thing we both know about this city, it's that you can't fight the Themes. Isn't that right?"

I nodded. "But you can talk to them," I said. "Correction: I can talk to them. You can't."

He laughed. "Not sure that I'd want to. But if you make them listen, you'd be doing me a great favour, believe me. Are there any more of those honey-cakes, do you think? They're really rather good."

13

"Now you've gone too far," she said.

"No," I said, "listen."

Sisinna's chaise had rattled away into the night, and we were alone in the house. I didn't have much time and she wasn't inclined to listen to me. Like the old days, really.

"It can be done," I said. "It's basically a lighting problem."

She thought about that and gave me a grunt of reluctant agreement. "No, it isn't," she added. "We've got to get them here first. If your keepers find out you're having secret talks with Theme bosses, they'll rip your lungs out."

Curiously enough, that thought had occurred to me. "They won't find out," I said. "And before you say it, yes, we can talk to the Theme bosses easy as pie."

She sighed. "I can, you mean."

God bless the theatre. Among other reasons, because it's a great gatherer-up of beautiful women; and once it's got all these gorgeous creatures, it doesn't pay them enough. Which means they need to supplement their incomes from other sources. It's not an ideal system, because contrary to popular belief not all actresses are as easy as the five-times table, and the ones who aren't have a rough time of it sometimes. That said, any means of earning a living in this man's town is likely to be nasty and unpleasant more often than not, and until they bring about Saloninus' ideal republic I don't see it changing any time soon. The point being: every self-respecting Theme boss has a popular actress as a fashion accessory. Therefore, we could talk to them anytime we wanted to. And the rest was, as I'd so acutely pointed out, just a matter of stage lighting.

"You're not ready for something like this," she said, as we waited in the dim light of a single small lamp for the Theme bosses to arrive.

"I'm as ready as I'll ever be," I told her. "And all this is your idea."

"You mean you're done thinking it over."

"I wouldn't go that far. But if we can impress Sisinna—"

"This isn't going to work. These people know you."

Which was true. The Blue boss, obviously not; but Parzenio the Green boss (properly speaking, the father-of-chapel for the Merchant Seamens' Guild) had fought in the arena with Lysimachus – alongside him, not actually with him, or he'd be dead – and shared a kennel with him, so she was quite right, it was a terrifying risk, if you stopped to think about it. But, like the lady said, the answer is, don't stop and think. Besides, we had the home advantage.

If I hadn't been a mediocre actor, I could've been a terrific lights man. Always been interested in what you can achieve, by way of light, shadow and the million degrees in between, with just candles, hoods and bits of coloured parchment. Take shadow, for example. You can stretch it, bend it, layer it, cast another shadow across it. Nobody ever notices it – why would you take any notice of what is, after all, basically only an absence – but it shapes and twists the way we perceive, you can mess with people's heads with it. As for light, don't get me started on light. You think you can trust it, but in the right hands there's nothing trickier, believe me.

The Blue boss was called Ascer, and he turned up first. "Why's it so dark in here?" he said, hesitating on the threshold.

"Get in here," I snapped back, in a hoarse stage whisper.

Yes, it was dark, but not so dark I couldn't see the knife on his belt. Ascer hadn't done time on the sand, but he'd been a Blue enforcer, same sort of job my dad used to do but higher profile. A wolf by the ears, I thought. But at some point in the past someone realised you could train wolves to fetch and carry and round up sheep.

"Elegaica was supposed to have explained to you," I said. Elegaica was the rising young tragedienne who looked after about half a dozen prominent Blues. "If anyone finds out about this, we're dogmeat."

A thump at the door they must've heard in Hill Street. "Get that for me, will you?" Well, Lysimachus wouldn't stir himself if he could send someone else.

Ascer glared at me, got up and opened the door. I couldn't see the expressions on their faces as the Blue boss opened the door for the Green boss, so I missed a treat, but never mind.

"Close that door, for fuck's sake, and keep your voices down. Over here. Mind out, there's a table by the window."

Two enormous men steered themselves successfully past the table in the dark and felt their way into chairs they could barely see. "What's all this in aid of?" Parzenio demanded. "Why couldn't we have met up at the palace or somewhere?"

"What this is in aid of," I said, same hoarse whisper, "is saving your arses. Is that worth it? You tell me."

I had a feeling I was overdoing it. Pull yourself together, I urged myself; keep your eye on that mirror. "I heard it was to do with the Fleet," Parzenio said, "that's all I was told."

"Then listen," I said. "Sisinna's asked the council to let him bring back the press. We told him yes."

That got me stony silence. I gave it three beats. "I take it you're not happy about that."

"No, we're not. The lads won't stand for it."

Not sure which one of them said that; not important. "Quite right, too," I said. "I don't like the idea much either."

"But you said—"

"Sisinna asked, we agreed. Rule one, you don't piss off the admiral of the Fleet. And that was just fine with my sugar-plum colleagues, because they don't know spit about the Themes and could care less."

"And you went along with it."

"To their faces, yes. I have to work with those idiots."

I could feel the character slipping away out of my hands like an eel; but amazingly the voice was still just right. It was Lysimachus saying words he'd never have said in his life, but it was Lysimachus, you'd bet your life on it. "So they're bringing back the press. There'll be trouble."

"Not if I can help it." Pause to let it sink in. Lucky for me Lysimachus was a slow talker at the best of times. "We're all here to make sure the press doesn't start up again."

Ascer said, "We're listening."

"You've got to let merchantmen join the Fleet," I said. "If you do that, I can get Sisinna to forget about the press, because he won't need it."

"You're kidding, aren't you?" Parzenio said. "You got any idea how much money that'd cost us?"

I named a figure. "Well?"

Pause. "About that," Ascer said.

"Glad we agree. And, yes, that's a lot of money out of your pockets, which means the pockets of widows and orphans in Poor Town, so we can't have that."

"Well, then."

"And we can't have the press-gang snatching any poor bastards they can lay their hands on, and we can't have fighting in the street, Greens and Blues against the marines. Something's got to give somewhere."

All this time I was trying to keep my eye on Parzenio without being obvious about it. He was angry, I could see that, but that was all. He was furiously angry because his old arena buddy was selling the Greens down the river. My heart was like the proverbial singing bird, but his wouldn't have been, so I kept it to myself.

"Like what?" Parzenio said. "Either there's press-gangs or there isn't."

"No press-gangs," I said. "And merchantmen can join the Fleet, because it's the patriotic thing to do and everybody knows the Themes are a hundred per cent behind the war effort every step of the way, plus the fact that your boys are itching to join up so they don't have to give you lot a tenth of their pay. And Theme funds won't lose a bent trachy, because I'll make it up to you somewhere else."

There comes a moment when you have to lay them down and see if the other guy has aces to your kings. I'm not a gambling man, as you'd probably have guessed.

"Somewhere else where?" Parzenio said cautiously.

Offstage, choirs of angels. "That'd be telling," I said. "Do we have agreement in principle or don't we?"

We had agreement in principle. So I told them about a few – a half-dozen, no more – of the gaping loopholes I'd noticed in the Imperial accounting procedures, when I glanced through all that stuff up in my tower cell, waiting to go on. At the time I was stunned that nobody had seen them and plugged them; a week or so with those three knuckle-heads and I reckoned I could see why. Uptown and Poor Town don't think the same way. Poor Town, Green, the son of a boss, it had been in the air I breathed and the water and the food, because everything back there and then was about the scam, the angle, the crack you could get the tip of your penknife into. Uptown, all they could see was doing a job efficiently and cost-effectively.

"Anyhow," I concluded, "I think that'll more than cover your losses, if your boys are anything like the fixers in the neighbourhood I grew up in. Yes, I know, nothing in it for the Sailors' Guild, which is your pitch, so you might want to see about spreading your interests a bit before anyone else finds out where the new pickings are coming from. But I think I can safely leave all that to you."

I could practically hear the little wheels going round. "Isn't anybody going to notice? At the Treasury end?"

"Eventually," I said. "And probably we'll tighten a few loopholes, by which time you'll have picked open a few more. That's tomorrow; I'm talking about today. We have an agreement."

Statement, not query. They confirmed it. Good, I told them; oh, and one other thing. If anybody outside of this room ever found out that this idea had come from me, I'd have the two of them killed. On that, as on the other matters we'd been discussing, they had my word of honour.

I'd told Hodda to make herself scarce, but naturally she hadn't. She'd been next door the whole time, with a cup held against the wall. "You were born lucky," she told me.

"Funny, I never noticed."

"You must've been. You realise you lost it completely at least twice."

I nodded. "I know I did," I said. "And still they didn't suspect anything. I think that must've been the Invincible Sun giving me a second chance."

She glared at me. She doesn't like people to know, but she's religious. "It's like you've got a death wish or something. You were hamming it up."

"Yes, I *know*." Hadn't meant to shout. "I couldn't help it. I lost him for a minute or so. But I found my way back, and it was all right. I got away with it."

"Yes, you did." A hard look crossed her face, just for a moment. "I'll give you that. By the way, did you ever get round to making up your mind?"

"I told you. If we get Sisinna on our side—"

"We could rule this city. We could *own* it."

One time I was crossing the stage and some fool had opened the trapdoor. I went through it, still saying my line, and suddenly I was in a crumpled heap in the cellar. "Hodda. I thought you said this city's finished."

"Oh, don't be stupid. It's the City. They'll never take the City."

"You said—"

"Never mind what I said. You fooled that ape, and he's known you for years."

"In the dark," I said. "And just for ten minutes."

"Then we'll get rid of him. All your old pals, gradually, one at a time."

I think I backed away a step. "I can't believe you just said that."

"Nor can I, actually." She blinked, as though I'd just lit a lamp in a dark room. "No, we can't go around slaughtering people wholesale, that's ridiculous. But the rest of it – we could do it, you know. We could run this place."

On the other hand, she's always been my harshest critic. If she thought I could do it, maybe I could.

"Hodda," I said. "Do we really want to?"

"Are you kidding?"

"I've seen what ruling a city involves," I said. "It's not exactly fun. It's endless hard work, people mad at you, everything you do pisses somebody off, nobody listens to what you actually say—"

She grinned at me. "Not *permanently*, idiot," she said. "Just long enough to cream off a great deal of money. And then we get on our private presidential yacht and don't come back." She has a lovely grin. It suits that angel face of hers. "Had you going there for a minute, didn't I?"

Paunching rabbits. Such a graphic image. Hard to get it out of your mind once it's found its way inside. "One step at a time," I said. "Let's see what the admiral does."

14

The Greens made their announcement first, followed by the Blues later on the same day. It had come to their attention that guild regulations made it difficult for merchant sailors who wanted to do their bit for the war effort to sign up with the Fleet. Those regulations were withdrawn, with immediate effect.

Admiral Sisinna came to see the three conspirators and me. Word had obviously got about, he said (he didn't wink; I don't think he was physically capable of it) and now there was no need for press-gangs. He didn't look at me once during the meeting. Later I got a note from him, passed from Auxentia to Hodda and Hodda to me, because I was allowed private letters from her now, for being good. Thank you, the admiral said. Good job well done.

My first thought was that it was a forgery, she'd faked it or had it faked, so I snuffled about among the archives until I found dispatches in Sisinna's own handwriting. Perfect match.

Time to think about it a whole lot more.

*

Time out, while I'm thinking about it, for some tangential reflections on the Public.

There's a saying in our business, as old as the hills and as perpetually relevant as death; *everybody loved it except the public*. Exactly. You get hold of a red-hot script, and by some amazing stroke of luck the exactly perfect cast are all available. Soon as you start rehearsing, you can tell you've got something really special on your hands – the buzz, the thrill, taking on a life of its own. So you send out invitations to the great wise men, the arbiters of taste, men who've loved and studied the theatre all their lives and know what works and what doesn't, and they all tell you, don't worry, you've got a hit on your hands there. Opening night, the air is thick with cheers and flying flowers, and six nights after that, you close, having just played to an audience of five, four of them your cousins.

I have spent my adult life trying to amuse and entertain the public, and maybe it would be worth asking the question, why? For money, yes; but there are a lot of ways of making money, many of them involving a lot less hard work and aggravation. Come to that, if money had been the one and only motivation in my life, I'd have stayed in the Greens and beaten it out of small shopkeepers.

No; the money matters because it means you can stay in the business, and so long as you're in the business you're in the game, in with a chance of making the big breakthrough. And if you do make that breakthrough, what happens then? You get lots of money, granted. So what do you do? Do you retire, buy a couple of farms, a cloth mill and a half-share in a trading ship, relax into a life of leisured ease? Like hell. You keep going in the business, because now the people are paying to see you, not the stupid play. And with every massive success you notch up, you ask for and get more money, not because you want it to buy things with but because it's the only reliable way in this business of keeping score. If you're getting x every night but your best friend and deadliest rival is getting $x+1$, it's enough to break your heart. So you try harder, and harder still.

Try and do what, exactly? You perfect your already perfect art, only a bit more. And your art is entertaining the Public. Remember them?

They all say it at one time or another; I do it all for my public. So let's consider them, shall we?

I do it all for my public, they all say. Really? Let's break the collective noun down into its component parts. You've got the stalls: people with money, who wouldn't be seen with you in the street, although if you're a pretty girl they might condescend to have sex with you. You've got the gallery: shopkeepers, tradesmen, clerks, Theme and guild officers, their wives and noisy children, the class of people you joined the profession to get away from, because that's where you were born and used to live. Can you honestly lay your hand on your heart and say you do it all – the grinding hard work, the boredom, the standing around, the frustration, the failures, the humiliation, the holes in your boots, going without food for a week until you get your first wages, spending your last fifty trachy on a fake-silk scarf rather than bread because you've always got to look smart – to bring some joy into their dull but moderately contented lives?

Thought not. So, do you do it because you want them to love you; you want to sway them, command them, own their hearts and minds? What, that lot? Them? The Public?

I knew a man once. He was a rich man's son, very rich; he thought he was untouchable. His favourite trick was walking into a dockers' bar, striking a dramatic attitude and calling out, "Ah, the people!" He got glared at a lot but never actually thumped, not even by me, and eventually he gave it up and got married, which served him right. Ah, the people. My country-men, my fellow citizens, my brothers.

Mind you, some of them are all right, when you get to know them. But a lot of them aren't; and here's a funny thing, because when you mix them together, the ones that are all right and the ones that aren't, as often as not the resulting blend is far worse than the sum of its parts. Greedier, more cowardly, more stupid. Don't know why, it's alchemy or something like that. There's probably a book about it somewhere that explains everything.

All my adult life I've been working my fingers to the bone for the public. And what have I been trying to do, and what do I want from them? I want them to find me entertaining – not such a big thing to ask, for you to have a good time, enjoy yourself; give it a go one of these days, you might even like it.

So maybe we should explore the other extreme, rather like my dad used to do. Out there in the streets and alleys are a hundred thousand head of cattle, and most of them have got some money, even if it's just a few trachy, and they can be made to do what you want if you know the trick. Fleece them, flay them, sell them to the savages on the other side of the wall for anything you can get for them, what does it matter? You don't owe them anything, and what the hell did they ever do for you?

I told her I would think about it and here I am, still think-ing about it, I guess. The Public, my fellow citizens, the City. Make 'em laugh, make 'em pay, make 'em bleed, so what? Nicephorus and Artavasdus and Faustinus could've filled the pockets of their coats with small items of great value and hopped it halfway across the world; instead, they stayed on stage, playing their hearts out – because they were born into noble families with traditions of service to the state, for whom high public office is the only way of keeping score, like money is in our game. Not, I venture to suggest, because they liked the dirty, scruffy, ungrateful people, but because – because they never stopped to think about it, I guess. If you stopped to think about it you'd never do it, so don't stop and think.

I think that, when I stand on a stage and look in front of me at that sea of faces, I'm looking at a mirror, maybe the only mirror in the City where I can catch a glimpse of myself. I also think that from time to time I'm not the sharpest knife in the drawer.

15

"Don't give me that," Nicephorus said. "You did something. We told you not to interfere, and you did something."

"You don't know the Themes," I replied. "I do. They got wind of what Sisinna had in mind, they weighed up the costs and the benefits and made a business decision. Regardless of what you may have read, they're not savages and they're not stupid."

Artavasdus grinned at me. "Well, you'd know more about that than us. But I always thought they were stubborn as hell. Worried sick about backing down and losing face."

"Which is why they decided not to pick a fight with the Fleet," I told him. "Isn't that what it says in the *Art of War?* The best way to win a fight is not to fight at all."

That got me the grin redoubled. Interesting man, Artavasdus, in his way. Grins at you when he despises you, grins at you when he likes you, and always the same grin.

"People are saying we give in to the Themes all the time," Faustinus said. "It's causing a lot of bad feeling."

"Really?" Nicephorus looked at him over his shoulder. "Who from?"

"Well, the House for one."

"Don't think I'll lose too much sleep over that."

"We ought to close that place down," Artavasdus yawned. "We don't need them and they're no good for anything."

"Technically," Faustinus said, "they have to approve all new legislation."

"Except for measures passed under the Imperial prerogative and the emergency powers," Artavasdus replied. "So, screw them."

"People like to know they're there," Nicephorus said mildly.

"You both keep saying *people*, but I don't think you know what you mean by it. What people?"

The Public, I thought. "The citizens of this city," Nicephorus said, in his sleepy-lion voice, which isn't nearly as effective as he thinks it is. "Ordinary decent, right-thinking—"

"Balls," Artavasdus said. "Purely mythical creatures, like elves and gryphons. No, things have changed and you know it. Time was, the old families ruled the Empire, and then along came the siege, and now it's the provisional government, meaning the military. Us."

"I'm not military," Faustinus pointed out.

"And Admiral Sisinna," Nicephorus said. "The Fleet's got more men and more money than the army, and Sisinna swore an oath to uphold the constitution, same as we did. How seriously he takes it I really wouldn't care to say."

"He's never here," Artavasdus replied. "Besides, he's a realist, and he's got far too much on his plate to bother about politics. Whatever we decide, he'll be fine with that, so long as he gets his new ships."

Faustinus was getting uncomfortable. "You really ought to think before you speak, Arta."

"I do."

"Then that just makes it worse. There's a world of difference between bypassing the House and overthrowing the constitution."

Artavasdus yawned again, this time making a performance of it. "You're probably right," he said. "Let them just wither away of their own accord, and nobody will notice or care." He smiled. "Why are we having this conversation anyway? I thought we were bollocking Notker for poking his nose in where it's got no place being."

I held up my hands. "I didn't do anything."

"We believe you," Nicephorus said, making *believe* sound like a dialect word for *forgive*. "And don't do it again."

I expected them to put me on a shorter leash after that, but apparently they reckoned I'd been spoken to and would therefore have learned my lesson. To be honest, I don't think I was exactly uppermost in their minds just then. There was bad news from the war – they didn't tell me, but they were careless with their bits of paper and I can read upside down.

We got the news from the Telpessians, a bunch of chancers who we did a lot of business with at one time. They liked us; they also liked the quicksand agglomeration of unlikely allies camped on the other side of the wall; they liked everybody, it's their nature. Because of this overwhelming brimming over with friendliness and love, they were able to buy from us all those unique and irreplaceable things that only we can make and you can't get anywhere else, and sell them to the hundred and one nations joined with King Ogus in the universal crusade to obliterate us. They got away with it because they weren't too obvious about it, and they were prepared to go the extra mile – the extra nine hundred and seventy miles, to be exact; from the City across the open sea to the southern tip of the Jotrai peninsula, where they handed the stuff over to the Lanquan Lijorn, who carried it across the mountain passes to Wamey, where caravans of desert nomads picked it up and carted it across the sand dunes to Ithbine Seauton for retail distribution among the members of the Anti-Robur League.

King Ogus wasn't happy about it, but what could he do? The Lanquan Lijorn were too far away to hit – so far away that in their country the sun rises in the west, or so I read somewhere – and trying to punish the nomads would be like trying to swat very small flies with a claymore. Since he didn't have a fleet, any sort of punitive expedition against Ithbine would involve going the very long way round on land and would tie up tens of thousands of men for the best part of a year, and Ithbine is no pushover, apparently. He made all sorts of roaring noises at his allies, who promised faithfully they'd do everything they could to stamp out the illicit trade inside their own jurisdictions, and then did nothing, mostly because the profits of the trade were helping them pay the ruinous expense of taking part in Ogus' ridiculous war.

Anyway, that's the Telpessians for you, and I've never met one and probably never will. But, according to them, Ogus had done a deal with the Hus. Just in case you don't know, the Hus live right up in the far north, where it's bitter cold nine months of the year, and there's a lot of them, living in flat valleys between mountain ranges. Milkfaces, naturally; in the past they had no beef with us, because our paths have never crossed, but the petty kings and chieftains who rule them have an insatiable appetite for pretty, shiny things, and honour and status can only be achieved through military prowess. So Ogus had done a deal for seventy thousand Hus mercenaries, all seven feet tall and strong as bears; but that wasn't all. About three hundred years ago the Hus conquered and enslaved the Ilse, a race of small, dark milkfaces who live just south of them, and who the Robur knew a bit about because the Ilse used to export iron ore. Their country is all barren mountains, but under the mountains there's enough iron to plate over the Middle Sea, so quite early on they packed up farming and took to mining, and as time went on they got rather good at it, particularly in the field of cutting galleries through living rock, something we in the soft south have never really got the hang of. Ogus did another deal with the Hus bosses and bought twenty thousand Ilse miners, and three guesses what he wanted them for.

As if that wasn't enough, he'd also been talking to the Aelians, our nearest and biggest trading partner. The Aelians live on a big island, so as long as they and their allies control the sea they're safe; except that, like the Ilse, they don't do their own farming. Instead, they buy food from the milkface tribes on the other side of the Friendly Sea; and those tribes, not wanting to be exterminated by Ogus' legions, had joined his grand alliance.

Ogus was too far away to bully the Lanquan Lijorn, but the Friendly Coast savages who supplied corn to the Aelians were right in his back yard, a few days' ride for light cavalry. So he gave the Aelians an ultimatum: stop trading with the Robur, or you get no more grain shipments.

The Aelians are milkfaces, but a different sort to Ogus and his lot; and we've tried to push them around in the past, but every time we sent an army or a fleet they wiped the floor with us, so they bear us no ill will. They're a bumptious lot, full of themselves and inclined to be snotty with anyone who tells them what to do. They slapped us down when we tried it, and they weren't any more impressed by Ogus and his feather-clad savages. Fine, they said; we'll buy our food from the Harpagenes instead, which is no big deal to us, and you can explain to your new allies why they no longer have a lucrative market for their agricultural surplus.

Fine words; but Harpagene is quite a bit further from Aelia than the Friendly Coast, and a lot of it is open sea, which nobody in his right mind likes crossing. My guess is, the Aelians were bluffing and didn't expect to be called on it. So far they'd been as good as gold as far as we were concerned, but they were starting to make little noises; seeing as how they'd been put to a lot of expense and inconvenience on our part, how about lower prices at the dockside, low or no customs charges, tariffs for their competitors, that sort of thing? Under the circumstances it would've been churlish of us not to agree, but it put a strain on our finances at a time when things weren't going quite so well for us commercially as we'd have liked.

None of this was the conspirators' fault, it goes without saying. But as soon as word got about, a lot of people in the City started feeling unhappy about it. The Hus mercenaries didn't scare anybody, because when the enemy campfires beneath your walls are more numerous than the stars, what's a few more here or there? But the Ilse miners were another matter. I gather that the main reason why Ogus hadn't tried to sap his way into the City recently was that most of his skilled sappers were wiped out in a botched attempt to undermine the walls shortly after the siege began, and he had no way of replacing them.

Rather more serious in political terms was the Aelian problem. Most of our end of the Aelian trade was controlled by a hard core of old families, big noises in the House, who'd been doing business with Aelia since long before the war and who'd kept up their contacts – to everybody's benefit, let's not forget, but if we found ourselves cut off from Aelia and forced to trade with other people, they'd lose a fortune, something they were reluctant to do. Even if the Aelians stuck by us, the lower prices would eat into their profits considerably; and, since their taxes paid a substantial proportion of the cost of guarding the City and manning the Fleet, they couldn't just be brushed aside as whining parasites. Hence, I realised, Faustinus' concern with the views of the House and Artavasdus' sudden interest in constitutional reform.

All of which was food for thought for someone who was spending a lot of his time thinking, and I wished I understood more about it than I did. As far as the sappers were concerned, I knew we'd beaten them once, so presumably we could beat them again, unless there was something about the previous occasion that had made our victory hard to repeat. I looked in the glass and discovered that I wasn't too bothered about the sappers. The Aelians, though, were another matter. The City was surviving because, for the time being, life wasn't just as good as it had been but better, and that was what made it possible for people, the Public, to turn a wilfully blind eye to the monster crouching under the walls and not wake up in the night screaming. Also, if trade dried up and money dried up, the provisional government wouldn't be able to afford to drown the Theme cats in cream; whereupon the temporary ceasefire between Themes and government and Blues and Greens would crumble away, and there'd be no need for Ilsen sappers and Hus mercenaries. They'd dig under the wall and burst into the streets and find we'd all slaughtered each other.

So if a man was thinking about going abroad to try his luck, this might be a good time. You won't be surprised to learn that the thought had crossed my mind a few times before all this Lysimachus business kicked off, just as it must have occurred to every single one of my fellow citizens at one time or another. Most of them resolved to stay because life had actually improved, see above, and the fields on the slopes of the volcano were beautifully fertile and grew fat crops of grapes and strawberries. Also, we were well aware (the government had seen to that) of the fact that Ogus and the milkfaces had sworn to annihilate the Robur race, which meant that as and when the City fell, he wouldn't be leaving it at that; furthermore, he was offering cash money for every overseas Robur anyone cared to bring him. Not everyone can work miracles with whiteface like I can; in the cold, hard world across the sea, how far would we have to go to be safe, and was there any realistic prospect of getting there? Chances were that if the enemy took the City, they'd capture at least some of the Fleet as well; even if they didn't, without Sisinna's men ruling the waves, it wouldn't be long before Ogus built or acquired warships of his own, at which point Aelia wouldn't want to shelter us, thank you very much, and neither would any of our other tried and trusted friends this side of the Sashan Empire. Add to that, in my own circumstances, the sad truth that the theatre as I know it is entirely a Robur phenomenon, so I had no skills to earn a living with over the wide blue yonder, and on balance I'd rather die by the sword than starve.

*

"Do you know what day it is today?" Artavasdus asked me.

I don't have hackles, but if I'd had some they'd have shot up like ducks off a pond. "Enlighten me," I said.

"It's the Old and New Moon."

"Ah."

Now I could see what he was grinning about. The Old and New Moon marks the start of the Absolution Day festival, which to ninety-nine per cent of my brother Robur means only one thing: the beginning of the new season in the arena.

Brief digression on opinion, prejudice and morality. There are a few things, a very few things, that I don't hold with. Some of them, like war and cholera, are pretty unpopular with most people, so no real issue arises. One or two of them are things I disapprove of but other people don't.

Might as well come straight out with it: I disapprove of arena fighting. I believe it's barbaric and horrible, it brutalises and corrupts the people who watch it, and there's nothing good to be said about it. To my credit, I also believe that my opinion is precisely that, an opinion, of interest and concern to me and nobody else; and a lot of people would say about the theatre what I say about the arena, and maybe they're right. And, since the arena doesn't affect me directly, I don't have and shouldn't have any say in the matter. One man's opinion is another man's prejudice is another man's bigotry. Have opinions, by all means, but keep the nasty things to yourself.

That said, I don't like watching the sand-fighting. My dad loved it, and, being who he was, we always had really good seats; in the North stand mostly, second tier, where you can see absolutely every damn thing that goes on. I would sit beside him and he'd do this running commentary, in a loud and carrying voice – bet you they could hear it out in the middle, not that he'd have cared about that. People used to come up to him afterwards and thank him, which was fair enough, I suppose, because he was very knowledgeable and well informed. If he ever caught me closing my eyes, he'd give me a clip round the ear that made my head spin. I don't know, maybe that's why I've never liked watching that stuff, though I can't honestly say watching strangers die ever really did it for me. Mind you, there's more sword fighting and more bodies on the ground at the end of the third act of *Scaphio and Phantis* than you get in the whole of Festival Week in the Hippodrome, and I regard that as high art. See above, under exactly what my opinions are worth.

Anyway, the point being Lysimachus would, of course, be the President of the Games; he'd lead the opening ceremony and be there in the Imperial box right through all five days, taking a keen professional interest and awarding the prizes.

"I can't do it," I said.

"Bullshit," said Artavasdus. "Of course you can. Just sit there and enjoy yourself. Wish I could afford the time."

"They won't be able to see you," Nicephorus said. "They'll be facing the sand, same as you. And they'll all be glued to the fighting."

"If I have to watch all that killing, I'll probably throw up."

The conspirators were hard men to shock, but I'd managed it. There was a stunned silence, then Nicephorus said, "You'll do no such thing."

"You were Green champion," Faustinus said. "Undefeated. Fought forty-six, won forty-two, drew four."

God help us, a fan. "I'm really sorry," I said, "but it's like seasickness, it's not something I can help."

Nicephorus closed his eyes for a moment, asking Heaven what he'd done to deserve me. "We'll have three lines of guards standing at the front of the box," he said. "If you're going to puke, duck down low."

"Can't have that," Artavasdus said firmly, "it'll make it look like he's scared of being assassinated. Bodyguards are a political issue. We'd be sending some very bad messages."

"He's right," Faustinus said. "It'd look awful."

"Not as bad as the iron man of the arena chucking his guts up at the sight of blood," Nicephorus said angrily. "It'd be one sure way of putting doubt in people's minds."

"If you're right at the back of the East stand, you can look directly down into the Imperial box and see everything," Faustinus pointed out. "I know, because that's where my father and I used to sit when I was a boy."

"Fine." Nicephorus held up both hands. "Forget the guards, then. He'll just have to pull himself together and not be a big girl's blouse about it."

"That," I said, with all the strength of character I could dredge up, "might not be possible. I think I'm going to have to be ill."

"Lysimachus would have to be at death's door to miss the opening days of Ascension."

"Then that's where I'll be," I said.

We compromised. Somehow or other I'd battle my way through one day of ghastliness, and then I'd be allowed to have a high fever and convulsions.

Oh, and there was one other thing. The rumours about Lysimachus' sexual proclivities showed no signs of dying down, so I'd need a red-hot female escort. Just as well we had one on the team, so to speak.

"I've never been to the arena," Hodda said to me, as we drove there in a covered coach. "I'm looking forward to it."

"Count yourself lucky. It's revolting."

She loved it. Just like the very best fight scenes in the theatre, she whispered to me as some poor fool got his hand chopped off at the wrist, but with real blood. And when the reigning champion skewered one opponent then whirled round on his heel, decapitated the man creeping up behind him, then pirouetted back to disembowel a third, she was on her feet yelling and waving her scarf in the air, just like my dad used to do. I lurched onto my feet and yelled too; now that's acting.

"Amazing footwork," she said, when we'd sat down again. "That's something we never get right, we just stand there and have at it, no wonder it never looks real. We should hire one of these people to do some arranging for us."

"Keep your voice down," I said.

"God, sorry. Only, it's so exciting. When I think what I've been missing all these years."

Of course, I know all about footwork. I learned it under my father's heavy, accurate hand. Footwork, he'd say, is everything: if you aren't there, you can't get hit. And there's a lot of truth in that. I'd taken him at his word and not been there for a long, long time. Now, it seemed, I was back, watching one man destroy another and having to act like it was a good thing. Childhood, they tell you, best days of your life. Well, that's their opinion.

In the seats in front of us, my three fellow conspirators were completely engrossed, caught up in the action. I think what Faustinus liked best was the fighting, which is what I'd expect from someone who hasn't been in a fight since he was seven years old. Nicephorus was following all the moves, seeing if there was anything he could learn – a serious-minded man, with a strong sense of his own inadequacy, which circumstances made him deny utterly in public. Artavasdus was enjoying the blood. Fair enough; as Saloninus says, the man who's tired of killing is tired of life, and at least he made no bones, no pun intended, about it. As for Hodda, I believe it was all three of the above, though I wouldn't care to speculate on the exact proportions. She's one hell of a fencer, by the way, in breeches parts; put a man's eye out once, and though she swears it was an accident I think she got carried away.

I wasn't enjoying myself, so I decided it was time for the onset of serious illness. About the only appropriate thing I'd ever experienced myself was mountain fever – no joke, trust me – so that's what I decided to do.

Lysimachus, the way I read it, had been suffering from the early symptoms all day, but being a man of iron he'd shrugged them off, ignored them, treated them with the contempt they deserved. Ideal for my purposes. I closed my eyes and remembered the pain, which wasn't difficult to do. Then I remembered the shivering, which starts in your knees and spreads upwards; then the muscle spasms, and I realised I was actually sweating, I don't know why but it saved me having to dab my face surreptitiously with spit. Then I stood up, fighting to keep my balance, lost the fight and toppled slowly forward, like a felled tree.

The trick is, if you want to fall convincingly, aim at something soft to fall on. I chose Artavasdus. He was entirely wrapped up in the sword fighting, so he had no idea what was going on until I fell on him, pushing him forward out of his seat and nearly braining him on the rail of the box. He let out a howl they must've heard down on the sand, and I'm guessing a few people must've looked round, then a whole lot more, because a second or so later the whole stadium was so quiet.

All I could hear was swords clanging away down on the sand, where those poor fools were still battling furiously for their lives, with nobody watching.

Someone grabbed me and I was lifted up in the air, and all hell broke loose.

I ought to explain that I hadn't entirely abided by the terms of my agreement with my co-conspirators. Under the agreement, I was supposed to pass out tomorrow, not today. Later I explained to them that if we'd done it the way we'd agreed, they'd have known what was coming, and they'd have been thoroughly unconvincing. As it was, the spontaneity of genuine shock carried us all through. They gave me a hard time about it, but eventually conceded that it had gone down very well, and therefore, by implication, I'd been right.

By this point, of course, we were having trouble hearing ourselves think. There was a mob under the window, singing hymns to the Invincible Sun for my recovery. Artavasdus said he put the number at roughly forty thousand, though I think he was exaggerating. Nicephorus, rather more plausibly, reckoned the whole of Sunrise Square was packed solid. If so, that was a lot of people, and all begging the Invincible to spare my life. Which is probably the weirdest experience I've ever had, in a somewhat unorthodox life.

Artavasdus reckoned I'd nearly broken his collarbone. I told him not to be such a girl.

16

I said I ought to see a doctor. It'd look really strange if I didn't, and someone would be bound to notice; leading medical practitioners wanting to know why the father of the country was dangerously ill and they hadn't been consulted. Nicephorus told me I was getting above myself, and not to be so stupid.

"You see?" Hodda was sitting by my bedside; I daren't get up just in case a servant came in. "They love you. It's pathetic, but they really do."

They'd been there all night, apparently, praying and chanting; how not being able to get any sleep was supposed to aid my recovery wasn't entirely clear to me, but that's the public for you.

"Why do I get the feeling you want to use that to make me do something stupid?"

"I remember when Mostellaria was dying," she said, "and ten thousand people stood under her window all night holding lighted candles. And she staggered to the balcony and took one last bow."

"Were you one of them?"

"Was I hell as like. I never liked her. But it was beautiful."

"You do realise," I said, "we're this close to getting our necks pulled. And I seem to be the only one of us talking this thing *seriously.*"

She looked at me. "You're doing fine," she said, "relax. You're well into your stride now. Follow your instincts and everything will be just swell."

Smart as paint, but not all the time. "I've been thinking," I said. "Sell out the City to Ogus, yes, but how? We can't just write him a letter and give a kid five trachy to drop it round to him."

She frowned. "You'd have to set up a private meeting," she said. "Just you and him."

"You're not helping."

"Be quiet and let me think. The invitation would have to come from him."

I was about to say something clever, but I didn't. "Go on."

"He would need to say that he's willing to talk peace, but he'll only talk to you, one on one."

"That would get those three idiots off my back, granted."

"Someone must know someone," she said, looking past me with her dreamy face on. "This city's crawling with spies, if you believe half what you hear."

In my case, about a tenth; which meant I believed the City was crawling with spies. Obviously, with foreigners dropping in and out on merchant ships every day of the week. I was starting to feel nervous.

"Leave it with me," she said. "I'll arrange it."

"No, for crying out loud, don't do that." I was about to jump out of bed, but I remembered I was sick. "You'll go blundering in and give the whole show away."

"Give me credit for a little common sense," she said, cool as a mountain stream. "I'll ask around, discreet enquiries; nobody'll know it's me asking. Obviously you think I'm stupid or something."

As soon as the Games were safely over, I made a miraculous recovery, for which thanks were duly given in the form of a huge outdoor Blessing of the Sacrament and Transfiguration of the Host in the Hippodrome, with all the top priests up there doing their stuff. I was back in the Imperial box but I didn't mind that, since nobody was getting killed. What I wasn't so keen on was the three-times-life-size statue of me they put up right in the middle of the arena, where the Bronze Tripod used to be before it got struck by lightning. Apparently it had been paid for by popular subscription, which meant the Public dropping their handfuls of trachy into hats on street corners, either voluntarily or by order of the Theme bosses, and of the two I don't know which would be worse; I didn't ask and nobody told me. It was a horrible statue, of me – I do beg your pardon – of Lysimachus in his glory days as a sand fighter, finishing off a sprawling foe with a huge spear.

"It's all fixed," she said. "I've arranged it."

What counts as a virtue in one context isn't necessarily a good thing in another. In the theatre it's a tremendous asset if your voice can be heard right up at the back of the gallery, even when you're supposed to be whispering. "For God's sake, Hodda," I hissed at her. "Keep your voice down."

"You don't need to know the details," she carried on blithely, "but an invitation will be issued; just you and him, face to face, time and place to be agreed. Finally, we're getting somewhere."

"What have you done?"

"What we agreed. Or had you forgotten?"

I didn't want to talk to her any more, but she was full of it, the buzz. "Of course, we need to figure out exactly how we're going to do it," she went on, "but there's plenty of time for that. You need to keep your ears and eyes open. I've been thinking. Opening the gates is probably going to be too difficult, but what if you take the entire garrison out on a night raid and lead them straight into a trap?"

Just when you think you understand, something always happens to prove that you don't. Forty thousand people had prayed for me under my window, and then somebody tried to kill me.

I was on my way back from that singularly annoying interview with Hodda. We always did the journey back and forth the same way: a closed carriage, always the same driver, always the same two palace guards, one inside with me, the other up on the box. You can't see where you're going in a closed carriage, but I fancy we were somewhere around Coppergate, because we'd just been going downhill a long way and were starting to climb. I remember thinking, "Hello, why are we stopping?", and the guard, who always sat opposite me looking like he'd been stuffed and frozen, leaned forward a little; and then there was this terrific thump on the roof, and then something smashed through the carriage door.

The guard wasn't moving. "What's happening?" I shouted at him, then I saw that the thing that had punched through the door was a big wooden fence post, and as well as the door it had gone right through the guard

I thought it must be some sort of bizarre accident. I stood up to bang on the roof, to get the driver's attention. Then the other door was wrenched open, I saw the frame splinter and someone climbed in. I assumed it was the driver or the other guard. "He's hurt," I started to say. I couldn't see the man's face because it was dark. "I'm all right but he's—"

He had a knife. The penny dropped.

There was a voice in my head, faint but perfectly clear: *The way you go about taking a knife off someone is this.* My dad, when I was eleven or twelve. We practised it over and over again. You'll be glad I taught you this one day, he'd say.

I took the knife away from him. He tried to take it back. I stuck it in his eye, as far as it would go.

First time I'd ever done anything like that. Let's not go there.

They were foreigners, Faustinus told me later: four Jazygites. No papers on them, but the Jazygite resident made a list of all the ships they could have come in on. We do a lot of business with them; they're nice people, friendly, on our side. We're guessing, Faustinus said, that someone hired them to do it. And for that they pay him the big bucks.

"What we don't know," Nicephorus said, "is whether they were hired by the enemy or someone in the City. Could be either, there's no way of telling."

I'd killed one, the guard on the roof got two more and the fourth ran away, got chased down half the alleys in Old Stairs and dropped down dead, would you believe, of heart failure. In case you're interested, they blocked the road with a donkey cart, then rammed the side of the coach with the fence post, hoping to take out everyone inside. "Amateurs," Artavasdus said, and I agreed with him. Not the way my dad would've gone about it. "From which it seems likely," he went on, "that someone went down to the docks and asked around for some out-of-towners who wanted to pick up some quick money. Rather than sending to the old country for the cream of the profession. Which doesn't get us any further trying to figure out who was behind it."

I pointed out that whoever it was had known I was in that particular coach in that particular street at that particular time. Artavasdus said that didn't help much either; the City was crawling with enemy spies, who probably knew more about what went on than we did. "Though if I were you," he added, "I'd think carefully about that girlfriend of yours. She knows all the arrangements, obviously."

"She would never—" I began, and then remembered why I could vouch for her absolutely, and why I couldn't tell them about it.

"We're keeping a lid on this," Nicephorus said. "We don't want riots, or all the Jazygites in the City torn limb from limb. If word got out someone tried to kill you, it could get very nasty indeed."

Keeping a lid on it; bless his naïve soul. And, yes, there were riots, twenty dead and whole rows of shops burned and looted; and roughly forty completely innocent Jazygite sailors and traders were killed in one night, and we had to lock the rest of them up in the Guards' barracks for their own safety. Nice to know that people care, but I'd have preferred it if they'd sent flowers.

Act 2

1

I woke up and there were six men standing over me: five soldiers and a fat man. "On your feet," the fat man said.

The soldiers had drawn swords in their hands. I got out of bed, looked for my slippers; they'd got kicked under the bed, presumably by the soldiers. I didn't bother with my slippers.

The fat man led the way down the long, narrow spiral staircase to the room where I spent most of my time, talking to the conspirators or reading or just lying on a couch. There were four more fat men there waiting for us. Four chairs, incidentally, in that room, plus the couch. I stood.

"That him?" asked one of the four. My escort nodded.

"Funny," said another. "He's not as tall as I thought he'd be."

"Oh, that's him all right," said a third. "I used to watch him in the arena. I'd know him anywhere."

"What's going on?" I asked.

One of the fat men hadn't spoken yet. He wasn't the fattest, or the tallest, or even the best dressed, though they were all pretty damn smart, in an austere sort of way. But he was clearly the boss. "Do you know me?" he said.

No, I was about to reply, but then something clicked into place in my mind. Yes, I'd seen him, even tried to impersonate him a few times, with pillows shoved up my front; but nobody in the audience knew who he was supposed to be, so we cut him out of the act. "You're Gelimer," I said.

He smiled. "Senator Gelimer to you," he said. "Leader of the House. Unlike you, you see, I have a real job in this town."

All over, then. I'd been found out. Ah well.

Before I could say anything, Gelimer went on: "These gentlemen are representatives of the four main parties in the House. They've formed a coalition to provide a government of national unity."

He paused. That's nice, I didn't say. Couldn't really see what business it was of mine, if I'd been found out.

"There's been a change of management," he went on. "The military junta is out, and the House is back in charge." He grinned. "Thanks to you, incidentally. Probably the most valuable contribution you ever made to the wellbeing of this city, and you didn't actually do anything."

"Steady on," said one of the other fat men. Gelimer turned his head, nodded, turned back to me. "The attempt on your life," he said, "has given us the pretext we needed. Obviously there was a conspiracy, to overthrow the state and deliver the City into the hands of Ogus and his barbarian hordes. But there's no need to panic. The conspirators have been apprehended and are in custody, and the Senate is in charge, making sure everything runs smoothly."

It occurred to me that maybe I hadn't been found out after all. "The others," I said. "Nicephorus and Artavasdus and Faustinus. Are they all right?"

Gelimer beamed at me. "Would you like to see them?"

"Yes."

He nodded, stood up, walked to the window, opened it, pointed. I looked where he was pointing. I saw the door of the inner courtyard, into which someone had hammered two big iron staples. Hanging from the staples by their hair were two heads.

"Faustinus wasn't at home when we called," Gelimer went on, "but he won't get far. We've got men down at the docks, and he'll probably try and get on a ship. He's not very bright. My third cousin, as it happens."

I moved away from the window. Severed heads are a real pain in the backside in the theatre. No matter how hard you try, they always look comic and someone in the back row is bound to snigger. Weird thing is, real ones look just as grotesque and improbable as the fakes do.

"You've got a choice," Gelimer went on. "Join us, or we were too late to save you and you were cruelly murdered by the traitors before we had a chance to get to them. No skin off our noses either way."

"I'm not Lysimachus," I said.

There was a dead quiet moment. "You what?"

"I'm not Lysimachus," I told them, in my own voice. "I'm an actor, called Notker. Lysimachus was killed by a trebuchet shot, weeks ago. Nicephorus and his lot made me pretend to be him. They told me if I didn't, they'd kill my mother. It's true. Everybody knows me in the theatres, they'll confirm it."

Utter silence. Then Gelimer laughed.

"You know," he said, "you had me going there for a moment. Trouble is, you don't know your history."

"It's *true*," I yelled at him. "I'm an impressionist, I do impersonations. I tried to do you once, in a burlesque at the Rose."

I don't think he was listening. "After the fall of Mistragon in AUC 447," he said, "King Pausanias escaped from his pursuers by claiming he was the king's body double, and they believed him. Then he raised an army, tried to take back the City and was killed. Don't kid a kidder, son, you're Lysimachus all right. Isn't he, Totila?"

The fat man who liked to watch the sand-fighting nodded. "I'll prove it to you," he said, and stood up. "That one," he said, prodding one of the scars Nicephorus had carved into my face, "I saw him get that, fighting Atucca in the New Years, ten years ago. He got that one from Pleusius the year after that; the judges called it a draw, but the fix must've been in, he won that fair and square. Take your shirt off. There," he went on, "that's where Ogus' goons stabbed him in the back when he rescued the milkface engineer."

Gelimer came up close and picked at one of the scars on my face with his fingernail. "That's not sealing wax and grease-paint," he said. "You're Lysimachus."

"Nicephorus did that with a razor," I said.

Totila shook his head. "That's an old scar," he said.

"We aged them, with saltpetre."

"Can't be done. Everyone knows that. You can't make a new scar look old."

"For crying out loud," I said. "Do I sound like Lysimachus?"

"Don't know, never met you before. I imagine you sound like Lysimachus, because that's who you bloody well are."

"Now then," Gelimer said, "that'll do. You had a good crack at it, fair play to you, but it didn't work. So let's get back to business, shall we?"

My mother used to say, don't pull faces or you'll stick like it. And did I listen? "Fine," I said. "What do you want?"

Gelimer leaned back in his chair. "Just now I offered you a choice," he said. "Cooperate with the legitimate government of this city or we'll kill you and bury you in a dung heap. We know you've only ever been just a figurehead, and during the early days of the siege you did absolutely nothing; you were just a bodyguard who happened to catch the public imagination. Fine, we have no problem with that. You can be our figurehead, and it'll make life easier for us. Otherwise we say you were murdered by Nicephorus, and the people will be very angry and terribly sad, but sooner or later they'll get over it. In case you were wondering," he went on, "the army's right behind us, and Sisinna's one of us, so don't expect anything out of him. All we want from you is to look pretty and wave, and not to do anything at all unless we say so. I imagine you can manage that, can't you? It's what you've been doing for the last seven years, after all."

Suddenly I had to know. "Was it you who tried to kill me?"

Bewildered silence, just for a moment. "Good God, no," Gelimer said. "Why would we want to do that? Like I just told you," he went on, "it worked out very well for us, marvellously convenient, but it wasn't us."

"We assumed it was Nicephorus and the junta," put in one of the fat men whose name I didn't know. "That's what gave us the idea. They've overstepped the mark this time, we thought; we can have them for that."

"He hasn't told us what he wants to do yet," Totila pointed out. "I think we need a decision, don't you?"

I couldn't help laughing. "Between doing what you tell me to and having my neck twisted?"

"Yes."

I pulled a big, cracked smile. "I'm with you," I said, "body and soul. Long live the revolution."

Totila gave me a weary look. "Don't call it that," he said, "there's a good fellow."

In the theatre there's a legend, or a ghost story, that we all know; it's called the haunted play. There's this play, so the story goes, and it's one of the best plays ever written. It has it all: great speeches, fantastic leads, wonderful can't-miss cameos, the best comic relief ever, but it never gets revived, and do you know why? It's haunted. There's the all-time greatest strong kick-ass female lead in this play, and nobody will ever play it again.

The story goes that the actress who won the part in the original production was poisoned by her understudy on the opening night; and with her dying breath she put a curse on the play. Anybody who played that part thereafter would be taken over by her, become her; see with her eyes, remember her memories, play the part exactly how she'd have played it if only she'd had the chance; die as she died, just as the curtain falls. Great story. For years I've been pitching it as an idea for a play, but for some reason nobody wants to touch it.

Do you think you could get trapped in a part that would never let you go? There was one old boy who'd done nothing all his life except the herald in the *Cuckold's Tragedy*. It's not a big part but it's got the best speech in the play, which is a classic; and he made such a hit with it when he was thirty-odd that every time it got put on after that, they said, get whatsisname for the herald, until the public wouldn't stand for anyone else. So: forty years saying the same sixty-eight lines of rhyming couplets every night: don't knock it, at least you're working. They say that towards the end he forgot his own name and would only answer to Vesanio, which is what the herald is called in the play. How sad, people say, what a waste of a life. Only I talked to his brother once, and apparently in real life he was the most boring, objectionable, obnoxious piece of work who ever emptied a room by walking into it – and he knew it, but he'd been born that way and couldn't do anything about it; but when he was being the herald everybody liked him, sat through the big speeches waiting for him to come on, paid money to see him. When he was up there, his brother told me, he was somebody. Out of costume, he was just another piece of shit.

2

The Senate, better known as the House, dates right back to the earliest years of the Robur empire, or the commonwealth as it was called back then, and the same one hundred and sixteen families have had the monopoly on it all that time. Good story about that. When Andronicus the Great became the first emperor, back in the year dot, he had the senators dragged in front of him in chains, the way you do, and one of them, head of the oldest and proudest of the hundred and sixteen, told him he was nobody, human garbage, didn't even know who his own father was. Quite true, Andronicus said. But my family begins with me; yours ends with you. Then, to show his magnanimity, he spared all their lives, and fifteen years later they had him stabbed to death in his bath; moral, don't neglect an opportunity to get rid of your enemy for the sake of a great one-liner.

The name of the snotty senator is not recorded, but bet you anything you like he was an ancestor of Gelimer. Quite a safe bet, actually, since the House families are hopelessly and inextricably interbred, like bindweed growing up through a honeysuckle, so everyone is everyone else's cousin, uncle, nephew, often all three at the same time. Whoever that senator was, he and Gelimer definitely had a lot of qualities in common: pride, enough arrogance to poison the Middle Sea, and a big fat chunk of raw courage.

There was more to Gelimer than that, however, as I found out fairly quickly. He sent for me. I'd spent a troubled couple of hours up in my tower, with guards on the locked-from-the-outside door, and I'd come to the conclusion that my only chance of staying alive was to find a way to make myself useful. How I was supposed to do that, I had no idea.

Gelimer had parked himself in the C Sharp Chapel – so-called because if you hold a C sharp for more than a few seconds there, the walls start shaking so much that bits of plaster flake off, or so the story goes. Since half the anthems and introits in the old liturgy are scored in the key of C sharp, maybe it's not surprising that for the last six centuries or so the place has been used as a sort of office come quiet room by successive Masters of the Vestments, the men who used to run things under the emperors. The last Master had been on the first ship out of the City when news of the siege broke, and he hadn't been missed; in the intervening seven years, I don't think anybody had been in the room except to clean the rather fine stained-glass windows and dust the few pieces of austere, utterly magnificent furniture.

Gelimer was sitting on a narrow, high-backed, uncomfortable looking chair made from walrus ivory, which I'm given to understand is the most valuable material in the world that isn't a metal or a stone. The only other seat in the place was – I recognised the pattern straight away as a spinner's chair, low, wobbly and prone to fall over backwards as soon as you try and stand up. I grew up in a house where both the chairs were like that. But not like this one, because it was carved out of whalebone in the captive-ball style; you know the sort of thing, where inside one ball there's another, and another one inside that, and some poor devil has spent years of his life picking the material away through tiny gaps with a tiny hook on a stick. Inside the legs of this chair, therefore, was a mountainside with grazing sheep and shepherds and shepherdesses dancing to the music of a double flute. My guess is that it used to belong to an empress who liked to play at spinning, no doubt in pursuit of the simple life.

He looked up at me. "Sit down," he said.

I considered the chair. "It won't take my weight."

He grinned. "You'd be surprised. That chair was made for the Empress Carbonopsina. They had to widen half the doors in the palace so she could get through them."

I sat down. Solid as a rock. "You wanted to see me."

He contemplated me for a moment, as if I was a piece of algebra, maybe the dying genius's last theorem that nobody's ever been able to solve. "My colleagues and I have been talking about you," he said. "In the end we took a vote. Three votes to two."

Not sure I liked the sound of that. "What was the motion?"

"Is this man Lysimachus or a burlesque actor by the name of Notker?"

"Right," I said. "Who won?"

"Three votes say you're Lysimachus."

"Which way did you vote?"

"But it's largely academic," Gelimer went on, obviously not having heard me. "Everybody outside this wing of the palace believes you're Lysimachus, so even if you really were an impostor, it wouldn't matter a damn in practical terms. And we don't care because, regardless of who you are, you're going to do exactly what we tell you to, or we kill your lady friend."

He paused to let the threat sink in. I was supposed to wait for him to continue. "The truth is," I said, "I am Lysimachus, and I can prove it if you want me to. And as far as Hodda's concerned, there's plenty more where she came from. But that's academic, too, because I'll be more than happy to fall in with anything you gentlemen have in mind."

"Son," he said, "I don't trust you further than I could sneeze a pig."

"Likewise."

That made him smile. "Of course," he said. "And between you and me and the doorposts, I trust my esteemed colleagues even less. We've only been allies for a month. Before that, we hated each other to death. You know, there's a lot of bullshit spoken about trust. Actually, you don't need it at all, you get on much better without it."

"A bit like truth, really."

He frowned at me. "For the time being," he said, "we need each other, that's all that matters. Which is why I'm making you the emperor."

My father had a trick punch, which he loved to show off. He'd hit someone just right, and the poor sod would stand there, completely winded and stunned, until my dad gave him a gentle little prod with the tip of his finger, whereupon he'd measure his length like a felled tree.

"Haven't we already got one?"

Gelimer shook his head. "He died about eighteen months ago. Merciful release, he'd been in a whatchacallit, coma, for four years, just lay on his back with his mouth open, couldn't move so much as an eyelash. I gather there may be a distant cousin somewhere near Olbia. You know where Olbia is?"

"No."

"Me neither. To all intents and purposes, there is no emperor. Not that it matters a damn, in fact we prefer it that way, but we've got popular opinion to think of."

"The people love the emperor."

He nodded. "Goes to show just how stupid people are," he said. "But, yes, they do. And they love you. But right now, you don't have what you might call official standing. You're not a minister or a councillor or a general or anything, so we can't use you to actually *do* anything." He paused for breath. "So, the story is, the emperor on his deathbed called for you and pressed the Great Seal into your hand and anointed your forehead with the holy oil and muttered long live Lysimachus I with his dying breath, and now you're it. You all right with that?"

"Lysimachus II."

"You what?"

"There's already been a Lysimachus I," I said. "About three hundred years ago. I was named after him, as it happens."

He frowned. "You know what," he said, "I do believe you're right. Learned about him at school. Didn't he build a bridge or something?"

"Aqueducts."

"Same thing. Are you all right with that or aren't you?"

There's a very old saying: when you're falling off a cliff, learn to fly. I've never flown myself, but I've seen it done heaps of times, and so has anyone who's ever been to the theatre. If you look really close, of course, you'll see a rope tied to a sort of harness thing worn under the flyer's shirt; but so what, they're still up there moving through the air, and that's a pretty good working definition of flight. "That's treason," I said. "And sacrilege."

He beamed at me. "Bullshit," he said. "It's not like anyone murdered the old fool. He died of natural causes, on my word as a gentleman. There's no blood successor. Under such circumstances, which have never actually arisen but the principle's there in the statute books for anyone to read, the choice of emperor lies with the House. We choose you."

I hadn't thought of it like that. "But all those lies," I said. "The holy oil and his dying breath."

"Oh, that. Merely corroborative detail, as the poet says. If we say you're the emperor, you're the emperor. That's the law."

"Me."

"You."

Once upon a time there was a caterpillar who wanted to be an angel, floating through the sky on gossamer wings. And one day he woke up and found that he had gossamer wings and could fly; and he was still him, no lies, no greasepaint, no deception. And besides, there's one's own personal opinion, and then there's the indisputable truth. A properly constituted committee of the House had just declared that I was Lysimachus and legally appointed me emperor in accordance with the constitution. Set against that the word of a disreputable burlesque actor, and who do you believe?

"It's not like I've got much choice," I said.

"You haven't."

"In that case, I accept."

"Long live the emperor." He yawned. "And the first thing you're going to do once you've been crowned is abolish the Themes."

Another trick of my dad's was the left-hand feint to the jaw, inducing his opponent to lean back out of the way, thereby opening his solar plexus to a devastating right cross. "You what?"

"The Themes," he repeated. "They're choking the life out of this city and they've got to go. It was bad enough in the old days, but legalising them was a total bloody disaster. So you're going to unlegalise them. That's what we need you for."

"You're crazy. They'll tear the City to pieces."

"It's possible," Gelimer said gently. "But it's got to be done. And I'll tell you what, you've got a bloody sight better chance of getting the people to agree to it than we have, that's for sure."

The ground rushed towards me, flat and hard and as far as the eye could see, and I thought: if birds can do it, it can't be all that difficult. "I'll do whatever you want me to," I said.

A few years ago I did a private after-dinner entertainment for the Faculty of History at the University. It went well; I did the Chancellor and a few of the senior lecturers, one of whom came up to me afterwards and actually thanked me, said it would make him ever so popular with the junior fellows. Anyway, after that I hung around for the free food, and I listened to a bunch of them, great scholars who knew everything there is to know, discussing some abstruse point, something along the lines of, was the post of Count of the Stables introduced by Cleomenes II or Strabo IV? One faction said there was good evidence (which they recited in detail) to say it was Cleomenes. The other lot adduced equally good evidence to say it was Strabo. Then someone passed round a bottle of the really good stuff, and when it was all gone, someone said, I know, let's vote on it. So that's what they did. Nine votes for

Cleomenes, seven for Strabo, and that's how we know, as a matter of cold scientific fact, which emperor created the post of Count of the Stables. And if you don't believe me, look in the history books – the latest editions, of course, incorporating all the new advances in the sum of human knowledge – and you'll see I'm right.

What, after all, is belief but knowing something without actually being able to prove it? Millions of people believe in the Invincible Sun. And anything believed by so many must be true; and if you disagree, it can only be because you don't quite understand the subtleties of the true definition of truth. If it wasn't true before, my dad used to say, when fifteen respectable householders swore on oath he'd been playing cards with them on the night that some unfortunate was stabbed to death in an alleyway on the other side of town, it's true now.

And it's what's true now that matters, sure as eggs is eggs. Think about it logically. Unless you're a bit wrong in the head, you can remember what happened one minute ago clear as day. But you'll be forgiven for being a bit hazy about the details of something you did or said twenty years ago. So, if there's a discrepancy, the minute-old truth is far more likely to be correct than an inconsistent version dating back twenty years.

Twenty years ago – longer than that – I was Notker. Right now I'm Lysimachus, and this time tomorrow I'll be Lysimachus II. And I have the scars to prove it.

"I hate you," she whispered in my ear.

Wonderful thing for a bride to say to her husband on their wedding day, don't you think? On the other hand it was probably true, at least at that precise moment.

The moment in question was just before I led her up the

aisle, between the rows of distinguished guests, to the twin thrones they'd dug out of storage and set up in the Long Hall on the ground floor of the New Palace. It goes without saying that the New Palace is the oldest part of the palace complex and dates back nearly a thousand years, and that the Long Hall is very, very long. Gelimer had chosen it because it was the biggest space available. I forget how many people were crammed in there to see the show. It was well over a thousand, all in their smartest clothes, all turned out to watch the mighty Lysimachus crowned and married on the same day.

(That had been my bright idea. What we need, I'd suggested, is to make me as popular as possible.

Why would we want to do that?

Because then, when I turn round and abolish the Themes, maybe they'll hesitate just a moment or so longer before they set fire to the City.

Good point, they conceded. So?

So, I said, coronations are popular. So are royal weddings. Let's have one of those as well.

Dead silence. Then someone, I think it may have been Senator Nasica, said that wasn't such a bad idea. All right, said Gelimer, let's do that. Of course, we'll need a bride.

You could've heard an ant fart, as the dozen or so senators present all thought of their unmarried daughters, nieces and similar livestock. Yes, it's always nice to have an empress in the family, but on the other hand—

"The People's Emperor," I went on, "should have a People's Empress."

Gelimer looked at me. "That sounds good," he said. "What does it mean?"

I pointed out that the emperor, alone out of all the Robur

nobility, could in theory marry whoever he liked. He had no need to marry money, or rank, or an old and distinguished family. Compared to the effulgent glory of the emperor, all commoners were so far beneath his notice that they were practically interchangeable – dukes, counts, farmhands, the man who goes round in a cart emptying the piss-pots, given the vast perspective distance, what possible difference could it make? Candaules the Great had married a milkmaid. Eudora, the wife of Marcian the Wise, had been a prostitute. The two most popular emperors in our history; because by marrying wives who weren't just commoners but the commonest of the common—

"Yes, point taken," Gelimer said. "Where's this leading?"

On the other hand, I pointed out, you needed someone who was at least presentable. Someone who knows how to look good in public. Someone very definitely of the people, but nevertheless with a touch of class—)

So up the aisle we walked; and that's one of the really important things you learn on the stage, how to walk. A walk can be so many things, a strut or a pace or a waddle or a prance; we can do all of those and a thousand more. We can tell you who we are (hero, villain, ingenue, low comedian; prince, peasant, soldier, feisty kick-ass chick, crone) without saying a single word, just by the way we put one foot in front of the other. To some of us it comes naturally. Some of us have to think about it and practise for hours in front of a mirror. A great actor I knew when I was starting out was practically in tears one time because he couldn't get his character's walk; then he hit on the idea of sticking a quarter-thaler coin between his buttocks and clenching them tight so it wouldn't fall out; and from that he got the character's walk, and from the walk he got the whole character. I don't know how Hodda figured out her empress-bride walk, but however she did it, she got it absolutely spot on. Me, I relied on my inner mirror, same as always, and I think it did the trick.

It had been my idea to have the Blue and Green bosses as crown bearers. Needless to say, they'd nearly come to blows in the anteroom over which one of them was going to carry the emperor's crown and which one would be stuck carrying the empress's. I told them to toss a coin for it; the Greens won. The Blue boss said that wasn't acceptable and predicted gutters running with blood before nightfall if his Theme was insulted in this way. Fine, I said. Green got to carry the emperor's crown to the steps of the throne, whereupon he would hand it to Blue, who would hand it to the Precentor of the Temple. Then Blue would fetch the empress's crown and hand it to Green, et cetera. The Green boss said that he could, and would, put five thousand armed men in the streets if he was forced to hand the crown to a Blue. We compromised. Accordingly, the crowns were brought in on a little trolley, which I'd remembered seeing in an anteroom somewhere, pushed by Blue and Green equally, side by side.

It's not just the crown, though; far from it. The Imperial regalia consists of seven distinct items – lorus, divitision, dalmatic, crown, orb, buskins, sceptre. Together they weigh seventy-two pounds twelve ounces, which is nearly twice what a heavy infantryman carries into battle. Yes, the weight is distributed fairly evenly about your person; the dalmatic goes on first, over your head and shoulders, followed by the divitision, which is a sort of massively embroidered cloth of gold dressing gown; then the lorus, which is seven feet of jewelled scarf, twisted and twined round you like one of those snakes in

Blemya that crushes its prey to death. The buskins are knee-length and purple, and I'm guessing that generations of Robur emperors have had very slim calves, because I could only get my leg two-thirds of the way down the bloody things before I got stuck. My crown balanced on the top of my head like a bird sitting on a statue. Hers came right down over her eyes.

No matter. The priest mumbled the magic words, and it was done. Then the next bit; do you, Lysimachus, take this woman, Hodda, and that was done, too. I must say she did her part very well, exactly the right soft breathlessness, but still perfectly audible at the back of the hall. But then, I'd have expected that, since less than a year ago she'd married an emperor forty-seven times on consecutive nights in the third act of *Only a Life*. First time ever for me, but I flatter myself that I coped pretty well.

They don't clap or cheer at coronations, or royal weddings. They sit there in stony silence. I think that's rather a shame, myself.

3

"Three reasons," I told her.

She was pretending not to listen. We were alone in the Imperial bedchamber, and some halfwit had covered the bed three inches deep in rose petals.

"One," I said, "Gelimer and his happy band of cutthroats told me that if I didn't do exactly as I was told, they'd kill you."

For that, I got to carry on looking at the back of her head. No matter.

"I figure, they'll find it that bit harder to carry out their threat if you're the empress. Two, I thought we agreed we're in this together. In which case, we need to be able to talk to each other without involving half a dozen people who don't like us and a platoon of the royal guards."

She was still wearing the dalmatic, and one buskin. She'd kicked the other one halfway across the room. The empress's buskins are four hundred years old and each one has embroidered into it enough seed pearls to buy all the big houses on the fashionable side of Hill Street, on the left as you go up.

"Three," I said.

"Oh, shut up." She turned round and scowled at me. "You know what? I'm sick and tired of the sound of your voice."

"Actually, it's not my voice, it's Lysimachus'."

She blinked. "So it is," she said. "I guess I must have got used to it. Makes no difference," she went on. "I've had to listen to it all day and I really don't want to listen to it any more, so if you'll please just shut the fuck up I'll be ever so much obliged."

Curious, I thought, that a woman justly famous for her ability to express the whole spectrum from ecstatic joy to hopeless misery should choose to convey her true emotions by sulking. Still, you don't do the day-job work on your day off, and if nobody's paying to watch, why bother? "Fine," I said.

"You sleep in the chair."

I could have pointed out that I was the emperor of the Robur, and emperors don't sleep in chairs, but I decided not to. Nor did I offer to help her shift the rose petals.

It was, as it happens, a supremely comfortable chair and a pleasure to recline in, and I was sound asleep a few minutes after I closed my eyes. How long I stayed that way I couldn't tell you, but I don't suppose it was very long.

"Since you've got me into this mess," she was saying, "I suppose it's up to me to get us out again."

"It's hardly a mess," I yawned. "I'm the emperor and you're the empress. Really."

"Yes, and if we do anything those horrible men don't like, they'll murder us."

"I've been thinking about that," I said. "And yes, probably they would, though they might not find it as easy as they think."

"Bullshit."

"Maybe," I said, "maybe not. They run the City, sure, but inside the palace I think it may be different. You saw the guards."

"Hard to miss them," she said. "Milkfaces."

"Sort of," I replied mildly. "Actually they're Lystragonians."

"So bloody what."

"The emperors have hired Lystragonian guards for over three centuries," I bleated on. "They have a strong tradition of absolute loyalty. We tell them what to do, they do it."

No reply. In context, that was encouraging.

"So long as we're alive," I went on, "they'll fight to the last drop of blood for us. Soon as we're dead, of course, their loyalty reverts to the next emperor, even if he's the one who just slit our throats. But from what I gather, they take it seriously. Anyone wants to kill us has got to go through them first."

Pause. "I wouldn't have thought your pal Gelimer would let you have your own personal army."

"Ah," I said. "Hardly an army. There's forty-six of them. Ought to be fifty, but four of them got sick and went home. Four replacements are on their way, apparently. I got talking to their captain," I explained. "Nice man. Saw you in *The Pirate Bride*. From what he said, I think you could rely on him no matter what happens."

"You must point him out to me some time," she said. "But, as you just said, there's only forty-six of them. And once they've died heroically to the last man—"

"Sure," I said. "But it makes it a little bit harder, that's all I'm saying. That's a step up from all they have to do is snap their fingers and we're dead. More to the point, we're safe so long as we do precisely what we're told. Do you have a problem with that?"

She was about to speak, then hesitated. "Depends, doesn't it?"

"I don't," I said. "I sign things and wave from balconies, and the rest of it's mostly eating and drinking. There are worse things."

"Notker." She hardly ever uses my name. "You remember when we were rehearsing *Tried in the Furnace.*"

"What's that got to do with anything?"

"And everyone said it was a sure-fire hit and it'd run for a year, and I said I didn't think people were going to like it. And it closed after a week."

"You always say everything's going to end in disaster. From time to time you're right. Proves nothing. Either say something positive or let me go back to sleep."

"Did I mention that I'm already married?"

No, she'd never mentioned that. "Doesn't matter," I heard myself say. "Look, hasn't it sunk in yet? We're not faking it any more. This is real. We are genuinely the emperor and empress. Isn't that what you always dreamed of?"

"Not like this."

"How's it different? We've got all the money and stuff we could ever want. We don't rule the empire, if our faces don't fit we'll probably be killed. Read some history, for crying out loud. That's being a real emperor. That's what they really do, in real life."

"Don't you want to know who my real husband is?"

Oh, for crying out loud. "No," I said. "Shut up and let me get some sleep."

No chance of that now, of course. I leaned back in the chair, which wasn't as comfortable as it had been a few minutes ago, and tried to figure out what I was going to do next.

*

The emperor's wedding night symbolises, in some way I'd rather not dwell on, the marriage between the supreme ruler, Vice-Gerent of Heaven and Brother of the Invincible Sun, and his loving and obedient people; so maybe it was only fitting that I spent it wide awake slumped in a chair, while my lovely bride snored like a walrus.

Up bright and early next morning for the investiture ceremony. This consisted of the two of us putting all those stupid clothes on all over again, but this time in the Blue Chapel of the Single Teardrop temple. Dressing up in absurd costumes and walking and sitting in an impressive manner in front of an audience, while other people did all the talking; that's not even acting. That's what you do when you're learning to be an actor, or if you're not good enough to be trusted with a few lines. And after the ceremony, I was due to give my maiden speech from the temple steps, in which I was going to outline the general thrust of my policies as emperor.

I told her what that was going to be as we walked through the cloisters that take you round three sides of a square from the Blue Chapel to the magnificently ornate main gate. They've ordered me to abolish the Themes, I told her.

She stopped dead in her tracks, nearly causing a disastrous pile-up of equerries and ladies-in-waiting. "You can't. They'll tear us limb from limb."

I gave her my most loving smile. "If I don't, we'll be murdered," I said. "But don't worry, it's fine. I've thought of an idea."

Fortunately we were intercepted at this point by the archdeacon, dean and chapter of the temple, denying me the chance to hear what she thought about that.

Time for my big speech.

(Gelimer had given me the text that morning. "I can't learn all this in that time," I told him.

He looked at me, and I wondered which way he'd voted, and whether he was wondering whether he was having second thoughts. "Of course you can't," he said. "You read it out."

"I never read speeches," I told him, snapping back into character like a set bone. "Half the people in the Themes would be horrified if they knew I can read. They'd think I'd sold out."

He shrugged. "That's your business," he said. "If you'd rather put it into your own words, fine. Just so long as you get across the general idea."

At the back of my head I heard trumpets. "Leave it with me," I said. "I'll manage.")

The steps of the Single Teardrop; many's the time I've thought what a wonderful venue it'd make for the right production. Fabulous acoustic, because of the tall buildings on three sides. Great sightlines, and if you were doing the classics you wouldn't need scenery, just a backcloth stretched across the columns; you've got the gate itself for your upstage centre entrances, the ends of the portico for entrances stage left and right and the gallery that runs along the architrave of the temple façade for balcony scenes and the like. Excuse me if you think I'm pathetic because I always reduce things to my terms, but I reckon it's a basic survival instinct. If you can turn any place you find yourself in into the back streets of your home town, you'll never be lost. And it makes it easier to plan ambushes.

My big speech.

Enter UC, proceed DC, stop. Pause. Look impressive. Speak. That's what was in the script. A bit bald and obvious,

I thought. So, when we were in the lobby waiting to make our entrance, I turned round and whispered in the ear of my new best friend, the captain of the Lystragonians—

(See above: Hodda's devoted fan. His name was Its Very Essence. I'd asked him, is it all right if I call you Very for short? Call me whatever you like, he'd replied. Very Essence of what? I asked him. Everything, he said. Fair enough.)

With the result that, when I walked out on stage, I was escorted by thirty of the forty-six formed up round me in closed order, while the other sixteen stayed backstage, in a ring round Hodda. I left my thirty in two ranks spread across the gateway; one rank facing forward, the other facing the gate. My distant predecessor chose Lystragonians because they're very tall and broad and have a reputation for, among other things, cannibalism. Good people to have between you and your potential worst enemies. In front of me, however, nothing but the imposing rose marble steps of the temple and the serried ranks of my fellow citizens. If they wanted to rush the platform and disembowel me, there'd be no pesky guards to interfere. Therefore, obviously, I trusted them implicitly. A fine statement to make; tyrants have bodyguards, but the Father of his Country doesn't need them (and goes without saying, even forty-six Lystragonians wouldn't slow up an angry mob for as much as a single heartbeat).

Even so. I'd asked Captain Very how far a man could throw a brick hard enough to kill somebody. Thirty-five yards max, he told me. From the front of the steps to the crowd, forty yards plus. Fortune favours the brave, but don't push your luck.

Advance downstage centre. Stop. Look impressive.

Showtime.

"Citizens," I said, "you know me, I don't do speeches. But

I do make promises. I'm going to make one now, and if I don't keep it – well, you know where to find me, and—" (unwinds lorus to expose neck and upper chest) "look, no armour. Don't need any. You are all the armour I need to keep me safe.

"Seven years ago, I legalised the Themes. Let me tell you why. I was born in a Theme, grew up in one. I was proud to fight for my Theme in the arena, and I've gone on doing just that, and that's what I'll always do, so long as there's breath left in my body. This city isn't walls and houses and temples, it's people, and who's always looked out for the people, fed and clothed them, kept them safe? The Themes. So I promise you, as long as I'm emperor, the Themes will play their vitally important part in running this city, looking out for ordinary decent working people, feeding them, clothing them, keeping them safe. You have my word on that.

"There's just one thing wrong with the Themes, and once we've fixed that, everything's going to be just fine. There's two of them. Blue and Green, Green and Blue. And it's in the nature of things, if you've got two rivals, they fight. And Blue against Green and Green against Blue is the curse on this city. Is there anyone here who hasn't lost a friend or a loved one because of it? That division is tearing us apart. And it makes it so easy for our enemies to say, We don't really need the Themes, they're more trouble than they're worth, they're just a bunch of gangsters and racketeers, let's get rid of them. I want you to think about that very seriously. Every time a Blue beats up on a Green or a Green sets fire to a Blue house, you're digging your own graves. It's got to stop.

"So from now on, there won't be any more Blues and Greens. Instead, there'll be one Theme. Purple. Yes, that's right. For four hundred years it's been treason for anyone except the emperor to wear purple in public. From today, you'll all be wearing it. My colour, my Theme colour, your colour. One Theme, purple, with the emperor as Theme Leader. My Theme, your Theme. My city, your city. Our Theme. Our city.

"And to prove to you that I mean what I say, in due course all the officers in the Purple Theme will be elected, by you, the people. No more favouritism, no more graft, no more jobs for the boys. You'll get to choose who runs the Social Fund, who's responsible for welfare and arbitration, who's in charge of night watches and keeping your streets and homes safe. You can choose the men who are doing those jobs now, if you think they're doing it well, or you can have someone else, it's up to you. But it's you they'll answer to, and if you don't like them, you can get rid of them. No more bosses, and that's a promise. Your servants, not your masters.

"Well, that's all I've got to say. If you don't like it, here I am. My whole life I've lived for you, and if you want me to die for you, that's fine by me. Any takers?" (Pause: long enough but not too long.) "That's settled, then. Long live the Purples. Long live the Empire."

Dead silence. Then a cheer. Then deafening cheers on all sides; purple, purple, purple. Wishing I could've thought of a suitably Imperial colour with only one syllable, I turned round and marched smartly off, and my Lystragonians closed in round me like a suit of armour.

4

"I did exactly what you told me to," I said. "I abolished the Themes."

I've never seen anyone so angry in all my life. But I had Captain Very and ten guards between me and him, and they were watching him the way a good dog watches a stranger: one move and I'll have you.

"Like hell you did," Gelimer said.

"Oh, for crying out loud," I said. "Were you listening? I just abolished the Blues and the Greens, and nobody raised a finger to stop me. If we'd done it your way, we'd be cowering in here while that mob out there bashed down the gates with rafters."

"Elected officers—"

"In due course, I said. Meaning sometime, meaning probably never. You really ought to listen, you know. You might learn something."

If looks could kill. But they can't, can they?

"As and when we have elections," I went on, "the people

will get a chance to vote, yes. They can vote for you and
the Optimates, or for Popilius and his Commonwealthers,
and everything will be exactly the way it is now, except that
instead of being at war with the Themes, you'll be running them."

There's the old phrase, the penny drops. And if you drop
a penny from the top of the Beacon tower in Old Town and it
lands on someone's head, it'll smash his skull like an egg. The
penny dropped, and landed. Gelimer looked at me. Didn't say
a word, just gazed.

"Meanwhile," I went on, "we do a bit of winnowing. The
small Theme bosses stay in place, because they know their
turf and how to get things done. The upper echelons have
got to go, naturally; you can arrest them for treason or they
can meet with unfortunate accidents, doesn't really matter
which so long as it's discreet and done very quickly. Then
we announce the new provisional upper hierarchy of the
Purple Theme. Me, then you, and you can choose who you
want for everything below that. That'll be the caretaker
hierarchy pending elections, which unfortunately can't
be held until the state of emergency is over. You'll have to
arrange for an emergency, but that shouldn't be a problem."
I paused, as chivalry demanded. Even in the arena, you give
the other man a chance to get up again before you finish him
off. "That's what I just said out there, clear as day, only you
weren't listening."

I glanced sideways at Captain Very. He was standing
perfectly still. It occurred to me that all I had to do was
provoke Gelimer into a word or gesture that Captain Very
could interpret as threatening, and I'd be rid of Gelimer,
and probably all the senators standing huddled behind

him into the bargain. My hands would be clean, of course; an overzealous officer, you can't really condemn a man for doing his job, particularly when it's guarding the life of the emperor. All Gelimer's fault, certainly not mine. I considered what I'd need to say to trigger the desired reaction. Just a few well-chosen words, that was all. Playing with people's emotions is what I'm paid to do, and it's not nearly as difficult as you might think. Should I? If Gelimer was in my shoes, he'd do it like a shot; and so, probably, would Artavasdus, rest his soul, maybe also Nicephorus, also of blessed memory; my dad, almost certainly, if he'd thought of it. And Hodda; you bet. A man is known by the company he keeps. I decided not to.

There was once a king in a far-off land who said, when you have them by the balls, their hearts and minds will follow. "Well?" I said.

"That was pretty smart," said Gelimer.

"Thank you."

"I was wrong about you," he said. "I thought you were a two-bit actor pretending to be a no-brain sand fighter."

"Easy mistake to make."

"Instead, you're a real piece of work." I saw Captain Very's hand twitch, but that was all. I don't think Gelimer noticed. He was preoccupied. "Very smart. I can see how you've got to the top. Not bad, for a two-bit Theme bruiser."

"We all have to start somewhere," I said, as mildly as I could. "Half the emperors on the list started off as infantry privates, worked their way up through the ranks, staged a coup. That's the wonderful thing about the empire, anybody at all can be emperor. Not a senator or a commissioner or a priest, or even a doctor or head of department in the civil service. But emperor, hell yes, why not? It's one of the things I love about our great country."

Gelimer took a deep breath. "You did a good job," he said. "Only next time, you might tell us what you're going to do before you do it."

I nodded. "Next time you'll listen," I said.

5

Back to the palace along the Royal Circle, in the state coach, with cheering crowds every step of the way. I wondered if they'd been in front of the temple when I did the big speech, or if they knew what had been in it.

All that cheering meant you couldn't hear yourself think, so Hodda didn't have an opportunity to express herself till we were back in the Imperial apartments, with the door bolted and ten Lystragonians standing to attention outside.

"What on earth possessed you—?" she started.

"Desperation." I hadn't meant to shout. "The prospect of standing up in front of all those people and getting my arms ripped off. Have you ever seen a man kicked to death by a crowd? I have. It's not uplifting or aesthetically pleasing, and I'm damned if it's going to happen to me. So I took a chance."

She nodded; from her that's garlands of flowers and a gold medal. "But you shouldn't have taunted Gelimer like that. You got carried away. You were showing off."

I lay down on the bed and closed my eyes. Never been so

tired in all my life. "Yes, I was rather," I said. "I got into it a bit too much and I couldn't make myself stop. I felt this need to say clever things."

"Bad idea. You don't want to get him riled up."

"I know." I sighed. "Why is it nobody's prepared to admit that my Purple Theme idea is a stroke of genius? It is, you know."

"I'd have made it gold, personally. Purple sounds silly."

"Purple's the emperor's colour."

"Yes, I know, and you explained. But purple sounds silly."

"I've just saved all our lives and solved a major social problem, and that's all you can say. Purple sounds silly."

"Well, it does."

"And you can make a cheap fake purple dye by mixing blue and red. If I'd said gold, only the rich bastards could've afforded it."

"Or white. White would've been good."

"There's a quarter of a million milkfaces camped outside the City and you want us all to call ourselves Whites."

"Purple." She said it in a clown's voice. "Purple, purple, purple. You can't even say the word without spraying the front three rows with spit."

I really don't like the feeling of going to bed (or in this case, chair) not knowing whether the world will still be there in the morning. I don't particularly mind knowing in advance that something bad is going to happen. It's been the case for so much of my life that I've got used to it. Obviously I'm delighted when I have something nice to look forward to. But uncertainty; when things could go either way, wonderfully good or catastrophically bad, and you have no idea which, and there's nothing whatsoever you can do to influence the outcome – I hate that.

How much notice would I get if the world was about to end? As I leaned back in my chair, which had gone from being luxuriously comfy to an instrument of torture, don't know why, I figured that in the worst-case scenario it would take overwhelming force somewhere between fifteen seconds and a minute to slaughter the ten Lystragonians standing guard outside our door, and one or two minutes to smash the door down; it was pretty solid, cross-ply oak three inches thick, three bolts as thick as your thumb. Between one and three minutes, therefore. There are some contexts where three minutes can be an eternity, but not this one.

Thinking about how little I could accomplish in three minutes, I fell asleep, and was woken up by a gentle, discreet tapping at the door; not a battering ram, just someone's knuckles. Of course, the best way to get through a three-inch oak door is to have someone on the inside open it for you. "Who's there?" I stage-whispered, so as not to wake Hodda.

"Captain Qobolwayo, Majesty."

Who? Then I remembered. *Qobolwayo* is Its Very Essence in Lystragonian. I'd fixed up a sort of signal with Captain Very, for just this sort of thing. If he wanted to come in and there was no danger, he was Captain Qobolwayo. If he was knocking on the door with a bunch of assassins holding a knife under his chin, he was Captain of the Guard. "Hold on," I said, "I'm coming."

Hodda lifted her head. "What's the matter?"

"Go back to sleep." I shot back the bolts, lifted the latch and opened the door a hand's span, just enough to afford me a clear view of Captain Very's deceptively gormless-looking face.

"The Senate's compliments," he said, "and would it be convenient for you to meet with them?"

That needed thinking about. "Come in," I said, and held the door open.

I don't think I've ever shocked anyone more in my life. The idea of actually setting foot inside the Imperial bedchamber, except for the purposes of defending the emperor to the last drop of his blood, was clearly something he'd never even considered. As for entering the Imperial bedchamber while the empress was in there, too, possibly in her nightie, or nothing at all—

"Come on," I snapped. "You're letting the draught in."

I think, given the choice, he'd have preferred to be massacred to the last man; but since that option wasn't available he did as he was told. Hodda, yawning, with the sheet under her armpits, said, "Who the hell's that?" I told her, Captain Very. "Oh, right," she said, and flopped back onto the pillows.

"Say that again," I said.

"Majesty?"

"Repeat the message."

Which he did, word for word. "What, now?" I said.

Captain Very was gazing at a spot on the wall just behind my head. "They didn't say, Majesty. Just, would it be convenient?"

It's hard not to like someone who's genuinely prepared to be cut to pieces defending you from all harm, even if he is ridiculously large and painfully shy. Also, on those occasions when I could get past all the Vice-Gerent-of-Heaven, Brother-of-the-Invincible-Sun stuff and talk sensibly to him, he was bright, down-to-earth and a good sort generally. "What do you reckon?" I said.

He thought for a moment before answering. "Something happened last night," he said, "but I don't know what. I tried to find out but nobody's talking to me."

"I don't like the sound of that."

"No, Majesty."

I looked over my shoulder. Hodda had gone back to sleep. She's like a snail out of its shell in the early morning. "You know this place better than I do," I said. "I want a room where you can get all your lads inside lining the walls without it being too obvious, and where we can fight our way out into the street if we have to."

Took him maybe a second and a half. "The Peacock cloister, Majesty."

"Is that the one with the little square of lawn in the middle, and a fountain?"

"Yes, Majesty."

"Exits?"

"One into the Ivory Chamber, one out into the rose garden. Or we could retreat onto the lawn and form a circle."

"It'll do," I said. "Tell the Senate I'll meet them in the Peacock cloister in twenty minutes. Then get your boys and come straight back here."

Twenty minutes, to put on all the gear. Just as well I've had plenty of practice changing in and out of ludicrous costumes in no time flat. "What are you doing?" she said, propping herself up on one elbow.

"Just popping out for a bit," I said.

"Dressed like that."

"I've got to go and meet some people. Just routine stuff."

"I'm coming too."

"Not allowed. Protocol."

"Fuck protocol."

"I don't think it's the fuckable sort."

She glared at me. "After yesterday's performance, I'm coming too. You're not fit to be out on your own."

And why not, I thought. Besides, on balance, she'd probably be safer with Captain Very and our guardian angels than stuck on her own where everyone would know where to find her. "You'd better get dressed, then. You'll have to hurry."

She swore at me, which I think was uncalled for, and dived into the clown outfit. All credit to her; I'd had five minutes start on her, but she was all ready and looking definitively regal when the captain came back to fetch us.

The message had said "the Senate" but that didn't mean anything; could be the whole lot of them, or a delegation of twenty, or a subcommittee of five, or just Gelimer using the collegiate plural. In the event, I'm guessing there were between fifteen and eighteen – principal magistrates, party leaders, that sort of thing. One face, though, was missing. They stood up as I walked in, and the guards fanned out round them.

"Where's Gelimer?" I said.

There was this tall, skinny man with a triumphal arch for a nose. I'd seen him before but hadn't caught his name. "Gelimer no longer speaks for the Senate," he said.

"Since when?"

"In an emergency session held last night at the House, it was resolved—"

"Who the hell are you, anyway?"

He looked at me, and I think he caught sight of Captain Very standing right behind me. I'm tall. Very's a head taller than me. Then he glanced round. Not sure what at, but wherever he looked, all he'd have seen would've been guards. "My name is Materculus," he said. "I lead the Patriotic Alliance, and the House has chosen me—"

"Is he alive?"

I got the impression I'd touched on a sore topic there. "Yes, of course," Materculus said, in a tone that implied that there was no *of course* about it.

"Where is he?"

"It was felt necessary to place him in protective custody. For his own safety, it goes without—"

"I know what protective means, thank you. Fetch him. Now."

Behind me I heard a hiss, as it might have been a sharp intake of breath, but I ignored her. Materculus looked at me for maybe a whole second, which was absolutely the longest possible time I could allow for disobedience if I was going to go through with this idiotic strategy. Then he nodded. "Majesty," he said; then he turned and looked at one of the senators, who got up to leave. I half turned to Captain Very, but he was way ahead of me; he snapped his fingers and pointed, and five of his men fell in beside the departing senator, who looked rather miserable, as well he might.

"On behalf of the House," Materculus started to say but I cut him short.

"Not a word out of you," I said, "till Gelimer gets here. And that goes for the rest of you."

Which left us with a rather fraught quarter of an hour of silent sitting around, during which Hodda leaned across and whispered in my ear, "Are you out of your tiny mind?"

"Be quiet," I whispered back.

"You can't talk to these people like that."

"I can't not talk to them like that," I pointed out. "It'd be out of character."

Puzzled look. "Whose character?"

"Mine."

At which point she gave up and started picking at a loose thread on the hem of her divitision, and not long after that the soldiers came back, with the sad-looking senator and Gelimer, with a swollen jaw, one eye closed and his left arm in a sling. He looked absolutely terrified, and there were significant stains on the crotch of his snow-white senatorial robe.

"That's your idea of protective, is it?" I said. "You're not very good at it."

It was one of those moments – you get them occasionally in the theatre and they're terrifying – when nobody knows what's going to happen next. And they were all waiting for me.

"Don't any of you try and explain," I said (as though I dealt with this sort of thing every day). "I can guess what's been happening here. Captain, if your men would be so kind as to escort these gentlemen to the Ivory Chamber and keep them there. I'm going to have a few words with Senator Gelimer."

Lambs to the slaughter – actually, I saw plenty of lambs being led to the slaughter when we lived in a sixth-floor tenement room overlooking the stockyards, and the stupid creatures obviously had no idea where they were going or what was going to happen to them when they got there. Captain Very sent about half his men with them, and the rest stayed where they were. I tweaked a corner of his sleeve and took him aside for a moment.

"If these jokers order the army to come and get me, what do you think will happen?"

That moment of intense thought; or maybe he wasn't

thinking deeply, just figuring out how to say what he wanted to say in Robur. Anyway, it was always most impressive. "Hard to tell," he said.

"That's not helping."

"I'm sorry. I think if they tried that, only about a quarter of the company commanders would obey. After all, you're not just the emperor, you're Lysimachus. I think between a quarter and a third of the army would actively support you, to the extent of locking shields against their comrades-in-arms. If that happened, the pro-senatorial quarter would almost certainly back down. It's one thing to obey an order that's technically within the established chain of command, quite another to slog it out in the street against your own side, with a fair chance of losing and getting killed now or hanged later. That's how I read it anyhow," he added. "I could be wrong."

Well, I asked. "Thanks," I said. "Is there any way those bastards in there could get a message out of the palace?"

This time he didn't think. "No, Majesty."

"That's all right, then."

I went and sat down beside Gelimer; and if I hadn't got to know him so well lately, I'm not sure I'd have recognised him. I don't know what they'd done to him – just a few light smacks, by my dad's standards, but for a man like that, more than enough to destroy him entirely.

"What happened?" I asked.

He turned to look at me. "They told me you were out of control and I wasn't fit to run you any more," he said. "I tried to reason with them, and they—"

"Yes, I can see that."

"Popilius wanted to kill me," he said, and the pain in his voice would've made a brick weep. "Ennius and Laeso wouldn't let him; they said I'd be useful as a hostage. They put me in a cellar, in the dark. They said if I made so much as a sound, they'd break my arms and legs."

"Don't think about it," I said gently. "I've got them locked up safe for now; they can't talk to anyone."

He gazed at me, then reached out, grabbed my hand and squeezed it.

"Much as I'd like to," I said, "I can't just slaughter the lot of them, so what I was thinking is this. We put the ringleaders on trial for treason, in public, where everyone can see. We'll make them out to be enemies of the people, dead set on bringing down the Themes, and we'll nail their heads up on an arch somewhere. Then I'll pardon the rest of them, at your passionate request. And we'll get rid of all the company commanders who might be on their side and put our people in instead. How does that sound?"

He nodded. I think he'd run out of words. I felt sorry for him. His world had just collapsed around his ears, and nothing would ever be the same again. And that's what we in the trade call tragedy.

6

We still didn't really know whether we'd got away with the Themes thing. I couldn't think who to talk to about it. I hardly knew anybody around the palace, apart from Captain Very. Out there somewhere, on the other side of my substantial oak-ply door, were a couple of thousand clerks who ran the empire and were supposed to know everything, but I had no idea how to get in touch with them. It's always quiet in the palace. Nobody shouts or runs in the corridors. They talk in soft voices with their heads close together and wear felt-soled shoes. Anything could be happening outside (riots, the enemy breaking through the wall, the end of the world) and you wouldn't know about it. Every day the same, and the only new faces are ambassadors.

There's also a very specific way of doing things, designed to stop things getting done. Nothing wrong with that, since ninety-two out of every hundred things done by any government will turn out to be counterproductive and just plain stupid, but you can take checks and balances too far. I wanted to know if I was a hero, or if I'd sparked off a civil war, and I didn't know who to ask.

So I asked Captain Very. "I need a clerk," I said.

He looked at me gravely. "They're afraid to talk to you," he said.

"Afraid in what sense?"

He looked down at his hands, which meant he was telling me something I wouldn't want to hear. "They don't know if you'll still be the emperor this time tomorrow," he said. "So they don't want to be associated with you, if they can help it."

I could see their point. "Bring me the most senior clerk you can catch," I said. "Quick as you like."

She was lolling on the bed, looking at me. "Don't start," I said.

"Charming. I was about to say, that was pretty smart."

"I doubt that, somehow."

"Suit yourself." She propped herself up on one elbow. Nobody can do languid like she can. "It's what I'd have done. That's a compliment."

I sat down. "What would you do next?"

"Find out what's going on, obviously. Until we know that, we can't decide anything."

"Agreed." I put my feet up on a priceless ivory occasional table. One of the legs broke. She laughed. "What can we do till he gets back?" she said.

"I don't know. Try and figure out some sort of backstop plan, I guess."

"Let's play Auditions instead."

I couldn't help it; I burst out laughing. In case you don't know, Auditions is the word game we play while we're hanging about in the wings waiting to go on. I won't try your patience with the rules, which are silly and inconceivably complicated, and unless you know the rules the game makes no sense. Suffice to say we had a thoroughly enjoyable game, which I won, though she maintained I cheated; and then Captain Very came back, with one of his sergeants and a clerk.

I've played eunuchs loads of times but never actually met one before. Most of the senior officials in the palace administration are eunuchs. It's the only known cure for nepotism and it doesn't really work; key jobs get handed out to idiot nephews instead of idiot sons. It strikes me as rather a drastic way of getting on in the civil service, but in most aristocratic families the fourth son in each generation gets chopped and they think nothing of it. I got the impression that this particular specimen hadn't come willingly.

"Name and job title," I said.

He was a short man, skinny, with a round face and short, curly hair. "My name is Spado," he said, in a high, very refined voice. "I'm the permanent deputy secretary to the Count of the Stables."

I glanced at Captain Very, who nodded; a big shot. "You'll do," I said. "Do you know who I am?"

"Yes, Majesty."

"Splendid. I'm new at all this, and I need somebody to look after me. Tell me what's going on, how to do things, stuff like that. You can do that?"

"Of course."

"Marvellous. You start straight away. Go and find out if the Themes are out smashing and looting, and if so what anybody's doing about it. And I want to know what the army thinks about all this, the Themes and the spot of bother we had with the Senate." I paused. "You know all about that?"

"Yes, Majesty."

"Right," I said. "And when you've done that, I want a list of who's who and who does what in the civil service, and who I need to talk to about what. Then the same for the army and the navy. And you'd better find me a dozen clerks I can trust, to handle letters and reports and all that."

Not a flicker. "Yes, Majesty."

"Good. Oh, and in case you were wondering, the captain here will stay with you wherever you go, and if the thinks you're up to anything, he'll stab you to death. For the time being, anyway. Sort of a probationary period."

Maybe his eyes opened a little bit wider, maybe not. What the hell. The ability to stay calm is an asset in administrative work. "Understood," he said. "Is there anything else I can do for you?"

"Yes. Find me somewhere I can use as an office, not too big, and where the captain can control who goes in and out. He can advise you on that."

When they'd gone, she said, "So you're taking charge, are you?"

I nodded. "I think I've got to. Otherwise—" I let her think for a second or two. "You saw what happened with the Senate. We're this close to getting our throats cut, so we need to be in charge of *everything*."

She contemplated me, as if she was considering a play for the Gallery. "Fair enough," she said. "If that's the way you want to go."

"It absolutely isn't. But like I said, I don't really see we've got a choice."

"Not if we stay here."

That took me by surprise. But I didn't need any distractions.

"I don't think we've got a hope in hell of sneaking out quietly through a downstairs window, if that's what you're thinking."

She smiled. "Besides," she said, "you want to stay. Of course you do. You're the fucking *emperor*."

I felt I hadn't deserved that. "And you're the empress," I said. "Isn't that every girl's dream?"

"Not mine. Not like this."

"Nor mine," I told her. "Doing this job makes me realise how ungrateful I've been all these years. It's true, you really don't know when you're well off."

7

When I was a kid – you're sick of hearing about my irrelevant and unedifying childhood, but bear with me just one more time – there was a Theme boss in the Greens, colleague and friend of my dad, who ran half a dozen wards adjoining Dad's turf. They were very much alike in lots of ways. Because of, or in spite of, that they were great friends; Uncle Luto, I used to call him, and every time he came to our house he gave me a honey-cake or fifty trachy; and flowers or a couple of yards of silk for my mother, and a bottle of the good stuff for him and Dad to share. I remember him as a big, round man with bushy white hair. It gushed up from the front of his shirt, scrambled up his face like ivy and exploded in a luxurious tangle on top of his head. I never gave him a moment's thought, except as a bringer of treats and a nice man generally.

Then one day I was inside the house and I heard the most appalling racket outside, mostly angry voices, male and female. I went to look out of the window, but my mother held me back. I wasn't having that. I was twelve years old, reckoned I was a grown man, like you do at that age if you're stupid. I ducked under her arm and headed for our front door, which was open.

There was Dad, standing out in the street, and on the ground in front of him was Uncle Luto, with his arms round Dad's knees, sobbing. Behind him was a big crowd, with axe-handles and bricks and God knows what else. I saw that Uncle Luto was bleeding.

"Well, did you or didn't you?" my dad said.

"For God's sake," said Uncle Luto, "what does that matter? I'm your friend."

I couldn't see Dad's face, he had his back to me. But he must have known I was there, because he said, "Come here, son."

I wasn't sure I liked the look of the crowd, but if Dad was there I knew there was nothing to be afraid of. I went round and stood next to him.

"You see this man here," Dad said, loud enough to carry to the crowd. "He's been stealing Theme funds." Uncle Luto shook his head and mumbled something, but I didn't dare look at him. "What do you think about that, son?"

"It's bad," I said.

"Speak up, son, I can't hear you."

"It's very bad," I said.

"That's what I thought," Dad said. "If a man does a thing like that, you can't let him get away with it, can you?"

"No, Dad," I said.

"What do you think we ought to do with him, son?"

I looked at the crowd, then at my dad. Then I kicked Uncle Luto in the mouth, as hard as I could.

Dad smiled as he shoved me well clear; then he brought the heel of his boot down hard on his friend's ear, and took a long step back. The crowd did the rest. It lasted about three minutes, but two minutes was just crunching up a dead body. Then Dad clapped his hands three times and the kicking stopped. He gestured with his thumb and the crowd sort of melted away. He looked down at the mess on the ground, then grabbed me by the elbow and marched me inside and shut the door.

A year or so later, he told me that he'd killed Luto with that boot strike; it was the least he could do for an old pal, even though he'd betrayed the Theme. I didn't say that I'd seen Luto move several times after that, because I knew Dad had seen it, too. He never mentioned the matter again after that.

What I did had no effect on the outcome, so it made no difference, so it didn't matter. At the time I believed I was destined to be a good little Green soldier. If you'd asked me then what I'd learned from Uncle Luto's death, I'd have answered: never, ever embezzle Theme funds.

Ask me the same question now, I'll give you a different answer. The original answer is still true, and the facts haven't changed, but I believe the answer I'd give you now is equally true, though back then I'd have denied it absolutely.

So, the truth isn't immutable; it can change. I'll go further; inevitably it changes as we change, just as the twelve-year-old kid who booted his dad's best friend in the teeth isn't the man just crowned emperor – undeniable fact, susceptible of objective proof. Measure them: different heights. Weigh them: different weights. Ask them about their core values: get two diametrically opposing answers. Two entirely different animals: the same man. The kid who stomped a Theme traitor: the emperor who abolished the Themes by a trick.

In fact, the truth is so flexible it can accommodate practically everything. The kid who was Notker, the man who used to be Notker, became Lysimachus, became His Majesty Lysimachus II. You'll argue that Lysimachus wasn't my name; big deal. Cleophon IV, nicknamed the Invincible, wasn't called Cleophon when he was twelve years old. He had a different name, eight syllables long, meaning Blue Horse in Euxine. He changed his name to Cleophon when, as captain of the palace guard, he assassinated Lerus II and seized the throne. He chose Cleophon because Cleophon III, fifty years earlier, had been the last of the glorious Manethrite dynasty and people loved and trusted the name. Perfectly legitimate, statesman-like act, and Cleophon IV saved the empire from the Aram no Vei, and if there's one thing nobody can deny in this life, it's that the end justifies the means.

The hell with it. If the truth really was absolute and immutable, how could someone like me be expected to live with himself?

Don't get me wrong. I don't hate my father. I learned so much from him. From him I learned how to defend myself; how to push people around, either by bullying or cajoling; how the Themes work; how people en masse think and react; how to use other people to get what you want; how to do all the above and still be loved. If it hadn't been for him I'd never have been emperor – and just think how deeply, genuinely proud he'd have been of me, his little boy, on the Imperial throne. I've never for one moment doubted that he loved me; and really and truly, what more can you ask than that?

The news, said Secretary Spado, was that there was no news. No riots, no looting, no angry mobs, no mobs of any sort. This might be because the Senate, either before or shortly after making its move against Gelimer, had ordered its sympathetic senior officers in the military to arrest and detain the hierarchies of both Themes, right down to divisional level. Shrewd move, smarter than I'd have given them credit for (or maybe they'd actually been listening to what I said). No riots, because nobody ranked high enough to organise a riot. The junior officers of both Themes weren't going to make a move on their own initiative, because they'd been taught from infancy that it takes a divisional rep or higher to authorise any kind of militant action, and unauthorised action would earn its instigator a street kicking at the very least. In the past, in my dad's day, it had never been possible to paralyse the Themes in this way because the authorities never knew who all the Theme bosses were; one or two in each quarter, maybe, but not all of them. It was only because the Themes had won their long, bitter fight to be recognised and given a share in government that it was now possible to kill them off.

Army officers unswervingly loyal to the Senate were listed in Schedule B, and the clerk who'd compiled the list had helpfully written next to each entry the name of a suitable replacement, so all I had to do was initial the bottom of each page. Loyalist civil service officials were Schedule C, and I'd have to rely on Spado to come up with substitutes, but that wasn't quite so urgent, and, besides, there were only a couple of dozen of them and they were in relatively lowly positions –

"Hang on," I said. "What about all the youngest sons of senatorial families? There must be hundreds of them."

Spado gave me look, half-scorn, half-pity, appropriate for someone trying to deal with something he can never hope to understand. "The service is institutionally loyal to the emperor," he said. "The Senate is an irrelevant relic."

"But it's their own fathers and brothers."

"That's how things work. The service runs the empire. The emperor allows them to do so. The Senate only gets in the way." He gave me his you-just-don't-get-it look, which I was to come to know well. "Yes, we feel a degree of loyalty to our families and our class, that's only natural. But there's a supervening loyalty to the service."

You mean the empire, I almost interrupted but fortuitously didn't.

"It's a bit like when a woman marries," he went on. "She leaves her father for her husband. When you join the service, you become part of the greatest institution in the world."

Oh, for crying out loud, I thought. Still, my father felt that way about the Greens. "What about policy?" I said. "I thought you weren't supposed to interfere with that."

Bless the child, said the look in his eyes, how sweet. "We don't concern ourselves with abstract issues, if that's what you mean. The Senate, of course, thinks about nothing else. That explains why it's gradually dwindled away over the last three hundred years. And the emperor is mostly preoccupied with ceremony and protocol, except when there's a crisis, of course."

"And then?"

"We advise him of his options and carry out his instructions."

I nodded. "The siege is a crisis."

"Of course."

"So you'll do what I tell you."

"Naturally," he said, face of stone, "in all matters pertaining to the crisis. As to ordinary everyday administration, we wouldn't dream of bothering you with trivia."

Such as raising money or organising labour or procuring and distributing essential materials. Quite. It occurred to me

to wonder whether Nicephorus and Artavasdus and Faustinus
had ever bothered to talk to this man, and whether they'd still
be alive if they had. And the Themes; now I could see why the
Blues and Greens had to go. Because there was a third Theme
we hadn't known about when I was a kid, and the town wasn't
big enough for the three of them.

All my life I've found it useful to pretend to be slightly more
stupid than I am. "Thanks," I said. "That sounds like a very
sensible arrangement."

"It's worked pretty well for a thousand years."

"And if it ain't broke," I said. "Get me the names for
Schedule C as soon as you can. Oh, and I'd like a secretary. Not
your sort of secretary, someone who writes letters. A clerk."

"You mentioned that before," Spado said. "I have someone
in mind. When will it be convenient for you to see him?"

8

Enter Usuthus.

Around three hundred and sixty years ago, the Robur planted a colony, one of many, on the bleak shores of the Friendly Sea. For some reason it got forgotten about – clerical error, probably, left off a list, confused with somewhere else with a similar name – and so it was left to its own devices for a century and a half. About two-thirds of the colonists died in the first five years; those who survived did so because they threw themselves on the mercy of the local savages, who patiently explained to them how to grow food, how to build wattle-and-daub huts, how to cure animal hides, how to smelt copper and knap flint, useful stuff like that. When the Mother City finally remembered them and sent out a governor to collect a hundred and fifty years of back taxes, he found a tribe of barbarians, distinguishable from their neighbours only by the colour of their skins. The Coribands, as they'd taken to calling themselves, were quickly reabsorbed into the Robur nation and taught to be civilised and properly ashamed of themselves, to the point where exceptionally bright Coribands were allowed to settle in the City and do the sort of jobs the pure-blood Robur didn't fancy. Usuthus was one of these. His father, he told me, had been a district chieftain – *uSutu* is the name of the Coriband royal house – with sixteen wives and four thousand sheep; he slept in a hut we wouldn't keep pigs in, and his most precious possession was a pair of military-issue boots.

Note the past tense. The Coribands were wiped out by Ogus. The hundred or so of them living in the City were all that was left.

As soon as I saw Usuthus, I realised – with joy, with *great joy* – that Spado had made a mistake. He'd underestimated me, just as I'd hoped he would. I'd asked for a personal clerk: fine. Spado had hand-picked a smart young man debarred from any hope of ambition by accident of birth, someone who owed everything to the service, who could be relied on to run and manage me as directed by his true superiors and faithfully report back every relevant word I said. He'd stitched me up and tamed me, and everything would be grand.

Usuthus was a short, broad lad with an oversized head and hands as big as frying pans, light-skinned (a touch of the limewash, as they charmingly put it in the service) with a wonderfully extravagant tattoo of stylised peacocks fighting all over his face and the visible parts of his neck. The peacocks, he told me, signified noble birth. I knew all about that, having carried a supernumerary spear in *Auronia, or The Princess of Coriband* more years ago than I care to remember. Eudoxia (remember her? Best Lady Fleta ever) came on in Act 2 with the most amazing peacock painted right down her back. It was pointed out to her that actually the Coribands only tattoo the face. Yes, but if we did that, they wouldn't be able to see it up in the gallery. Anyway, Usuthus' peacocks weren't nearly as good, being merely the real thing, but they were pretty impressive nonetheless, and he didn't have to come in an hour early every night to draw them on; they were permanent.

"You don't mind them?" he said, mildly stunned.

"What's to mind?" I said.

"Everyone says I ought to wear a veil," he said. "Master," he added quickly, having forgotten who he was talking to. "But I think a veil would look even worse."

"I agree. You'd look like an idiot. Tell yourself, in ten years' time everybody's going to be getting tattoos, just so they'll look like me."

He laughed. Then it occurred to him that the Brother of the Invincible Sun was going out of his way to be nice to him, a thought that shut him up like a door. Like I said, smart.

"Sit down," I said. "No, over here where I can hear you. I want to ask you something."

"Master."

I poured myself a drink. Nearly offered him one, but that would've been weird, even for Lysimachus. "How well do you know the service?"

"Like the back of my hand. Master."

"Well, you would do," I said. "Your family's dead, your people have been exterminated, the service is all you've got left."

He hadn't learned the granite face yet, though he was well on the way. "Yes, Master."

"How do you feel about that? What happened back home, I mean."

So far out of his comfort zone, even the stars looked different. "How do I feel?"

I nodded. "Come on, it's a simple question. Sad? Angry? Suicidal? No great loss?"

"Sad. And angry."

"Scared?"

"Yes, Master."

"Me, too," I said. "And I'll tell you for why. While we're all sitting here playing musical chairs with the governance of the City, Ogus and a half-million savages are getting ready to do to my people what they did to yours. Does that worry you?"

"Yes, Master."

"I wish you wouldn't call me that. Sorry, where was I? It worries me, too. People in this city seem to have forgotten about it. There's this feeling that because we're still alive and life is going on just about as normal, somehow we've won. We haven't, though. Rather the reverse."

"Majesty?"

"Actually, that's worse. Forget I spoke." I leaned back in my chair and picked up a sheaf of papers. I'd found them on Gelimer's desk, which he hardly ever used now. "See these?"

"Master."

"Reports," I said. "Foreign affairs committee of the House, about nine months old. Very, very boring. But if you manage to wade through all the diplomatic shit, they're scarier than werewolves." I handed them to him. "Read them," I said. "Let's see how smart you are."

Next time I saw him he handed them back. "Well?" I said.

"I see what you mean," he said.

"Tell me what you make of them."

"Ogus is tightening the noose," he said. "He's overcommitted militarily, so he's using diplomacy to cut us off from our food supply."

I nodded. "Just diplomacy?"

"No, Master. He's smart. He's started building factories."

I clapped my hands slowly. "I was right," I said, "you're smart."

"He's not doing it himself," Usuthus went on, "but he's behind it. All the money that's going into setting up factories and buying or hiring skilled craftsmen, right across the East and the North; there's only one place it can have come from. Nobody else has got that much money, not even the Sashan or the Echmen."

"Who are at war, and therefore have no spare cash. Go on. Why's he doing this?"

"At the moment, we're indispensable. We make things people abroad want and can't get anywhere else. Also, City-made's got the most amazing prestige. If you're a chief of some savage tribe somewhere, and you've got a lamp or a wine cooler made right here in the City, even if you don't drink wine—"

"Like your dad and his army boots," I said.

He smiled. "About a year ago Ogus bought a hundred thousand prisoners from the Sashan. The prisoners were Echmen, from a city way out East, where they used to make fine porcelain, textiles, fancy metalwork, before the Sashan captured it and burned it down. We make fine porcelain, textiles and fancy metalwork."

"In a totally different style."

"People can learn. But what else would Ogus want with a city full of craftsmen? His people aren't interested in that sort of thing. Well, some of them are, but it's not advisable to let on about it if you know what's good for you. Ogus is planning to put us out of business. And then we starve."

I nodded.

"Or, rather," Usuthus went on, "we dig our own graves first. When people abroad stop buying our goods, we send out the Fleet and try and take over their cities, to protect our trade. We've got to do this; we have no choice. The foreigners won't like that, not one bit. So they'll turn to their mighty neighbours for protection, the Sashan and the Echmen."

"Who are at war, so they're too busy."

"A land war," Usuthus said. "Both empires have substantial fleets, presently standing idle. In a long, nasty war you're always looking for new allies. It won't be long before our fleet comes up against theirs; one or the other, quite possibly both. Now the Robur fleet is the best in the world, but it's left over from when we had an empire almost as big as the Sashan, or the Echmen. If we sink sixty of their ships, they can replace them in a month. If they sink twenty of ours, we'd be lucky if we could build new ones inside six months. More likely a year, assuming we can get the materials. All the timber and stuff has to come in from abroad by sea. If we've got ourselves into a war with the Sashan—"

I raised my hand. I hadn't thought of that; not beyond the putting-us-out-of-business stage. "That'll do," I said. "Where did you get all that stuff? About the Sashan and so on."

"It's obvious," he said. "When you think about it."

"Absolutely," I said, having thought about it and not found it obvious. "So presumably the service has a range of contingency plans drawn up."

"I don't think so." He looked puzzled. "For a start, I don't know which department it would come under."

God almighty. "So in the whole of the City there's just two men clever enough to recognise something so obvious: you and me."

"I didn't say that," Usuthus said. "Probably it's occurred to a lot of people, especially in the higher grades. But not officially."

"Ah."

"Officially, there's not a problem. And wild speculation isn't encouraged."

"I bet it isn't," I said. "Well, that's about to change. What do you think we ought to do about it?"

He looked at me. "About Ogus and the factories?"

"Yes."

"I don't know. It's a problem. There doesn't seem to be an obvious easy answer."

"Ah."

He looked down at his hands. "That's why the higher grades don't want to think about it," he said. "They've thought about it, privately, like this, and decided there's nothing that can be done."

"A bit like death," I said.

"Excuse me?"

"We all die," I said. "Now you'd have thought an intelligent species like us, faced with something like that, we'd devote all our energy and our cleverness and all our money and spare time to finding a cure for death. But we don't. We accept it. By the time we're thirteen years old we just don't think about it. We put it out of our minds and turn our attention to other things. If we didn't, we wouldn't be able to function. And that's what the Senate and the service have done."

"I suppose so," Usuthus said. He didn't seem very happy

about it. "But that's how it is, surely. Some problems can't be solved."

I stood up. "Actually," I said, "that's not true."

"Majesty."

"Oh, don't look at me like that. I know, I sound like an idiot. But actually, you'd be amazed what can be done, if you've got absolutely no choice. Like, an alley rat from the Themes can become emperor. How unlikely is that?"

He laughed. Fair enough. It was a good line, and I did it just right. "True," he said.

"And half of that," I told him, "was luck, and the other half was the thought of what would happen to me if I didn't make the most of the luck. That's why the Invincible Sun gave us fear. It makes us smart. Show me someone who's afraid of nothing because he's got nothing to be afraid of, and I'll show you a cow. Humans are at their very best when they're scared shitless."

That was my exit line, only I had nowhere to go, so I sat down again. Usuthus looked at me. Then he said, "You have something in mind."

"No," I admitted. "Right now I'm staring up at the sky waiting for luck to drop at my feet. But when it does, I want to be ready for it. And that's where you come in."

9

"What are you up to?" she asked me.

I hadn't seen very much of her for a few days, and she was clearly bored out of her mind. Of course. No job on earth as boring as being empress, if you let it. What you're supposed to do is loll about in gorgeous splendour surrounded by a hundred ladies-in-waiting, all of noble birth, so with very little conversation. A woman who's been used to managing a theatre would obviously go mad after a few hours of that, so she'd chased the noble ladies away and found a quiet room at the top of a tower where she could put her feet up and read poetry, which she quite likes. But two days of that had been more than enough. Right now, she was ready to start breaking things.

"I'm stealing the civil service," I said.

She nodded approvingly. "That extraordinary little man with the chickens on his face."

"Peacocks."

"I stand corrected. He's part of it, I imagine."

"He's the key," I told her. "Right now, we're banjaxing all the official channels so that everything's got to go through him."

"Like the main sewer."

"Good analogy. In order to be valid, every order in this man's town has to be sealed with the Imperial seal. Not the Great Seal, of which there's only one, it's sort of the next seal down. And at the moment there's, what, thirty of them, all identical: one for each major department of state."

"With you so far," she yawned.

"By this time tomorrow," I said, "with luck, there'll be five, and all in one room."

Her eyes widened a little. "Clever."

"I thought so. There's six Coriband clerks working in the service. My pal Usuthus is one of them. The other five are sitting in a little room somewhere waiting for the seals to arrive. Usuthus is arranging for all the departmental seals to be called in, for an audit or something; then twenty-five of them will mysteriously vanish, and the Coribands take charge of the remaining five. Once they do, they're going to be very, very busy."

"And that's how you steal the civil service." She grinned at me. "Everything's got to go through that office, and your people control the logjam. You'll never get away with it."

I shrugged. "Vorderic and the giant," I said. "The giant traps Vorderic in his cave and says he's going to eat him at sunrise. During the night, Vorderic blinds the giant. The giant is very big and strong, but he can't catch Vorderic because he can't see him. If you want to tame a giant, put out his eyes."

"Actually, that is quite clever. Whatsisname thought of it, presumably."

"Yes. He's smart. And I'm smart, for recognising that."

"Of course you are, dear. Out of interest, though, why are you bothering?"

"Excuse me?"

"You just stole the civil service. Why? What do you want it for?"

Trouble is, so many people are smart, and not necessarily the ones you want to be. "There are two people in a room, and one knife. Who would you rather had it, you or him?"

"Throw it out the window."

"There is no window." Trust me, there's never a window. "Either we control it, or it's a threat. That's why I'm collecting things: the throne, the Senate, the army and now the service."

"And the Themes."

"Yes, them, too."

"But they're all irrelevant," she said. "You know that. So long as *he's* out there."

"Fine." I got up, walked over to the window and looked out. From our tower, you could see the sea. "Here's an idea. We get hold of a couple of big winter coats and fill the pockets with—"

"Small items of great value."

"Yes. When nobody's looking, we slip out of the palace disguised as jobbing musicians. We stroll down to the docks and get on the first ship that'll take us out of here. After that, our lives will be nothing but sheer uninterrupted pleasure." I paused. "Why haven't we done that?"

She looked at me. "We'd never get out of the palace."

"Exactly. The two most conspicuous people in the City can't just slip out of anywhere."

"In the middle of the night—"

"Past all those guards. And don't say, give them the night off, it doesn't work like that. It's the price we pay for not getting our throats cut in our sleep."

She lifted her head and gave me her best look. "Let's try it."

"You what?"

"Right now. A dummy run. Let's see how far we can get. Bet you we make it out into the street."

"It's broad daylight."

"Well, then. If we can make it out of here in the middle of the day, we'll know that the middle of the day is a good time." She paused and looked at me again. "You do want to go, don't you?"

"Are you crazy? Of course I do." Pause. "Actually, I was going to ask you the same question."

"Me?"

"You."

"Oh, come *on.*"

"Being empress," I said. "Best job in the world."

"Balls." She smiled at me. "I've been here, what, two months—"

"Less than that."

"I really don't know, time just sort of all runs together in this place. It feels like two months. It feels like twenty years. I've never been so *bored* in all my life."

"Yes, but even so—"

"If I have to stay in this place much longer, I'll kill someone. You know what I do all day?"

I'd asked myself that, certainly. "Nothing?"

"Exactly." Her eyes were blazing. And when they do that, you really can see them from the back of the gallery. "Beats me why anybody with half a brain would ever want this job.

Makes no sense. What do people see in it? Dressing up in quaint costumes? Sitting still looking regal? I can do that at the Gallery of Illustration and *get paid* for it. Dear God." She picked up a tea bowl, blue and white porcelain, very old and rare, dropped it and ground it into dust under her heel. "If I wanted to be an empress, I'd hire a writer to write me a play with an empress in it. That way, at least I'd be centre stage. I'd have something to do and people would listen to me. Being one for real—" Words failed her, never a good sign. "You can stuff it."

"Fine," I said. "Same goes for me, too."

"Oh, you," she said irritably, "you've got it easy compared to me. You get to leave the Imperial apartments. You don't have to spend all day banged up with a mob of silly rich women."

"No," I said, "I spend my days a couple of lengths ahead of getting killed, like the deer in a stag hunt. I tell you what, this job brings out the best in a person. I never realised quite how smart, imaginative and resourceful I am. And if I stopped being supremely all three for two minutes, my head'd be nailed up on a door somewhere. Bored? God, how I wish I could be bored. It must be sheer bliss."

We looked at each other.

"We'll need costumes," she said.

Thoughtful moment. It seemed like a lifetime since I'd last had any clothes of my own. As things stood, I didn't even know where my clothes were kept; they were brought to me, several times a day, and whisked away again as soon as I stepped out of them. Even if I knew, it wouldn't help. Apart from sheer silk underwear and linen shirts so fine you could barely feel them, my wardrobe consisted of dalmatics and divitisia, about a dozen of each, all identical, plus the buskins and lorus, both unique, which almost certainly hadn't been washed for three hundred years and which stank. She was better off; they let her wear pretty frocks under the uniform, substantial enough that she could go out in the street in them without getting stared at. But inconspicuous, no. Even round the palace, cloth of gold embroidered with seed pearls gets you noticed.

"We could make some," I suggested, "out of blankets."

She gave me a don't-try-my-patience look. "Really?"

Good point. Our bed linen was only marginally less gorgeous than the Imperial regalia. "Don't ask me to knock out a couple of guards so we can steal their kit," I said. "I'm in enough trouble as it is."

"There must be servants in this building," she said. "I mean proper servants, not Lord High Groom of the Chafing Dish servants. People who work for a living."

"There are," I said. "I've seen them."

"So," she said, "we sneak out, find where they sleep, and steal their spare clothes."

She hadn't said it with any real conviction, so I didn't bother answering. Instead, I pulled the red bell-rope. I had six bell-ropes, all colour-coded. The red one brought me Usuthus.

"For purposes of our own," I said to him, when he materialised scarily quickly, "Her Majesty and I need two battered old overcoats, the sort of thing the grooms in the stables wear."

"Master."

"I want you to fetch them. Don't send anybody else. Don't tell anyone who you want them for."

"Master."

"Quick as you like. And thank you."

He bowed and withdrew. "I don't like that," she said.

"Nor me," I told her. "He now knows that we're up to something. I think I can trust him. By the same token, Gelimer thought he could trust his boyhood friends in the Senate, and Nicephorus thought he could trust Gelimer. Probably for much better reasons."

She sat down wearily on a chaise longue and put her feet up. "That screws that, then."

"For today," I said. "But if we act normally for the rest of the day, maybe he'll forget about it."

"Is that likely?"

"No."

When Usuthus came back with the coats, I told him to leave them on the bed and go away. Then we examined them. Hiding them would be a problem in itself, because the royal bedchamber was painfully short of storage space. We tried lifting the mattress, but it was far too heavy, and the bed was boarded in (with exquisitely carved reliefs of scenes from scripture and pastoral fantasy) right down to the floor. Finally, by standing on a chair and tiptoe, I managed to stow them on top of the canopy over the bed.

"We put them on under the divitision," she said, "and take them somewhere where there's a cupboard."

"Great idea. Where?"

She thought, then pulled a face. "We sneak out and find somewhere with a cupboard."

The coats slid down off the canopy and landed in a smelly heap on the floor. I picked them up and threw them in the corner of the room. She gazed at them with utter distaste. "Saloninus says," she said, "that the unexamined life is not worth living. Our lives are so examined we can't even hide a coat. We've got to get out of here."

I sat down next to her, reached out and took her hand. She pulled it away. "I agree," I said. "But it's going to take some thinking about."

"Think quickly."

I always do. Quick as a flash, me. I can come up with something truly stupid in the time it takes you to blow your nose.

10

So there you are (to revert to an image I've used earlier), living a life of luxury and ease in your mountaintop villa, with magnificent views over the valley below and all the piping hot water you could ever want—

People do it, though. Fact is, I've never been outside the City in my entire life, but I'm given to understand that there's a great big city somewhere in Sashan territory built all round the base of a huge volcano. It's on an island, with the most amazing natural harbour, and the idea is that the moment the volcano starts playing up, everyone rushes down to the ships and gets well clear. They have a full dress rehearsal once a year, and everybody is taught from birth what to look out for, where to go and what to do; and the City does so well out of trade, because of its harbour, that everyone pays a half per cent tax, and with that money the City fathers have bought great big estates on the mainland so that the islanders will have somewhere to go when the big day comes. Not if, when; it's inevitable, they know that for a fact, like death. But, unlike death, they can see no reason why they shouldn't take it with them.

I can see you could live like that, at a pinch, if you know what's coming, what to look out for, where to go and what to do. By the same token, you could live like that if you *thought* you knew all that useful stuff, even if it turned out in the event that you'd got it dreadfully wrong.

I guess we were a bit like that island, only in reverse. We were the mountaintop, and the volcano was living all round us on three sides. But we, too, have a magnificent natural harbour and make our livings from trade, and there's loads of ships at the docks; and none of us know where to go or what to do, and there's no plan. I guess it would all be different if the volcano on the island had tried to blow up, once years ago, and all the people had rallied round with human chains of buckets and put the horrible thing out.

People get cocky is the truth of the matter. I think I neglected to mention that, in honour of my coronation, Ogus deployed his biggest trebuchet yet and launched a huge rock at the Yarnmarket district; not only did he miss, falling short and not even clearing the walls, but the throwing arm snapped, making the trebuchet overbalance and fall over, squashing its crew. The sentries saw the whole thing from the top of their tower, and it added just an extra smidgeon of joy to the municipal celebrations.

"We've felt for some time that Ogus' artillerymen have gone as far as it's possible to go with trebuchet design," the colonel of engineers told me, when I sent for him. "You can only make those things so big, and then they tear themselves to pieces. There's a limit to the stress you can put on wood and rope and nails, and we believe they've reached it." He gave me a cheerful smile. "I can show you diagrams and calculations, if you'd like to see them."

"I'll take your word for it," I said. "But they can still build machines that can clear the wall."

"Yes," he conceded, "but only just."

"Only just is enough," I said. "I was—" Stopped myself just in time; nearly said, *I was killed by one.* "I was nearly killed by a trebuchet shot, only a month or so ago. I was due to go to a dinner at a house down by the walls. I was too busy and gave it a miss, and that night the house was flattened."

"Lucky for all of us that you changed your mind," the colonel said. "But the solution's pretty obvious. Evacuate the houses directly under the walls, and you'll have no more trouble."

I gave him a look. "Good heavens," I said. "Why didn't I think of that?"

Later I made enquiries, but the chiefs of staff told Usuthus there was no suitable alternative candidate for colonel of engineers and they had full confidence in the present incumbent, so we were stuck with him.

A few days afterwards, I happened to look out of my tower window. I remember thinking, that's a particularly beautiful sunset. Then it occurred to me that it was later than that and, besides, the sun sets in the west.

I grabbed the red rope and nearly yanked it out of the wall. I needn't have bothered; a second or so later there was the most appalling hammering on the door. I asked who was there and got the all-clear signal: Captain Qobolwayo.

Usuthus was with him. I pointed to the window. Usuthus nodded.

"Fire," he said, "in the Tanneries. The bastards are shooting fire-pots."

No need to ask who the bastards were, in context. Nobody's tanned anything in the Tanneries for seventy years. Now it's one of the districts where the people from the Old Flower Market settled; hundreds of little shacks with wooden walls and thatched or shingled roofs. Also not that close to the walls. Of course, a fire-pot is considerably lighter than a bloody great rock, therefore travels further.

"I didn't know if you'd want to be disturbed," Captain Very said apologetically. "But he insisted."

Couldn't be bothered to answer that: I was looking round for something to put on over my Imperial silk nightshirt. I caught sight of the mouldy groom's coat in the corner. "You stay here," I snapped at Hodda, who was just starting to surface out of deep sleep.

"What's going on?" she muttered.

"Fire in the Tanneries."

"Right," she said, and snuggled her head back into the pillows.

I hadn't tried on the coat before. It was too short and tight across the shoulders. "Let's go," I said.

On the way, they told me that the captain of the City fire brigade was called Diocles, but he was under arrest for being a Senate loyalist; besides, the fire brigade never went east of the Butter Cross because they weren't welcome in Theme territory. I know, I said.

And I did, too. When I was a kid, there was a fire in the neighbourhood next door to Dad's patch. It should have been up to the local boss to deal with it, but he had a bit of a falling-over-drunk problem and was completely useless after dark, so Dad was hauled out of bed and had to take charge. Which he did, very effectively; it was one of the things the

Themes were genuinely good at, fighting fires. They had to be. And, of course, I went with him, and acted as his aide-de-camp and general runner, so I knew the drill. Under normal circumstances, I could've relied on the local Theme boss to take charge and see that everything was taken care of. But the circumstances weren't normal, because some idiot, who wore my underwear and shaved with my razor, had had the boss of the Tanneries judicially murdered.

"Excuse me," Captain Very asked, as we hurried though the streets. "What are we doing, exactly?"

"We're going to put out a fire," I said.

"You mean you, *personally?*"

I stopped, because I was out of breath. Shame on me: soft living. "Yes," I said. "And while we're at it, you—" I pointed at his sergeant, who'd been tagging along with us. "Go back and get the rest of the guard, all of them, and meet us at Tannery Stairs. No, don't look at him, do it."

Captain Very nodded and the sergeant ran. "With respect," Usuthus said.

"Shut your face."

Because, if not me, then who the hell? I knew what to do. Presumably there were other people who knew it too, but I didn't know who they were or how to find them, and a fire in the Tanneries wouldn't stop there. If the wind got up from the south the whole city could go up – I remember stopping dead and closing my eyes, trying to picture myself and seeing my father.

You need buckets, naturally, and hooks on long poles, for dragging thatch off roofs – they'd be in the Theme house, ready – and picks and shovels and sledgehammers and axes, for tearing down houses to make a firebreak. When we got there – the smoke was as thick as stew and I could feel the heat sunburning my face – we found the guards had beaten us to it. "Where is everybody?" I yelled, over the crackling.

Then I realised what I wasn't hearing, and the penny dropped. "Get over to the Theme house and ring the bell," I said. "And fetch the long hooks; they'll be up in the rafters. You lot, start pulling down that row of houses there." I pointed. The guards looked at me, and it occurred to me that maybe they didn't know how to pull down a shanty-town house real quick. Specialist knowledge, though commonplace in the Themes. "All right, leave that and go and collect buckets. The nearest well's over there, just behind the Pride & Endurance."

Usuthus and the captain were staring at me; how the hell did I know that? "If we take down these rows here," I said, pointing, "it'll stop the fire sweeping down south and getting to the lumber warehouses and the tar stores in Princesgate. If they go up, we've had it."

I heard a funny noise, a sort of swishing, and something flew over our heads. I thought at first it was some sort of bird. "They're still shooting," the captain said, and a fat orange bloom burst out of the ground about fifteen yards from where we were standing. Scared the life out of me.

"Nothing we can do about that," I heard myself say, and then I heard the Theme bell.

When the bell goes, everyone knows what to do. You drop everything and run to the Theme house, where the boss tells you where to go. Only, I remembered, there wasn't a boss. People would be flocking in and nobody to meet them. Idiot.

By the time we got there, the little square was crowded. They saw the guards and made way to let us through. I jumped up on the top step and took a deep breath. I couldn't remember my lines – it was a long time ago, for pity's sake, and I only heard it once. But I opened my mouth, and thank God it all came back to me.

"You lot—" (points) "—housebreaking tools. Two rows need to come down right away; the soldiers'll show you where. Women to the well, we'll need a bucket chain to damp down the firebreak. You lot, firehooks and drag the thatch off, four rows back from the fire on all sides, then work backwards from there. The soldiers will tell you what to do as we go along. That's all. Let's get to it."

It was only when they'd all run off to do what I'd told them that I realised, I'd been doing my father: voice, gestures, body language. Worked, though.

It was a long night, and I wasn't actually doing anything, just rushing about yelling orders and getting under people's feet. It didn't seem long at the time, because I was too busy thinking to notice. That's what you've got to do, if you're the boss in a situation like that. You need to form a picture in your mind and see all the pieces on the board, not just where they are now but where they ought to be and where they might get to if things start going horribly wrong, and where everything needs to be to counter that – all at the same time, seen from all angles. I coped because I'd seen my dad doing it, and because I've watched real professionals – Hodda and Momas and Olethria – staging a play. I asked Olethria how she did it once, and she said, you need to see it all in your head; oh, and back home she'd got a little toy theatre, and blocks of wood, three inches tall for the men, two and a half for the women, and she worked out every move to the inch the night before. I didn't have that luxury, but I could visualise the Tanneries as a stage, with Prompt and OP, wings and front and centre; not really very close, but close enough. All the world's a stage, according to Saloninus; that's not actually true, but if you pretend it is, it helps, when you're managing a fire.

As to the outcome, opinions differ. I think I made a pig's ear of it, because forty-six people died, seventeen of them because while we were scrambling about like blue-arsed flies ripping down Glory Row, the wind turned and sent the fire roaring like a furnace down Greenside, which I hadn't had time to evacuate. Also there was a godawful jam in the bucket chains because I had three teams drawing from one well, when there was a perfectly good conduit we could've punched a hole in only fifty yards up the street; and there were other things, too, which I'm too ashamed to mention. I distinctly remember standing on the steps of the Poverty & Silence, gazing hopelessly at an advancing wall of flame and watching bundles of dragged-off thatch on the ground bursting alight from the sheer heat, even though the fire was fifteen yards away; at which point, Captain Very came bounding up, drenched to the skin, and telling me it was all over—

"No it's not," I said, lying to myself. "If we could only get more buckets up here—"

"No, it's *over*," he said. "It's under control. We did it."

I pointed at the fire. "You call that—" and then it occurred to me that in front of that fiery wall was a wide-open space, just rubble and dirt and muddy pools of water, and that the captain might just possibly be right.

He was drenched to the skin because every few minutes he'd poured a bucket of water over his head before rushing back to where the action was; if he hadn't, he'd have been roasted to death. As it was, his hair and eyebrows were gone and the skin on his cheeks and hands was all blistered to hell;

about the only visible part of him that wasn't burned raw was his smile.

As I said, opinions differed. Just before dawn I realised I was too tired to think any more and I was doing more harm than good, so I handed over command to a couple of random Themesmen who'd been the real heroes of the hour and limped back to the palace with Captain Very, Usuthus and two guardsmen. All five of us were in a real mess and I was wondering aloud, in an abstract sort of way, how the hell we were going to prove to the sentries who we were.

"Don't worry about that," the captain said quietly. "I know a back way."

I was almost too tired to appreciate the significance of that. "Don't be silly," I said. "There's no back way into the palace, everybody knows that."

"Ah." He gave me a big grin. "Wait and see."

Interesting. Meanwhile, Usuthus was jabbering in my other ear about a triumph, and how it couldn't have come at a better time. "The emperor," he was saying, "leading the firefighting *in person*. Actually literally saving the City. No other emperor in living memory could've done that. He wouldn't have known how. He wouldn't have *wanted* to. This time tomorrow you'll be a *god*. We'll be able to do anything we want and nobody will be able to stop us."

"That's all right, then," I said.

"It'll have fixed the Theme question absolutely once and for all," he drivelled on. "Whose job is it to fight fires? The local Theme officer. Who fought the fire? The leader of Purple Theme. Perfect. It really couldn't have been better if we'd arranged it ourselves – only they won't be able to accuse us of setting the fire deliberately, because everybody saw the fire-pots whistling through the air. I can't think of anything that could've consolidated our grip on power better than this; it's what legends are made of. Lysimachus and the Great Fire. We'll have to see about a statue, of course."

If I hadn't seen Usuthus an hour earlier dragging an old woman out of a burning house, I'd have smashed his teeth in.

"And the coat," he went on, "the coat was just perfect. If you'd shown up in dalmatic and lorus, it'd have been a flop, you can bet. But the emperor in an old docker's coat, directing the rescue efforts—" He stopped. "So that's what you wanted it for. How did you know?"

"Shut up," I told him. "You're making my head hurt."

"We'll have to get it carefully cleaned and mended," he said, defying a direct order, "so you can wear it whenever you address the people. It can be your signature garment. It'll be how everyone visualises you, the old coat over the silk gown, that's an amazing metaphor."

"Captain, make him shut up. He won't listen to me."

But the captain only grinned at me. Apparently he'd stuck like it, just like his mother warned him. "It certainly won't have done you any harm," he said. "You were popular before, but now—"

"It's the best thing that could possibly have happened," Usuthus said.

I managed to forgive him for that, just about, eventually. Meanwhile, we'd fetched up outside a long grey stone building, with massive oak double doors. "I know where this is," I said. "This is the east side of the cavalry barracks."

Captain Very nodded. "Follow me," he said. "Probably best if we kept the noise down. We're not really supposed to be here."

He counted seven doors down, gave the eighth a shove and it swung open. Up a narrow flight of stone stairs, pitch dark, to a landing with a door on the left; through that. "We're in the roof space above the main stables," he whispered, as we trod warily on uneven wooden planks that creaked horribly with each step. "Watch out for the rafters, they're quite low."

I was trying to picture the layout in my mind. The cavalry barracks back onto the palace, but where, and next to what? It felt like it took an hour to get from one end of the roof to the other, but eventually the captain stopped and groped around for something; the latch of a door I couldn't see until he opened it and let through a shaft of pale yellow light.

We followed him through, and came out in a wide attic, illuminated by a slit in the roof covered over with parchment. "And this," the captain said, "is the roof directly above the laundry room in the east wing of the palace. That's why it's so hot in here."

He was right about that. Standing close to the flames had made my skin raw all over, and the heat was making it tingle like hell. "You mean to tell me," I said, "that anyone who can get into the stable yard, like we just did, can walk right into the palace."

Captain Very went all solemn. "It's a scandal," he said. "I'll get it seen to straight away."

"No," I said, "don't do that. After all, nobody knows about it except us."

"That's not quite true." He looked sheepish. "Actually, it's common knowledge for us, the Lystragonians, I mean. The fact is, we knocked that door through, about forty years ago."

"Is that right?"

"I'm afraid so. Back then, I don't know the details, but the emperor wasn't exactly popular at the time, and he wanted a bolt-hole only he and us knew about. And there it's been ever since."

"It can be our secret," I said.

"Yes, but anyone could find it."

"I don't think so," I said firmly. "Let's leave it as it is. You never know when something like that could come in handy."

If he'd been a dog, he'd have put his head on one side. Instead, he nodded. "Understood," he said. "Now, to get to the state apartments from here, we go this way."

I tried not to look as though I was committing every turn and distance to memory. When we came to a big horseshoe-top door, he sent the two guardsmen ahead to make sure the coast was clear. It was a while before they came back. We crossed a wide corridor, like a cloister, with about fifty doors on each side.

"The Exchequer offices," Usuthus explained. "Always a lot of people about at this time of day."

Noted, I thought. After that, we went up a lot of narrow spiral stairs and in and out of a lot of narrow passages, and I realised that my sense of direction, which has never been my best point, had given up entirely. Still, I had a fixed point – the Exchequer – from which I was fairly sure I could navigate my way to the laundry room. Or I could just ask one of the maids.

"And here we are on the top landing," Captain Very announced, opening a door for me. "Now we just go through the servants' door there, and they've got a straight run to the bottom of your tower."

I was exhausted: all those stairs after a long night. The backs of my calves were killing me. "I need a bath," I said. "I stink of smoke."

"I'll see to it," Usuthus yawned.

I'd forgotten. It takes sixteen people for the emperor to have a bath. "Don't bother about it," I said. "Send someone up with a bowl of water and a towel. Then go and get some sleep, for crying out loud."

I went into the bedroom and sat down on a chair.

"What the hell did you think you were playing at?" she said.

I turned my head. "Now what have I done?"

"Rushing about being the hero. I ask you."

I let my head loll onto my chest. "We put out a fire. What's the big deal?"

"You're not a hero." Real hissing, like a snake. "You're just an actor playing one. If you'd fucked it up—"

"But I didn't."

"But you could have, so easily. And it wasn't necessary. You could've ordered the soldiers to go and deal with it. Not our soldiers, the real soldiers, the army. But, no, you had to go charging off—"

"They wouldn't have known what to do."

"Are you kidding me? They're the *army*. Of course they can put out a fire."

And she was quite right, as ever. That was what the emperor would have done. Even Lysimachus. We pay their wages, it's what they're there for, et cetera. But going out there myself, taking charge, playing at being a Theme boss like my dad always wanted me to be; that was what *I* would have done. Did. Go figure.

"God, you smell bad. Go and have a bath."

I'd been meaning to tell her all about the secret way into the palace, which could so easily double as an exit. But you know what it's like, when you can't get a word in edgeways.

*

Usuthus was right. By late afternoon, a huge crowd had gathered in front of the palace, and they made it clear they were staying there until I came out and waved to them or something. So I did that, and the noise—

Old actors I've talked to tell me that the applause is what they miss. You think you can live without it, they say, when you quit the stage, but you can't. It's what the profession is all about; every night, hundreds of people tell you that you've done good, or at the very least you've done all right, and so you don't have to ask yourself that question. In no other walk of life do you get that affirmation and reassurance, they tell me, and really, how can a human being be expected to live and carry on living without it? How could you possibly tell if you're doing all right or not?

To which I tend to reply: have you ever actually looked at the sort of people who go to the theatre? The idle rich; the fat, complacent tradesmen; the scum of the earth; do you really value their opinions so very much? To which they reply: the audience is the people, the community, Mankind. What other opinion could possibly matter?

I know exactly what they mean. There's that moment, when you're taking your bow at the end of the show. It's done, of course, in strict reverse hierarchical order, starting with the walking gentlemen, then the minor support, then the soubrette, the comic, the stars. You stand there grinning while your immediate inferior goes up and bows, and then it's your turn. You can tell by the weight of the noise; does it go down, or up, or does it stay the same? If it goes up when you go forward, there's no better feeling. In scripture, one or two of the prophets are occasionally permitted to talk to the Invincible Sun face-to-face and find out what He thinks of them. In the theatre, we get to find out every night.

Of course, there's always the remote possibility that they're applauding the play, not you; but really, that's a meaningless distinction, like saying I didn't steal the money, it was the evil part of me. Particularly meaningless when you've written the script – though, as I think I've said (see above), I'm not a writer.

Anyway, whatever it was they were cheering, didn't they ever cheer; my fellow citizens, my countrymen, my brothers. They cheered, they waved bits of purple cloth, they shouted my name and purple, purple, purple (she was right; it did sound very silly). I stood there with my arms spread wide, basking in it like a salamander; and somebody shot me.

11

I don't remember much about it. I remember looking down and thinking, hello, there appears to be a small tree growing out of my thigh; and then I noticed the blood soaking through the divitision (hard to spot blood against a purple background, but it caught the light and sparkled). Captain Very noticed it, too, and dragged me out of the way, and I was hustled inside. I missed the riot and the bloodbath that followed. I always miss the exciting bits.

Fruit and the occasional egg you learn to take in your stride. Arrows are something else. You don't get shot at in the profession, except possibly at the Rose, on a bad night. I vaguely recall being manhandled into a chair and held down by four Lystragonians; I assumed I was being assassinated and they were in on the conspiracy, and as far as I can remember I wasn't particularly upset by that; oh well, I thought, probably I've asked for it, so what the hell. But instead of slitting my throat, Captain Very knelt down beside me and had a good look at the arrow – surely he's seen an arrow before, I thought, in his line of work – then he looked up at the four guards who were holding on to me and nodded, and then there was this moment of sheer agony as he pulled the nasty thing out. Then he sniffed the arrowhead, and then – it was all a bit surreal but I really didn't expect that – he yelled, "Get me a chicken, now." I assumed he'd gone off his head, but the other guards seemed to think it was a perfectly reasonable thing to say, and where they got a chicken from at such short notice I really don't know but they did; a live one, upside down, clucking and not happy. Then Captain Very stuck the point of the arrow into the poor thing's foot and started counting aloud, one, two, three. Nobody was looking at me, just the chicken. Then the captain got to ten and the chicken turned its head and clucked (instead of dying from the poison, of which there wasn't any, as I later figured out) and everybody relaxed. Where's that fucking doctor, someone yelled, and then I sort of drifted off into sleep.

Act 3

1

She was sitting next to me when I woke up. "Hello," I said.

"You were born lucky," she said. "A quarter-inch to the left, it'd have cut the artery and you'd be dead."

"What happened?"

She scratched her nose. "We don't know. The City prefect thinks it was a disgruntled Themesman, so he's been rounding up the little that's left of the old Blue and Green hierarchies; not a big job, since the mob evidently shares his view and they've torn all the old bosses they can find into tiny bits."

"Did somebody try and kill me?"

She scowled at me. "Yes," she said. "The army thinks it must've been a hired killer in the pay of the enemy, and apparently there's lots of technical stuff about the arrow and the type of crossbow used to support that, and they're arresting any foreigners who came in recently who survived the riot, not that many of them are left, but they say if it really was a trained assassin he'd have planned his escape route carefully in advance, so quite probably he got away."

"Since when did we have a City prefect? Didn't he get killed by the senators?"

"That was ages ago. There's a new man now, your pet clerk chose him. I'm a bit concerned about that man, to be honest with you. I think he's getting above himself."

"The prefect?"

"Your clerk, whatsisname." It's a point of honour with her not to remember the names of people she doesn't like. I made a big effort and decided she must mean Usuthus. "Too big for his boots, if you ask me."

"You leave him alone."

"Don't worry, I won't hurt him. Personally," she went on, "I think it was the senators. Of all the people who hate you, I think they hate you the most."

"People don't hate me. You heard them. I'm really popular."

The you-halfwit look. "I told the army people I thought it must be the senators and they said they'd look into it, but I don't suppose they'll actually do anything. Which is a pity. We could get rid of the whole lot of them, after something like this."

"I'm very tired," I said. "Please go away."

"I can't," she said. "I'm your devoted empress. I have to stay here. And this chair's murder and I've got cramp in my leg."

2

While I was lying there drifting in and out of sleep, Captain
Very and Usuthus had a difference of opinion, which by all
accounts you could hear right down the hall. The captain said
no more standing waving on balconies, period. Usuthus said
he's got to do that, if he starts skulking around behind a bunch
of guards they'll think he's scared. He should be scared, said
the captain, people are trying to kill him. What about a mail
shirt, suggested Usuthus, or one of those metal-lined coats, a
brigantine? A brigantine is a type of ship, the captain said. You
know what I mean, said Usuthus.

So, in addition to all that horrible, hot, heavy stuff I had to
wear concealed armour, which weighed a ton and made me
sweat like a pig. That, however, was the least of my concerns.

As soon as I was up and about again, I sent for the military.
I got a representative sample: General Aineas, commander-
in-chief, General Pertinax, officer commanding the City
garrison, and the idiot in charge of the engineers, who I'd
already met. Yes, they told me, the enemy were continuing

to bombard us with fire-pots, but not to worry because now the Themes were cooperating with the City fire brigade, everything was under control. Yes, there were fires in various parts of Poor Town practically every day, but the engineers had drawn up a scheme of wholesale demolition for the shanty districts, which were by far the most flammable parts of town, and once those had been cleared away there really shouldn't be a problem. Yes, the bombardment was having an effect on morale, but since the worst affected areas were mostly slum neighbourhoods—

I stopped them there. How come, I asked, the enemy could now shoot fire-pots over the wall? Ah, said the engineer, that's because they've solved, or at any rate partially solved, the problem of the mass-versus-velocity trade-off, basically the reason why you can throw a stone further than a feather, with their latest generation of trebuchets; it was either a modification to the throwing arm or a new type of clay for making the pots out of, they weren't quite sure which—

"And that means they can lob a pot over the wall?"

"That's right."

"How high over the wall?"

He didn't know. "Quite some way, I assume," he said, "or they wouldn't reach so far inland, so to speak."

"What I want you to do," I said, as quietly and calmly as I could, "is get a load of very tall poles, and a load of nets. Do you see where this is going?"

"With respect," said the engineer, "it'd take an awful lot of nets and poles to protect the whole circumference of the walls."

"Then that's how many nets and poles we'll need."

"Yes, but how will we know if we've got the nets up high enough?"

Colonel of engineers. By definition, one of the smartest men in the empire. "I'd have thought you could work it out by the angles the pots come over at. You know where the trebuchets are, roughly. You know where the pots are landing. And if the nets turn out not to be high enough, use longer poles."

(The world is full of idiots, and always has been. But sometimes I wonder why such a disproportionate quantity of them end up running other people's lives.)

The nets worked, for a while. Then they didn't; the pots came sailing over the top of them. So we put up longer poles, and the bombardment stopped.

"That's all very well and good," said General Aineas, when he reported that fact; I'd insisted on meeting him at least once a week for a regular briefing, and he was gradually getting used to me. "But we can't just react to that sort of thing, we've got to start making the running. We need to hit them. Hard."

I nodded. "Such as?"

"A full-scale strike against their artillery."

"I see," I said. "So when you get stung by a bee, you think it's a good idea to go and kick over the hive."

"Excuse me, Your Majesty, I don't quite—"

"No full-scale strike," I said. "If we fail, we lose hundreds of men we can't replace. If we succeed, we make Ogus look stupid, so he finds some other way to hurt us, to save face. I thought it had been decided long ago, we can't achieve anything worthwhile by fighting them, at least not on land. By sea, maybe, except they haven't got any ships."

The general looked at me as if I was babbling. Maybe I was.

"We've got ships," I said. "Tell you what. If you really feel we ought to give Ogus a bloody nose, why not put some of your men on board some ships, sail off somewhere where

Ogus' people think they're safe, and make life miserable for them? Moral: if you hit us, we'll hit you back, only we can do far more damage."

I gathered I'd suggested something faintly obscene. "I would need to discuss that with Admiral Sisinna."

"Fine," I said. "Do it. Write him a letter. I want a list of potential targets. Make them places where we can go in and out with minimal risk, where we can do a lot of damage and be well away long before Ogus can get his soldiers there. Also, for choice, places that supply stuff he needs for the war effort. Not just food but other stuff: clothes, rope, tools, barrels. Barrels are a good thing, actually; you can't fight a war without barrels. Where does Ogus get his barrels from?"

Pause. "I'd have to look that up."

"If we do this right," I said, "we can make life really hot for him, and there's nothing he can do about it. Not unless he wants to pull lots of soldiers away from the siege to defend every town and city in his empire that happens to be on the coast. Which an awful lot of them are, by the way, in case you hadn't noticed."

I was getting on his nerves. "It would mean committing our naval reserve," he said, "possibly to a dangerous extent."

"Not really. At the moment our whole fleet's a reserve. The enemy have no ships."

"Also," he went on, "we would need to take a substantial proportion of our fighting infantry away from the City, thereby seriously weakening the garrison."

"You forget," I said. "I was here when Nicephorus and Artavasdus defended this city with a few hundred engineers and a bunch of armed gardeners. I'm sorry," I added, "didn't mean to raise my voice. Actually, I'm agreeing with you. You said we need to hit them hard. You're absolutely right. And this is a very good way of doing it."

The look on his face as it dawned on him that there was a serious risk of it turning out to have been his idea; I'd have felt sorry for him if he hadn't been an idiot.

Usuthus brought me the list. They'd done a good job; locations (see map), together with estimated sailing times there and back (not necessarily the same, because of tides and stuff), known defences and estimated level of resistance, also value as military and economic targets. I called in Captain Very, and the three of us went over it. Captain Very wanted to hit an arrow factory a hundred miles up the Friendly Coast; not a bad idea, except they weren't shooting a lot of arrows at us right then, on account of being out of range. Usuthus pointed out that trashing a couple of small towns just down the coast would disrupt food supplies to the enemy camp. Smart, I said, but they can just as easily bring what they need in overland, so they'd be back to normal inside a week. Instead, I suggested, what about these here? Namely, towns and small cities, practically undefended, where Ogus had established his factories, to put us out of business by manufacturing copies of everything we had to offer.

"Actually," Hodda said, over my shoulder, "that's not a bad idea."

I hadn't heard her come in. "It's got to be worth a try," I said. "They've been there for seven years, and all that time nothing we've done has really hurt them. All we've managed to do is try their patience. If we can show that this war isn't necessarily all one-sided, maybe we can change a few minds. Not his, obviously, he's obsessed. But he must have people he relies on, supporters, allies. If they get it into their heads that maybe the game isn't worth the candle, we might just get somewhere. At the very least, it'll give the generals something to do. I worry they'll get bored and try something stupid."

So we attacked Locaria. Locaria is, or was, a small city on the south-western coast of the Friendly Sea. Until about seven years ago, it was a loyal member of the empire, paying its taxes, sending men to serve in the auxiliary forces, desperately keen on the latest City fashions in clothes, food and popular music; I vaguely remember someone taking a touring company out there years ago, in the off season, playing some worn-out old melodrama. They'd always been good metalworkers, because of the rich ore deposits in the nearby hills, and when Ogus told them they were free of us and working for him, it meant hard times for a while, since we'd always been their best customers. But then Ogus set up a big factory in Locaria, making cooking pots, trivets, door hinges, nails, firedogs, all the stuff we do so well, and life was just starting to get back to normal when we turned up.

I read the reports, which were terse and to the point: mission accomplished, basically. Forty ships carrying three thousand heavy infantry suddenly appeared off the coast early one morning. I imagine the Locarians were able to recognise Imperial warships from a long way off; only seven years ago, everybody made money when the Fleet was in. Quite likely they assumed that the ships had come to liberate them from the oppressor, which would explain why the Locarians stayed in their city weaving garlands of flowers instead of running like hell.

I didn't order the soldiers to slaughter unarmed civilians. Then again, I didn't order them not to, and you know what soldiers are like, apt to get carried away, like a fox in a hen coop. These things happen in war, so they tell me. I wouldn't know. Also they told me that it was necessary, in order to strike terror into the enemy, which had been my idea. Define enemy; seven years ago, they were our friends, they were *us*. But there; identities change, don't they, and we aren't necessarily the same people we were seven years ago, or seven weeks, even. Seven weeks or thereabouts (I lost track of time as soon as I set foot in this bloody palace) I was someone completely different. We *evolve* (I think that's the word), like caterpillars turning into butterflies, and the truth evolves with us. And, as the dear old saying goes, you can't make an omelette without breaking eggs.

3

Applause takes different forms, depending on context. In the theatre, people laugh, clap, cheer, throw flowers. In war, your enemy expresses his appreciation for a particularly clever move on your part by doing his best to rip your throat out. His way of showing affection, I guess.

Ogus' version of a bunch of roses and a big hug was an all-out assault on the wall, the first time he'd done that since the early days of the siege. He kicked off in the middle of the night with a furious artillery barrage, which ripped up the nets and made the walls shake but achieved nothing of any real use. At first light our artillery opened up and made kindling out of the trebuchets and mangonels he'd brought in close during the night. Round one to us.

I didn't know that, though. I was woken up by Usuthus and the City prefect, bundled into my loathsome armour and that bloody coat and hustled out of the palace into a covered coach. "Where are we going?" I remember asking, but nobody gave me a satisfactory answer.

It wasn't long before the noise told me everything I needed to know. I'll never forget the early days of the siege, when it felt like there was a heavy bombardment every other day. The ground really does shake, you feel and hear the noise simultaneously, and after a while it gets so that you can't stand it any more, but it goes on and on and there's absolutely nothing you can do about it. I remember we were playing *Acis and Philostratus* at the Crown to a good house and the bombardment started. People knew the score by then, how to clear a building without trampling each other to death; Olethria was Acis and she was doing the big speech, and by the time she got to the end the building was completely empty, just a dozen of us standing like idiots on an empty stage, which bounced under our feet every time a rock pitched nearby.

At Fourways we transferred from the closed coach to an open one. "People need to see you," Usuthus said.

The streets were, of course, deserted. "What people?"

"The soldiers, on the wall."

"I'm not going up there, you lunatic. The air's full of rocks."

"*Near* the wall," the prefect amended. "That's where all the work's going on right now. We've got artillerymen setting up, carters bringing ammunition, masons, carpenters. Once they've seen you, word'll get around. It'll be great for morale."

Well, I thought, fair enough. Being seen is what I'm there for. "Then can I go home?"

"There's a meeting of the joint chiefs of staff at the war ministry," Usuthus said. "Then we'll need you to talk to the Theme leaders; we need volunteers, lots of them."

"Then?"

"I think that depends what happens next," the prefect said.

What happened next was Ogus bringing up more

artillery – basically, everything he'd got, and as fast as our boys trashed a row of his machines, he brought up another two rows. Once he had a couple of full batteries in place, he opened up on our artillery. Every one of machines he took out cost him a dozen of his own, but it didn't matter; if things went how he wanted them to, this time tomorrow he wouldn't need them, so what the hell. We had spares, of course, dozens of them, all ready to be winched up, assembled and installed in the blink of an eye. But he smashed them, too.

In the event, he ran out of artillery before we did, but it was a close-run thing, and what we had left wasn't enough to rake the open space in front of the walls with enough shot to stop Ogus bringing up his scaling ladders and siege towers. He'd been banking on shutting down our artillery, so his towers didn't get very far; we killed them all long before they got in range. Also, three of his five covered rams, and the other two we managed to catch with grappling hooks and overturn, like woodlice. Not to worry. Ogus had half a million men, as against our twenty thousand.

Of those twenty thousand, nine thousand were archers. I think it was Nicephorus who instituted the archery prizes: gold medals and large sums of money for the best shots in the army, organised into leagues and running four competitions a year. If it was him, he was a genius. The soldiers spent hours of their free time practising, and so did a great many civilians, so we had an extra three thousand-odd trained bowmen on the wall just when we needed them most. Of course Ogus' men advanced behind great big shields and horse-drawn pavises, but by that point the flat ground out front was liberally scattered with spent artillery shot – big boulders to you and me, and no troop of soldiers, however well drilled, can advance across that sort of terrain and keep in perfect step. So gaps started to appear, and once that happened they unravelled like a laddered sock. They shot back, of course, but mostly they shot wild – short or over the top, and the rising sun was in their eyes, which really puts you off your aim. We killed fifty or so of them for every one of us they hit, and the heaps of their own dead and dying made holding a straight line that bit more awkward, and still they came. All this time, of course, our mangonels and scorpions were pounding them with round stone balls, at a low trajectory with the springs partly relaxed, so the balls bounced and rolled instead of just hitting the ground and burying themselves in the dirt. They couldn't reach the front, archery range, but they made a horrible mess of the fresh troops coming up. We had artillerymen who could drop a ball so precisely that it pitched at the front of a column of men and didn't stop until it had reached the back, taking roughly a third of the poor bastards with it. Now that's skill.

"He's proving our point," said some high-ranking army type as we watched from a relatively safe tower. "This is precisely why he hasn't tried something like this for years. We're wiping the floor with him."

"I'm guessing he's overestimated the number of men we sent to Locaria," someone else said. "He thought there'd be nobody home to mind the store."

Curious he should say that, because originally the idea had been to send ten thousand men on the raid, until Captain Very advised me that three thousand would be plenty, and I told the joint chiefs to trim it down accordingly. Two things Ogus had got wrong, then: he'd expected he'd be able to knock out our artillery and use his siege towers, and he'd anticipated fewer archers. On that basis, he might well have been in with a chance. As it was—

"Why's he doing this?" I said. "He must know it's not working."

"I think he's good and angry," said the prefect. "And with the manpower at his disposal, I guess he can afford to indulge the occasional tantrum."

He kept it up for the rest of the day; then, as night fell, he broke off abruptly and pulled back his forces to their original position, leaving nothing but mess behind him. We spent a sleepless night on the walls. All I did, all I could do was walk up and down being shown things, saying well done in a patronising tone of voice to men and women who'd saved us all by some of the most extraordinary acts of stupid courage you could possibly imagine; for this I was cheered hysterically everywhere I went, which made me feel strange. Shortly before midnight Hodda joined me, in full costume, escorted by nine ladies-in-waiting. Remember what I told you about taking bows, and the volume increasing? Of course a lot of people recognised her from the theatre. She did the patronising smiles and nods much better than I did, so maybe she deserved the applause. For once in my life, I didn't resent it. More than enough to go round, in any case.

Just before the sun rose we could hear a sort of creaking; here we go again, the soldiers said, and everybody limped and rolled to their duty stations, ready to start all over again. But the creaking wasn't a new assault. It was the distant squawking of about a million crows, settling down to make the most of a once-in-a-lifetime opportunity before some cruel bastard shooed them away.

4

They showed me a list of casualties. Thirty-seven artillery-men, three hundred and sixteen regular infantry, fourteen militia and sixty-three civilians, mostly hit by overshooting arrows or run down by munitions wagons. We'd loosed off seven hundred thousand arrows (but we still had over a million in store, so that was all right) and just over half our artillery shot; two-thirds of our artillery was out of commission, but it wouldn't take long, they assured me, to make up for that; a week at the most. Ogus, on the other hand, had practically no artillery left, and his dead and wounded—

Quite. For two days the sky was full of black spirals, as the crows wheeled and circled in desperate frustration, swooping and pitching and being driven off before they'd had a chance of more than a peck or two. My heart bled for them.

Around midday, Ogus sent out men and wagons to collect his dead. I told the soldiers to shoot at them, which they did, quite effectively. The burial party drew back.

"That's a bit harsh, isn't it?" General Pertinax said. "It's one of the conventions of war—"

"Stuff the conventions," I said. "They started it. Let them wait till sunset and grope about in the dark."

Next day the ships got back from Locaria, having missed (as their commodore put it) all the fun. No problem, I said, and sent them out again. This time they were going to Menaroa, a pretty seaside town where Ogus had set up a porcelain factory; and after that, they were to swing north up the east coast and take out the potteries at Onnaco and the silk weavers at Deusambor. On their way home, if they felt like it, they could stop in at Trysa, where the craftsmen at Ogus' new glassworks were reckoned to have developed the most amazing new techniques for blowing and moulding; if they could pick up a few prisoners, so much the better, but not to worry if they couldn't.

"What's got into you?" she said. "You're crazy. You're out of control."

"Far from it," I said, dumping the horrible armour on the floor with a thump. The only way out of that thing was to lift it over your head, then bend over and let it slide off you. It chafed my neck and pinched at the waist, and it was giving me chronic backache. "I'm conducting the war in a logical and efficient manner. That's what the generals are saying. Usuthus overheard them at the last staff meeting, before I got there."

"You care what the generals think."

"Well, they ought to know."

"You're mad, do you know that? What the hell do you think you're playing at, Notker? No, look at me when I'm talking to you. This is all your fault."

"Define this."

"*This.*" She took a deep breath, to calm herself down. "The attack on the City. The raids on all those little towns. All those people getting killed. You did that. Those people would still be alive if you hadn't interfered. Think about that, will you?"

"I have thought about it, oddly enough."

"Then what in God's name are you doing it for? It's not helping. You're just making things much, much worse for everybody."

I took a moment to reply. "That's what you think, is it?"

"Too bloody right it is. Things were ticking along, just about all right, until you came along and decided to make trouble. What's got into you, Notker? Why are you doing this?"

"I don't know," I said. "I guess it's in character."

I could see she couldn't trust herself to speak for a moment. She actually jammed her hand into her mouth. "Bullshit," she said.

"No, not really. It's what Lysimachus would do. No, listen, just for a second. I've been reading the reports and despatches, from the early days of the siege."

"You're starting to believe you're actually him. You're delusional."

"The reason why we won the other day," I went on, "is because we were ready, we were organised, everybody knew what to do. And why was that? Because someone worked out a drill and made sure everybody knew it and practised it regularly. I wanted to know who that was. I assumed it must've been Nicephorus, but no, actually it was Lysimachus. He saved us the other day. He stopped them taking the City."

She clapped her hands slowly three times. "Bravo," she said. "Well done. Only, they wouldn't have attacked if you hadn't sent those ships to burn down that stupid city. Lysimachus didn't do that. You did. And you won't even let them bury their dead. That's *sick*. What's that all about, for crying out loud? Is it because they're milkfaces? Is that it?"

"It's nothing to do with—"

"Because if it is, let me tell you something. They aren't that colour any more. You ever seen a body that's been left out in the sun? It changes colour. The skin goes purple, then black. So they aren't milkfaces any more, Notker, they're as black as you and me."

"It's about making a point," I said.

"Really. And what point would that be?"

I couldn't put it into words. Maybe I didn't understand it myself, I don't know. "They came here," I said. "They came here to wipe us out, like an ants' nest or wasps in the rafters. And all we've managed to do up till now is stay alive, with them crowding round us, in our faces, just waiting for a chance to murder the lot of us. And because they haven't succeeded yet we just shrug our shoulders and carry on like nothing's happened, like they were high winds or an earthquake, something random, with no spite in it. But there's spite all right."

She nodded. "What was that very clever image you were telling me you used the other day? A man gets stung by a bee, so he kicks over the hive. Very intelligent. Or maybe I'm getting that mixed up with what you said just now, about wiping people out like they're a wasps' nest. Are they the wasps, Notker? Is that what you want? To kill them all, till there's not a single milkface left?"

"Chance would be a fine thing. No, I didn't mean that. I meant, that's not going to happen ever, so it's not worth thinking about."

"Crossed your mind, though. Hasn't it?"

"*No.*" I hadn't meant to yell. She hadn't raised her voice, so who was I shouting down? "Since when did you care about the enemy? You know what that word means, don't you? Or would it help if you looked it up?"

"I know what it means," she said. "It means what you want it to mean. It means you can do what you damn well like. Do you like having people killed, Notker? Does it make you feel big and strong?"

"Enemy means someone who wants to hurt you," I said. "Them or us, simple as that."

"Simple." She gave me a look I won't forget in a hurry. "I don't think there's any point talking to you. Remember Andronica in *The Golden Mask*? That's you, just the wrong way round."

Did you see that show? If not, you missed a real treat. Andronica was this princess, born butt-ugly so she had a beautiful golden mask; and when she wore it she was so happy she started being nice to people, and they loved her, and she was even nicer to them, and so on and so forth. Then one day she took the mask off, and lo and behold, she was just as beautiful without it. Only the other way round.

"We were going to get out of here," she said, quiet now. "Remember? We were going to fill our pockets with treasure and get the hell out of here and leave all these idiots to it."

"Yes," I said.

"You've changed your mind about that, evidently."

"No," I said. "Only we can't get out of the palace, remember?" Yes we can, I thought. "But while we're stuck here, I can't just stand by and do nothing—"

"Can't you? Why not? That's what everybody else does."

"Not if you're the emperor."

"Ah."

242 K. J. Parker

"It wouldn't look right," I said. "It's not in character. For him."

"You know what, Notker? I'm amazed you can still breathe. You're so full of it, there can't be room in there for a pair of lungs."

Hodda very rarely hits people. Why hurt your hand, maybe risk skinning a knuckle, when you can do so much more damage with a word and a look? Also, what you need to bear in mind is, the actual words are just the arrowhead. The arrow is how she says them.

"I mean it," I said. "I want to get out of here, alive, in one piece, preferably with a lot of money. As soon as it can be done—"

"You know a way out of here. And you're not telling me."

"Don't be silly."

"That night when there was the fire," she said. "You came in a back way."

Don't bother trying to figure out how she knows things. She just does. "Yes," I said. "But there's guards and sentries. We came in that way because Captain Very was with us. You don't seriously believe there's a way in and out of here that isn't guarded, do you?"

She believed me. Just goes to show. I'm not a bad actor, when I really try hard.

5

Old joke. What's the difference between a lawyer and a rat? Answer: under the right circumstances, you can grow fond of a rat. Substitute war for lawyer and you've got my views on the matter, concisely and memorably phrased.

Nevertheless.

Things change, you see; everything changes, we all change, just like the truth, see above. Five minutes into the first act, and the audience are sitting there grim-faced, like you're personally responsible for everything that's wrong with their lives, and you're trying to remember who's hiring for what, because tomorrow you'll be out looking for a new job. But sometimes, things change. I remember once, at the old Harmony, they were stone-cold all through the first two acts, but come the end they were standing and cheering, we took so many bows we nearly sprained hamstrings. Things change.

In war, apparently, as in everything else; and in war, according to the books I'd taken to reading, change can come suddenly, unexpectedly, catastrophically (in the literal sense of turning things upside down). In battles, Act 1 can be entirely with one side, to the point where the opposing king or general runs for his life, with his attendant lords and luxury furniture rattling along after him in a string of carts, but in Act 2 the winners make a stupid mistake, and Act 3 is either a ghastly, bloody draw or the previous winners getting slaughtered. Moral: never take your eye off the ball, and never assume it's over till you're actually dead.

Of course, if it's melodrama rather than legitimate tragedy, you can and should expect more twists than a corkscrew, and a lot of wars seem to me to have been melodramas of the worst possible sort. This war started really badly for us. We lost the empire practically overnight and came within a whisker of losing the City. Act 2, heroic defence by Nicephorus and Lysimachus, the City preserved. Properly speaking, the third act should be Lysimachus rallying the defence and driving the barbarians into the sea.

Not really an option, since the sea's on the wrong side of town, but you know what I mean. Dramatic necessity should dictate a glorious and conclusive victory. That's what the audience will be expecting, and it's up to the author to provide it. Which makes me glad that, as I've mentioned earlier, I'm not a writer.

Nevertheless. I'd tried something, and it seemed (very early days, of course) like it was working. Now you were with me, so to speak, when I got the idea, so you can testify that it wasn't part of a grand strategy for victory. General Aineas wanted to send men out to attack the enemy positions and get themselves killed; I thought of something on the spur of the moment to distract him, and then we had to go ahead and put that frivolous suggestion into action. Then, purely by chance,

I remembered what I'd been told about Ogus' master plan to finish us off by driving our trade out of foreign markets, and I thought: two birds, one stone. Probably I wouldn't have thought of turning my two bright ideas into a coordinated plan of action if Ogus hadn't paid me the compliment of sending six thousand of his men to their deaths (that's the figure they came up with, by the way; a conservative estimate, they told me) in a fit of ungovernable rage. If it made him that mad, I thought, there's got to be something in it.

But it was all made up as I went along, not carefully plotted out beforehand; and that's how and why things change, because no matter how good the outline on paper looks when you're pitching it to a manager, when you sit down and actually write the bastard, things inevitably turn out different. Big events you were relying on turn out not to be in character. You get Andronica or Messanus for the leads, but Andronica can't or won't do such and such a scene, and Messanus is best in blood-and-thunder roles, so you need to shoehorn in some anguish and gore, which shifts the balance; any play, I've always found, that ends up being recognisably what the manager originally agreed to buy will be rubbish, and only the author's mother will want to see it.

Things change, everything changes, we change. Pun intended. I can change in two minutes flat, from a clean-shaven king to a bearded funny peasant; you'd never know in the gallery that they're both me, but they are. Except that I've changed, and where I was in character for a king, now I'm in character for a clown. And if I can do that, so can a war.

Actually winning the horrible thing – now there was a thought. I'm sure it never occurred to Nicephorus and Artavasdus, rest their souls; to be honest with you, I'm not sure

Gelimer and his honourable friends in the House ever gave it any thought – because war is the army's job, and senators are brought up from babyhood on the doctrine of separation of powers; war's none of their business, so they don't really take any interest in it, their whole attention being taken up with the glorious game of politics. As for Lysimachus; I'm prepared to bet that, simple soul that he was, he genuinely believed that the Robur race would triumph and the enemy would be utterly crushed *one day*; but not necessarily in the near future or his lifetime. Actually, I bet you that Lysimachus was a sucker for the old-style melodramas. They would have made sense to him, because that would've been his idea of how the world worked.

And, of course, there was Hodda, probably the smartest person I've ever known. She was quite definite about it. The City was dead meat, because of the arithmetic. There's no shrewder manager than her, because she understands what people do and don't want, what they'll do and what they can't be induced to do, even with bribes and horrible threats. She doesn't get many runaway hits but she virtually never has a flop. She doesn't sit down and work it all out with numbers and an abacus. She just knows.

Winning the horrible thing; define victory.

6

They did good business (as we say in the trade) at Menaroa,
Onnaco, Deusambor and Trysa – sounds like a tour of the
provinces and I suppose in a sense it was, trying the Grand
Plan out on the road and achieving a reassuring level of success. The thing is, an awful lot of people live by the seaside,
and one thing you really don't want is the Imperial navy turning up out of (literally) the blue and burning your house down.
At least, at Menaroa and Deusambor they had the sense to run
away when our sails appeared on the skyline.

No rest for the wicked, I always say; so I sent the wicked off
to Picron Oistun and Timaressa, where Ogus had recently
spent a lot of money on looms and a ropewalk. Picron and
Timaressa are both due south, on the Blemyan Gulf, many
hundreds of miles away from the Friendly Sea. Moral: we are
everywhere the sea is, and you have no idea where we're going
to turn up next.

At least ten thousand reinforcements showed up in Ogus'
camp, and the carpenters were busy throwing up shacks for

them all to live in. We had a little surprise for them. You'll recall that our wonderful colonel of engineers expressed the view that Ogus had gone as far as it's possible to go in refining and improving the trebuchet. I took that as meaning that if they could improve their versions of the loathsome device, so could we, up to that ultimate point that Ogus had apparently reached; see to it, I said grandly, and sure enough they did. Knowing something can be done is a great incentive to figuring out how, I guess; anyway, we had prototypes of the new improved version ready before you could say sudden violent death, and as soon as Ogus' carpenters had finished the new wing of the camp, we reduced it to splinters in less than an hour. Naturally, that meant that the more-or-less permanent settlement Ogus had built up over the last seven years was no longer safe and had to be moved back a hundred yards. Cue great trouble and expense, and tens of thousands of soldiers having to camp out in the pouring rain while the work was being done. It's the little things, I always find, like having to sleep in the mud soaked to the skin, that really get you down.

I had a fairly shrewd idea of what would happen next, having taken the trouble to read up on the early days of the siege, and I knew that if I was right we faced a serious problem. Sure enough, as soon as the carpenters had finished moving the camp, they set to work on a whole new shanty village, which they finished just in time for the residents to move in. About eight thousand of them, not soldiers but civilians, and you didn't need to be a genius to figure out their trade or profession. Miners, from all over what used to be our empire, here to dig under our walls and bring them tumbling down.

Of course, Ogus had already tried that and it hadn't worked. But the mood he was in, it was only a matter of time before he tried it again. I'm guessing the trebuchet thing tweaked his tail to the point where he really didn't care about looking stupid if he failed. Just as well, really, that Nicephorus had seen something of the sort coming and signed a treaty with the Tanagenes.

In case you don't know, Tanage is a peninsula on the Lerosian coast, nominally inside Sashan territory, but what the eye doesn't see the heart doesn't grieve over. Once upon a time the Tanagenes exported copper and tin all across the world, but the seams are almost completely worked out now, leaving Tanage with thousands of trained miners with nothing to do. Nicephorus had bribed the Duke of Tanage, at eyewatering expense, and in return we could call on up to six thousand Tanagene miners, at a moment's notice, provided we paid them a ridiculous sum of money. Personally, I always feel that survival is cheap at any price and it puzzles me that so many men in authority don't seem to see it that way.

Nevertheless, the cost of hiring the Tanagenes was rather more than we had on hand in the Treasury. The finance ministers proposed a forced loan on all registered citizens, plus increased tariffs at the docks. I figured that since Ogus had made us incur all this expense, he really ought to pay for it. So when the Fleet got back from Timaressa, I sent them straight off to loot the cities of the Osmala delta.

Maybe you're old enough to have been there. It was a popular destination for affluent City dwellers before the war – beautiful scenery, elegant dining in luxurious seaside villas, sophisticated ladies employed in the hospitality and leisure sector, everything a man could ask for. No sea walls, no defences of any kind, and we were in and out of each one of the five main cities in less than a day, taking with us a fortune in second-hand luxury goods and leaving behind a heap of rubble and cinders. A squadron of Iasolite merchants rendezvoused with the Fleet just off Sear Point and gave us a sensible price for the entire haul sight unseen. A pleasure doing business with you, they said, let's do this again soon.

"You realise," she said, on one of the rare occasions when she was speaking to me, "this is exactly the sort of thing that made Ogus decide to get rid of the Robur for ever."

"I didn't start it," I said.

"Civilian targets," she said. "People who've never done a single thing to hurt us, not even trying to make vases cheaper than we can. You're no better than pirates. It's disgusting."

"So's wiping out a whole city."

"You should know."

I pride myself that I bring out the best in her sometimes.

7

"It's working really well, according to our sources," General Aineas told me. "His allies are starting to complain that nowhere's safe, and of course they can't prepare in advance because they have no idea where we'll turn up next."

"That's significant," said some official from the war department whose name I didn't catch. "Not so long ago, none of the allies would have dared complain about anything Ogus did. Now they're whining like mad and he hasn't had their heads cut off. Which shows he's worried."

"The allies all signed up on a promise that he'd finish us off once and for all," Aineas went on. "And it's seven years later and he's signally failed to do that, and now we're fighting back. And it's no secret that he's a hard master, far worse than we used to be when it was all Imperial territory. All we need to do is keep it up for long enough, and cracks are bound to show. And the way Ogus' regime is put together, once it starts to go it'll all come tumbling down, you mark my words."

"If he pulls men away from the siege to defend the provinces," said someone else I didn't know, "which, incidentally,
he's sworn he'll never do, his opponents can point to that and
say he's going back on his original promise. If he stays put and
does nothing for the provinces, he's a heartless monster and
high time he was got rid of. He can't win."

"Talking of things tumbling down," I said, "what do we
know about the mining operations?"

By this time, the Tanages had arrived and were settled in
and spending freely in the downtown bars. Ogus' men had
started work, but the best guess was that they'd hit the annoying seam of granite that runs from the Bluehorn right across
the City's front lawn to the South Road. Last time, Ogus
hadn't had to bother about it, because he'd been able to start
substantially closer to the walls.

"My scouts have been keeping an eye on the amount of spoil
coming up at the pithead," said General Aineas. "It seems to
have slowed down considerably over the last couple of days,
which would seem to indicate that they haven't got through
the granite yet. Which means this would be a good time for
a pre-emptive strike. I could send out two regiments, under
cover of darkness. We could breach their main gate, and then
one regiment could secure and destroy the pithead while the
other staged a diversionary attack on the main camp. With any
luck we could set their operations back a month, with losses
well within acceptable parameters."

Oh God, I thought. "Let's not do that," I said. "No good
ever came of fooling about in the dark, and I need a full brigade
for the cities in the Bay of Mahec. That's a week's sailing each
way, so while they're out of town we'll need everyone we've got
up on the wall, just in case he fancies another assault."

A stroke of bad luck for the three cities that nestle in the warm water of the Mahec estuary; they were the first places that sprang to mind, and I had to think quickly before the others started agreeing with him. That's how bad things tend to happen, I guess, only we don't usually find out about it.

Be that as it may. Aineas was perfectly satisfied with my reasoning and agreed to shelve the pre-emptive strike, so for every fifty Mahec civilians whose lives I took with my arbitrary spur-of-the-moment choice, I saved the life of one Robur soldier. I know; usually it's the other way round, but I was pushed for time.

"The Mahec," I explained to her, once she'd paused to draw breath, "is where Ogus has been recruiting lately. So; all the men go off to war in a faraway country of which they know little, and while they're away the enemy swoops down on their defenceless home and razes it to the ground. Suddenly Ogus' grand alliance doesn't seem such a good idea."

She told me what she thought about that. She had a point, which she didn't hesitate to drive home up to the hilt. Leading me to ask myself, would she make me feel more guilty if she didn't give me such a hammering over everything I did? The more she sticks the knife in, the more I resent it, the less I actually think about what she's been saying. That, of course, presupposes that the object of the exercise from her point of view is to change my mind about what I'm doing, as opposed to beating me to a pulp.

Lysimachus probably wouldn't have listened at all. More likely, he'd have smacked her across the face. Funny, really. I could unleash violence and death on women and children in Mahec, but I could no more hit a woman than fly in the air; because I'm civilised, I suppose. I guess the difference is between what happens offstage and on. A manager once told me, you can have your hero butcher entire nations in a messenger's report, but for God's sake don't have him hit a woman or a child on stage. You'd lose all sympathy.

8

Funny old stuff, granite. Way out east in the Sashan country, I gather there are mountains of it, literally; huge spiky towers, like a castle, or the backdrop in an old melodrama. You see them on imported porcelain – people say it's the best way to tell if it's genuine Sashan or not, because artists who've never seen those mountains can't possibly imagine them clearly enough to paint them, because they're so utterly unlike anything else on earth.

Our granite is the pink stuff. Years ago, we did a roaring trade in it, mostly to the Echmen royal court. They built great temples and palaces out of our pink granite, while we imported equal amounts of their bluey-grey granite (which you don't get west of the Friendly Sea) to build our temples and palaces out of; go figure. The barges they built to cart the stuff backwards and forwards across a thousand miles of treacherous sea were the biggest ships anywhere ever, and at one time there were hundreds of them. In recent years the quarries next to the City have all closed down, because the deposits close to the surface are all worked out, and all that's left is the thick underground ribbon that crosses the plain, more or less precisely underneath where Ogus had drawn his siege line, before our improved trebuchets forced him to draw it back.

Cutting through solid rock is a bitch, they tell me. You have to bank up huge underground fires, which heat the stone white hot. Then you pour buckets of vinegar on it, which cracks and splits it enough so your miners can get in there with wedges and picks. We saw the smoke and the steam, and an endless column of wagons carrying logs and charcoal to the pit head. All that went on for days, and then it stopped.

"We beat them before and we can do it again," said the idiot engineer cheerfully. "My predecessor managed it and he was a milkface, so it can't be all that difficult."

A clown; except that I've known some very wise, shrewd clowns over the years. He wasn't one of them. Also, he wasn't remotely funny. "Didn't he flood their tunnels out?" General Aineas said.

"Diverted an underground river," said the City prefect. "Wiped out the enemy miners and cleared up bad flooding in Poor Town all in one go. Pity we can't do that again."

"Can't we?" I asked.

The prefect shook his head. "Ogus has diverted the river of which our underground river is a tributary," he said. "He did it to form a reservoir so his camp always has plenty of drinking water, but it means we can't use the same trick twice. Still, it doesn't matter. We're ready for them. We've got the Tanagenes."

"Oh, them," said one of General Aineas' yes-men. "More trouble than they're worth if you ask me. Have you heard the latest? They're demanding more money."

"Give it to them," I said.

"None of them's done a stroke of work yet, and they're already getting twice what a cavalry trooper gets. I say, send them home and be damned to them."

"Not much call for cavalry in a siege," I said. "But we need miners. Give them what they're asking for."

After the meeting I sent for Usuthus.

"Have a look through the files," I said, "and see if anyone's ever drawn up contingency plans for evacuating the City."

He gave me a sad look. "Is it that bad?"

"No," I said, "not yet. But it's a possibility we need to consider."

"I don't need to check the files," Usuthus said. "I can tell you without looking, the answer's no. There's never been a plan, because it can't be done."

"Ah." I waited, but Usuthus seemed to think the conversation was over. "Why not?"

"Loads of reasons," he said. "Even if you could get a hundred and fifty thousand people onto ships, where would they go? Ogus controls a third of the known world. Also, merchantmen aren't like warships. Ships big enough to carry a lot of passengers have to stay close to shore, and all the coasts round here belong to Ogus. They wouldn't be able to put in for fresh water, let alone taking on food. Remember, you'd need to be providing three hundred thousand rations of food and water a day. It's bad enough keeping the City fed and watered on dry land. You'd need supply depots set up at sixty-mile intervals all the way to where you're going. Those depots would need to be established beforehand, on enemy soil, then fortified and garrisoned and held until they'd fulfilled their function. We simply don't have the manpower for that."

"We control the sea," I said. "Doesn't that count for anything?"

"Not really, no. Not unless we all grow fins and learn to live off seaweed. The successful formula is control of the sea *plus* an impregnable city wall. One without the other just won't do. Believe me, if it was possible to get everybody out, we'd have done it years ago."

Art is such a subjective thing, don't you think? Personally, I think all those Neo-Primitive and Mannerist icons are hideous and indescribably vulgar, particularly the ones with all the gold and jewels stuck on all over them. But they're extremely popular, especially abroad, where people pay silly money for them. A genuine Callicrates, for example; one of those would set you up for life, even if your favourite hobby was breeding pedigree racing elephants. Ridiculous, if you ask me. For one thing, they're so small. You could fit five of them into a coat pocket.

There were seventy-two Callicrates icons on one wall in the palace; twelve sequences of the Six Stations of the Passion. I gather that complete sequences are worth about double what you'd get for six individual pieces. Fools and their money, as the saying goes.

"I'm sick of the sight of those horrible things," I said to the Chamberlain, as I walked down the corridor where the Callicrateses were hung. "I've got to walk up and down this passage three times a day, and every time I look at them they make me feel depressed. Get rid of them, for crying out loud, and put up something cheerful."

Next time I walked that way, the icons had gone and in their place were selections from Apsimar IV's monumental collection of erotic ivories. Of course, people pay a lot of money for that sort of thing, too.

I sent for the Chamberlain. "Good joke," I said. "Congratulate yourself on having scored a point off me. Now get rid of the horrible things and put up something *nice*."

"Majesty."

"Actually," I said, stopping him as he turned to leave, "we may have stumbled onto something useful here. Do we have a lot of artwork in store in the palace?"

"Yes, Majesty."

"Safely under lock and key?"

"The vaults are the most secure location in the City, Majesty. It's inconceivable that anyone would ever be able to break into them."

"That's good to know. More to the point, though, all that stuff must be worth a lot of money."

I'd offended his delicate sensibilities. Ah well. "I should imagine so, Majesty. Although a considerable amount of the finest material has been sold since the start of the siege."

I nodded. "And a good thing, too. I mean, if it's all down there locked away, what's the point in keeping it? I want a complete inventory made, with valuations. At times like these, we really ought to have some idea of what we've got."

That afternoon, on my way back from meeting the Lords of the Treasury, my eye was caught by a series of the ghastliest landscapes, oils on wooden board, that it's ever been my misfortune to set eyes on. I asked, and was told that they were the work of his late Majesty's mother.

The Tanagenes set to work. They started off by digging a series of tunnels parallel to the wall, one on top of another.

The idea was that as soon as the enemy came close to the wall, they'd be able to detect the vibrations they made – all you do is put lots of bowls of water on the tunnel floor and wait till the surface of one of them starts shaking – and locate fairly precisely where the enemy were coming from. Then they'd be able to dig their own countersap (I think that's the proper word) and take the appropriate measures.

There are quite a lot of those. The one the Tanagenes favoured was sulphur and a big double-action bellows. You punch a hole in the wall of your enemy's tunnel, set light to the sulphur and use the bellows to blow in the sulphur fumes, which are guaranteed to kill pretty much anything. From which you'll gather that it wasn't in the Tanagenes' nature to muck about.

Will it work? I asked. Of course it will, everybody told me. It's a time-honoured method of dealing with enemy sappers, in all the standard books on the subject. Works like a charm every time.

The trouble with books is, however, that there's a danger that someone on the other side has read them, too. When the first enemy sap was located, the Tanagenes were ready: sulphur lit, bellows standing by, sledgehammers and drills poised to smash a hole through. At which point, they heard a tapping, about fifteen yards behind them down the tunnel. It was the enemy, breaking a hole.

The sulphur fumes worked like a charm, sure enough. Seventeen Tanagene sappers were killed by it, blasted through the breach by Ogus' own double-action bellows. The rest of the Tanagenes fell back double quick and broke down the supports of their own tunnel, to stop the enemy pouring out into the City streets. As soon as they were safely above ground, they asked for their pay and said they were going home.

I think they probably meant it, and about a third of them actually went; those that stayed grudgingly agreed to double pay, plus a substantial death-in-service benefit. Meanwhile, we had an enemy sap about fifty yards from the wall. It was obvious, the colonel of engineers told me, what had happened. Ogus' men had their own pails of water on their floor, and had guessed what our countermeasure would be.

"So if we try and break into their saps, they'll smoke us out."

He shrugged. "It's what I'd do, in their shoes," he said.

"How long will it take them to undermine the wall?"

"Hard to say," he said. "One to three days, at a guess."

I waited for him to suggest something. He didn't.

Luckily, while I'd been talking to the colonel, Usuthus had been chatting in the anteroom to a couple of junior captains who'd come along to carry the colonel's papers. What we might try, said one of the captains, a tall, skinny youth with a ridiculous plummy voice and the faintest wisp of hair on his top lip, is dig seven or eight countersaps, intercepting the enemy sap at decent intervals, and break through all of them simultaneously. Chances were, he explained, that they only had one bellows, two or three at the most; even if they accurately located all eight countersaps they'd only be able to smoke out a few of them; we'd be able to rush men through the ones that weren't flooded with deadly fumes, and then it'd be good old-fashioned knife-fighting in the dark. Not an inviting prospect, he was prepared to concede, but probably better than the alternative.

Usuthus grabbed him by the arm, put him in a little room and locked the door. When I'd got rid of the colonel, he took me to see him.

"I'm sorry, Majesty," he said, when he'd stuttered through it all again. "It was only a suggestion."

"What's your name?"

"Apsimar, Majesty."

I knew him, of course, though I'd never set eyes on him before. At least, I knew his type intimately. They're the ones who hang around the back door of the theatre, waiting for the chorus girls to come out.

"Take this," I said, giving him the bit of paper Usuthus had just written out for me, "to the colonel. It's a – what's it called, Usuthus?"

"Mandate."

"Mandate," I said, "relieving the colonel of command and putting you in charge instead. Get those tunnels dug as soon as you possibly can."

Colonel Apsimar – twenty-one years old, according to his docket; looked and sounded four years younger – led the raiding party himself. It was, of course, pitch dark in the saps and there wasn't room to stand upright, let alone swing a sword or use a spear; and armour clinks when you move, so they didn't wear any. It was, as Apsimar had said, knife-fighting in the dark, with a sulphur-fume garnish to add a touch of piquancy. After they'd killed forty-six of Ogus' best sappers, Apsimar's boys dragged the pile of brushwood they'd brought with them about sixty yards down the enemy tunnel and set fire to it. The props burned through and the roof came down, after which the Tanagenes set about backfilling with rocks and baskets of rubble. We lost twenty-eight men, all regular infantry.

"Trouble is," Apsimar told me, when he'd stopped shaking enough to be spoken to, "every clever wheeze we think of, they get to use against us next time. I think we've probably seen the last of the sulphur, because once you've let it loose you can't really control who breathes it in, if you see what I mean. I think from now on it'll be sapping and counter-sapping and – well, that sort of thing."

He had a bandage wrapped round his left arm, and the blood was starting to seep through it. "Can we keep it up?" I said.

"If they can, so can we," he said, "but it's a hell of a way to earn a living." He glanced at me, suddenly scared he'd offended against protocol by the use of mild bad language. I grinned at him; he grinned back. "For one thing," he said, "in the dark you can't tell the good guys from the baddies."

Hadn't thought of that, and it made me shudder.

"Years ago," he went on, "they used to daub themselves with scent, so you could tell each other apart by the smell. But that only works up to a point. Our lads go down stinking of roses, their boys start splashing it on, too, and you're back where you started. In theory you're supposed to have a picture of the tunnels in your mind and know exactly where your own people are, but that doesn't actually work when you're down there. It's so easy to get turned round, you see, specially after a bit of a scrimmage, and next thing you know—"

He didn't want to finish that sentence. "Do the best you can," I said and sent him away, feeling like I'd just stamped on his face.

9

In case you've been wondering, I no longer slept in the chair. It was making my neck hurt. Instead, I used to heap up cushions on the floor, which was fine. I've slept on worse, believe me. As for the snoring, it hadn't bothered me back when we were an item, and it didn't bother me now.

"Did Lysimachus snore?" I asked her.

"Like a sawmill. Almost as bad as you."

"I do not snore."

"My God. It's a miracle the roof doesn't cave in."

"You're just saying that to be spiteful. I do not snore."

"How would you know? You're always asleep when you do it."

"I have it on good authority," I said.

She gave me a pitying smile. "It's so sweet that you believed her."

"Actually, it was the male chorus of *Astonished by Joy* at the Sceptre. It was the start of the siege and we slept at the theatre because of the bombardment. And if I'd snored, you can bet they'd have mentioned it."

Her can't-be-bothered-to-argue look. "You snore," she said. "Get over it."

That from a woman who could scare rooks off laid barley. Still (in case you were wondering) we were back on speaking terms, shortly after I'd told her about the Callicrates icons.

"The Chamberlain's department's the most efficient part of the service," I told her. "Usuthus says so, and he should know. They've got where everything is written down in a file or an inventory. And they can find it in no time flat."

"They'll be in the vault," she objected. "They're worth a fortune."

"For now, yes," I said. "And then, when we're ready to go, I announce that Her Majesty wants them hung up in her private dressing room. An hour later, that's where they'll be."

Her eyes glowed with fierce longing. "Are you sure about that?"

"Of course. They're our bloody pictures."

She frowned. "I suppose they are. Yes, they are," she decided. "Let's send for them right now."

I shook my head. "We still haven't got a way out of here," I said.

And then she grinned at me. "We'll see about that," she said. And then Captain Very came to escort me to my next meeting.

"We've driven them back at least a hundred yards," General Aineas said. "At this rate, quite soon we'll have them pinned up against the granite, and then we can really lay into them."

Colonel Apsimar wasn't at the staff meeting. He was leading a sortie, down there in the dark. So far, we'd lost about five hundred men; meanwhile, we'd recovered about eight hundred of Ogus' dead from the tunnels we'd captured – we threw the bodies over the wall every morning, and let them come and collect them; Apsimar's idea, to give their colleagues something to think about – and there were plenty more we hadn't picked up. No prisoners on either side, of course; too much trouble to go to, under the circumstances.

"I don't understand," I said. "Why aren't they driving us back by sheer weight of numbers?"

"Doesn't work that way," Aineas said blithely, as though it had been him down there killing men by feel. "More than exactly the right number and they just get in the way. And they make a racket and we can hear them, and they can't hear us. No trouble at all to bring the roof down on 'em before they even know you're there. No, it only goes to show what I've said all along. In a tight corner, milkfaces simply don't have the stomach for it."

After the meeting, which was a complete waste of time, a young engineer subaltern popped up out of nowhere and tried to intercept me. Fortunately, I was able to stop Captain Very from killing him. "What is it?" I said.

The young subaltern explained that he was a friend of the colonel's; actually, they'd been to school and military academy together, and their families had always been close. The thing was, he went on, so embarrassed he could barely breathe, before all this lot kicked off, the colonel, who would flay him alive if he ever found out he was doing this – well, he went to the theatre a lot and he'd always had the most tremendous admiration for, well, back then she was just Hodda, of course, in fact he'd sent her heaps of notes asking her to have dinner with him after the show, she hadn't replied, of course, not being that sort of, um, lady, but what he was getting at was, the colonel had been feeling a bit blue lately, what with having to go down the mines all the time and really, it's not a lot of fun down there, and it would buck him up most awfully if Her Majesty sent him a note or something, just two words on a bit of paper saying good stuff, keep at it, it'd mean ever so much to him if it could be arranged somehow, and if it couldn't, of course he understood and he hoped he hadn't given offence by asking.

Hodda laughed like a drain when I told her. But I nagged her and she wrote *For a true hero* on a scrap of parchment and signed it, and sent it to him along with a handkerchief. "He'll wear it next to his heart, bless him," she said. "They always do."

There's a stall in the market where the actresses buy handkerchiefs; ten trachy a dozen, or a gross for a quarter-thaler. Rose- or lavender-scented, two trachy extra. But Hodda had hers delivered on a cart, in bales. Still, it's the perceived thought that counts.

10

Lots of ships come and go at the docks, but let me draw your attention to two in particular.

The first one didn't actually make it to the dockside. It anchored about half a mile out and raised a certain very distinctive flag. Everybody knows what that flag means. Plague.

"We ought to send a warship and sink it," said the City prefect.

"Counterproductive," said Rear Admiral Gainas, who spoke for the navy at staff meetings when Sisinna was out of town. "In order to sink it, our ship would have to come into physical contact with it. That's the last thing we want to do. No, just leave it alone and let nature take its course."

"That's completely irresponsible," the prefect said, and he never raises his voice or gets upset, ever. "What if there's a storm and it gets blown into harbour? Or some fool coming in might feel sorry for them and drop them off some food or water. You can't tell what might happen. You've got to sink it, right now."

"It's a Synaean ship," Gainas said calmly, "they're allies of the Sashan. If we sink one of their ships, it's an act of war."

"Under the circumstances, I hardly think—"

"We tell the Sashan ambassador there was plague on board," Gainas said, "but what if he chooses not to believe us?"

"It's flying the green flag, for crying out loud."

"The Sashan ambassador doesn't know that. He'd only have our word for it. And like I said, if he *chooses* not to believe us—"

"Have you any idea how quickly plague can spread in a city this size?"

"Depends," put in someone else I didn't know. "There's three or four different types of plague, and they spread differently. Of course, we don't know what kind they've got on the ship."

"Gentlemen," I said, and they all shut up and looked at me. Then I turned to Usuthus, on my left. "Find someone who knows about the different sorts of plague, and get him here stat." Usuthus nodded and got up. "Our first and only priority is to make sure the plague doesn't come here. The prefect's point about the ship getting blown in here is a valid one, and so's yours, about having to get in close enough to ram them. Remote chances both, but plausible, so the hell with that. How about sinking the poor devils with a catapult?"

Gainas frowned. "We could do that," he said. "But sinking her in any fashion is dangerous. I'm thinking about the tides. If we sank her where she's riding right now, there's a danger the bodies might wash ashore."

"Fine. Tow them out into the middle of the sea and do it."

"Which would involve even more contact."

The prefect made a soft moaning noise. "We can't just leave

it out there. Have you read Anser's account of the plague at Antecyra? It doesn't bear thinking about."

Some navy type sitting on Gainas' right muttered something about towing the ship thirty miles down the coast, where Ogus had a big supply depot. "Absolutely not," the prefect shouted, "what if it's airborne? It's that kind of reckless attitude—"

"I don't think that was a serious suggestion," I said firmly. "Gentlemen, we're trying to make a decision without any facts to go on. Let's hear what the expert has to say and then decide."

Enter the expert: an Echmen doctor with thirty years' experience with plague epidemics, which are an everyday fact of life out there. It all depends, he said. Some kinds of plague, you're fairly safe touching the patient, so long as you wash your hands afterwards. Other kinds are carried on a kind of miasma of poisonous air and can strike you down fifty yards away. If he knew which sort we were dealing with, he'd be able to advise accordingly. But the green flag just meant plague; and for all we knew it could simply be that the ship's captain was a hysterical type misdiagnosing a bad cold.

The City prefect changed his mind. Sinking the ship was clearly out of the question; if the plague could be contagious at fifty yards, we couldn't take the risk. Gainas changed his mind, too; leaving it there would be madness. What if another ship came in off course and blundered into it at night, in the dark? How would it be, I suggested, if we sent a warship to sink it, and then quarantined that warship out in the middle of the Friendly Sea for a month? Gainas explained that no warship could stay out at sea long enough to sit out the maximum incubation period; they'd have to put in to land for food and water, and the only places they could do that were used regularly by the navy; if anything went wrong, it could spread through the Fleet like wildfire.

"We need a decision," the prefect said. "The longer it sits out there, the more danger we're in."

I looked at Gainas. "Can your ships' artillery hit something a hundred yards away, guaranteed?"

He thought for a moment. "I'll have to say no," he said. "But you've got artillerymen on the wall here who could do it."

"Find them," I said. "Use at least a dozen fire-pots and burn the bloody thing right down to the waterline."

The other ship was a Fremmer cog. We get about three dozen of them a day; short-haul traders who work their way up the Blemyan Gulf, trading dates for raisins, raisins for olives, olives for rye flour, so on and so forth, a small profit each step of the way; by the time they get to us, they have a hold full of either wheat or lumber, dirt cheap everywhere else but valuable to us. The Fremmer live on an archipelago off the coast of Blemya and are the best of friends with everybody, to the point where, like starlings, you barely notice them.

Very occasionally they carry passengers. You'd have to be determined or desperate to take a ride on a cog, unless you like sleeping on a coil of rope and being thrown around like dice. The passenger on this cog was probably both.

He stepped off the ship onto the quay and asked the first man he saw where the harbourmaster might be. Over there, the man points. He goes to the harbourmaster. I'm an envoy, he said, from Emperor Ogus. Take me to your leader.

Reasonably enough the harbourmaster assumed he was a lunatic and had him arrested. At the Watch house, the envoy produced his credentials; impressively illuminated in red and gold on snow-white parchment, quite a work of art, sealed in lead with a seal as big as your fist. The Watch captain decided that most lunatics don't have access to expensive accessories like that, so he escorted him up to the palace and made him the duty officer's problem. Thirty-six hours later – by palace standards, that's like lightning – he was my problem. Lucky me.

"Do I need an interpreter?" I asked.

He looked at me. He was a short man, square shoulders, slight pot belly, thin moustache and a tuft on his chin, nearer sixty than fifty, pale brown eyes. He was plainly dressed and didn't seem remotely scared. "No, Majesty," he said. "I speak tolerable Robur."

"So you do," I said. I picked up the work of art. "This says you've come from Ogus to arrange a meeting."

"That's right."

"Ogus has never agreed to a meeting before."

"With respect, that's not true. He met with Colonel Orhan several times."

"The man who did Apsimar's job at the start of the siege," Usuthus whispered in my ear. "You know, the milkface."

I nodded. "Wasn't he a traitor?" I replied, loud so the envoy could hear.

"That was never proved."

"So you see," the envoy went on, "there's a precedent. I can assure you, the emperor is very keen to talk to you."

"What about?"

"That I couldn't tell you."

I looked at him. He was good. Absolutely no idea what was going on in his mind. "You're just here to make arrangements."

"Yes, Majesty."

I turned to Captain Very. "I don't trust this jerk further than I could spit him," I stage-whispered. "What do you think?"

The captain pursed his lips. "On the other hand," he said.

I nodded, and turned back. "We would be happy to grant Ogus safe passage into the City," I said.

"That wouldn't be acceptable, I'm afraid."

"I'm not going over there, not for all the rice in Blemya."

"Understandable," the envoy said. "What we had in mind was this."

I'd have assumed he was trying to be funny, except that apparently diplomats do this sort of thing all the time. Since Ogus didn't trust us by sea and we wouldn't trust him on land, the idea was that his men would build a jetty half a mile long and ten feet wide. I would row out in a small boat and meet Ogus at the far end of the jetty. He could bring one other, so could I. I would stay on the boat, he'd stay on the jetty. We could talk to each other, then go our separate ways.

Then we got the maps out. I wanted a spot where there was no chance of the current running me ashore. They needed somewhere they could build a jetty that wouldn't get washed away. Unbelievably, there was a spot on the north coast that answered all the above, but it was two miles straight across the open water from the harbour mouth. Absolutely no way, I pointed out, that I could row two miles, even if paddling a rowing boat accorded with my Imperial dignity, which it didn't.

Compromise. I could have two oarsmen, if Ogus could have two men on his side. I didn't like the sound of that. They'd have to be naked, I said, so there was no chance of concealed weapons. The envoy said, if it came to concealed weapons, I could easily hide a spanned crossbow in the bottom of the boat, but Ogus was magnanimously prepared to take that risk; the least I could do was reciprocate by letting him have two clerks, and no clerk can do his job properly if he's frozen numb to the bone.

Fine, I said. I would turn up in a warship, with sixty archers. He could have sixty archers on the jetty. If we're going to be stupid about this, let's be stupid in style.

The talks went on for a very long time and at various points in the discussion tempers frayed a bit; but eventually we reached an agreement. Me in a boat, with one aide and two oarsmen. Ogus on the jetty, with three aides. No weapons anywhere. "How about if it's raining?" I asked.

I think the envoy had had enough by that stage, too. "You'll all just have to get wet," he said.

"I'm going with you," she said.

"Don't be bloody ridiculous," I told her. "I'll need Usuthus, or Captain Very."

"You can have both of them. They can row a boat, I assume."

"It's dangerous," I said. "It's almost certainly a trap."

"I doubt it," she said sweetly, "you've been awfully thorough. And I don't get seasick. Remember, I've done loads of tours of the provinces. I'm a good sailor."

"You're not coming. Why would you want to, anyway?"

"You idiot. This is our chance."

"I agree," I said. "If Ogus really wants to negotiate—"

"You clown," she said. "You really don't get it, do you? He'll be expecting me."

I do have a brain, though for most of my life the only part of it I ever used was the memory. "You what?"

"Keep your voice down, you moron. He'll be expecting me. Both of us. Don't you remember?"

"No."

"Yes, you do. We agreed. We decided we needed to do a deal with Ogus so we could get out of the City safely. You said, there's no way we can get in touch with him. I said, leave it to me. So I arranged it."

Various things jostled in my throat trying to get said. What came out was, "That was ages ago."

"These things take time."

"What things?"

She explained (I use the term loosely). A few years ago she toured the Dosmoi peninsula with a travelling production of – I can't remember, some hack show. While she was out there she met some rich traders – what a surprise – and got to know them quite well. So, when she wanted to get a message to Ogus, she found a Fremmer captain, gave him a certain amount of money and told him he'd get twice as much from So-and-so in the Dosmoi when he handed him a certain letter. The Dosmorines, we know for a fact, have a virtual monopoly on the supply of vinegar to Ogus' army. Simple, she had the nerve to conclude, as that.

"But that's crazy," I said. "What on earth made you think Ogus would want to meet *you*?"

"Because he'd know I was Lysimachus' mistress," she said. "Only now I'm the empress, so the original scheme's been overtaken by events. Not to worry, the end result's the same."

"I don't think your hare-brained scheme's got anything to do with it," I said. "I think Ogus wants to talk peace because we've been wiping the floor with him lately."

"Do you? That's so sweet. I know he wants to see us because of me, because my Fremmer pal told me so."

"Bullshit. You haven't met any sea captains."

"He got a letter to me curled up inside a perfume bottle. See for yourself." She unstoppered one of the million trillion little bottles on her dressing table and handed it to me. Inside was a tiny scrap of rose-scented paper. I could just make out the writing on it.

"He wants his money," I said.

"Because the Dosmorine wouldn't pay him his bonus. Also, if you look there, he says the meeting is all arranged and we'll hear about it shortly. That was two days before the envoy showed up. So, you see, I did all that."

"A letter in a random bottle of perfume. What are the odds you'd open that particular one?"

"Attar of roses. My Dosmorine friend knows I happen to like that particular scent very much."

I could see the weathervane swinging round from Plausible to Likely. "All right, that covers How," I said. "I'm rather more interested in Why."

"You know why. Or weren't you listening? We can't get out of the palace. This is our only chance."

"You want to jump off the boat and swim for the shore. In the full regalia. You'll drown."

"No. *Listen.*"

11

Everything changes, see above. Nothing changes more often, more rapidly or more radically than the past. Yesterday's heroes are today's villains. Yesterday's eternal truths are today's exploded myths. Yesterday's right is today's wrong, yesterday's good is today's evil. And tomorrow it'll all be one hundred and eighty degrees different, on that you can rely.

Which is odd, since the past has already happened; it's done, complete, finished, signed off, sealed, delivered; dead. But, then, dead things change a hell of a lot, as the smell testifies. I tend to think of the past as compost; drifts of dead yesterdays rotting down into a fine mulch, in which all sorts of weeds germinate, sprout and flourish. Of course, the past changes, it can't not change, and what was true yesterday—

See above, passim. Change and decay in all around I see; everything changes, except for *me*. And that's what I told her. I'd made up my mind, I said to her, to get the hell out of this doomed city while I had the chance, as soon as I had the chance, and I intended to stick to that, come what may.

"God, I'm relieved to hear you say that," she said. "I was starting to worry about you."

"That's so sweet."

"I was afraid you'd started believing your own bullshit."

I smiled at her. "I do a lot of really stupid things," I said. "But that, never."

Usuthus had to learn to row a boat.

"You'll get the hang of it," I told him. "Look at the sort of people who spend their lives rowing boats. If they can do it, so can you."

Usuthus is terrified of water. So I asked Rear Admiral Gainas to find someone to teach him, and off they went in a little dinghy. Usuthus came back shaking like a leaf. "I can't do it," he said. "I'm not strong enough and I'm scared stiff."

"That's what I thought when they made me emperor, and now look at me," I said. "Now pull yourself together and get on with it."

I felt sorry for him, I really did. Also for Captain Very, who came from a landlocked country surrounded by mountains. He didn't like the sea much either, but he was determined not to let it beat him; *die, you bastard*, you could almost hear him say every time he thrust an oar into the water. It was me who suggested they really ought to practise rowing together, since teamwork is the cornerstone of oarsmanship. Funniest thing I've seen since Chalco played the Archduke in *Love's Alchemy*.

The envoy came back and said the conditions we'd asked for were acceptable, except for one. Let me guess, I said; and I was right. I'd asked that Ogus suspend the mining operations, as a gesture of good faith. No chance.

So, while Ogus' carpenters built a half-mile jetty, the

horrible war in the tunnels continued. I'd insisted on Colonel Apsimar taking a break from leading the attacks on their positions himself, with the result that we'd lost ground and been pushed back a hundred yards, at horrific cost to both us and them. So Apsimar resumed personal command, took back the lost hundred yards in a single desperate night, and carried on driving them back, one step at a time, until they reached the granite ridge. That was what Ogus had been anxious to avoid. It had cost him an infinity of effort, materiel and lives to breach the ridge. If we managed to capture and block the breach, he'd have to start all over again.

"It's all a matter of timing," General Pertinax told me at the next staff meeting. "If we can block the hole in the granite before you meet with Ogus, obviously you'll have a much better position to bargain from. Of course, it works both ways. If we make an all-out attempt to capture the breach and we get beaten off, it'll weaken your hand tremendously."

Thank you so much for that, I thought. I couldn't bring myself to tell Apsimar face-to-face, so I chickened out and sent him a written order; you have five days to capture the breach, failure isn't an option. "Not that we give a damn really," Hodda said, when I explained why I was looking so miserable. "But you're right, we've got to make a show of taking it seriously or someone may get suspicious."

Defending the breach was much easier than fighting in the open tunnels. They brought out the sulphur and the bellows and killed seventy-six of our most experienced tunnel-fighters in a couple of minutes. Apsimar retaliated by building a bellows of his own; only this one didn't blow, it sucked. As fast as they puffed out poison smoke, Apsimar pumped it out into a side-tunnel left over from a previous stage in the action.

Meanwhile, our sappers dug yet another tunnel, parallel to the one everyone was fighting over; then, when they came up against the granite, they turned ninety degrees, following the line of the ridge until they came out right next to the breach. Ogus' men managed to turn the nozzle of the bellows just in time and snuffed out forty men like a beekeeper smoking bees; that was when Apsimar led his main assault, up the original tunnel, before they had a chance to turn the nozzle back to where it had been. After about five minutes of the bloodiest fighting of the entire siege we broke through, slaughtered about three hundred of their engineers and barricaded the tunnel on their side while our stonemasons dragged up twelve solid basalt blocks, carefully designed in advance to block the hole. They were made so they interlocked, with no need of mortar, and when they were in position they were more solid than the original granite. Our men scrambled through before the last block dropped into position. Job done, with two days to spare.

I'd have liked to have been able to congratulate Apsimar personally, in front of the entire City, but it wasn't possible. I spoke to the men who were with him at the end, but it wasn't clear what had happened. The young subaltern who'd been the last man to speak to him said they'd been together on our side of the breach, just after the big push; Apsimar had led the attack, but had come back to our side of the hole to bring up reinforcements, since we'd lost more men than he'd expected. Then the subaltern told me he'd smelled roses and panicked—

"What do you mean, smelled roses?" I asked.

"Lately the bad guys've taken to wearing rose scent," he told me, "so they can tell their own people apart from ours. It's an old trick."

"I know. It doesn't work."

"Exactly. But they're stupid."

Anyway, the subaltern thought he could smell roses, got the wind up and refused to go any further. Apsimar said that was perfectly all right, sent him back down the tunnel to fetch the reinforcements and went back into the breach, and that was the last anyone knew.

But he was definitely dead. We knew that, because Ogus had his body tied to a buggy and dragged up and down in front of the wall, just out of bowshot, until eventually it broke up and fell to bits.

I think I know what happened, for what it's worth. By all accounts, when Apsimar went back through the breach the enemy had all been cleared out, temporarily, though they rallied for one last unsuccessful push; but one of our side must have heard someone coming through, and smelt a very faint scent of roses, and stabbed him, thinking he was a bad guy. The mistake arose because Hodda is particularly fond of attar of roses and soaks her handkerchiefs in the stuff till they stink the place out.

12

Still, never mind. We'd secured the breach, and that was what mattered. General Aineas, Rear Admiral Gainas and the City prefect told me we had Ogus on the run and I shouldn't settle for anything less than a complete withdrawal of enemy forces; I should also press for some of our territory back and at least a hundred million angels in war reparations; if I couldn't get that, I must absolutely insist on Ogus closing his factories, or at the very least agreeing to pay some sort of royalty.

The boat they'd built specially was a thing of beauty: painted purple, with the details picked out in gold leaf; the hull was oak, guaranteed arrowproof, so if they started shooting all I had to do was duck; they'd even listened when I asked what if it rained, because there was a huge purple umbrella, spring-loaded so it would fly open at the touch of a lever. "Let's hope it does rain," the new colonel of engineers said, "so you'll be nice and dry and he'll get sopping wet." He told me Apsimar had designed it himself; he had a flair for silly gadgets, apparently.

Hodda had a new frock for the occasion. The Chamberlain

had wanted us both in the full getup. I said, show me where it says in the book that the emperor and empress shall wear complete regalia when negotiating in person with the enemy from a rowing boat. Besides, Hodda said, the Imperial regalia were holy symbols of the Imperial dignity, and if they got ruined by saltwater or fell overboard, it'd be a national disaster. So Hodda embarked in a gown of flowing white silk, curiously reminiscent of the one she'd worn in *The Storyteller and the Slave*, while I wore the uniform of the Imperial brigade of cuirassiers, minus the stupid cuirass.

"God, it's wonderful to be back in real clothes again," she yelled in my ear as we rowed out into the bay.

I was scanning the horizon for ships, small boats, swimmers with knives clamped between their teeth. "That's your idea of real clothes, is it?"

When I said that I was wearing a red knee-length tunic edged with a key pattern in gold thread, under a quilted red velvet habergeon embroidered with the double-headed boar emblem of the cuirassiers in gold and silver wire, red cross-gartered stockings and red suede boots. She had the grace not to say anything, although she really didn't need to.

Usuthus and Captain Very were making a pretty good job of rowing the boat, even though it was much bigger and heavier than the one they'd been practising with. The sea was calm and flat and Hodda and I had silk cushions to sit on. I didn't feel sick at all. Then we were far enough out to see the jetty, and I felt my insides squirm.

Ogus, for crying out loud; himself, the most evil man in the world, the devil incarnate. Actually, I'd never thought about him much. I knew he hated all the Robur, therefore by implication he hated me. It was because for centuries the

Robur had oppressed and enslaved his people, which I guess was fair enough. The only answer to the Robur problem, he said, was total extermination; until that happened, the world wasn't safe. When the siege started I'd assumed he was a nutcase, insane, frothing at the mouth; now that I'd learned a bit about how things work and how they come to be done, I could sort of understand his reasoning. I could imagine one of those miserable, dreary meetings, with three powerful men bickering over whose deeply flawed plan to adopt; and I could picture myself saying, fine, let's just slaughter the lot of them, and that'll be that solved; and everybody agreeing with me so they wouldn't have to agree with either of the other two. No, actually I couldn't, but maybe that's simply because my imagination isn't strong enough. Not so different, after all, from some of the orders I'd given lately: burn down such and such a town I'd never heard of before the meeting; round up all the Green and Blue bosses and dispose of them; capture the breach, without fail. When you give the order, it makes sense. If a few people have to suffer in the process, it's a small price to pay. Let's get rid of this menace, once and for all.

So, Ogus and I had both paid subscriptions to belong to the same club; I'd be able to look him in the eye and see some sort of human being, not a demon or a monster. As for being scared of him – when you've stood up in front of a thousand paying customers with nothing to defend yourself with but twenty lines of rhyming iambic pentameters, people don't scare you just by being people. Unless he brought along a hundred archers dressed in invisibility cloaks, there wasn't anything to be frightened of.

Even so.

My experience as an emperor has enabled me to put together

a simple rule of thumb, which I'm pleased to be able to pass on to any kings, rulers, governors or members of representative assemblies who may happen to read this. *Let's get rid of this menace, once and for all* is always wildly popular, because it appears to promise a solution and nobody will have to think hard about the real problem or do the things that actually need to be done; instead, just blot a few people out and move on. The crucial element is numbers. Kill several million, and inevitably you're a monster. But if you restrict yourself to a relatively modest number, say one or two per cent of the population, fifty thousand people at the absolute maximum, you're a statesman and a hero and the father of your country. And there you have it. Please feel free to refer to it as Notker's Law, if you think it'll help.

But some people just don't give a damn, do they? And one of them was waiting for us at the end of the jetty. Nobody knew what he looked like, of course. The only hard data we had to go on, handed down by someone who'd known them both, was that he was on the tall side for a milkface and that he looked a lot like his father. Apart from that, nothing at all. In which case, the man waiting for us at the end of the jetty might not be Ogus at all. For all we knew, it could have been a stunt double, or an impostor.

The question has probably been addressed and dealt with by a scientist or a philosopher, but if so I haven't heard about it; at what point does a tiny dot on the horizon resolve into something you can identify? First, there's just a dot. Then you get closer, and it's still a dot. Then it's a shape, but still abstract. Then there comes a moment – the subject of my enquiry – when it *could* be a man or a horse or a dog, and then another moment when it definitely is.

"I can see him," Hodda sang out. She's got ridiculously good eyesight.

"You do realise," I said, "this is the furthest from the City I've ever been in my life."

Hodda glared at me, then glanced at Usuthus and the captain, who had their backs to us. I realised what she meant; what was true for me wasn't necessarily true for Lysimachus. I cursed myself under my breath, but I was fairly sure they were too busy rowing to have heard me.

"I can see them, too," I said.

They'd made a beautiful job of the jetty. Dead straight and dead level, none of your rustic charm, and the pale wood blazed like pale gold in the morning sun. Hardly surprising, I guess. Their carpenters had had a lot of work lately, and the more work you do the more you hone your skills.

I looked back at the City. Everyone says the best way to view it is from the sea. They're right. From the sea, on a sunny day, you don't see the dirt and the squalor and the people, just towers and gilded roofs and white domes against a blue sky. A thing of beauty, pretty as a picture. I'd never seen it before, of course. It looked curiously small.

"He's alone," she said.

"No," I corrected her. "The agreement was, we could each bring three aides."

"He's alone."

She was right, as always. Half a mile of jetty – first, you drive poles thick as a man's waist into the seabed, using special drop hammers mounted on barges; then you plank them over and add railings; then, if you're desperately keen to show off, you paint the railings crocus yellow – and just one man, right at the end, sitting on a folding stool. Now that's how to do arrogance.

We stopped about a hundred yards away, so Captain Very could talk to me. He couldn't turn round, so I was talking to the back of his head. "Is he really alone?" the captain said.

"Yes."

"He hasn't got men hidden anywhere?"

"You couldn't hide anyone on that thing."

"He could have divers underwater, holding their breath."

"I don't think so."

"In that case." Captain Very lowered his voice, which was silly, if you think about it. "In that case, we could kill him. No, listen. You engage him in conversation, I slip over the side, swarm up one of the piles—"

"No," Hodda said.

"We could end this war at a stroke," the captain said urgently. "No Ogus, it all falls to pieces. I can take him, I know I can. We'd be back in the boat and out of bowshot long before his men could reach us."

"No," Hodda repeated. "If you try it'll all go wrong, and there's our one chance of peace out the window. I absolutely forbid you to do anything of the sort."

"Majesty?"

Meaning me.

Just think. At a stroke. The sort of brave, impulsive seizing of the moment that changes history. Lysimachus the Great saves the Robur nation. "She's right," I said. "Nice idea, but better not."

Captain Very nudged Usuthus in the ribs, and they lifted their oars; a moment later, we were under way again. Nice idea, I thought. Exactly what Lysimachus would have done – hero, arena champion, best fighting man of his generation, he'd have pulled it off, too. I wished he was there in the boat, and I wasn't.

"Take us in to about five yards," I said.

"We can't see," Usuthus said. "You'll have to say when."

The closer we came, the higher up Ogus was. As soon as I saw him, I knew him; the type, I mean. I'd grown up with it. He was the typical Theme bruiser who's made his pile and taken to indulging himself; pot belly, double chin, fleshy face, bags under the eyes, but all sort of added on, like modern additions to an old house, and under it you could see the man who made the pile, by hurting and scaring people and being more than usually smart. He was about the same age my dad would have been, had he lived.

I stood up. The boat rocked horribly. I sat down. Ogus laughed.

"Who are you?" he said.

"Lysimachus. The emperor."

"No, you're not," Ogus said. "I've met Lysimachus, and you're not him."

Then I noticed Hodda glaring at him, same as she'd done at me a moment ago, only about five times fiercer. "No matter," Ogus said. "You're the emperor."

"Yes."

He got up, came to the edge of the jetty and squatted on his heels. "Let's get down to business," he said.

"Sure," I replied. "What can we do for you?"

Grin. "We ought to talk," he said. "But not like this, it's ridiculous."

"Agreed."

"There's an island," he said, "about six miles up the coast, Lapizaria. Tiny scrap of rock with one croft and a dozen sheep. We'll meet there. Your men clear it out, including the sheep. My men row over and make sure it's empty, then your men and my men pull out. You row over in a boat, so do I. We meet in the crofter's hut, one aide each. Deal?"

I turned to confer with Usuthus and the captain, but Hodda scowled at me. "That sounds fine," I said. "When?"

"Noon, day after tomorrow. When your boys have cleared the island, raise a white flag and my boys'll come over. When we're all done, I row back, and you don't signal to your warship to come in until I'm back on shore." He paused and grinned. "Got that, or do you need your clerk to write it down for you?"

"I think we can remember that, between the four of us."

He stood up. They'd been right: he was a tall man, about my height, though not quite as broad across the shoulders. He looked at me, frowned, turned and walked away down the jetty. He had a sort of a swagger and a roll, which brought back memories.

Eight hours later, they told me, the jetty was gone, as if it had never been. A team of engineers came out and dismantled it, packed the planks and beams onto carts and rattled away. All that timber would come in useful for building tunnels.

13

One question I wanted an answer to, but couldn't face asking, so I didn't. Meanwhile, preparations to make, for the summit conference.

"We want you to wear your armour," the City prefect said. "We didn't last time, because of you being in a small boat, and if it capsized you'd sink. But this time we'll take you right to the island in a warship, and fetch you off in one, so you'll be able to wear it safely."

"No," I said.

A certain amount of dialogue followed, in which the words *stupid* and *pig-headed* weren't spoken aloud, but for once I put my buskinned foot down. There's two basic schools of defence: armour, and not being there. My dad was a firm believer in the latter. All that ironmongery is strictly for the military, he used to say; on the street you don't want it, just slows you down. If the other bastard looks like he's about to have a go at you, get out of the way. If you aren't there, you can't get hit.

Words to live by. Dad and I differ on the precise meaning

of *out of the way*; for him it meant a quick step back and/or sideways, then nip in smartly while he's off balance and punch him in the kidneys, whereas I interpret it as running away and not stopping until you're sure you're safe. In any event, no armour for me. I was sick to death of the bloody thing anyway.

"We've already been over the island," General Pertinax told me. "Nobody's lived there since the siege started. Some farmer puts a few sheep there during the summer and a shepherd uses the hut, that's all. We've patched up the roof and rehung the door, and put in a table and some chairs." He lowered his voice and leaned forward. "The floor's covered with flagstones," he said. "We could lever one up and hide a weapon under it."

"Please don't," I said.

"Think about it," the general hissed in my ear. "Your aide could distract him, you make a show of dropping something on the floor, you stoop down, lift the slab, get the knife; your aide grabs his arms, you stick him in the guts. You could end the war at a stroke."

"No," I said. "It's a stupid idea and we're trying not to do stupid any more. We're doing smart instead."

"We've got time; we could rehearse it beforehand, so you'd know exactly what to do. Amazing what a difference that makes, you know."

So true. "Something always goes wrong," I told him. "Read your history. Assassinations always screw up somehow. His aide will be watching me like a hawk. And what if Ogus is wearing armour under his shirt? No, we do this properly. Probably best if you clear out the flagstones and put down a nice rug or something. If I was Ogus' chief of security, I'd suspect a trick like that."

Still, it was worth thinking about. "Hairpins," I said to her.

"What about them?"

"A nice long hairpin," I said, "with poison on it. Someone told me once about some stuff they brew out of white hellebore roots: prick your finger and you're a goner. While we're talking, you're fooling about with your hair; women do it all the time, nobody even notices. Then you pull out the hairpin and stick it in his arm, I smash his aide in the face, we run for it. Well?"

"Are you serious?"

"It's worth thinking about."

"No," she said, "it isn't. And white hellebore only grows in the mountains of Permia; there wouldn't be time."

"There's probably something else just as good."

"Forget it," she said. "It's a really stupid idea."

I nodded. "I thought so, too. Only—"

"What?"

"I don't know. It's the sort of thing Lysimachus would've—"

"You're not Lysimachus."

At which, something woke up in the back of my head. I told it to go back to sleep. "Agreed," I said. "Just thought I'd run it past you, that's all."

Interesting that she knew so much about poisons and where to find them. Still, she's a very well-informed woman. "You're still thinking about staying here, aren't you?" she said.

"If there's no Ogus, there's no reason to leave."

"Yes, there is. Of course there is. I can't stay here the rest of my life, in these stupid clothes, locked up with a load of stupid women. We need to get out of here, with money, lots of it. You agreed to that. Well, didn't you?"

"Yes."

"You've changed your mind. You like pretending to be the emperor."

"I am the bloody emperor," I snapped. Then: "But you're right, of course. I can't live like this, any more than you can. Long runs are great, but not a lifetime. We've got to get out."

"*Yes.* As soon as we can. Tomorrow."

I stared at her. "You're kidding."

"Do I look like I'm kidding? No, when Ogus goes back to the mainland, we go with him. That's the plan. Are you in or not?"

"It won't work. It's too soon. We can't just rush into anything."

"Tomorrow or not at all. I've got it all figured out. You just leave all the talking to me. Keep your mouth tight shut, and everything will be just fine."

Around the time Hodda and I were having that conversation, Ogus' miners broke through the granite shelf, about five hundred yards south of the previous breach.

We picked it up on our pans-of-water mining detectors, and there was no doubt about it. If at first you don't succeed; patience, perseverance, an admirably strong work ethic.

"Chances are," said the new colonel of engineers, a fifteen-year veteran who'd got the job because everyone better qualified was now dead, "it's just a blind, and he'll be putting his main effort into the old workings. But we can't just ignore it, obviously, or he'll make the new breach his main assault and play around with the old one as a diversion."

"We've got the resources to counter him, haven't we?" I said.

He nodded. "I've got the Tanagenes digging a countersap right now," he said, "and we've got nine sets of burners and bellows. I imagine he'll have something new up his sleeve after getting beat the last time. No guessing what it could be, so we'll just have to wait and see."

Hrabanus, his name was; I'd read his record and he seemed quite bright, though a plodder rather than an inspirational hero in shining armour. "Have you read Posidonius on siege-craft?" I said.

"Been meaning to get around to it for ages," he replied. "But you know how it is."

"Posidonius," I said, "says that if a besieger has sufficient resources, a besieged city attacked by sapping and undermining will inevitably fall. It's just a matter of time, expense and political will. The defenders' job is to make it more trouble than it's worth, and four times out of ten they succeed; the besieger runs out of time or money, or the government changes at home and wants peace, or plague breaks out in the besieger's camp – that happens a lot – or something happens that stops him pressing on to the bitter and otherwise inevitable end. But in purely technical terms, assuming the besieger has the resources, it's impossible to defend a city against undermining indefinitely. That's what Posidonius reckons, anyway."

"Haven't read him," said Hrabanus. "Sorry."

Once I'd got rid of Colonel Hrabanus I had time to think. Posidonius lived three hundred years ago; he was the chief engineer for the Vesani empire, on whose behalf he besieged and captured no less than twenty-six cities; still a record, apparently. He wrote his book in a city under siege, in the intervals of defending it with all the skill and experience at his command, and died bravely when the city was undermined and sacked by the enemy. But that was two hundred years ago, history, the past; and, as we've seen, nothing changes like the past. Take your eye off it for a split second and it's unrecognisably different. You can set too much store by precedent, if you ask me.

"I've had enough of this," I said to her. "Let's do something. Let's go to a theatre."

She looked at me. "What, and watch?" she said. She made it sound indecent. "We can't do that. It takes three days to organise if we set foot outside the palace."

"Fine," I said. "We'll have a royal command performance. We can do that. We can send out for any show we want."

"If you insist," she said.

"One thing's for sure," I told her. "Where we're going, wherever we end up, there won't be theatres there. Not what we know as theatres, anyhow. This is our last chance."

She shrugged. "Can't say the thought bothers me much," she said. "But if that's what you want."

I sent for the Chamberlain. "We're out of touch," I explained. "What's the best show in town?"

He didn't know, but he'd find out. Half an hour later, he came back. The consensus of the younger clerks, he said, was that you couldn't beat *The Girl from Emarus* at the Sword, with Olethria in the title role and Psaolus as a comic doctor. The senior clerks recommended *The Liar's Tragedy* at the Sceptre, with Einhard as the king.

"We'll have the comedy," Hodda said. "Send for them."

"What did you have to go and choose that for?" I said, after the Chamberlain had gone.

"Because I'm not in the mood for three hours of Saloninus. Anywhere, *Girl from Emarus* is a good show."

"I don't like it."

"Really? Why not?"

"I wrote it."

296 K. J. Parker

"So you did," she said, "I'd forgotten. Or at any rate you did the second act and several of the songs. Come to think of it, I still owe you money for that one."

Actually, it wasn't bad. The first and third act went well, Olethria did her sword dance and someone had replaced one of my songs with a dance routine involving nine girls dressed as fish. After it was over, she went backstage to say hello to her old friends, because it would've seemed odd if she hadn't, while I sent for the Chamberlain.

"I forgot to mention it earlier," I said, "but Her Majesty would like the paintings in her dressing room taken down and replaced with something with a bit more class. Her words."

"Yes, Majesty."

"She thought maybe the Callicrates icons."

"An excellent choice, Majesty."

"See to it, there's a good chap."

14

The most famous icon in the world is, of course, Our Lady The Averter Of Evil, which hangs above the altar in the Golden Spear temple; it's black as coal from a thousand years of incense smoke and almost certainly not the original, which disappeared sixteen hundred years ago; it miraculously reappeared a century later, when nobody who'd ever seen it was still alive, and I suspect it of being an impostor, like someone else I could mention. But for a thousand years it's performed regular miracles – healing the sick, restoring sight to the blind, bringing victory against our enemies – so it's clearly doing a grand job, even if it's a fraud.

The second most famous icon is Our Lord Of The Bronze House, and on the first day of each month ever since the siege began the priests of the Studium had carried it in procession round the walls; which, according to about eighty per cent of the population of the City, was the only reason we were all still alive.

We do like our icons. We have them as godparents at

298 K. J. Parker

baptisms; they witness wills and important commercial con-
tracts; they give the bride away at weddings if the bride's actual
father is dead or absent. A sick man would far rather have an
icon than a doctor – Our Lady Of The Golden Skein is the
only known cure for the bite of the black diamond spider and
several sorts of poison toadstool – and the venerable series of
the Transfiguration above the White Gate is practically down
to bare boards, thanks to the habit of generations of soldiers
of scraping a tiny scrap of paint away under a fingernail, to
protect them from death on campaign. Actors and dramatists
especially revere Our Lord Of The Balances; I used to have a
copy of it myself, egg tempera on limewashed board, which I
kissed just before going on stage.

After all, they work, or they work every bit as well as anything else does in this life. The Emperor Corineus, according
to some book I read, used to go into battle wearing armour
made entirely of icons, overlapping like the scales of a fish, and
once during the assault on Auxesis he was hit square on by a
catapult arrow at point-blank range. The arrow bounced off,
and he wasn't even bruised.

What was good enough for Corineus, Hodda explained to
her ladies-in-waiting, is good enough for my husband; so she
had them sitting up all night carefully stitching the seventy-
two Callicrates icons in between two layers of red velvet to
form a holy brigandine. For her own protection she sent one
of the girls down to the Chapel Royal to borrow the venerable
and exquisite Our Lady Of The Waterlilies, which she hung
round her neck on a gold chain. Once that was done, we were
good to go; so we went.

On the way to the docks we heard the latest from the mines.
We'd put out half a dozen exploratory saps, only to find (the

hard way) that the enemy were much further forward than we'd thought. We'd had to fall back and fill our main sap with rubble mixed with sand and mortar, to keep the enemy from driving through it right into the City. Hrabanus was proposing to dig deep under the enemy's main gallery and undermine it – dig a wide chamber twenty feet below it, collapse the chamber roof and bring their gallery crashing down – but that was bound to take time and he wasn't exactly precisely sure of where the gallery actually was, so it was just possible that he was directing all our energy and resources into something that wasn't going to work. Still, it was better than sitting around playing cards waiting to have your throat cut.

15

Somehow word had got about, and there were thousands of people at the docks, mostly wearing Theme purple, to see us off. Hodda stood up in the carriage and held the holy icon over her head, which got her the most tremendous cheer – and why not, it was a scene she was born to play. I stayed sitting down, looking miserable. No need to act for that.

The sea wasn't quite as calm as it had been the last time. I felt sick, just managed to keep it down. First time I'd been on a warship, of course; we're a seafaring nation, salt in our veins and all that, but as far as I'm concerned you can stuff it.

The island wasn't what I'd been led to expect. It was closer to the mainland, for a start, and bigger. I'd got it into my head that we were headed for a rock sticking up out of the water with a little hut perched on top of it. Instead, it was bigger than the Haymarket; the biggest open space, in fact, that I'd ever seen up close. In the distance, I could make out a building. As we tramped across the grass, with great big rocks the size of your head lying about where anybody could trip over them, I figured that must be the shack everyone had been talking about. Some shack. In Old Stairs, you'd have five families living in something that size.

He was there waiting for us, sitting on the porch steps. "I'm alone," he called out, "it's quite safe."

Here we go, I thought. The last part of the walk was a steep climb, and I arrived out of breath and sweating.

Ogus stood up. "Come inside," he said.

"Here'll do me," I said.

"Inside. That was the agreement."

True; so we went indoors. The shack was horrible; the walls were white with mould, the air was damp, and there were rat holes in the walls and rat shit on the window-sill. Hodda hates rats. As soon as we were inside, Hodda slammed the door shut and stood with her back to it. Hello, I thought.

"Right," Ogus said, not to me. "Who is this clown?"

I looked at her. She was looking at him. "It's a long story," she said.

"Answer the question."

"He's an actor," she said, "called Notker. Lysimachus got killed by one of your stupid catapulty things."

Ogus was grinning. "You're kidding, right?"

"No. Notker looks like Lysimachus—"

"No, he doesn't. I met Lysimachus. This idiot's taller and stockier, and his nose is a different shape."

"He's an *actor*," Hodda said. "Anyway, he's now the legitimate crowned emperor of the Robur, and that's gospel truth."

"Excuse me," I said.

"Be quiet," Hodda snapped. "I've brought him, here he is," she went on, "and I've kept my end of the deal. All right?"

There was a window but it was too small and narrow to get out of. The door or nothing, should you wish to leave in a hurry. "What deal?" I said. "Hodda, what's going on?"

Ogus turned his head and frowned at me. "Be quiet," Hodda repeated. "Well?" she went on. "Have I or haven't I?"

I remembered – Ogus had reminded me – that I was a big, strong man, almost a head taller than Ogus and at least twenty years his junior. I took a long stride forward and grabbed him by the shoulder.

You tell me what's going on right now, I was planning to say, but I couldn't, because by then I was on the floor in a heap, unable to breathe. My dad knew that punch, he used it a lot. You barely move at all, and the other guy's as helpless as a baby.

"Don't hit him," I heard her say.

Ogus kicked me. Actually, it hardly registered; when you're completely winded, you can't feel anything. I heard her yell at him; a soft, disinterested voice in the back of my mind said, she doesn't want to do that, he won't like it. Sure enough, a moment later I heard a loud slap, a scream and another slap, this time no scream. "Don't you tell me what to do," Ogus said, not raising his voice. Three guesses who he reminded me of.

"I've had enough of you," he went on. "You're a pain in the arse, that's what you are. Now shut your face and get away from the door."

"This isn't what we—"

"No, I changed my mind. Shift."

I managed to drag some air inside me. It was like swallowing a brick. I opened my eyes. She was on the floor, in a heap, in front of the door. He was bending down, grabbing a handful of her hair. Useful stuff, hair, in my dad's line of work. "All right," he said, and tried to yank her to her feet.

I'd have grinned if I'd been able to. Hodda gets her wigs and hairpieces from the Curali brothers, in Long Acre. She pays a lot of money for them. Worth every penny.

The hair came away in Ogus' hand, and he staggered backwards. That gave Hodda just enough time to scramble to her feet, open the door and hurl herself outside. Full marks to her, she had the wit to slam the door behind her as she left. It only took Ogus a split second to open it again, but a split second can be a very, very long time, in context. Long enough – to take an example purely at random – for me to haul myself up off the floor and smash a chair over his head.

Didn't actually work like that. We use fake chairs, made of some light, fragile wood. This one was heavier and clumsier to swing, so the best I managed was to clout the side of his head with one leg.

Still, it doesn't have to be perfect, and there was no audience to criticise or throw nuts. I'd clearly hurt him enough to stop him thinking, let alone doing anything, and that's all you need to achieve; trust me, I know about this stuff. I had plenty of time and just enough strength left to hit him properly: a stab in the kidneys with the legs. Now that hurts. He dropped to his knees, leaving me a clear shot, at my leisure, at his head. With a nice heavy, solid chair like this one, I could finish the war at a stroke.

Except I couldn't. I maintain it's because I was too weak, after being winded and kicked, I mean. I looked at him, on his knees, and stepped back, keeping the chair legs directly between him and me. On the floor, I saw half an icon. He must have broken one of them when he hit me.

He put his hands on his knees and stood up slowly. "She won't get far," he said.

"What's going on?" I asked him.

He laughed. "You cheated," he said, "you're wearing armour. She said she wouldn't let you do that."

I unbuttoned the coat and opened it. "What're those?" he said. "They look like little pictures."

"Icons."

"Really. You people are pathetic, you know that?"

He lunged at me, but I was ready for him. Even my dad grudgingly admitted that I have good footwork, when I'm expecting an attack. I sidestepped, he rushed past me and nearly collided with the wall. I swung the chair as he went past, but I'd underestimated the headroom. The legs hit a roof beam, and one of them snapped. I dropped it. He turned to face me. He had a knife in his hand. Of course, by this point so had I.

Didn't I mention that? My idea, not hers, for once. I'd stuck it into the lining of the coat, where my dad taught me, the place where only the most careful frisking will find it. It wasn't a wonderful knife, but it was the only one I could get at short notice.

"Seriously," he said. "You're an actor."

"Was."

"Like her."

"You obviously know each other."

"Oh yes. She's my wife."

He didn't need a chair to make my head hurt. "Your wife."

"Yeah, she insisted. All my wives come to a bad end. Talk of the devil," he added, as the door opened.

My guess is, she hadn't got far but had put up a fight. The milkface soldier with her looked like he'd had a torrid time of it. Scratched face, that sort of thing. He pushed her inside, shut the door and stood in front of it.

"You're useless," Ogus said to the soldier. "I could've been killed while you were larking about out there. My aide," he added. "I don't cheat. Well," he added, sticking the knife back in his belt, "no more than you do."

I kept mine where he could see it. "You can't get off this island," I said. "They'll see you from the warship."

He grinned at me. "There's a blind spot," he said. "The shack covers a way back to our boat. Not the one we came over in, goes without saying. You people are stupid."

I looked past him. "Are you really married to this oaf?" I said.

She scowled at me; on her knees, picking up her wig and putting it back on. At a time like this, I thought; still, she's Hodda. Presumably the soldier counted as an audience. "Yes," she said.

"If I were you," Ogus said to me, "I'd put that knife down, before you cut yourself. Him and me, we can take you easily, but accidents happen."

"I don't think so," I said. "If I do, you'll kill me."

Ogus sighed. "We're going to kill you anyway, son. Hadn't you worked that out?"

Then something unexpected happened. The soldier slid to the floor. He wriggled a bit and made a funny noise, then lay still. Hodda was looking at me. "Hairpin," she said.

Ogus swung round, took in the altered circumstances at

a glance, then glowered at her. "You stupid bitch," he said. "What did you do that for?"

"You promised me," she said. "You weren't going to kill him."

"The hell I did."

"That's when he was Lysimachus. This is Notker."

"I'm not interested who he is."

"In my last letter, I said, don't kill him. We had a deal."

That's so like her. She sets terms and assumes you've accepted them. "You changed it," he said. "Anyway, why not? He's nobody."

"Leave him alone."

"If I do that, what's the point of the exercise? The deal I agreed was, you bring me Lysimachus, I kill him."

"Pretend he's dead," she said, "that's just as good and we aren't going to contradict you. We'll go off somewhere."

"You and him?"

She nodded. "I don't think I want to be married to you any more."

"I don't think so," Ogus said. "I need a head to stick on a pike, otherwise who'll believe me?" That grin again. "God, I wish you'd told me Lysimachus was dead. We needn't have bothered with all this nonsense."

I was thinking about it. Hodda and me against him; it would probably work, assuming Hodda was really on my side. Could I count on her? Probably not, even though I was the one with all the valuable icons. What mattered, though, wasn't the truth. It was what Ogus believed. "She's stitched you up," I said.

"You be quiet," she yelled. I ignored her.

"You die," I said, "the war's over, she's the empress of the restored Robur empire. Not to mention your widow. Would that make her empress of your lot, too?"

"Shut *up*," Hodda screamed at me.

"Bring a knife, she told me, just in case. And if that didn't work, there's always her trusty poisoned hairpin."

He laughed. "I don't think so," he said.

"Believe what you like." I took a step forward. "Get behind him, Hodda, that's a good girl."

Ogus took a long, graceful step back into the corner, just like I wanted him to, to where I wanted him to be. Of course, Hodda's the experienced director, not me. Still, you pick a few things up.

In this instance, the chair. I threw it at him and darted towards the door. It only opened halfway, of course, because the stupid dead soldier was blocking it, and in the time it took me to kick him clear, Ogus was on to me. So I stabbed him.

I remember him looking at me, then down at the blood soaking into his shirt. I pulled the knife out. "You might want to get that seen to," I said. "Come on, Hodda, we're leaving."

She didn't want to go but I got her arm behind her back, like Dad taught me. He had a wonderful way with women, and kids, too.

We ran about a hundred yards, which was all I could manage before I dropped to my knees, gasping like a landed fish. I managed to turn my head. We weren't being followed.

"Get up," she screamed at me.

No, I thought. What's the point of being emperor if I can't indulge myself in the occasional luxury, such as breathing? Hauling the air in was like dragging a cart uphill; it really didn't want to go, and I wasn't sure I had the strength. So she grabbed my ear and hauled me to my feet. You can't argue with that.

We ran, with her towing me like a tug with a grain barge, until we could see the warship. She let go of me and waved her hands over her head.

I was back on the ground. "You killed someone," I said.

"What?"

"That soldier. You killed him."

"Yes, I suppose I did." She waved again. "Never done that before. Just as well I did, or you'd be a dead man right now."

"How could you do that?"

"My lucky hairpin," she said. "I've had it for years. Oh, you mean how could I bring myself to? Easy-bloody-peasy, in the circumstances."

I saw the warship lower a boat. "You set me up," I said.

"Not you. Lysimachus."

"I ought to break your neck."

"Don't be stupid, Notker. If you hadn't screwed everything up, we'd have been fine."

The boat was a third of the way over to the island. "Come on," she said.

I staggered to my feet. "What was the plan?" I said. "The one I screwed up."

She sighed. We started to walk. "Originally," she said, "I was to seduce Lysimachus and talk him into a meeting, like this one. Ogus would kill him, and that'd be that. Of course, that's when we all thought Lysimachus was the heroic genius who saved the City."

"In your last letter, you said to him."

"I wrote to him after he realised you weren't Lysimachus," she said. "Letter in a scent bottle. I told him, let us go and pretend you've killed Lysimachus. But he welched on us, the bastard."

"You're really his wife?"

She nodded. "I could've sworn he was nuts about me," she said sadly. "It was when I did that tour of the Cartwheel Islands. I slipped across to the mainland on a fishing boat and went to see him. I can give you Lysimachus, I told him. We got on famously, so I thought." She stopped, turned round and looked at me. "You stabbed him. Will he be all right?"

"Oh, I should think so," I said. I showed her the knife. Then, with the tip of my left index finger, I pressed the point right down into the handle.

"Oh, for crying out loud," she said.

Theatre knives, like theatre everything else. It's spring-loaded, so it looks like you're driving five inches of steel into somebody and in fact you haven't broken the skin. And when the blade goes into the handle, fake blood squirts out through a little tube. I'd palmed it off one of the actors at our command performance. It was the only knife I could get.

"He'll be very confused for an hour or so," I said, "all that blood and no hole. Other than that, he'll be fine. I'm not a killer," I added. "Not like some people."

She gave me a look of pure refined contempt. "You're a clown, Notker."

"I like to think so," I said. "We don't get the girl, but we get all the laughs. You might have said something. I really thought we were going there to negotiate."

"Really? God, you're dumb."

"Really. You neglected to say anything that would tend to make me think otherwise."

"You're lying," she said. "Or you wouldn't have brought the icons."

"They were for you, you stupid bitch." Moment of silence. "You were desperate to get out of the City. I assumed that was the plan. You set up the meeting so he and I could talk peace, and the valuable artwork was your commission."

"Oh." She was still gazing at me. "Thick as a brick," she said. "You really thought that."

"It seemed plausible," I said. The boat had reached the shore. We were about two hundred yards away from it. "I thought he might actually want to talk. Silly me."

"You'd have let me go."

"Not up to me, is it? You want to go, you go. Why didn't you let him kill me, by the way? That was your original deal, wasn't it?"

"No, that was Lysimachus."

"I'm Lysimachus," I said. "Ogus seemed happy enough with it, but you said no."

"That wasn't the deal," she said. "And anyway—" She scowled at me. "I don't know," she said. "Come to think of it, it would've worked out pretty well. You wanted to go," she added angrily, "you told me so. You said, we've got to get out of the City."

I nodded. "That was one of the things I was going to ask for," I said. "In the peace negotiations, which never happened. I don't know. This is what comes of not talking to each other."

Captain Very was walking toward us, with two soldiers. "You're not going to tell anyone," she said.

"What, not mention the fact that you tried to betray the emperor to the enemy?"

"Notker—"

"Keep your voice down, please."

Captain Very closed to within earshot. "Well?" he called out.

"Balls-up," I called back. "Let's get out of here quick."

16

A trap. A cowardly, treacherous attempt on the life of the emperor. It went down like free beer.

"People are saying it's because he's desperate," General Aineas told me, "because he knows he's losing the war. It's done wonders for morale."

"Jolly good," I said.

The holy icons, according to the best medical opinions, had saved me from at least one broken rib. Which proved, according to expert theologians, that icons really do work. Meanwhile, as soon as the news of the cowardly, treacherous attempt reached the poor bastards in the mines, they launched a counter-attack that drove Ogus' sappers right back to the second breach, and gave Hrabanus time to finish his undermining in peace and quiet.

"You're not talking to me," she said. "That's childish."

"What the hell is there to say?" I told her. "If you can think of anything that won't make things worse, I'd love to hear it."

"Childish," she repeated.

"For God's sake, Hodda." When she makes me shout, she

knows she's won. I lowered my voice, but by then it was too late. "You know what you've done. I don't see talking about it's going to make it any better."

"I see. That's the thanks I get for saving your stupid life."

I could feel history changing all around me. "Let's forget it, shall we?"

"I know you," she said. "You'll keep banging on and on about it until I want to scream."

"Let's talk about something else." I took a deep breath and let it out slowly. "What next?"

She cast her eyes up at the ceiling in silent prayer for strength. "I don't know," she said. "All my plans have gone the way of yesterday's piss, thanks to—"

"Yes, thank you."

"I'm stuck here," she said. "Stranded, until Ogus smashes his way in and murders the lot of us. All thanks," she added, "to you. If it wasn't for you, I could get on a ship and sail away. I'd be broke, but at least I'd be alive."

"Was that what you wanted from Ogus? Money?"

"Ever such a lot of it, yes. And I could see the war could only end one way."

"You really think that."

"Yes," she said, "I do."

"I agree with you," I said.

Not just intuition, in my case. Latest from the mines; since our unfortunate meeting, Ogus had opened up six new saps. His miners now knew everything there was to know about breaking through a granite shelf, so it wouldn't be long before we were fighting on six fronts, at least, down there in the pitch dark. Hrabanus' men were still fighting like lions for every inch of tunnel, killing Ogus' men at a ratio of over ten to one, but it was getting harder and harder to replace the experienced men we lost.

He can't keep it up, my wise advisers told me. Sooner or later the provinces will rebel, especially if we step up the pressure with the Fleet. He can't keep on conscripting whole cities. Already there were entire regions where nobody lived and the land was drifting back into a jungle of briars and thistles, because all the men had been marched away to the war and never come home. People won't stand for that sort of thing. They just won't.

I'd have agreed with him, except for a book I'd read. Apparently in north Blemya there's a desert, thousands upon thousands of square miles of sand. Hundreds of years ago, that was all wheatfields, the breadbasket of the First Blemyan Empire. But then there was a civil war, two nephews scrapping over who was to succeed their uncle. Both of them were brilliant generals, and they fought many remarkable battles, wonderful displays of military science, in each of which tens of thousands of men died but with no clear result. So more and more men were recruited, and the war went on; one of the rivals died and was replaced by his equally brilliant son; the other rival married his only daughter to the finest general in the world, Robur it goes without saying, who in due course inherited his father-in-law's claim. The war only ended when the whole of Blemya was over-run by nomads – simple people, no match for civilised armies, but by then there was practically nobody left to fight them, and they burned down the empty cities and grazed their goats on the weedy, overgrown fields. Now goats will eat anything and everything, and before long the high winds they have in those parts blew away all the overgrazed topsoil, leaving nothing but the sand underneath. Moral: it's amazing what people will stand for, if the government tell them to.

17

So I started to read about granite.

I had plenty of time for reading, since I refused to spend my evenings stuffing my face with indigestible luxury foods in the company of stupid, boring aristocrats. The Imperial palace library has a copy of every book ever written; all I had to do was tell Usuthus what I wanted, and armies of dedicated librarians scrabbled around like moles till they found it for me. There is in fact a ridiculously large literature on the subject of granite, but the librarians winnowed out the irrelevant stuff and only brought me what I needed to see.

All sorts of useful information: what it's used for, where it comes from, the different sorts of granite, how much a square foot of it weighs, what volume a ton of it occupies. Granite, I realised, held the key to all our difficulties, if only I could make people do what I wanted. Compared to people, of course, granite is easy as pie to work with. Of all the components that go towards building a city, human beings are the most intractable, unreliable, expensive and dangerous. Didn't need a book to tell me that. I learned that lesson at my father's knee, or, properly speaking, his toecap.

Relevant, in its way. I had a team of (relatively) good, knowledgeable men to advise me about the stones and bricks of the City and how to keep them from being torn down; where to reinforce the battlements, the importance of mamelons and ravelins and the mysterious science of the flying buttress, just how much pounding a wall can take, all the minutiae of digging over, under, round and through the many and various kinds of dirt, gravel, clay and rock. As far as brick and stone went, I was reasonably confident that we had it covered.

But Saloninus says, it's not bricks and stones that make a city, it's men and women. And concerning them, who the hell could I ask or trust? Thousands of years of history and the actions of great men, inspiring leaders, wise statesmen – they were all the funnel down which we'd slid to find ourselves in this ghastly, appalling mess. The great-great-grandsons of those wise leaders made up the House, and as far as I could tell they'd all inherited their ancestors' way of thinking along with the money and the gold dinner services. Professional soldiers, who'd lost us the empire more or less overnight; no, I can't say I put a lot of stock in what they thought about things, specially since I'd got to know them. The Themes, sorry, Theme; the voice of the people, united we stand and divided we fall, and until very recently there had been two of them, do the maths. I grew up in the Themes, as I may just possibly have mentioned, and my father was so much a part of his Theme that even now I find it impossible to evaluate the one without the other. As you'll have observed, I owe a vast deal to my father and the Theme; my instincts, the ability to think on my feet; nothing less than my life, on countless occasions. He taught me to think as if every moment of my life could turn into a fight, and I can't imagine any more valuable gift. In comparison, the inheritances of the great senatorial families are so much trash. But the Themes can't run a city, no more than maggots can bring what they're feeding on back to life. No; we may have sorted bricks and stones, but as far as people go we don't understand them and I don't see that we've ever seriously tried to.

Stones and people; what they call a symbiosis. Stones piled up into a wall keep you safe. Stones lobbed over a wall squash you flat. Why does everything in life have to be so ambivalent?

There was a bit of a scuffle in the street as I processed, in all the horrible gear, to the Annunciation Day service in the Red Heart temple. "Nothing to worry about," Captain Very assured me, "just some mad woman." He laughed. "Reckoned she was your mother."

After the service, I told the captain we were going to the Watch house. Which one? The one where they'd taken the poor unfortunate mad woman who made the disturbance in the street. The emperor, I pointed out, is the fount of all clemency, and people like that sort of thing.

"If you insist," he said. "You'll be late for the Privy Council."

"Fuck the Privy Council."

Just so happened I knew that Watch house quite well. I spent eight hours locked up in it once, on an entirely baseless and malicious charge of disorderly conduct after a wrap party. The cell they took me to was bigger than mine, but without a street view.

"Hello, Mother," I said.

"Notker? What the hell do you think you're playing at?"

"Not so loud, *please.*"

"It *is* you," she said, "I knew it was. I saw you up on the steps at the Old and New Festival. What the *hell*—?"

So I told her. She listened in stony silence. Nobody, not even Hodda, does silent disapproval better than my mother. Of course, she's had so much practice.

"You're mad," she said.

"What else could I do?" I complained. "At every point there's been people with weapons threatening to kill me if I don't do as I'm told. I didn't ask for any of this. It just happened."

"No, it didn't."

"Yes, it—" Deep breath. "I got picked up and swept along on a wave," I said. "Yes, as it's gone along I've tried to make the best of it, with the result that I'm still alive. If I could've got out of it at any point, I'd have done just that. But I couldn't. It wouldn't let me."

"Rubbish," she said. "It's all just you telling lies. You always were a liar, Notker. You tell lies even when you don't have to. Half the time, I think you don't know what's true and what isn't."

"Fine," I said. "Suppose you're right. You're my mother. Tell me what I should do."

She gave me that look, the sort that turns grapes into raisins. "Putting your own mother in prison," she said. "Never been in a jail cell in all my life, until you put me in one."

"Yes, all right."

She looked at me, without the shrivel effect. "You're a fool, Notker. All you've ever done your whole life is lie and run away. You broke your poor father's heart."

"No," I said, "I didn't. He was proud of me."

Shrug. "He wanted you to have a better life than he did. And now look at you."

Well, I thought, yes and no. "What do you think I should do?"

She thought about it, for what seemed like a long time. "Get out," she said. "Get away from here, as far as you can possibly go, where nobody knows you and you can start again, with a proper job."

"I can't do that," I said. "I told you, I'm trapped."

"You'll have to find a way, that's all," she said. "Tell a lie or two. You're good at that."

"I wish I was," I said.

"Don't ever wish that," she snapped at me. "It's lies got you into this mess. No good ever came of lying."

I wanted to explain to her; I really am the emperor. Doesn't matter how I got there. Half the emperors in the list had no right to the job until they actually got it. What about Tisander the Liberator, conqueror of Ballene and friend of the poor? He was a clerk who worked his way up to head of department. When the old emperor died, he was in charge of the arrangements for the coronation. He was supposed to help the crown prince on with all the gear – lorus and dalmatic and divitision and all that shit – but, instead, he climbed into it himself, dashed out into the Great Hall, plonked his arse down on the throne and proclaimed himself emperor; only the emperor could wear the regalia, he explained, he was wearing the regalia, therefore he was the emperor. And *he got away with it*; in spite of the fact that he'd got the dalmatic on inside out and the buskins on the wrong feet. I really am the emperor, so how dare you say I've been a disappointment to you, even if it's true?

Couldn't say that, of course. "So that's your advice, is it? Lie and run away."

She knows me all too well. No matter what I become or who

I turn into, she knows me. Everything changes, but not that. "I don't see what else you can do," she said. "Not after the mess you've made."

"Lie and run away," I repeated. "All right, then."

I released an official statement, to be read out in every marketplace and temple in the City; you know the sort of thing, there's two or three of them every day about something or other. This one said that the emperor had taken pity on the poor mad woman who tried to assault him in the street. On enquiry, it turned out that the woman had lost her reason after her son was killed in action against the enemy; her tragic loss had addled her wits, so it was impossible to believe a word she said about anything. Nevertheless, she was therefore a heroine of the commonwealth, and as a mark of respect to her and others like her, the emperor had graciously awarded her a substantial pension for life and free accommodation in a grace-and-favour apartment, together with the purely honorary title of Mother of Her Country. Just as you'd expect, it was wildly popular with the people, and Usuthus said he wished he'd thought of it.

Lie and run away, two things I'm good at. Well, I thought, marking my place in yet another book about granite with my handkerchief, why the hell not?

18

In which case, there wasn't a moment to lose. I sent for the First Lord of the Treasury. "How much money have we got?" I asked him.

He looked at me. "Majesty?"

"In actual coins," I said. "How much?"

He gave me a respectful scowl. "I really couldn't say, Majesty. The specie reserves fluctuate from day to day, depending on a wide range of factors."

"At a guess."

I think he'd have liked me better if I'd asked him to eat a turd salad. "Really, it's impossible to make a meaningful estimate. I can find out for you, if you'd like me to."

"Do that."

"Of course, Majesty, it will take several days. And by the time I have a consolidated figure, the situation may have changed substantially, rendering the stated total meaningless."

"You've got till this evening," I said. "And I wouldn't want to be in your shoes if the figures aren't accurate."

I got my answer, on time and guaranteed bang-on right. Based on my thumb-and-fingers estimate, it wasn't enough. So I sent for the president of the central bank. "How much money have we got?" I asked him.

Same rigmarole. Result: ready cash added to the value of loans already agreed, mortgages on future revenues and other concrete intangibles (I kid you not; that's what he called them) would be just about enough. So I sent for Colonel Hrabanus and Rear Admiral Gainas.

I told them what I wanted them to do. There was one of those silences.

"You don't think it'll work," I said.

"Far be it from me," said the colonel, "but it's a bit—"

"Radical," I said. "Yes, I know. But let me tell you something. We're way, way past the point where anything that's been done before can possibly help us. Did you read Posidonius, like I told you?"

"Yes, Majesty. However—"

I glared at him, but he carried on regardless.

"Things have changed since Posidonius' time," he said. "Defensive techniques have come a long way since then. We've made great strides in earth-moving and tunnel construction."

"I know. So has the enemy."

"I refuse to acknowledge that it's a foregone conclusion." He stopped short, desperately ashamed of himself for yelling. "I firmly believe that a conventional defence will be effective. It's got to," he added.

I shook my head. "It's not a conventional attack," I said. "Against us we've got a lunatic who rules a third of the known world, and he doesn't care what it costs, in money or lives. That's pretty unconventional, if you ask me."

"Even so—" He raised his hands, that old words-fail-me gesture. "If you give the order, I'll do my very best to carry it out. But I have strong reservations—"

"Noted," I said. "Admiral, what about the ships? Do you see a problem?"

He shook his head. "Not if the ships exist," he said.

"Oh, I imagine they do," I said airily. "They were built out of oak and tarred and caulked within an inch of their lives. I know it's a long time ago, but I bet they're still around."

"In that case," he said, "yes, it's entirely feasible, if that's what you really want to do."

"And the escort side of it? That's very important."

"We can do *that*, certainly," he said. Which was all I needed to hear.

So I sent for the senior officers of the Purple Theme; not the dummies I'd installed to appease the House, the real ones, leftovers from the old days who'd wisely decided to play ball with me. "I need a hole dug," I said.

They didn't like the sound of that. "Sapping and counter-sapping are skilled trades," one of them said. "We don't have anyone experienced enough to—"

"Don't worry," I told him, "I'm not asking you to send Themesmen down the mines. Not yet, anyway," I added, just as he was beginning to relax. "No, this is a strictly civilian hole. Big, but civilian."

They looked at each other. My *not yet* hadn't been wasted on them. "Consider it done," they said.

"Oh, and one other thing," I said as they got up to leave. "We haven't had a proper census for years. I think we ought to have one."

"With respect, there was a census the year before last."

"That was a government census," I pointed out. "Naturally, people lie to a government census, it's expected of you. I mean a Theme census. A true one, done by us. How many people there really are and where they really live. I think I ought to have that information, if I've got to plan for emergencies. Otherwise, people might end up with no food and nowhere to sleep, just because I didn't know they existed. See to it, would you? No rush, this time next week will do."

After that, all I had to do was send for the captain of the fastest ship in the fleet and give him his orders.

"All that money, Majesty."

"Nowhere safer than the hold of an Imperial warship," I said. "Besides, nobody except you and me will know what you're carrying."

He looked straight at me. "You trust me with all that money?"

I nodded. "You have a wife, a mother, two sons and a daughter," I said. "Get back here with a sealed receipt before Ascension Day and they'll be released."

"Ascension Day." He stared at me. "That's not—"

"Bet you it is," I said gently. "Let's find out, shall we?"

(Hodda said: "You don't really mean that, do you? That poor man's family—"

I shrugged. "Probably not," I said. "If this doesn't work, it isn't going to matter very much."

"What's that supposed to mean?"

"This is our last chance," I said, "don't you understand that? If it doesn't work, we're out of time, and money, and soldiers, options, everything."

"But it's a stupid idea. It won't work.")

And then I'd done all I could; it was up to other people.

The word went round: double the going rate for digging a bloody great big hole, picks and spades provided if you haven't got your own. Naturally, people wanted to know what it was for. Drains, we told them. Of course, nobody believed a word of it.

Two more Synaean ships showed up, flying that horrible flag that only means one thing. That got me worried. I had the harbourmaster trawl through his records, every Synaean ship that had landed for the last three months. There had been fifty-nine of them, and their crews had done the usual tours of the bars and brothels. No sign of plague anywhere. But three plague ships in such a short time; I sent for Gainas and told him to turn back all Synaean vessels at the five-mile line. "But don't go on board," I told him. "And if one of them refuses to go back, ram it. And the ship that does the ramming had better go off somewhere for a month, just in case."

"What about the two quarantine ships?" he asked. "Sink them, like last time?"

"That seems a bit heartless," I said. "Tell you what. That island, where I met Ogus. Escort them there. At least the poor bastards can die on dry land, and there's no chance of their ships drifting into the harbour once they're all dead."

He looked at me. "You're hoping Ogus will send soldiers over there, and they'll take the plague back to his camp. Actually, that's not a bad—"

I shook my head. "They're not that stupid," I said. "Also, I wouldn't do that to anyone, not even him."

"It's not a bad idea," Hodda said.

"No," I said. "It's a horrible idea, and I'm not doing it."

"You could end the war at a—"

"We tried that, remember?" She scowled at me. I went on: "Anyway, I've been reading a book about it. Pacatian's account of the plague at Coseilha."

"Where?"

"It was a long time ago," I said. "There was a siege. Plague broke out in the besiegers' camp. Five thousand men died in a week."

"That's not bad."

"So what the besiegers did," I went on, "they loaded corpses onto catapults and tried to chuck them over the wall into the city. But their catapults weren't strong enough and they fell short."

"There you are, then."

"So they cut the bodies into bits. A bit of a plague corpse does just as well, they found. Six weeks later, they rammed open the gate and found they had the place to themselves. Everybody inside was dead. Moral: you don't mess with Mister Plague. He is not your friend."

She shrugged. It's a beautiful thing to watch when she does that. "You do read a lot of books," she said.

"Full of good ideas, some of them."

She got up to leave the room. It was time for her to go and sit doing nothing in the company of the flower of Robur womanhood for the rest of the day. "Just a moment," I said.

"What?"

"Sit down."

"I can't be long, they'll be waiting for me."

"Do you care?"

"I hate them," she said simply. "Forty-six simpering rich women, aged between seventeen and sixty-nine. Each one wearing enough diamonds and pearls to fill a bucket. There's this fat woman."

"Do tell."

"I mean *fat*," Hodda said. "Melt her down, you could make enough candles to light the Gallery for a month. And she's got this ruby and sapphire ring."

"Nice?"

"Horrible. It's so horrible I can't help staring at it. And it must be worth – I don't know how much it'd be worth. I long to stab her in the neck and rip it off her finger."

"Don't do that," I said gently. "It's against the law."

"And they talk," Hodda went on, "all the damn time. And don't ask me what about, because I really don't know. People I've never heard of, mostly, doing stuff that bores me stiff. Who went to dinner with who and who else was there and what they were wearing. It's *stupid*."

"It's called Society."

"It's what we do plays about," Hodda said bitterly, "only in the plays we all know it's ridiculous. But they don't seem to realise that. They seem to think it's real life."

"Real life. Haven't heard that expression in a while."

She sat down, elbows on knees, head slumped forward. "It's killing me, Notker. I can feel my brain turning to cheese. I've got to get out of here or I'll die."

If she was acting, she was playing herself. I put my arm round her shoulders. "But that's the life every actress dreams of," I said. "Respectable and rich. Every chorus girl from Old Stairs who ever fluttered her eyelashes at a senator's son—"

She glared at me. "Got what she deserved," she said. "Didn't someone say once, the punishment for wanting something too much is getting it?"

"Depends what you want, I guess."

"I want to manage a theatre," she said, so loud they must have heard her through the door. "I want to choose plays, hire and fire actors, yell at the painters and the costume designers, drill the chorus like they're a Guards regiment and make a great deal of money. Not to spend," she added quickly, "just to have, to prove I'm a success. That's what I want, Notker. And you know what? I used to have it, till you came along."

I took my arm away. "Just one thing," I said. "You and Ogus."

"Oh, that."

"That," I said. "You went out of your way to seduce our mortal enemy, with a view to selling him the City. For, presumably, a great deal of money."

She looked at me. "He's going to win," she said. "You know he is."

"Yes," I said. "I've known that for a long time."

"That's why I did it," she said. "I thought, everything I know and love is going to go up in smoke and everybody I know and love is going to die. Well, not me. I'm getting out, and I'm going to make damn sure I get a lot of money out of it to take with me." She stopped and looked at me. "You can't blame me for that, can you?" she said. "If they're all going to die anyway."

"Everybody's going to die," I said gently, "it's a medical fact. Not everybody helps murder a whole city."

"True." She gave me her ingenue look, the one a thousand men in this city would gladly die for; the one she pulls five times a night, for money. You know it's completely fake, of course, but like the man said, what is Truth? To which I answer without a moment's hesitation: overrated. "Just as well I didn't get away with it, really."

"Probably just as well," I said. "It was a bloody stupid idea, you know."

"No, it wasn't. You screwed it up."

"Probably just as well," I repeated.

She nodded; perfectly done, but I wasn't convinced. Nor did I care. "Notker," she said, looking straight at me, "what are we going to do?"

I looked directly ahead, so I couldn't see her. "I asked my mother that," I said. "She gave me some really good advice."

"Go on."

"She said, tell lies and run away. She knows me so well."

"Notker, I'm serious. What are we going to *do*?"

I thought about that for a moment. Then I made up my mind.

"If I can get us out of this," I said, "alive and in one piece and maybe even obscenely rich, though that's not guaranteed, will you marry me?"

It was as though she'd asked me for bread and I'd given her a slug. "You what?"

"You heard."

"But we're already married," she said. "And you don't like me very much."

"True," I said. "But that wedding was just acting. And, yes, there's things about you that make me want to jump down a well just to escape. But you're very pretty."

I'd said that to annoy her. "Notker."

"And," I said, "you're smarter than anyone I've ever met, and you can run a theatre like nobody else in history, and you were an amazing Princess Toto."

"I don't love you, Notker."

I nodded. "I don't think you're capable of loving anyone,"

I said. "And why should you? It'd be such a waste. I think of you as a goddess."

"Oh, come on."

"I do," I said, "really. Spiteful, selfish, utterly self-centred, addicted to worship, callous, unfeeling and incapable of loving anyone but yourself. What do you say?"

Her exasperated face. "All right," she said. "On the strict understanding that it'll never happen, because there's no way out of this. If there was one, I'd have thought of it."

"I want to hear you say yes."

"Fuck off. Oh, all right then, yes. If it makes you feel happy."

Something I needed to ask. "The hairpin," I said. "Did you really just happen to have it by you?"

"What? Oh, that. Yes, I've had it for years. It lives in this little silver tube, look. Well, you never know, do you?"

"I could do with something like that. A brooch, maybe."

"I'll give you the recipe."

I smiled at her. "You're going to kick yourself when you hear what I've got in mind," I said. "It's like this."

19

I'd said a hole, but really it was a ditch. It ran parallel to the walls, thirty yards distance between them, all the way round the City, sixty feet deep. The spoil was piled up in the gap between the walls and the ditch, forming a bank that completely filled the space, so we had to build towers on our side, and a walkway, so the sentries could get to the watchtowers and the artillery bays.

Sixty feet deep, because that's as far down as you can go before you hit bedrock. We had all sorts of problems, as you can imagine. We hit four underground springs, which flooded the trench and turned everything into revolting sticky mud. They had to be located and diverted, a massive undertaking in itself. There was no money at all, so the workforce – basically every able-bodied member of the Purple Theme – was paid in scrip, which didn't go down wonderfully well to start with, until everyone got used to money being little bits of sealed clay rather than shiny metal. If it hadn't been for the Theme organisation, we'd never have got people to do it. But with the government paying silly money on one side and the Theme bosses explaining what would happen to them if they didn't show up for work on the other; two sides of the same coin, almost certainly counterfeit.

And on a schedule, too. It had to be done by Ascension Day. Actually, I was desperately worried that Ascension would be leaving it too late; Ogus had opened three more saps and was pouring men into the mines. Colonel Hrabanus was keeping him at bay with undermining. For the time being at least, we could dig down deeper than they could, thanks to an ingenious idea Hrabanus' people had come up with for pumping air down to the lowest levels, using the monster bellows we'd built for the sulphur and pipes made from hollowed-out birch logs. Ogus' men tried to copy it, but we found out, dug sideways, found his pipe, bored a hole in it and pumped in sulphur smoke; my guess is, when a thousand men went down that tunnel and didn't come back, Ogus' engineers didn't realise we'd sabotaged the ventilation system, and concluded that it simply didn't work.

Hrabanus was no longer leading the war in the mines. I put him in charge of digging the ditch and promoted one of his junior officers, a half-milkface called Cotkel. He was the one who'd come up with the birch pipes, and who blew the smoke into Ogus' copy of same. He was a disagreeable little man with a dreadful record of insubordination and striking superior officers, and he'd killed more enemy engineers with a knife or his bare hands than anyone else in the regiment of engineers, so I figured he'd be perfect for the job, and I wasn't disappointed. Hrabanus, on the other hand, was college-educated and knew all about maths and military architecture and stuff, and drew a whole load of exquisitely neat plans of the ditch, heavily annotated with numbers and figures. I don't know if they helped at all, but they were very pretty to look at.

"I thought you ought to know," I said. "I'm going to get married."

It was wonderful, people said. The emperor, busiest man in the City, still made time to go and visit the poor old mad woman who'd lost her son. I think the only person who wasn't impressed was the poor old mad woman, who bitterly resented being called mad when she wasn't. Fortunately, nobody took any notice of a word she said. Except me.

"I don't know why you bother telling me," she said. "It's a stupid time to get married, anyway. Haven't you got other things you ought to be thinking about, beside chasing after girls?"

"You'll like her," I said. "She's smart."

"Can't be all that smart if she's marrying you."

I smiled. "She took some persuading," I said.

She frowned. "Planning for the future, then."

"Yes," I said. "I think there's going to be one, after all."

"You're a fool. You can't win this war."

"Everybody tells me that." I stood up, then sat down again. The cushions were so soft they hurt my back. "Are you comfortable here?"

"It's all right. I'm bored. I've got nothing to do."

Sixty years chained to a spinning wheel. Take it away from her, she's bored; she's got nothing to do. Everything's always my fault. "Is there anything I can get for you?"

She didn't even answer. "You mean well, Notker, some of the time. But you don't care about people. You don't give a damn."

"That's not entirely true."

She sighed. "I know," she said, "it's not your fault, it never is. You're in trouble all the time, so you're always thinking about yourself, of course you are. When you're drowning, you aren't worried about whether someone else can swim. You never have time for people, because you're always running away from some stupid mess you've got yourself into."

"I don't think you're being quite fair," I said.

"Don't you? And borrowing money. You've never got any money."

"Right now," I said. Right now I've got plenty, I was about to say, but all the money in the Exchequer was on a warship bound for the Sashan empire.

"It gets in the way," she said. "You're so busy figuring out how you're going to kid people into lending you money, you haven't got a chance to think about their feelings and all. When was the last time you talked to me, when you weren't looking to borrow money?"

"I'll make it up to you," I said. "I'll make it up to everybody."

"Sure you will. You always say that."

"One of these days I'll mean it."

"And always the last word," she said, with a grin. "Always a joke, and always the last word. Who is she, anyway?"

"Her name's Hodda."

"Her." She shrugged. "No better than a common tart."

"I've been mad about her ever since the first time I saw her," I said. "I looked at her and I thought, that woman is a goddess."

She laughed. "Your father said that about me once. Didn't last long, though. But he was a good man, your father."

"Yes," I said, "he was, in his way."

"Better than you."

"That," I said, "remains to be seen."

Her no-point-arguing look. "What's all the fuss about in the street?" she asked. "People coming all hours of the day and night with scaffolding planks and wheelbarrows. What's going on?"

"We're digging a ditch," I told her.

"What the hell for?"

So I told her.

I explained that Ogus' engineers were bound to get past us sooner or later, because there were so many of them, and we couldn't defend against them. The only thing that had kept them back so far was the granite shelf, and they'd got the hang of breaching it by now, so we couldn't rely on it any more. But what if they got as far as the wall, undermined it and brought it crashing down, only to find a huge bank of earth? As good as a wall; better, in many respects. For a start, you can't bash it down with rams or catapults, like you can with a stone wall. It's soft: it gives instead of splintering. And if you drive a sap into it, as soon as you break through your sap fills up with loose dirt; as fast as you shovel it out of the way, more comes cascading down. So, you dig under the huge pile of dirt in the hopes of coming out on the other side of it, and what happens? You run into another granite shelf, twice as thick as the first one.

Ah, you say, there's no granite shelf on our side of the wall. True; not yet. But pretty soon there will be.

"We're demolishing all the temples and public buildings," I told her, "all the ones built or faced with granite, and when the trench is finished we'll fill it with blocks. It'll be almost as thick as the City wall, but deep underground. There's not enough quarried granite in the City, but I've sent away to the place where we used to get all our granite from, with instructions to buy up everything they've got. When it's finished there'll be a sort of mirror wall, sixty feet high and twelve feet across, only under the ground instead of over it. And when they try and sap holes in it, we've got a surprise in store for them. We came across four underground rivers when we were digging the ditch. A nudge of a sluice gate and all that water will go gurgling down right on top of them." I paused for breath, then went on, "At first I didn't think we could get it done in time, but we can. You'd be amazed what can be done if you've got the Theme bosses on your side and nobody arguing with you or saying there's no money. There *is* no money, of course, but there's food for the workers and everybody in the City, for now anyway, and as for later, we'll cross that bridge when we come to it. We'll just have to work flat out, that's all, to make enough stuff to sell and pay off the cost of it all. It'll take time, but we'll *have* time, instead of all being dead."

Her head was turned away.

"And you know what," I went on. "That's all me, that is. Nobody but me could've done it. Not the old emperor, because he didn't have the brains. Not Nicephorus, because he didn't have the power; he'd have had to talk other people into it, and they would've told him it'd never work. Not the House or the civil service, because they can't do anything, only stop things being done. Not even the real Lysimachus, because he'd never have got the Themes together and made them work for him; he was a Green through and through, just like Dad, and the Blues would rather die than do all that stuff for a Green, even if it'd save the City. The engineers couldn't have done it, the soldiers and the politicians couldn't have done it, the Themes wouldn't have bothered trying. It was me, a stupid two-bit song-and-dance man, your son. *I* did it. I lied and I cheated and I pretended to be a great hero and I told people I was doing one thing when I was doing something else, I bullied and stole and twisted people's arms, I did everything you're not supposed to do, all the stuff I'm good at, and as a result the City will not fall, and we'll all be here this time next year, and the year after that. So don't you dare say I'm no good, because it's not true."

I looked at her. She'd fallen asleep.

20

Why Ascension Day, I hear you ask? Because that's when the weather begins to change, according to the Admiralty manual. Horrible fierce winds start to blow from the west thirty days after Ascension Day, and sailing eastwards across open sea is bound to end in tears. Also, Ascension is the second biggest festival in the calendar, and the emperor traditionally delivers his state-of-the-empire address to the people on the last day of the festival. And, more to the point, Major Cotkel had given it as his considered opinion that after Ascension he couldn't guarantee to keep Ogus from coming up through the floor, like the devil in a pantomime, and slaughtering the lot of us.

Open sea, because if you draw a straight line across the chart instead of hugging the coast all the way to the Sashan border, you shave a whole two months off the trip. Most freighters can't handle the wind and the waves that far out, but I knew for a fact that the Sashan stone barges (I told you about them; biggest ships ever built) could do it and survive, because that was the route they used to take in the old days. I was gambling that the same ships would still be in service – a fair bet, given that they'd cost an obscene amount of money to build, so you'd need to operate them for about a hundred years before you got your money back, let alone showed a profit. I'd read the specification they were built to in one of the old books and I was deeply impressed, even though I didn't understand a word of it.

Meanwhile, we ripped down the Senate House and prised the architraves off the Golden Feather temple, we dismantled half of Hill Street; best part of a quarter of a million granite blocks, each weighing half a ton. The engineers and the Stonemasons' Guild and the carters and the artillerymen told me it couldn't be done, certainly not in the time available, probably not at all. But I'd closed all the factories and workshops, the shops and the market stalls, even (God forgive me) the theatres; if you wanted to earn money, you came and worked for me. Not real money, of course. Nothing I do is real. But my pretend money was good all over town; you could buy bread with it. All you had to do was suspend your disbelief, like the audience at a play, and everything went smooth as ironed silk. It was a pretty paradox – let's save the City by taking it apart stone by stone and burying it in the ground – but paradox is the gatehouse of truth, in my opinion. I have no idea what that means, by the way, but I bet you it means *something*.

I was paying them silly money and they had no choice; even so, I don't for one minute think they'd have done it but for one extraordinary thing. The people believed in me. The people loved me. You mean Lysimachus, she said, but actually no, I don't. Take the humble caterpillar, which changes its name and puts on a fancy silk costume, and instead of crawling along the ground, it flies. Two entirely different creatures, one a worm,

one a sort of very small bird, you couldn't possibly mistake
the one for the other, they bear each other no resemblance
at all. Same creature, though, inside. And maybe I wasn't
Lysimachus, but for most of my life I hadn't been Notker, or
at least not when I was working. I'd been me. For a long time
I crawled along the ground, and then I spread my wings. And
ask yourself this: when you go to a show and see Olethria play
Queen Eudicia, who do you clap and cheer for? Lysimachus
was a good part, but I flatter myself I'd played it pretty well.
Because of which, we dug the ditch, pulled down the buildings and laid the stones, and all with two days to spare before
Ascension Eve.

Smug bugger, aren't I?

Hope breeds in this city, like rats. Forgive me for repeating
myself; it's a good line, and nobody will notice that I used it
before. Not that I really understand what people have against
rats. They're small and furry, with cute whiskers, and all they
want to do is make a living, raise their very large families in
peace and quiet and not get exterminated by huge monsters
whose motivation they can't begin to understand. But: you
move into a new place and the first thing you say is, Yuck, rats,
they'll have to go.

By go you mean die, of course; so you make war against them
with every means at your command. You borrow someone's
terrier. You mix poison with a handful of wheat chaff. You set
traps, cunning, ingenious traps with mechanisms whose intricate workings are a delight to behold, taken out of context. If
you're really determined, you stop up all the holes but one and
puff sulphur smoke down it with a bellows. Maybe, if you're as
soft as butter, you feel a trifle guilty, because all life is precious,

even the enemy; but you know in your heart that they've got to go, because they're rats. There's a line in one of the poets:

> *. . . In ruined churches, where the bees*
> *And rats and mice build monasteries.*

It's a good line, though the rhyme's a bit dubious. Actually, it's *ants and mice*, but not to worry. Nobody likes sharing with an ants' nest, either.

Hope, though; now there's a real pest. Hope doesn't just nibble your cheese and chew holes in your skirting boards. Hope keeps you plodding on when it really is time to call it quits. Hope drags you to sixteen auditions in a single day, when there's a nice job in your brother-in-law's tannery just waiting for you. Hope keeps you going in Old Stairs or Paradise, even though there's no money and nothing to eat and the landlord just took your chair and your chamber pot. Personally, I can see no great merit in simply being alive if you're miserable and in pain, but Hope won't let you go. She's a tease, like bad children teasing a dumb animal, and I've made a point of avoiding her whenever I can. Still, sometimes she runs you down and there's nowhere left for you to go. You can turn and fight her and lose, or let her scoop you up and turn your brain to mush.

Hope against hope. We had human chains shifting those blocks with levers and rollers, through the narrow alleys where carts couldn't go. We had shifts digging the ditch by lamplight, in the rain. And in every working party there was at least one man who cheerfully announced that it wasn't going to work, the whole idea was stupid, the enemy'll find a way round this in two shakes, just you see; and even he didn't really believe it, because of Hope. Hope turns a hundred men and women ripping the skin off their hands on a coarse hemp rope into a street party. Someone tells a joke, or clowns around, or starts singing a favourite song from one of the shows, and Hope bursts through, like sappers, and next thing you know she's everywhere, like smoke, or floodwater, or rats. We're going to beat Ogus, she whispers in every ear, and this time it'll be different.

And then the ships came. I wasn't there, but I heard about it. At first they thought it was a mist blowing in from the sea. No, it was sails, hundreds and hundreds of sails, covering the sea in a line so long it curved; and some of them were warships, the Fleet coming home, but most of them were huge black-hulled things with ridiculously high forecastles, impossibly big and square and flat, with best part of a quarter of an acre of canvas towing them steadily through the choppy water as though it wasn't relevant. It was as though the giants had come to visit; people expected to see men twelve feet tall in their rigging, and rats the size of horses.

Those were the Sashan stone barges, on whose existence I'd gambled every trachy in the Exchequer, and here they were, a dream come true, deliverance swooping down on wires at the end of Act 3. I went down to the docks to see them put in, along with the joint chiefs of staff, the department heads of the service, the entire House and the chief officers of the Theme. I'd read about them, every detail, precisely how many nails and dowels there were in each one, but I'd never imagined they could be so big; and yet they strolled demurely into the harbour and snuggled up to the quays like kittens.

I knew they could do that, because they'd done it before. Because, according to the books, the whole of the docks were knocked down and rebuilt three hundred years ago to accommodate those monsters; a hundred of them at a time, with room to unload comfortably, turn and go out again.

But there weren't a hundred of them, there were two hundred and sixty-two; sixteen more than it said in the books, which sort of proves my point about history. I'd asked them to send the lot, and they had.

The cranes we'd built to handle the blocks were all there ready and waiting, and once the blocks were on the quay the teams took over, rollers and levers and ropes, because it'd be quicker to manhandle them from the docks to the wall than to lift them up onto carts and then lift them down again. I climbed up onto one of the observation towers, and from up there it was like a granite river running through the streets, like rainwater, or the lava from an erupting volcano. Ah, volcano imagery; how useful it's been to me in telling this story. Maybe this was the point where the lava starts flowing back up the hill, to fill in the fiery hole and make sure it never bursts out again.

21

She joined me on the tower. We watched as Purple Theme did the impossible: a whole city on the move, working together, doing what actually needed to be done. Which is a hell of a lot more unlikely than lava flowing uphill, I can tell you.

"Fine," she said, after a while. "You win."

"Really?"

"I know when I'm beaten," she said. "You did this. It's amazing, and we're going to beat Ogus. I can't believe I said that, but it's true."

"No," I said. "It isn't."

That oh-for-pity's-sake look. "Don't be silly," she said. "They're doing exactly what you told them to, and it's going to work. The City is safe. No power on earth—"

I took a good look, enough to last me the rest of my life. "Actually," I said, "no. It won't work. Not if Ogus can read. Or if he's got someone to read to him."

"What the hell are you talking about?"

I wanted to break it to her gently, but she's a big girl, she could handle it. "It won't work," I said. "I know it won't."

"You're talking drivel again. I wish you wouldn't do that."

Sigh. "You don't honestly believe I thought of this myself, do you?"

"Didn't you?"

"God, no," I said. "I found it in a book. *Elements of Military Architecture*, by Deodatus. And he didn't think of it, he only wrote about it."

She shrugged. "What the hell," she said. "Originality's overrated, if you ask me."

"Deodatus," I went on, in my plonking, boring voice, "wrote about the siege of Oppa, where the Echmen spent five years trying to beat the greatest military engineer of all time, a man called Posidonius. All this was his idea. It's not in any of his books, however, because he never lived to write about it. Posidonius did all this at Oppa – the trench, the underground wall – and it didn't fucking work."

She looked at me, eyes very round. "You're kidding."

"Sadly, no. It took the Echmen a whole year and a lot of money and dead people, but they got through it, and then Oppa fell and everybody inside it was killed, Posidonius included."

"But you said it would work."

"I lied."

I waited, but the storm didn't come. She was too stunned to say a word. When she'd recovered enough to speak, she said, "It might work."

"I don't think so."

"Bullshit." She glared at me. "It's all there in the book, is it?"

"Yes," I said. "What Posidonius did, and how the Echmen got around it. Technical stuff."

"Fine," she said. "You know what the bad guys did then,

so you can figure out a way to stop them. If you know what's coming, you can prevent it."

I shook my head. "We do something. Then they do something, so we do something. Trouble is, it's not exactly a fair fight. It's like the archer and the deer. They can lose over and over, and still try again. If we lose just once, we're dead. It's inevitable, Hodda. Didn't we both agree? Sooner or later the City will fall."

I'd made her angry. "Then what's all this in aid of? Just to make people feel better?"

I wanted to laugh. All my working life, all the effort and skill we put into it, structures we build out of words and costumes, greasepaint and pretty scenes painted on cloth; castles in the air. Do we change the world? No. We make people feel better, for a little while. I could almost hear myself pitching it to a manager. Castles in the air, I'd say, they've been done to death. Now a castle under the ground; that's something new.

Another thing we do in the theatre; we wait till the very last moment. "Not entirely," I said.

It was a wonderful Ascension festival. I can't remember a better one. They worked all day, dragging stone blocks and dropping them into position, until the job was finally done, a glorious wall of the hardest stone on earth, right where it needed to be. Then they moved off in solemn procession to the Hippodrome. The auditorium was built to seat sixty thousand, but you can double that if you cram them in like olives in a press; it was full. Everyone in the City who could walk was there; exhausted, happy, hopeful, proud to be Robur, waiting to hear their emperor speak.

I had a few things I had to see to, and then I was ready. For once I didn't begrudge having to put on all the gear, including my lucky coat and my armour. Anyone in the business will tell you, once you've got the costume on, suddenly you aren't you any more: you're who you're supposed to be. In my case, the emperor.

So: fanfare of trumpets. Everyone sits still, stops eating cashew nuts, turns and looks at me. I stand there for a moment, looking inexpressibly dignified.

Then someone taps me on the shoulder and hands me a note. I read it. Pause for effect.

Showtime.

"Citizens," I said, "it's bad news. The enemy have broken through the new wall."

I'd allowed myself a count of three; enough time for it to sink in, not quite long enough for mad panic. "We have to evacuate the City," I said. "Theme leaders, organise into wards and neighbourhoods and take your people directly to the docks. There are ships waiting. I repeat, there are enough ships. Everyone, do exactly as your Theme leaders tell you. If we panic, we're all dead. If you panic, you're not just killing yourself but your family and your neighbours, too. Do as your Theme boss says and you'll be fine, you have my word. Stay in your seats till your ward is called, then get up and leave quickly and quietly. Don't run, and it's best if you keep quiet so you can hear the instructions. Go straight to the docks, don't worry about the folks left at home, we'll bring them. I'm sorry, but you can't go back for your things, there just isn't time. That's all. Let's go."

Now that's a scene I'll never forget. Everyone stayed where they were. Then three rows at the back stood up and filed out, then two rows at the front, then three rows in the middle, and so on till there was nobody left in that huge space except me and my hangers-on in the royal box. Quite the most beautiful thing I've ever seen: calm, organised, even graceful. And we had the Themes to thank for that. Nobody else could've done it, and without them it wouldn't have happened.

Take away the people, about a hundred and sixty thousand of them, and who's left? The army and the navy had their orders and were carrying them out, too busy to think. I'd had the senators rounded up just before dawn; they were in their allotted places in one of the ships. The engineers were fully occupied flooding Ogus' saps with the water from those beautifully timely underground springs; they were the only real piece of luck I was given, and I think I made full use of it. I had a few other people running a few small-scale errands. That was it. Leaving just me and my immediate circle, who actually knew what was going on.

This is how I'd explained it to Hodda. It's all been a lie, I told her. The underground wall won't work. But that's not the point. The purpose of the exercise wasn't building a wall. Building walls never achieves anything. The purpose was getting those ships here.

Question: why didn't we evacuate the City years ago? Answer: because we'd never have got people to agree to it; because nobody in their right mind would try and organise something like that; but mostly because where on earth are you going to find enough ships to transport a hundred and sixty thousand people, all at once?

But, just like the rats, we've got to go. But, unlike the rats, we aren't going to die, just because our faces don't fit. Bricks and stones don't make a city, people do. The only way to save the City, therefore, is to leave it behind. Or, looked at the other way round, to take it with us.

As soon as I read about the stone barges, in the course of finding out everything I could about granite, I knew they were our last and only chance. There were these amazing ships; what's more, they were built to sail across the open sea, and the docks were made to suit them. If I could somehow kid the City into getting on board those ships—

And then (I told her) I remembered that fire at the Gallery of Illustration, four years ago, or was it five? You were amazing, I told her. You stood at the front of the stage and you told the audience, in a clear, calm voice; ladies and gentlemen, a fire has broken out, here's what to do and it'll be fine. And you did it so well, they all got up and filed out quietly, no running, screaming or people being trampled into mush; no hesitation, nobody turning round and asking, hang on, is there really a fire or are we being taken for a ride? And that, I thought, is how you evacuate a city.

Was there a fire? Bless you, there's always a fire. There was a fire in Poor Town and I saw how the Theme came together and handled it. Just because the fire's still a couple of blocks away doesn't mean you can be complacent. You bet there's a fire. It's leave now or stay and burn.

Lie and run away, my mother told me. Good advice.

There's room, I told her. Each one of those barges can hold six hundred and fifty people, I know that because I worked it out. If x is the number of granite blocks of dimensions y that a barge can hold – six hundred and fifty people with room to lie down. It won't be luxurious, but it's a lot better than death. Once we're out of the bay we go west, clear out of the Middle Sea. There are islands out there; we know about them because they send us

fruit and vegetables. On an island, we'll be safe, because of the
Fleet. Even Ogus can't dig a tunnel sixty miles long under the
sea. On the way there, the Fleet can feed us – wholesale piracy,
robbing and burning and leaving people to starve; it's all Ogus'
territory, if that makes any difference. And the barges will be
safe, because they don't have to put in to shore. We'll reach the
islands in five weeks. It won't be fun, but people can hold out
that long, if they have to.

What if they find out? They won't find out. Nobody will
know except us, and after a very short time the past will have
changed to suit us.

"And one day," she said, "we'll come back."

I didn't answer.

"We'll come back," she said. "And we'll drive out the milkfaces and take back what's ours. Won't we, Notker? One day?"

"One day," I said.

She nodded. "We've got to," she said. "We can't let him win.
Even if it takes fifty years, or a hundred. You can't let the bad
guys win. It's not acceptable."

For Hodda, life is drama. It falls into a set number of clearly
defined categories: tragedy, comedy, romance, burlesque, farce.
If it's a comedy, the good guys win and everybody gets married.
If it's a tragedy, the good guys win but everybody dies. But you
can't let the bad guys win. Nobody's going to pay to see that.

Me, I don't care about the bad guys, so long as they keep the
hell away from me. When they get too close, in my face, I tell
lies and run away. That means I'll never be a hero, but I don't
mind that. I do character parts and impersonations.

They wanted us on board the Imperial flagship, but I wasn't
having any of that. Our place is with our people, I said. We'll
be on the last barge out. So we waited, while the first hundred

barges loaded up with people and pulled out and the next hundred came in. It was extraordinary to watch: people moving slowly in long lines to where they were supposed to be going. They looked sad and anxious and a lot of them were crying, but in spite of that they had – hope. That old thing. But, just for once, it made itself useful.

The last barge was ready to leave. Two hundred and fifty massive ships, loaded with frightened but hopeful people, en route to Out Of Harm's Way; most of them were already out of the harbour, and there was still half an hour of daylight.

The last barge left. My mother was on it, carried aboard on a litter and bitching like hell. We weren't. Instead, we scrambled into a little pinnace, property of Captain Very. He'd had enough of being a mercenary, he'd told me; time to go home and settle down. I asked him if he'd mind giving Hodda and me a lift. With pleasure, he said, and I do believe he meant it.

"It's the only way I could be sure of getting away," I told Hodda. "Send the entire City on ahead."

We settled ourselves into the stern of Captain Very's boat. Crew of three, and three passengers; the crew were Lystragonians, all ex-guards. Both Hodda and I found it hard to get comfortable, partly because it was small and cramped, partly because it's murder sitting on a coat lined with icons. The captain's share of the haul was a duffle bag stuffed with diamonds, rubies and pearls. They aren't great art lovers where he comes from, he told me, but diamonds are diamonds wherever you go. You're welcome, I told him. Take as much as you want. He lifted the bag, feeling its weight. This'll do, he said. Doesn't do to be greedy.

"I wonder what they'll do when they find out we've gone," Hodda said.

"Who cares?" I replied. "I expect Usuthus will take charge, or Admiral Sisinna. Personally, I never want to see any of them as long as I live."

She smiled. "I can't believe it," she said. "It's actually happening. For real." Then the boat dipped and rose again, and she swung her head over the rail and threw up like – for want of a better comparison – a volcano.

One other thing. Ours wasn't the only small boat fooling about in the harbour after the barges pulled out. There was one more, crewed by the bravest men I've ever met. They were true heroes, and they should have got the girl. But they didn't. Real true heroes never do.

They were Lystragonians; I asked for volunteers, with the proviso that their families back home would be compensated with wealth beyond imagining, a promise I made sure would be kept. I sent them to the island where Hodda and I had met Ogus, and where I later directed the Synaean plague ships. There were six men in the boat; each one carried a little wicker cage and a bag of breadcrumbs. Their job was to go to the little hut on the island and round up as many rats as they could lay their hands on, then take them back to the City and turn them loose in the palace. Rats – I read it in a book – are what spread the plague.

I had no idea if it would work but I thought, what the hell, it's worth a go. Actually, it worked out rather well. It's hard to get accurate information about faraway events in Octiana, which is the city in the far east of the Sashan empire where Hodda and I wound up, at least for a while, but according to what we heard, the death toll among Ogus' army was somewhere between a hundred and two hundred and fifty thousand.

Enough, at any rate, for half of his empire to break away inside eighteen months.

Ogus, however, wasn't among the dead. He caught the plague, but he survived. Now there's several different kinds of plague, apparently; this sort attacks the nervous system and the brain. Ogus caught the plague and survived but he didn't make a full recovery. It left him blind and deaf, with no feeling in his fingers and toes. Last I heard, he's still alive. Long live the emperor. I hope he lives for a very long time.

These are the histories, as I think I may have mentioned earlier, of Notker, the professional liar, who told lies and ran away, thereby saving the City. Please accept my apologies if I've inadvertently made myself out to be the hero. I can't help trying to write a good part for myself, and, as my mother once told me, I do like to have the last word.

But why did you cut and run, you ask, when your people needed you? Seriously? Because when I looked into that mirror in my head, I saw Lysimachus, except that – call it a trick of the light – he looked just like Ogus. Anyone who thinks killing inconvenient people and sending soldiers to burn down cities is a good idea is Ogus, sooner or later. I wasn't him, not yet, just a man doing impressions, but that's the risk with staying in character. Sooner or later, the character stays in you. Or, as my mother used to say, don't pull faces, you'll stick like it.

I know I'm not the hero, because the hero always gets the girl. She left me in Octiana, taking most of the money with her, though what she left me with will be plenty. She said she was going to go to Sagbatan – that's the Sashan capital – and see if she could interest the people there in Robur-style theatre. If they have any taste whatsoever, she'll succeed; and I'll be there on opening night. I don't know if Princess Toto will translate well into Sashan. I'd love to watch her play it again. She was the best, ever, and it was worth being alive, worth being Robur, just to see her.

One day, perhaps.

extras

orbit

meet the author

K. J. PARKER is a pseudonym for Tom Holt. He was born in London in 1961. At Oxford he studied bar billiards, ancient Greek agriculture and the care and feeding of small, temperamental Japanese motorcycle engines. These interests led him, perhaps inevitably, to qualify as a solicitor and immigrate to Somerset, where he specialised in death and taxes for seven years before going straight in 1995. He lives in Chard, Somerset, with his wife and daughter.

For a comprehensive guide to the unreliable world of K. J. Parker, go to http://parkerland.wikia.com.

Find out more about K. J. Parker and other Orbit authors by registering for the free monthly newsletter at: www.orbitbooks.net.

if you enjoyed

HOW TO RULE AN EMPIRE AND GET AWAY WITH IT

look out for

THE LAST SMILE IN SUNDER CITY

The Fetch Phillips Archives: Book One

by

Luke Arnold

A former soldier turned PI tries to help the fantasy creatures whose lives he ruined in a world that's lost its magic, in a compelling debut fantasy by Black Sails *actor Luke Arnold.*

extras

Welcome to Sunder City. The magic is gone, but the monsters remain.

I'm Fetch Phillips, just like it says on the window. There are a few things you should know before you hire me:

1. *Sobriety costs extra.*
2. *My services are confidential.*
3. *I don't work for humans.*

It's nothing personal—I'm human myself. But after what happened to the magic, it's not the humans who need my help.

Walk the streets of Sunder City and meet Fetch, his magical clients, and a darkly imagined world perfect for readers of Ben Aaronovitch and Jim Butcher.

1

"Do some good," she'd said.

Well, I'd tried, hadn't I? Every case of my career had been tiresome and ultimately pointless. Like when Mrs Habbot hired me to find her missing dog. Two weeks of work, three broken bones, then the old bat died before I could collect my pay, leaving a blind and incontinent poodle in my care for two months. Just long enough for me to fall in love with the damned mutt before he also kicked the big one.

Rest in peace, Pompo.

Then there was my short-lived stint as Aaron King's bodyguard. Paid in full, not a bruise on my body, but listening to that rich fop whine about his inheritance was four and a half days of agony. I'm still picking his complaints out of my ears with tweezers.

After a string of similarly useless jobs, I was in my office, half-asleep, three-quarters drunk and all out of coffee. That was almost enough. The coffee. Just enough reason to stop the whole stupid game for good. I stood up from my desk and opened the door.

Not the first door. The first door out of my office is the one with the little glass window that reads *Fetch Phillips: Man for Hire* and leads through the waiting room into the hall.

No. I opened the second door. The one that leads to nothing but a patch of empty air five floors over Main Street. This door had been used by the previous owner but I'd never stepped out of it myself. Not yet, anyway.

The autumn wind slapped my cheeks as I dangled my toes off the edge and looked down at Sunder City. Six years since it all fell apart. Six years of stumbling around, hoping I would trip over some way to make up for all those stupid mistakes.

Why did she ever think I could make a damned bit of difference?

Ring.

The candlestick phone rattled its bells like a beggar asking for change. I watched, wondering whether it would be more trouble to answer it or eat it.

Ring.

Ring.

"Hello?"

"Am I speaking to Mr Phillips?"

"You are."

"This is Principal Simon Burbage of Ridgerock Academy. Would you be free to drop by this afternoon? I believe I am in need of your assistance."

I knew the address but he spelled it out anyway. Our meeting would be after school, once the kids had gone home, but he wanted me to arrive a little earlier.

"If possible, come over at half past two. There is a presentation you might be interested in."

I agreed to the earlier time and the line went dead.

The wind slapped my face again. This time, I allowed the cold air into my lungs and it pushed out the night. My eyelids scraped open. My blood began to thaw. I rubbed a hand across my face and it was rough and dry like a slab of salted meat.

A client. A case. One that might actually mean something.

I grabbed my wallet, lighter, brass knuckles and knife and I kicked the second door closed.

There was a gap in the clouds after a week of rain and the streets, for a change, looked clean. I was hoping I did too. It was my first job offer in over a fortnight and I needed to make it stick. I wore a patched gray suit, white shirt, black tie, my best pair of boots and the navy, fur-lined coat that was practically a part of me.

Ridgerock Academy was made up of three single-story blocks of concrete behind a wire fence. The largest building was decorated with a painfully colorful mural of smiling faces, sunbeams and stars.

A security guard waited with a pot of coffee and a paper-thin smile. She had eyes that were ready to roll and the unashamed love of a little bit of power. When she asked for my name, I gave it.

"Fetch Phillips. Here to see the Principal."

I traded my ID for an unimpressed grunt.

"Assembly hall. Straight up the path, red doors to the left."

It wasn't my school and I'd never been there before, but the grounds were smeared with a thick coat of nostalgia; the unforgettable aroma of grass-stains, snotty sleeves, fear, confusion and week-old peanut-butter sandwiches.

The red doors were streaked with the accidental graffiti of wayward finger-paint. I pulled them open, took a moment to adjust to the darkness and slipped inside as quietly as I could.

The huge gymnasium doubled as an auditorium. Chairs were stacked neatly on one side, sports equipment spread out around the other. In the middle, warm light from a projector cut through the darkness and highlighted a smooth, white screen. Particles of dust swirled above a hundred hushed kids who whispered to each other from their seats on the floor. I slid up to the back, leaned against the wall and waited for whatever was to come.

A girl squealed. Some boys laughed. Then a mousy man with white hair and large spectacles moved into the light.

"Settle down, please. The presentation is about to begin."

I recognized his voice from the phone call.

"Yes, Mr Burbage," the children sang out in unison. The Principal approached the projector and the spotlight cut hard lines into his face. Students stirred with excitement as he unboxed a reel of film and loaded it on to the sprocket. The speakers crackled and an over-articulated voice rang out.

"The Opus is proud to present..."

I choked on my breath mid-inhalation. The Opus were my old employers and we didn't part company on the friendliest of terms. If this is what Burbage wanted me to see, then he must have known some of my story. I didn't like that at all.

"...*My Body and Me: Growing Up After the Coda.*"

I started to fidget, pulling at a loose thread on my sleeve. The voice-over switched to a male announcer who spoke with that fake, friendly tone I associate with salesmen, con-artists and crooked cops.

"Hello, everyone! We're here to talk about your body. Now, don't get uncomfortable, your body is something truly special and it's important that you know why."

One of the kids groaned, hoping for a laugh but not finding it. I wasn't the only one feeling nervous.

"Everyone's body is different, and that's fine. Being different means being special, and we are all special in our own unique way."

Two cartoon children came up on the screen: a boy and a girl. They waved to the kids in the audience like they were old friends.

"You might have something on your body that your friends don't have. Or maybe they have something *you* don't. These differences can be confusing if you don't understand where they came from."

The little cartoon characters played along with the voice-over, shrugging in confusion as question marks appeared above their heads. Then they started to transform.

"Maybe your friend has pointy teeth."

The girl character opened her mouth to reveal sharp fangs.

"Maybe you have stumps on the top of your back."

The animated boy turned around to present two lumps, emerging from his shoulder blades.

"You could be covered in beautiful brown fur or have more eyes than your classmates. Do you have shiny skin? Great long legs? Maybe even a tail? Whatever you are, *who*ever you are, you are special. And you are like this for a reason."

The image changed to a landscape: mountains, rivers and plains, all painted in the style of an innocent picture book. Even though the movie made a great effort to hide it, I knew damn well that this story wasn't a happy one.

"Since the beginning of time, our world has gained its power from a natural energy that we call *magic*. Magic was part of almost every creature that walked the lands. Wizards could use it to perform spells. Dragons and Gryphons flew through the air. Elves stayed young and beautiful for centuries. Every creature was in tune with the spirit of the world and it made them different. Special. Magical.

"But six years ago, maybe before some of you were even born, there was an incident."

The thread came loose on my sleeve as I pulled too hard. I wrapped it tight around my finger.

"One species was not connected to the magic of the planet: the Humans. They were envious of the power they saw around them, so they tried to change things."

A familiar pain stabbed the left side of my chest, so I reached into my jacket for my medicine: a packet of Clayfield Heavies. Clayfields are a mass-produced version of a painkiller that people in these parts have used for centuries. Essentially, they're pieces of bark from a recus tree, trimmed to the size of a toothpick. I slid one thin twig between my teeth and bit down as the film rolled on.

"To remedy their natural inferiority, the Humans made machines. They invented a wide variety of weapons, tools and strange devices, but it wasn't enough. They knew their machines would never be as powerful as the magical creatures around them.

"Then, the Humans heard a legend that told of a sacred mountain where the magical river inside the planet rose up to meet the surface; a doorway that led right into the heart of the world. This ancient myth gave the Humans an idea."

The image flipped to an army of angry soldiers brandishing swords and torches and pushing a giant drill.

"Seeking to capture the natural magic of the planet for themselves, the Human Army invaded the mountain and defeated
its protectors. Then, hoping that they could use the power of
the river for their own desires, they plugged their machines
straight into the soul of our world."

I watched the simple animation play out the events that have
come to be known as the *Coda*.

The children watched in silence as the cartoon army moved
their forces on to the mountain. On screen, it looked as simple
as sliding a chess piece across a board. They didn't hear the
screams. They didn't smell the fires. They didn't see the blood-
shed. The bodies.

They didn't see me.

"The Human Army sent their machines into the mountain
but when they tried to harness the power of the river, something far more terrible happened. The shimmering river of
magic turned from mist to solid crystal. It froze. The heart of
the world stopped beating and every magical creature felt the
change."

I could taste bile in my mouth.

"Dragons plummeted from the sky. Elves aged centuries in
seconds. Werewolves' bodies became unstable and left them
deformed. The magic drained from the creatures of the world.
From all of us. And it has stayed that way ever since."

In the darkness, I saw heads turn. Tiny little bodies examined themselves, then turned to inspect their neighbors. Their
entire world was now covered in a sadness that the rest of us
had been seeing for the last six years.

"You may still bear the greatness of what you once were.
Wings, fangs, claws and tails are your gifts from the great
river. They herald back to your ancestors and are nothing to be
ashamed of."

I bit down on the Clayfield too hard and it snapped in half. Somewhere in the crowd, a kid was crying.

"Remember, you may not be magic, but you are still... special."

The film ripped off the projector and spun around the wheel, wildly clicking a dozen times before finally coming to a stop. Burbage flicked on the lights but the children stayed silent as stone.

"Thank you for your attention. If you have any questions about your body, your species or life before the Coda, your parents and teachers will be happy to talk them through with you."

As Burbage wrapped up the presentation, I tried my best to sink into the wall behind me. A stream of sweat had settled on my brow and I dabbed at it with an old handkerchief. When I looked up, an inquisitive pair of eyes were examining me.

They were foggy green with tiny pinprick pupils: Elvish. Young. The face was old, though. Elvish skin has no elasticity. Not anymore. The bags under the boy's eyes were worthy of a decade without sleep, but he couldn't have been more than five. His hair was white and lifeless and his tiny frame was all crooked. He wore no real expression, just looked right into my soul.

And I swear,
He knew.

2

I waited in the little room outside the Principal's office on a small bench that pushed my knees up to my nipples. Burbage was inside, behind a glass door, talking into the phone. I couldn't make out the words, but he sounded defensive. My guess was that someone, probably another member of staff, wasn't so happy with his presentation. At least I wasn't the only one.

"Yes, yes, Mrs Stanton, that must have been quite shocking for him. I agree that he is a rather sensitive boy. Perhaps sharing this realization with his fellow students is just what he needs to bring them closer together... Yes, a sense of connection, exactly."

I rolled up my left sleeve and rubbed the skin around my wrist. Tattooed on my forearm were four black rings, like flat bracelets, that stretched from the base of my hand to my elbow: a solid line, a detailed pattern, a military stamp and a barcode.

Sometimes, they felt like they were burning. Which was impossible. They'd been marked on to me years ago, so the pain of their application was long gone. It was the shame of what they represented that kept creeping back.

The door to the office swung open. I dropped my arm to let the sleeve roll back down but I wasn't fast enough. Burbage got a good look at my ink and stood in the doorway with a know-ing smile.

"Mr Phillips, do come in."

The Principal's office was tucked into the back corner of the building, untouched by the afternoon sunshine. A well-stocked bookcase and a dusty globe flanked his desk, which was cluttered with papers, used napkins and piles of dog-eared textbooks. There was a green lamp in the corner that lit up the room like it was doing us a favor.

Burbage was unkempt to the point where even I noticed. Brown slacks and a ruffled powder-blue shirt with no tie. His uncombed, shoulder-length hair began halfway down the back of his round head. He sat himself in a leather armchair on one side of the desk. I took the chair opposite and tried my best to sit up straight.

He began by cleaning his glasses. He took them off and placed them on the desk in front of him. Then, he removed a pristine white cloth from his shirt pocket. He plucked up the glasses once more, held them out to the light, and massaged the lenses softly in his fingertips. It was while he was rubbing away that I noticed his hands. I was supposed to notice them. That's what the whole show-and-tell was about.

When he was satisfied that I'd taken in his little performance, he put his spectacles back on his nose, laid both palms down on the desk and rapped his fingers against the wood. Four on each hand. No thumbs.

"Are you familiar with ditarum?" he asked.

"Am I here to take a class?"

"I'm just making sure you don't need one. I've been told that you have lived many lives, Mr Phillips. Experience beyond your years, apparently. I'd like to be sure your reputation is justly merited."

I don't like jumping through hoops but I was too desperate for the money that might be on the other side.

"Ditarum: the technique used by Wizards to control magic."

"That's correct." He held up his right hand. "Using the four fingers to create specific, intricate patterns, we could open tiny portals from which pure magic would emerge. The masters of ditarum – and there was only a handful, mind you – were crowned as Lumrama. Did you know that?"

I shook my head.

"No." A disconcerting smile hung between his ears. "I would expect not. The Lumrama were Wizards who had achieved such a level of skill that they could use sorcery for any exercise. From attacks on the battlefield to the most menial tasks in everyday life. With just four fingers they could do anything they required. And to prove this—"

BANG. He slammed his hand down on the desk. He wanted me to flinch. I disappointed him.

"To prove this," he repeated, "the Lumrama lopped off their thumbs. Thumbs are crude, primitive tools. By removing them, it was proof that we had ascended past the base level of existence and separated ourselves from our mortal cousins."

The old man pointed his mutilated hands in my direction and wiggled his fingers, chuckling like it was some big joke.

"Well, weren't we in for a surprise?"

Burbage leaned back in his chair and looked me over. I hoped we were finally getting down to business.

"So, you're a *Man for Hire*?"

"That's right."

"Why don't you just call yourself a detective?"

"I was worried that might make me sound intelligent."

The Principal wrinkled his nose. He didn't know if I was trying to be funny; even less if I'd succeeded.

"What's your relationship with the police department?"

"We have connections but they're as thin as I can make them. When they come knocking I have to answer but my clients' protection and privacy come first. There are lines I can't cross but I push them back as far as I can."

"Good, good," he muttered. "Not that there is anything illegal to worry about, but this is a delicate matter and the police department is a leaky bucket."

"No arguments here."

He smiled. He liked to smile.

"We have a missing staff member. Professor Rye. He teaches history and literature."

Burbage slid a folder across the table. Inside was a three-page profile on Edmund Albert Rye: full-time employee, six-foot-five, three hundred years old...

"You let a Vampire teach children?"

"Mr Phillips, I'm not sure how much you know about the Blood Race, but they have come a long way from the horror stories of ancient history. Over two hundred years ago, they formed The League of Vampires, a union of the undead that vowed to protect, not prey off, the weaker beings of this world. Feeding was only permitted through willing blood donors or those condemned to death by the law. Other than the occasional renegade, I believe the Blood Race to be the noblest species to ever rise up from the great river."

"I apologize for my ignorance. I've never encountered one myself. How are they doing post-Coda?"

My naïvety pleased him. He was a man who enjoyed imparting knowledge to the ignorant.

"The Vampiric population has suffered as much, if not more, than any other creature on this planet. The magical connection they once accessed through draining the blood of others has been severed. They gain none of the magical life-force that once ensured their survival. In short, they are dying. Slowly and painfully. Withering into dust like corpses in the sun."

I slid a photo out of the folder. The only signs of life in the face of Edmund Rye were the intensely focused eyes that battled their way out of deep sockets. He wasn't much more than a ghost: cavernous nostrils, hair like old cotton and skin that was flaking away.

"When was this taken?"

"Two years ago. He's gotten worse."

"He was in the League?"

"Of course. Edmund was a crucial founding member."

"Are they still active?"

"Technically, yes. In their weakened state, the League can no longer carry out their sworn oath of protection. They still exist, though in name only."

"When did he decide to become a teacher?"

"Three years ago, I made the announcement that I was founding Ridgerock. It caused quite a stir in the press. Before the Coda, a cross-species school would have been quite impractical. Imagine trying to force Dwarves to sit through a potions class or putting Gnomes and Ogres on the same sports field. It would have been impossible for any child to receive a proper education. Now, thanks to your kind, we have all been brought down to base level."

He was baiting me. I decided not to bite.

"Edmund came to me the following week. He knew that he wouldn't have many years ahead of him and this school was a place where he could pass down the wisdom he'd acquired over his long and impressive life. He has served loyally since the day we opened and is a much-loved member of staff."

"So, where is he?"

Burbage shrugged. "It's been a week since he showed up for classes. We've told the students he's on leave for personal matters. He lives above the city library. I've put the address in his report and the librarian knows you're coming."

"I haven't accepted the job yet."

"You will. That's why I asked you to come early. I was curious as to what kind of man would take up a career like yours. Now I know."

"And what kind of man is that?"

"A guilty one."

He watched my reaction with his narrow, know-it-all eyes. I tucked the photo back into the folder.

"It's been a week already. Why not go to the police?"

Burbage slid an envelope across the table. I could see the bronze-leaf bills inside.

"Please. Find my friend."

I got to my feet, picked up the envelope and counted out what I thought was fair. It was a third of what he was offering.

"This will cover me till the end of the week. If I haven't found something by then, we'll talk about extending the contract."

I pocketed the money, rolled up the folder, tucked it inside my jacket and made for the exit. Then I paused in the doorway.

"That film didn't differentiate between the Human Army and the rest of mankind. Isn't that a little irresponsible? It could be dangerous for the Human students."

Under the dim light, I watched him apply that condescending smile he wore so well.

"My dear fellow," he said chirpily, "we would never dream of having a Human child here."

Outside, the air cooled the sweat around my collar. The security guard let me go without a word and I didn't ask for one. I made my way east along Fourteenth Street without much hope for what I might be able to find. Professor Edmund Albert Rye;

a man whose life expectancy was already several centuries over-due. I doubted I could bring back anything more than a sad story.

I wasn't wrong. But things were sticking to the story that knew how to bite.

if you enjoyed

HOW TO RULE AN EMPIRE AND GET AWAY WITH IT

look out for

THE MASK OF MIRRORS

Rook & Rose: Book One

by

M. A. Carrick

Darkly magical and beautifully imagined, **The Mask of Mirrors** *is the unmissable start to the Rook & Rose trilogy, a rich and dazzling fantasy adventure in which a con artist, a vigilante, and a crime lord must unite to save their city.*

Nightmares are creeping through the City of Dreams....

Renata Viraudax is a con artist who has come to the sparkling city of Nadežra—the City of Dreams—with one goal: to trick her way into a noble house and secure her fortune and her sister's future.

But as she's drawn into the aristocratic world of House Traementis, she realizes her masquerade is just one of many surrounding her. And as corrupted magic begins to weave its way through Nadežra, the poisonous feuds of its aristocrats and the shadowy dangers of its impoverished underbelly become tangled— with Ren at their heart.

Prologue

The lodging house had many kinds of quiet. There was the quiet of sleep, children packed shoulder to shoulder on the threadbare carpets of the various rooms, with only an occasional snore or rustle to break the silence. There was the quiet of daytime, when the house was all but deserted; then they were not children but Fingers, sent out to pluck as many birds as they could, not coming home until they had purses and fans and handkerchiefs and more to show for their efforts.

Then there was the quiet of fear.

Everyone knew what had happened. Ondrakja had made sure of that: In case they'd somehow missed the screams, she'd dragged Sedge's body past them all, bloody and broken, with Simlin forcing an empty-eyed Ren along in Ondrakja's wake. When they came back a little while later, Ondrakja's stained hands were empty, and she stood in the mildewed front hall of the lodging house, with the rest of the Fingers watching from the doorways and the splintered railings of the stairs.

"Next time," Ondrakja said to Ren in that low, pleasant voice they all knew to dread, "I'll hit you somewhere softer." And her gaze went, with unerring malice, to Tess.

Simlin let go of Ren, Ondrakja went upstairs, and after that the lodging house was silent. Even the floorboards didn't creak, because the Fingers found places to huddle and stayed there.

Sedge wasn't the first. They said Ondrakja picked someone at random every so often, just to keep the rest in line. She was the leader of their knot; it was her right to cut someone out of it.

But everyone knew this time wasn't random. Ren had fucked up, and Sedge had paid the price.

Because Ren was too valuable to waste.

Three days like that. Three days of terror-quiet, of no one being sure if Ondrakja's temper had settled, of Ren and Tess clinging to each other while the others stayed clear.

On the third day, Ren got told to bring Ondrakja her tea.

She carried it up the stairs with careful hands and a grace most of the Fingers couldn't touch. Her steps were so smooth that when she knelt and offered the cup to Ondrakja, its inner walls were still dry, the tea as calm and unrippled as a mirror.

Ondrakja didn't take the cup right away. Her hand slid over the charm of knotted cord around Ren's wrist, then along her head, lacquered nails combing through the thick, dark hair like she was petting a cat. "Little Renyi," she murmured. "You're a clever one...but not clever enough. That is why you need me."

"Yes, Ondrakja," Ren whispered.

The room was empty, except for the two of them. No Fingers crouching on the carpet to play audience to Ondrakja's performance. Just Ren, and the stained floorboards in the corner where Sedge had died.

"Haven't I tried to teach you?" Ondrakja said. "I see such promise in you, in your pretty face. You're better than the

377

others; you could be as good as me, someday. But only if you listen and obey—and stop trying to *hide things from me*."

Her fingernails dug in. Ren lifted her chin and met Ondrakja's gaze with dry eyes. "I understand. I will never try to hide anything from you again."

"Good girl." Ondrakja took the tea and drank.

The hours passed with excruciating slowness. Second earth. Third earth. Fourth. Most of the Fingers were asleep, except those out on night work.

Ren and Tess were not out, nor asleep. They sat tucked under the staircase, listening, Ren's hand clamped hard over the charm on her wrist. "Please," Tess begged, "we can just go—"

"No. Not yet."

Ren's voice didn't waver, but inside she shook like a pinkie on her first lift. *What if it didn't work?*

She knew they should run. If they didn't, they might miss their chance. When people found out what she'd done, there wouldn't be a street in Nadežra that would grant her refuge.

But she stayed for Sedge.

A creak in the hallway above made Tess squeak. Footsteps on the stairs became Simlin rounding the corner. He jerked to a halt when he saw them in the alcove. "There you are," he said, as if he'd been searching for an hour. "Upstairs. Ondrakja wants you."

Ren eased herself out, not taking her eyes from Simlin. At thirteen he wasn't as big as Sedge, but he was far more vicious. "Why?"

"Dunno. Didn't ask." Then, before Ren could start climbing the stairs—"She said both of you."

Next time, I'll hit you somewhere softer.

They should have run. But with Simlin standing just an arm's reach away, there wasn't any hope now. He dragged Tess out of the alcove, ignoring her whimper, and shoved them both up the stairs.

The fire in the parlour had burned low, and the shadows pressed in close from the ceiling and walls. Ondrakja's big chair was turned with its back to the door so they had to circle around to face her, Tess gripping Ren's hand so tight the bones ached.

Ondrakja was the picture of Lacewater elegance. Despite the late hour, she'd changed into a rich gown, a Liganti-style surcoat over a fine linen underdress—a dress Ren herself had stolen off a laundry line. Her hair was upswept and pinned, and with the high back of the chair rising behind her, she looked like one of the Cinquerat on their thrones.

A few hours ago she'd petted Ren and praised her skills. But Ren saw the murderous glitter in Ondrakja's eyes, and knew that would never happen again.

"Treacherous little bitch," Ondrakja hissed. "Was this your revenge for that piece of trash I threw out? Putting something in my tea? It should have been a knife in my back—but you don't have the guts for that. The only thing worse than a traitor is a *spineless* one."

Ren stood paralyzed, Tess cowering behind her. She'd put in as much extract of meadow saffron as she could afford, paying the apothecary with the coin that was supposed to help her and Tess and Sedge escape Ondrakja forever. It should have worked.

"I am going to make you pay," Ondrakja promised, her voice cold with venom. "But this time it won't be as quick. Everyone will know you betrayed your knot. They'll hold you down while I go to work on your little sister there. I'll keep her alive for days, and you'll have to watch every—"

She was rising as she spoke, looming over Ren like some Primordial demon, but mid-threat she lurched. One hand went to her stomach—and then, without any more warning, she vomited onto the carpet.

As her head came up, Ren saw what the shadows of the chair had helped conceal. The glitter in Ondrakja's eyes wasn't just fury; it was fever. Her face was sickly-sallow, her skin dewed with cold sweat.

The poison *had* taken effect. And its work wasn't done.

Ren danced back as Ondrakja reached for her. The woman who'd knotted the Fingers into her fist stumbled, going down onto one knee. Quick as a snake, Ren kicked her in the face, and Ondrakja fell backward.

"That's for Sedge," Ren spat, darting in to stomp on Ondrakja's tender stomach. The woman vomited again, but kept wit enough to grab at Ren's leg. Ren twisted clear, and Ondrakja clutched her own throat, gasping.

A yank at the charm on Ren's wrist broke the cord, and she hurled it into the woman's spew. Tess followed an instant later. That swiftly, they weren't Fingers anymore.

Ondrakja reached out again, and Ren stamped on her wrist, snapping bone. She would have kept going, but Tess seized Ren's arm, dragging her toward the door. "She's already dead. Come on, or we will be, too—"

"Come back here!" Ondrakja snarled, but her voice had withered to a hoarse gasp. "I will make you fucking *pay*..."

Her words dissolved into another fit of retching. Ren broke at last, tearing the door open and barreling into Simlin on the other side, knocking him down before he could react. Then down the stairs to the alcove, where a loose floorboard concealed two bags containing everything they owned in the world. Ren took one and threw the other at Tess, and they were out the door of the lodging house, into the narrow, stinking streets of Lacewater, leaving dying Ondrakja and the Fingers and the past behind them.

PART 1

1

The Mask of Mirrors

Isla Traementis, The Pearls: Suilun 1

After fifteen years of handling the Traementis house charters, Donaia Traementis knew that a deal which looked too good to be true probably was. The proposal currently on her desk stretched the boundaries of belief.

"He could at least try to make it look legitimate," she muttered. Did Mettore Indestor think her an utter fool?

He thinks you desperate. And he's right.

She burrowed her stockinged toes under the great lump of a hound sleeping beneath her desk and pressed cold fingers to her brow. She'd removed her gloves to avoid ink stains and left the hearth in her study unlit to save the cost of fuel. Besides Meatball, the only warmth was from the beeswax candles—an expense she couldn't scrimp on unless she wanted to lose what eyesight she had left.

Adjusting her spectacles, she scanned the proposal again, scratching angry notes between the lines.

She remembered a time when House Traementis had been as powerful as the Indestor family. They had held a seat in the Cinquerat, the five-person council that ruled Nadežra, and charters that allowed them to conduct trade, contract mercenaries, control guilds. Every variety of wealth, power, and prestige in Nadežra was theirs. Now, despite Donaia's best efforts, and her late husband's before her, it had come to this: scrabbling at one Dusk Road trade charter as though she could milk enough blood from that stone to pay off all the Traementis debts.

Debts almost entirely owned by Mettore Indestor.

"And you expect me to trust my caravan to guards you provide?" she growled at the proposal, her pen nib digging in hard enough to tear the paper. "Hah! Who's going to protect it from them? Will they even wait for bandits, or just sack the wagons themselves?"

Leaving Donaia with the loss, a pack of angry investors, and debts she could no longer cover. Then Mettore would swoop in like one of his thrice-damned hawks to swallow whole what remained of House Traementis.

Try as she might, though, she couldn't see another option. She couldn't send the caravan out unguarded—Vraszenian bandits were a legitimate concern—but the Indestor family held the Caerulet seat in the Cinquerat, which gave Mettore authority over military and mercenary affairs. Nobody would risk working with a house Indestor had a grudge against—not when it would mean losing a charter, or worse.

Meatball's head rose with a sudden whine. A moment later a knock came at the study door, followed by Donaia's majordomo. Colbrin knew better than to interrupt her when she was wrestling with business, which meant he judged this interruption important.

He bowed and handed her a card. "Alta Renata Viraudax?" Donaia asked, shoving Meatball's wet snout out of her lap when he sniffed at the card. She flipped it as if the back would provide some clue to the visitor's purpose. Viraudax wasn't a local noble house. Some traveler to Nadežra?

"A young woman, Era Traementis," her majordomo said. "Well-mannered. Well-dressed. She said it concerned an important private matter."

The card fluttered to the floor. Donaia's duties as head of House Traementis kept her from having much of a social life, but the same could not be said for her son, and lately Leato had been behaving more and more like his father. Ninat take him—if her son had racked up some gambling debt with a foreign visitor...

Colbrin retrieved the card before the dog could eat it and handed it back to her. "Should I tell her you are not at home?"

"No. Show her in." If her son's dive into the seedier side of Nadežra had resulted in trouble, she would at least rectify his errors before stringing him up.

Somehow. With money she didn't have.

She could start by not conducting the meeting in a freezing study. "Wait," she said before Colbrin could leave. "Show her to the salon. And bring tea."

Donaia cleaned the ink from her pen and made a futile attempt to brush away the brindled dog hairs matting her surcoat. Giving that up as a lost cause, she tugged on her gloves and straightened the papers on her desk, collecting herself by collecting her surroundings. Looking down at her clothing— the faded blue surcoat over trousers and house scuffs—she weighed the value of changing over the cost of making a potential problem wait.

Everything is a tallied cost these days, she thought grimly.

"Meatball. Stay," she commanded when the hound would have followed, and headed directly to the salon.

The young woman waiting there could not have fit the setting more perfectly if she had planned it. Her rose-gold underdress and cream surcoat harmonized beautifully with the gold-shot peach silk of the couch and chairs, and the thick curl trailing from her upswept hair echoed the rich wood of the wall paneling. The curl should have looked like an accident, an errant strand slipping loose—but everything else about the visitor was so elegant it was clearly a deliberate touch of style.

She was studying the row of books on their glass-fronted shelf. When Donaia closed the door, she turned and dipped low. "Era Traementis. Thank you for seeing me."

Her curtsy was as Seterin as her clipped accent, one hand sweeping elegantly up to the opposite shoulder. Donaia's misgivings deepened at the sight of her. Close to her son's age, and beautiful as a portrait by Creciasto, with fine-boned features and flawless skin. Easy to imagine Leato losing his head over a hand of cards with such a girl. And her ensemble did nothing to comfort Donaia's fears—the richly embroidered brocade, the sleeves an elegant fall of sheer silk. Here was someone who could afford to bet and lose a fortune.

That sort was more likely to forgive or forget a debt than come collecting...unless the debt was meant as leverage for something else.

"Alta Renata. I hope you will forgive my informality." She brushed a hand down her simple attire. "I did not expect visitors, but it sounded like your matter was of some urgency. Please, do be seated."

The young woman lowered herself into the chair as lightly as mist on the river. Seeing her, it was easy to understand why the people of Nadežra looked to Seteris as the source of all that was stylish and elegant. Fashion was born in Seteris. By the time it traveled south to Seteris's protectorate, Seste Ligante, then farther south still, across the sea to Nadežra, it was old and stale, and Seteris had moved on.

Most Seterin visitors behaved as though Nadežra was nothing more than Seste Ligante's backwater colonial foothold on the Vraszenian continent, and that merely setting foot on the streets would foul them with the mud of the River Dežera. But Renata's delicacy looked like hesitation, not condescension. She said, "Not urgent, no—I do apologize if I gave that impression. I confess, I'm not certain how to even begin this conversation."

She paused, hazel eyes searching Donaia's face. "You don't recognize my family name, do you?"

That had an ominous sound. Seteris might be on the other side of the sea, but the truly powerful families could influence trade anywhere in the known world. If House Traementis had somehow crossed one of them...

Donaia kept her fear from her face and her voice. "I am afraid I haven't had many dealings with the great houses of Seteris."

A soft breath flowed out of the girl. "As I suspected. I thought she might have written to you at least once, but apparently not. I...am Letilia's daughter."

She could have announced she was descended from the Vraszenian goddess Ažerais herself and it wouldn't have taken Donaia more by surprise.

Disbelief clashed with relief and apprehension both: not a creditor, not an offended daughter of some foreign power. Family—after a fashion.

Lost for words, Donaia reassessed the young woman sitting across from her. Straight back, straight shoulders, straight neck, and the same fine, narrow nose that made everyone in Nadežra hail Letilia Traementis as the great beauty of her day.

Yes, she could be Letilia's daughter. Donaia's niece by marriage.

Follow us:

f **/orbitbooksUS**

𝕏 **/orbitbooks**

▶ **/orbitbooks**

Join our mailing list
to receive alerts on our
latest releases and deals.

orbitbooks.net

Enter our monthly
giveaway for the chance
to win some epic prizes.

orbitloot.com